The Rom-Com
Agenda

The Rom-Com Agenda

JAYNE DENKER

ST. MARTIN'S GRIFFIN
NEW YORK

First published in the United States by St. Martin's Griffin, an imprint of St. Martin's Publishing Group

THE ROM-COM AGENDA. Copyright © 2022 by Jayne Denker. All rights reserved. Printed in the United States of America. For information, address St. Martin's Publishing Group, 120 Broadway, New York, NY 10271.

www.stmartins.com

Designed by Jen Edwards

Library of Congress Cataloging-in-Publication Data

Names: Denker, Jayne, 1966– author.
Title: The rom-com agenda / Jayne Denker.
Description: First edition. | New York : St. Martin's Griffin, 2023.
Identifiers: LCCN 2022034035 | ISBN 9781250821485
    (trade paperback) | ISBN 9781250821492 (ebook)
Subjects: LCGFT: Romance fiction. | Novels.
Classification: LCC PS3604.E58553 R66 2023 |
    DDC 813/.6—dc23/eng/20220719
LC record available at https://lccn.loc.gov/2022034035

Our books may be purchased in bulk for promotional, educational, or business use. Please contact your local bookseller or the Macmillan Corporate and Premium Sales Department at 1-800-221-7945, extension 5442, or by email at MacmillanSpecialMarkets@macmillan.com.

First Edition: 2023

10 9 8 7 6 5 4 3 2 1

For Mom. On my way, as always.

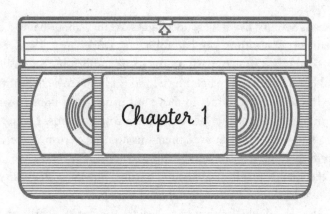

Chapter 1

Leah Keegan was positive she was not meant to be a superhero. Or an alien. Or whatever other life-form came in a peculiar shade of near-fluorescent lime green. A disturbingly large amount of her skin was sporting the lurid tint at the moment, proving that this was not her color. Besides, the last time she had seen this particular shade on a humanoid, the poor thing was being pursued by one Captain James T. Kirk, and no thank you to that. The green had to go.

She plopped down on the narrow boards ringing the inside of Ward Peterson's tiny, rustic bare-bones boathouse, just the right size for a small motorboat and nothing more. The interior was now painted said screaming alien-green, solely so Ward could more easily locate it and navigate his boat back in after a long day of fishing. His eyesight wasn't so good these days, he had told her, especially at dusk. Leah preferred not to speculate on how much his eyesight was affected by how many beers he had indulged in on any given fishing expedition.

Leah picked at the dried paint that had somehow managed to cover almost as much of her as it had the inside of the boathouse. But doing that tugged on the fine hairs of her forearm, which just plain hurt, so she let it be for now and admired her handiwork instead. Seventy-five dollars and flights of fancy about being a different sort of creature. Not bad for a day's work.

Now it was time to pack up the paint and brushes and rollers, haul her butt out of the boathouse, and get home to a cool shower. She forced her tired bones to move but paused mid-boost, a wash of melancholy knocking her back down to the boards. Except for the siren song of that shower, there was no need to rush home. She kept forgetting. It was a strange thing to get used to, and she hadn't succeeded just yet. It would come. In time. She knew that—in her head, at least. Her heart was still catching up.

She sat quietly, leaning back against the coarse boards of the boathouse, watching the gentle flow of the water. From here all she could see were other docks, other modest properties huddled up along the inlet. Follow this stretch of water, however, and it soon opened out onto the vast, powerful St. Lawrence River, moving northeast to the Atlantic Ocean. Beyond the huge vessels in the shipping lanes and the various small bits of land in the river that gave this part of New York State its name, the Thousand Islands, lay Canada. On this side of the river, the lush green flatlands gave no hint that the Adirondack Mountains would poke up, ancient and imposing, less than a hundred miles away.

But here, in this boathouse, on this inlet, a bit of peace—from the tourists, who were starting to wrap up their summer vacations as each day grew progressively cooler and shorter, from the river traffic, from the thoughts that filled her head day and night.

Leah took a breath. This was okay. This was good. By tonight she'd have money in her "gettin' outta Dodge" jar and food in her stomach. She'd scrub the alien tint off her skin, wash her paint-spattered clothes—er, throw away her paint-spattered clothes—and spend the rest of the night watching trashy TV. But for just one minute she closed her eyes, relaxed her aching muscles, and listened to the soft blipping sound of the tiny waves lapping the wooden posts under the boathouse.

"Aren't you going to miss this place?"

The voice was so close Leah almost answered the question.

But it was just a trick of acoustics, sound bouncing off the water's surface and funneled straight into the boathouse. Whoever it was wasn't talking to her. Nobody could even see her in here unless they were out on the water, pulling into the boathouse or cruising past it, and there wasn't much more to the inlet past the Petersons' property. In a few hundred yards it dissolved into a weedy marsh, just past the—oh, the bridge. Someone was on the bridge.

"Come on, admit it. You are."

The voice was measured, smooth, and deep, almost musical, but with an energy underlying it. The guy was tense, even though he sounded like he was joking, and it made Leah stiffen as well.

Another person responded with a tolerant sigh. "Of course I am."

A woman this time, also tense. Leah wondered if these two were wound up about the same thing.

"I wish you didn't have to go," the man said.

"It's just a sabbatical, Eli."

Eli. She wondered who he was, whether she'd seen him around. In a small town like Willow Cove, knowing nearly everyone was expected. Unless you were a hermit, and Leah had to admit she had been one for quite a while.

"Sure you don't want me to come with you?"

His tone was playful and sexy and Leah squirmed uncomfortably. This was obviously a private conversation, and she *really* wished she could teleport out of the boathouse without them seeing instead of hiding in here trying not to listen . . . and failing. But she was here and they were there and the only way out was past them, so she was going to have to wait until they moved on.

In the same intimate tone, Eli said, "You are going to miss me, right? Call me with all the news, text me at weird hours when I'm sleeping and you're drinking your morning espresso in some piazza in Rome?"

He was probably bumping his shoulder against hers, Leah thought, his forehead touching her temple, as they leaned on the bridge railing side by side, watching the dimming sunlight on the water.

The woman laughed softly. "Sure. That is, *if* I ever get to Syracuse to catch my first flight."

"Okay, okay. *Hang* on," Eli said, drawing out the words, and Leah pictured him throwing an arm over the woman's shoulders and pulling her to him. Obviously she was anxious to get going, and not just because of her flight. Eli, on the other hand, wasn't exactly ready to let her go. "There's something I want to say first."

"Eli."

"Victoria, just listen, okay?"

"Mm."

Victoria did not, in fact, want to listen; Leah was sure of it. Leah didn't either, because she had the feeling Eli was about to say something very private.

"I want you to know I'm going to miss you, and the next ten months are going to be torture—"

"Eli."

"We've been over this already, I know. It's only . . . I—I love you. I do. So much. You're going to say it's too soon, and I get that," he rushed to add, probably because Victoria was moving to protest again. "Most people would probably say it's too soon for a lot of things. I mean, four months, right? But I say when you know, you know. So . . ." After a moment he added, "It's not a diamond or anything."

Silence from the bridge. A long, heavy silence.

Leah dropped her forehead to her bent knees. *Oh no, Eli. No, no, no. Don't do it.* She could practically feel the resistance radiating from Victoria right through the boathouse planks at her back.

Despite Leah's silent pleas, he went and did it anyway. "I hunted down the jewelry maker you liked so much from the arts festival and had him make this. Consider it a, you know . . . okay, *promise* sounds a little high school. What's the equivalent for thirty-year-olds? Commitment? Anyway, I'm ready to commit. With you. I'll be here when you get back, and then we'll—"

"I can't—"

"Victoria," he protested over her, "take it, okay? I want to marry you. I want to build a life with you."

"Eli." Victoria's voice got stronger. "Come on. Look at what you're doing."

"It looks like I'm asking you to marry me because I lo—"

"It looks like you're angling for a way to 'lock it down' before I leave."

Eli laughed, but it sounded forced. "You make it sound like a bad thing."

"It *is*. It's like you're afraid I'm going to go off to Rome, hook up with some random guy, and go riding off into the Italian sunset on his Vespa. It's, I don't know, kind of desperate, don't you think?"

Eli didn't answer.

"I'm sorry," Victoria said, "but it is. And, to be honest, putting this on me right before I go is a pretty shitty thing to do."

"I thought it would be romantic. I thought . . . I thought we felt the same way about each other."

"You know I care about you," Victoria said, her voice soft now. "But four months, Eli? That's not enough time to be sure of anything."

Leah could barely hear Eli's answer as he murmured sadly, "I was sure."

More silence.

Oh my God, please just go, Leah begged silently. *Take this conversation somewhere else. It's excruciating and embarrassing and I have to pee.*

Nobody moved, though. Nobody spoke. Leah pictured Victoria fidgeting, itching to leave, while Eli leaned on the railing and glowered at the water below them. She found herself holding her breath, waiting for the resolution. She hoped it would come soon.

"So now what?" he asked reluctantly.

"Look, Eli, I'm sorry. This summer has been fun, but I think you're reading too much into . . . us. I need to go to Rome and focus on my research. Nothing else. You understand, right?" After a pause in which Eli didn't, in fact, say that he understood, Victoria pressed, "Tell me you're okay with this."

Leah thought Eli would renew his protests, but instead he

said in a clipped, tight voice, "You bet. Really. So, you know, safe travels."

Victoria sighed. "I have to go."

Another pause, and Leah thought she heard a small kiss.

"Take care of yourself, Eli. Be happy, okay?"

"Yeah, you too."

Leah stayed frozen while the sound of footsteps on the wooden boards faded away. *Thank God.* Now she *really* had to pee. She hopped up and lifted the latch on the rickety homemade wooden door. It opened with a creak, the uneven, swollen bottom sticking on the floorboards. Leah stuck her head through the narrow opening only to find Eli was still on the bridge.

Shit.

Even with his elbows on the railing and his shoulders hunched dejectedly, just as she'd imagined, Leah could tell he was tall and broad, with shaggy dark hair that had a wild wave and curl to it. A faded T-shirt, jeans that had seen better days, unlaced work boots. Light eyes, either blue or green. Leah couldn't tell, and she didn't take the time to find out, because they were staring into the middle distance, right at her.

Dammit.

Breathless, she forced the door closed again. Had he seen her? Wait—why did it matter? She didn't know this guy, hadn't seen him before. She would have remembered. And so what if she had been in the boathouse? It was a free country. He couldn't prove she was eavesdropping. Which she wasn't. At least, not intentionally. Hey, if they were going to have a conversation in a public place, they had to accept that somebody was going to hear it.

And yet her face was still flaming from being found out. *If* she'd been found out. He might not have been looking at her at all.

She could stay hidden and wait for him to leave—and pray that he wouldn't storm down to the dock and knock on the door, wanting to know what she was up to—or she could hold her head high and march out of there, as she had every right to do.

Leah did neither.

As she dithered, there came the sound of a deep, agonized sigh, punctuated by the distinctive *ploop* of something small and solid hitting the water.

And that'd be the ring, she guessed.

Eli's heavy footsteps walking away came soon after.

～

Leah had never been so happy to see the inside of the tired little house she called home. She slammed the door and leaned against it as though she had just outrun a pack of zombies.

Well, okay, one particular lovesick zombie.

After Eli had finally, *finally* walked away, she'd scooted out of the boathouse, not even stopping to find Ward or his wife for her money, and raced home, Eli and Victoria's excruciating exchange rattling around in her head the entire time. And it was still there. It wouldn't go away.

"Oh my *God*, Cathy, you won't believe what happened to me today," she called out, dropping her bag and sweatshirt on a chair in the living room. She related the whole painful story as she finally visited the bathroom, shouting over the water as she washed her hands at the sink, then stopped in the kitchen, paused to inspect the contents of the fridge, pulled out a peach, and walked back through the house.

"I swear," she said with a sigh, leaning in the doorway of the master bedroom and picking at the fuzzy surface of the fruit, "that poor guy is in for a world of hurt. I'd bet anything he actually thinks they can pick up where they left off when she gets back, but I'm pretty sure she doesn't have any intention of doing *that*, right?"

There was no answer. There hadn't been one for a month now. The hospital bed sat silent and empty, filling the small room so completely that the foot of the bed nearly reached the door. Leah sighed and patted the end of the plastic mattress nearest to her. She really had to call the medical supply place and have them pick it up soon.

"I miss you, Cathy," Leah whispered to the empty room, the empty house. "Mom."

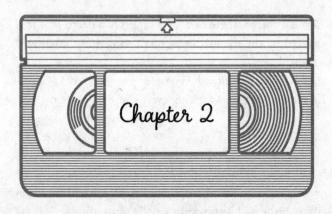

Chapter 2

"Life should come with a warning label. But it doesn't. Doesn't matter. Even if it did, we wouldn't pay attention. We never do. Be careful. Look both ways. Wear a helmet. Put your seat belt on. Do we listen? No, we don't."

"Dude."

"And then later, we get other warnings. Get your oil changed. Floss. Check your credit score. Change your passwords. Protect your Social Security number."

"Eli."

"Protect your heart."

"Aw, come on, big guy—"

"We never listen. Not to any of it. We're like toddlers let loose on a playground while our parents sit on park benches, chugging their Starbucks and checking their phones. And do we do anything differently, even after our seesaw partner gets off their end without *any* warning at all, and your nuts are crushed when your end slams into the ground? Nah. After we finish crying, we just find someone else for the seesaw and do the same thing all over again."

Jenna locked eyes with her husband over her brother's bowed head. "Maybe convincing Eli to come out tonight was a bad idea."

"Ya think?"

"Plug-stupid optimists, that's all we are," Eli declared.

"Oh boy." Ben shifted in his seat, took another swig of beer. "Let me try." Nudging away his basket of chicken-wing remnants and clearing his throat, he leaned his elbows on the table. "Okay, look, bro—"

"You were too good for her."

Ben gave his interrupting wife a look. She ignored it. They had been married for twelve years, after all. Eli didn't answer, just stared into the depths of his pilsner.

"Honey, you've got to snap out of this," Jenna pleaded, putting a hand on his arm. "So she broke your heart. I'll break her nose the next time she shows her face in this town."

"Please check your threats, sister of mine," came Eli's monotone, delivered in the direction of the fake woodgrain of the tabletop. "May I remind you that, if not for some unforeseen circumstances, she'd be your sister-in-law come June."

"Unforeseen? You mean the fact that she turned you down flat? And no surprise there, considering you ambushed the girl after only a few months. So that's your own fault." Jenna paused and reconsidered her approach. "You're a hopeless romantic and an incurable optimist. Uh, usually. And that's great. It's what makes you you and what makes everybody love you."

"Except Victoria," Ben snickered into his beer.

Jenna cuffed him in the back of the head and then continued, "*But* it also makes you, well, stupid sometimes."

That got at least one eyeball trained on her from under the brim of Eli's weathered baseball cap.

"Look at you. Five months since she dumped you, and you're still a mess."

"I'm reflecting and regrouping," Eli countered evenly.

"You're turning into a hermit, a wild man of the woods. One of those dudes who knows seven different ways to fricassee squirrel and whose best friend is their chemical toilet."

"I've been among people. I led fall-foliage kayak tours for two of those months, if you recall."

"And since then?"

No answer.

"Beard growing is not a competitive sport."

Ben perked up. "You know, actually, I think it is."

This time it was his wife who gave him the look, which he, in fact, did not ignore. They had been married for twelve years, after all.

"The beard *is* a bit extreme, dude," he said.

"Could you at least review your shower schedule, maybe tweak it a little?" Jenna sighed. "Because you're *looking* a lot like a wild man of the woods."

"I embrace my aesthetic," Eli responded, stubborn to the last. "If you are unable to do the same, I merely ask for your support."

Even if his magnificent facial growth, of which he'd lost control weeks ago, did itch like a sonofabitch, he wasn't going to concede the point to his sister and brother-in-law. It wasn't as if he'd cultivated his new look; it had just sort of happened while he was busy doing other things. Like being in a massive funk after his failed proposal and Victoria's departure for Italy.

It should have been like a movie. A nearly spur-of-the-moment proposal, her shocked but overjoyed acceptance, a bittersweet farewell, but only a brief separation before an incredibly romantic visit or two or three in sun-drenched southern Europe during Victoria's sabbatical. Then long-distance wedding planning, Victoria's return, and a joyous celebration followed by fifty or sixty years of wedded bliss. He'd been so sure, honestly hadn't expected any other outcome, hadn't even imagined her saying no. So when she did . . . well, it sent him on a downward spiral that included a lot of dark days marked by a distinct lack of fresh air, larger-than-is-normally-acceptable amounts of beer, and long stretches of video games in the dark.

When Eli realized beer didn't buy itself and he was in danger of losing his progress on his games because his electricity was about to be cut off—not to mention his vitamin D levels were probably alarmingly low—he reluctantly led a few kayaking expeditions.

That ended up helping his mood a bit. Being outdoors always did. He still ached for Victoria and what he'd lost, but physical activity and interacting with tourists got his mind off his misery for minutes at a time once in a while. The people were nice, the fall scenery a breathtaking display as only the Northeast can do in September and October, and if any of his clients of the female persuasion were inclined to flirt with him, he didn't notice.

All right, he did notice, but he pretended not to. His instinctive reaction was to hide—if not in his cabin, then within himself. His hair got longer, his beard bushier, his clothes bulkier and more misshapen. His sister's concerns about his hygiene, however, were unfounded. He might only use the mirror in his bathroom as a toothpaste-spittle collector instead of a grooming assistant, but he did, in fact, keep himself clean. He wasn't a heathen; he just wasn't inclined to feed his ego right now. Because his ego had been stomped flat on the boards of a particular nearby bridge last August and, as far as he knew, it was still lying there, twitching, perforated and pinned by Victoria's stilettos.

"Eli!"

The shout came hurtling in their direction, seemingly propelled on a blast of cold air when the door opened. Within seconds he was surrounded by more people than he'd spent time with in months.

"Was this intentional? Is this an intervention?" he asked his sister as Gillian, Delia, and Gray swarmed the table. Amid the general bustle of stamping snow off boots, unwrapping scarves, and fetching more chairs, Ben went to the bar for drinks.

"Don't be so self-centered, little brother," Jenna said, shifting over to make room for their friends. "It's January in the islands. What else is there to do except meet at the bar?"

"Ooh, Eli, it's so good to see you out of the house," Delia cooed, patting his cheek as she sat down next to him. "When was the last time we spent time with you, Christmas?"

"If by 'spent time with' you mean caught a glimpse of some hulking figure lurking in the shadows of our house while the rest of us celebrated, then yes," Jenna said.

"What the hell is this?" Gray laughed, scratching Eli under his scruffy chin. Eli good-naturedly swatted his hand away. "It's bigger. It's scarier. I don't like it."

"That's what she said," Eli muttered, but his heart wasn't in it.

"Doesn't he look awful?" Jenna asked of the group, seeking backup.

"What that woman did to him . . ." Gray tsked, sitting back in his chair and crossing his muscled arms. Gray always sported tight T-shirts, even in the dead of winter. He called it advertising— whether for his personal life or to get new clients, Eli was never sure. Then again, Eli wasn't sure there was a difference, as Gray was proudly a player and always seemed to find dates right there at work. And he was always at work. Right on schedule, Gray added, "Get your ass into my gym. We'll throw some hot workout shots up on Instagram, and she'll come running from Europe dying to get back with you before somebody else snaps you up."

"Very funny."

"I never joke about getting ripped and you know it."

"He doesn't want her back," Jenna declared. "Right, Eli?"

"Wrong, dear sister," Eli said, knocking back the last of his beer. He'd thought a lot about whether he was going to try to forget Victoria or not, accept their breakup as permanent or not. He'd decided the answer to both questions was "not." "I've been staying in touch with her while she's in Italy—*casual*, don't worry, just to prove I'm being an adult about how we left everything. I'm not stalking her. She told me to keep in touch, and that's what I'm doing. Leaving the lines of communication open, you know."

"Is she answering your messages?" Jenna asked.

A pause, then, "Sometimes. It's fine."

Jenna waited.

"Okay, okay, she answered twice. All right? Happy?"

"In five months? Oh, Eli . . ."

"It's fine. She's busy. I'll keep messaging, she can answer when she has the chance, and when she returns, I'll get her back. That is the plan, and don't even try to change my mind."

"And what, exactly, are the details of this plan?" Gillian asked, sizing him up. "*How* are you going to get her back?"

"I'm working on it."

"You don't have a plan, do you?"

Eli shrugged. Jenna was his only blood sibling, but Gillian and Delia served as his tough-love and nurturing fairy godmothers, respectively. Right about now, he knew, he was going to be tough-loved to death.

"I've got a few months to figure it out," he hedged. "In the meantime, I'm staying in touch with her. A little. As friends."

"You want her back, you've got to offer her something special."

"He's special just the way he is," Delia insisted. "Leave him alone, Gilly. If Victoria can't see how wonderful he is, it's her loss." Delia punctuated her last statement with another pat on his cheek.

Gillian just stared him up and down, one skeptical eyebrow hovering close to her honey-blonde hairline. "Mm-hmm," she grunted. "I'm not seeing it, and someone as classy as Victoria isn't going to see it either. I mean, an art professor, grew up in Georgetown . . . she's something else."

"Right," Jenna agreed. "Hyperintellectual, into gourmet cooking, theater fan if I recall correctly."

"And string quartets," Delia added.

"Ooh, right," Ben said, returning with more beer. "Yep, just your type."

"What are you implying? I'm not all of those things?"

"You're none of those things," Jenna said bluntly. "And there's nothing wrong with that . . . unless you're trying to connect with her beyond the basic physical attraction you guys had going for a few months. Sure, she had fun slumming with the backwoods guy for a bit, but really, Eli, you can't possibly think she belonged here."

"She said she liked it here. Remember? After that group kayaking trip she came back on her own. Said Willow Cove was magical."

Gillian sighed. "That doesn't mean she actually wanted to stay for the rest of her life, Eli."

"I prefer to take her at her word."

"Then you should take her at her last word, which was that she didn't want to marry you."

Eli said nothing, just hoped his stubborn silence would do the talking for him.

"Well," his sister said with a sigh, "obviously talking sense to you isn't going to work, so fine. Just know if you want to get her back, you'd better up your game."

Eli shifted, uncomfortable. He'd known Victoria was out of his league, but she seemed to like him just the same. He was happy to cling to the whole opposites-attract thing, and he was certain he could have held on to her if she'd stayed . . . well, pretty sure, anyway. Now, however, he faced some serious competition: distance, his botched premature semiproposal, and the lure of Europe. And European men. Could he compete with some dashing, urbane Antonio or Paolo—or literal Romeo—whisking her off to a classical music concert or a gourmet restaurant or the vineyard he owned in Tuscany? He wanted to think he could, but deep down he wasn't so sure.

"You've gotta get ripped," Gray said.

"You've gotta shave off that badger on your chin," Ben said.

"Show her you don't need her," Gray added.

"Yeah, cut her off—radio silence, man," Ben agreed. "Make her crawl."

The women exchanged glances, and Eli had a feeling this wasn't going to end well for anyone at the table with a preponderance of testosterone.

"Eli," Jenna said, with a cutting look at her husband and Gray, "if you really want to get Victoria back, then fine. I might not approve, but I'll support you. But do *not* listen to these Neanderthals. They have all the worst ideas, and no notion of what women truly want."

"Hey, I won you over, didn't I?" Ben protested.

His wife's lips twitched with a suppressed smile. "Oh, honey."

"What?"

Jenna leaned over and kissed him affectionately. "You didn't win me over. I decided you were the one in high school. After that, I orchestrated everything. But I respect you for working so hard."

"You're lucky I love evil masterminds," he grumbled, but with a pleased smile flashing like lightning, contrasting against his dark skin.

Delia took over the campaign. "Eli, you're a good person, but—and don't take this the wrong way, because you know I love you to bits—you're just not . . . husband material. Not for someone like Victoria. Not yet," she rushed to add. "You just need some time to take care of yourself, get your confidence back, spruce yourself up a little."

Her eyes widened, and Eli felt his stomach tighten. He'd seen that *I've got a brilliant idea* look before. A wave of telepathy rippled around the table.

"Makeover," Delia whispered.

"A project," Gillian breathed, swiveling her head to scrutinize Eli. "Perfection by spring."

"I *said* get ripped," Gray pointed out, miffed that his contribution had been ignored.

"Oh, he's fine there," Jenna said with a wave of her hand. "All that hiking and rowing?"

"But how's your six-pack?" Delia asked, to the annoyed groans of the men. "What? It matters! Have you looked at modern romance novel covers lately? Six-packs everywhere. The genre is lousy with 'em."

"She's right," Gray said. "There are muscles for show and muscles for go. You need a bit of show-off stuff. Lift up your shirt and let me see what you got."

"What? No!" Eli protested.

Gillian laughed. "Gray just wants to ogle you. Give the boy a little somethin'."

"Truth, I gotta admit."

"The whole package," Jenna interrupted. "He needs to be the

whole package by the time Victoria gets back. Looks. Style. Personality."

Delia added, "Manners. Comportment."

"What the hell is comportment?" Ben asked, completely lost. The women ignored him.

"Culture," Gillian said. "Knowledge."

"That's it." Jenna slapped the table. "Eli, we're turning you into husband material."

Chapter 3

Winter in the Thousand Islands was a test of resiliency. While it was easy to live there during the summer months, when the population swelled with tourists and summer residents and the towns were alive with crowded shops, packed restaurants, and nonstop activities, once winter descended it was another story. The entire region seemed to shrink with the cold, contracting in on itself bit by bit after Labor Day, growing quieter with every degree the temperature dropped. Sure, there was always a brief flare of life around Christmas, with parades and bazaars and festivals, but it was only temporary. After the holidays, the year-rounders might just as well have been living on the moon.

Not everybody could hack it there, Leah was certain. When the chainsaws were turned from ice sculpting to cutting more logs for the woodstoves, when music from outdoor stages had long been silenced and the only sounds were the squeak of your insulated boots on the snow and the whine of the snowmobiles in the distance, when most of the shops and restaurants remained closed from Christmas until the spring thaw . . . that was when the true islanders thrived and everyone else ran for the comparative liveliness of Syracuse or Albany or, barring the ability to get that far in the snow, Watertown, several miles away. Watertown had a mall, after all.

Here in Willow Cove, however, the first thing Leah had to do when she worked the day shift at the small clothing shop on Main Street was put out a sandwich board on the sidewalk. Its message read, in big, bold letters, YES! WE'RE OPEN! to remind residents that not all the shops went dark until May. Not that it made much difference. The locals knew what was open and what wasn't. If they needed clothes, they came by. Most of the time they didn't, and the days Leah took some of the burden off Mr. Lehman, the proprietor, she spent behind the counter with a good book from the library (open three half days a week in the off-season—one morning and two afternoons), never waiting on a single soul.

So when she spotted a cluster of four people bustling down the icy sidewalk, she was a bit startled. It wasn't so much the fact that the scene, bathed in the thin, pale sunlight of a winter's morning and highlighted by the tiniest of crystallized snowflakes that only drifted down when the temperature was below zero, looked like it could have been painted by Norman Rockwell (if Norman had painted women with purple hair and post-punk tendencies, and those ladies were herding what seemed to be a captured Sasquatch), it was that the entire parade took a hard right turn and strode right into the shop.

That didn't usually happen in Willow Cove in January. At least, not as far as Leah had experienced.

She carefully put down her book and tried to look attentive as the group sorted itself out. "Welcome to Thousand Island Dressing. How can I help you?"

One of the women, a statuesque blonde, spun around and brightened up immediately.

"Oh, hey!" Gillian exclaimed. "What are you doing here?" Before Leah could answer, Gillian tacked on, "Well, working, obviously. I didn't know you worked here, though."

Leah smiled. "I fill in sometimes."

"No moss growing on you. Oh, I'm so rude. Everybody, this is Leah Keegan."

Amid a general murmur of hellos, Gillian pointed out everyone by name: Delia Dupree of the purple hair, Jenna Masterson-Page with the studded leather jacket, and . . . Eli Masterson? Did she say Eli? *Her* Eli? Well, not *hers*, of course, but . . .

Leah took a closer look at the Sasquatch. Yep, under the red-and-black checked lumber jacket, faded baseball cap, and all that hair and beard was the man she'd seen on the bridge last year, getting dumped. Honestly, he looked terrible—thinner, she thought, although it was hard to tell under all the winter clothing, his face drawn and no longer tanned. Only his eyes were the same. She still couldn't quite make out their color, as he had the curled bill of the cap pulled low, but she recognized the arch of the strong, dark eyebrows, the shape of his eyes and their kind expression. Which was slightly hidden behind a veneer of irritation as the women fussed around him, filling the shop with their energy.

He looked back at her, frowning a little, and Leah felt her cheeks grow hot. Did he recognize her as well? God, she hoped not.

Before he could say anything, Gillian said, "Leah, I'm so glad you're here. Eli needs some serious help."

"Oh?" Leah busied herself with finding a notebook and pen. Anything to avoid those eyes watching her so carefully.

"He's having woman trouble. And look at the guy—do you think he's going to win the woman of his dreams looking like Forrest Gump after all that time running across the country? Of course not."

Fighting back a smile, Leah dared to steal a furtive look at Eli. Gillian wasn't wrong; he did bear a striking resemblance to Forrest, mid-movie. Maybe not as much hair. But pretty close.

"We need you to help us fix him up."

"My brother needs a new wardrobe," the woman named Jenna said. "Top to bottom, bottom to top. Pants, shirts, sweaters, jackets, shoes if you got 'em, even underwear if you've got that. If you work on commission, I'm paying your rent this month, baby."

Leah salivated at the notion. But she was only on a straight salary. She'd still do her best, though. She liked a challenge. "As stylish as we can make him?"

"He should walk out of here looking like he stepped off the

pages of *GQ*," Delia said. "He's our project, to pass the time during the long, dark winter."

"Couldn't you just, I don't know, knit instead? Or something?" Eli pleaded.

They soundly ignored him.

"Can you handle it?" Gillian asked Leah.

"No problem."

Eli, however, looked like he had a problem. In fact, he looked like he would rather ice skate on the St. Lawrence nude than stand there and let four women hold shirts and suit jackets up to him to decide whether they went in the yea or nay pile. Even so, he remained on his best behavior—occasional eyerolls and heavy sighs notwithstanding—as Leah plucked different items off the racks for consideration. The yea pile grew faster than the nay pile.

"These shirts, those sweaters, especially the shawl-collar one—so distinguished," Jenna said. "Jeans, pants—oh, I love the flannel and the tweed—and this blazer . . . hey, we'll take both jackets, why not . . . and this pile of socks. Do *not* ask what's wrong with your white gym socks," she snapped as Eli opened his mouth. He shut it again. "They're going in the trash. Oh, and this thing goes too."

Before Eli could stop her, Jenna grabbed his beat-up baseball cap and flung it a good distance across the store.

"Hey!"

Apparently Eli could put up with a lot, but he drew the line at losing his treasured hat.

"Oh my God, let it go. It's filthy."

"That's patina."

"I don't care what you call it. The ratty thing's gotta go. Sorry, Leah, I was aiming for the trash can, but I'm a lousy shot."

"I'll take care of it."

"A hat would be nice, though," Jenna mused. "A good one."

Delia lit up. "Ooh, a—"

Before Delia could say the word "trilby," Leah had one in her hand.

"Exactly!"

"Oh, come *on!*"

It was clear Eli had reached his limit. But Delia forcibly pulled on his collar to get him to lean down, plunked it on his head, and turned him toward the mirror.

"I look like a douche."

"You look like a *stylish* douche," Jenna corrected him. "Which Victoria will adore."

"Think of it as a signature look. Own it," Gillian said. "Strike a pose like you mean it."

"No. *No.*"

"Yes." Jenna grabbed his shoulders and turned him back to the mirror. "Look suave. Look sophisticated. Look like you belong with Victoria. No. You look like you have gas. Try again."

"I don't know what you want me to do!"

"No whining. Shoulders back. Relax—you look like you have a pole up your butt. Look confident. But look natural."

"You're not making any sense."

"Try to look seductive," Delia suggested. "Get a slow burn going."

"Set myself on fire?"

"In a manner of speaking," Gillian said. "Look like you want to tear her to pieces."

"I want to tear all of you to pieces."

"Not violent-like, sexy-like. Get your smolder on."

"Nope," Jenna declared as he tried out a couple of squinty looks. "You still look like you're experiencing intestinal distress. Never mind. We'll work on it later. But we'll take the hat," she said to Leah. "You have good taste."

Leah carried the huge pile of clothing to the register, nudging the forgotten baseball cap behind the counter with her foot.

While she rang up the items, she said, "Of course, buying new clothes is only half the solution, you know."

"It is?" Eli asked weakly from across the room where they'd left him, completely wrung out from the morning's ordeal. "What else is there?"

"Tailoring." She smiled at his agonized look. "It's not so bad. All you have to do is stand there. The tailor does all the work. And when the clothes are done, they'll look even better on you. Your girlfriend won't know what hit her."

"Yeah?" He seemed more interested when she added that last comment.

"Promise. Naturally I recommend the tailoring services of Stitch, Please, next door. You can take your purchases right through there and someone will be with you shortly."

Flush with their success and loaded down with Eli's new wardrobe, the women nudged him through the wide opening in the brick wall while Leah made her way to the back room, scooping up the baseball cap on the way.

In the tailor shop, Jenna, Gillian, and Delia pulled out the clothes to be altered, then looked up and started laughing when Leah came out of the back room of Stitch, Please with a tape measure draped around her neck. Mr. Lehman owned both places, and they were essentially one and the same, down to sharing a back room. They flung some pants at Eli and shoved him toward the dressing room.

While Eli was changing, Gillian asked Leah, "Hey, how are you holding up, honey?"

"Not bad, thanks."

"Can't say I miss seeing you in the pharmacy on a regular basis, but you know what I mean. I love your hair, by the way."

Leah self-consciously tucked a wayward curl of her dark pixie cut behind one ear. "It grew in faster than I thought."

Before Gillian could continue the conversation, Eli pushed aside the dressing-room curtain and walked over to them awkwardly, plucking at the fabric of his new trousers and shaking his leg like a dog with a twitch.

"Up on the platform, big guy," Leah commanded, happy that she didn't have to answer any more of Gillian's questions. "And stand still. I have pins, and they're going to be very close to some of your favorite body parts."

Eli obeyed, and Leah walked around him, studying his silhouette, pulling at the fabric, and nipping in the waist. Eli held his arms out so it would be easier for her to get to the waistband. She nudged them back down most of the way so his stretch wouldn't interfere with the natural drape of the pants.

He sighed uncomfortably. "So. Come here often?"

Leah laughed softly and started to pin. Eli fell silent. Jenna, Gillian, and Delia were across the room, staring out the plate-glass window at the snow blowing down the empty street. Every once in a while bits of their conversation drifted over to her.

Jenna: "Looks familiar . . . How do we know her?"

Delia: ". . . go to school with us?"

Gillian: "No, after us . . . had it rough lately . . . Cathy's caregiver. Cancer. Awful. Whole year."

Leah cleared her throat and shifted uncomfortably, then refocused her attention on hemming Eli's pants. She hated having to listen to her story related by someone else, and laced with pity at that.

Jenna: "Not just her, though? Cathy . . . biological son? Patrick?"

Gillian: "Oh, sure. MIA though. Dick."

Another round of muttering, except this round was bitter. Patrick they knew and obviously didn't like.

Gillian again: "So yeah. Just her. Had to have been awful."

Leah dragged a stool over while Eli pulled on one of the blazers. Even though she had asked Eli to come down off the small platform, there was no way she was going to get anywhere near his shoulders to mark the jacket without some extra height. She hastily climbed onto the stool and teetered a bit.

"Whoa, there." Eli steadied her with large hands on her waist. "You all right?"

"I'm fine," Leah murmured. "Just a little clumsy today."

"I don't mean your balance." Eli jerked his head at his sister and friends. "I mean that."

Leah looked up and met his eyes fully for the first time. They were blue. Not icy blue, but a warm medium hue that could go dark and masquerade as black in the right light, she suspected. No matter the color, though, they were kind, and currently studying her with concern.

"She may be tiny, but she's super strong," Gillian said.

Leah forced a smile. "My secret is out. I'm super strong."

Eli's voice was warm when he answered with a half grin, "I believe it."

"A tattoo!"

Both Leah and Eli jumped at Delia's outburst and her sudden appearance right beside them. Eli's hands instinctively went back to Leah's waist just in case she came close to toppling off the stool again.

"*No!*" he said, incredulous.

"Why not?" Delia demanded, hands on her hips.

"You know I have a low pain threshold."

Jenna shouted from across the room, "Little brother, you finished that one kayaking trip with a broken ankle, so don't go yipping about pain."

Eli bugged his eyes at Leah with a half-amused, half-exasperated look, then shouted over his shoulder, "Okay, *first* of all, it was a hairline fracture. And I was sitting down in the kayak, wasn't I?"

"Then how did you portage out of there afterward, huh?" his sister countered.

Eli closed his eyes and sighed. "No tattoos, okay? I'm letting you do all this other nonsense, but I've gotta draw the line there."

"I'm gonna need a third-party ruling," Delia said. "Leah, honey, what do you think? A nice armband or something? Hot, right?"

"Oh . . . well . . . I . . ."

Eli got her attention again, pleading silently, his eyes almost as wild as the beard below them.

"An armband might be a little cliché, I think."

"Yeah!" Eli was obviously grateful for the support. With a wink at her, he added, "Listen to this lady here."

Leah had absolutely no reason to still be standing on the stool, so close to Eli. None at all. And the warmth radiating off his large body, and the sudden, surprising flutter she felt in the vicinity of her navel from such a simple gesture as a conspiratorial wink, made her all the more anxious to get away. She forced herself off the stool, took a step back, and pointed him toward the dressing room.

"And stop trying to re-create me in your image," Eli shouted once he was behind the curtain. "Tattoos and Harleys are fine for you and Ben, but—"

"Hey, now *that* is a great idea—"

"No Harley!"

"Insta-badass! Think about it!"

Eli whipped aside the curtain as he buttoned another shirt. "I am not trying to be an insta-badass, or any other sort of badass. Keep your head in the game—one you invented, may I remind you. You said you were going to make me into the kind of guy Victoria couldn't say no to. I doubt she'd fall for a guy with tattoos and a Harley."

Jenna smirked. "Shows how much you know."

Leah just smiled politely. She could already see great gaping holes in their plan. While she didn't know Eli at all, she got a sense that tattoos and motorcycles wouldn't fit with what she'd seen of him already, and changes that were too drastic would never take. Turning him into a badass was too high a risk, she thought. They should focus on a little refining instead. Subtle things. If they were needed at all. Really, he seemed fine from what she'd already ob-served. Unless he ate with his feet, what did they think he needed to change?

The tailoring only took a little while longer, and the relief Eli felt when Leah finally told him he was free to go was palpable. He said a polite goodbye and thanked her for making the process as painless as possible, but he couldn't get out of the shop fast enough.

Gillian, Delia, and Jenna took their time packing up.

"I'll call you when Mr. Lehman is finished with the tailoring," Leah told Jenna. "He'll be able to take care of it right away."

"Thanks, honey. You're a godsend."

"What do we do with him next?" Delia asked.

"Hair," Gillian and Jenna chorused decisively.

"We're going to have to go someplace really professional for that," Delia mused.

"What about Poppin' Locks?" Leah suggested. "They do a good job."

"If they did your pixie cut, then you're right," Jenna said. "I love it. I could never pull off a short style like that."

Gillian caught Leah's eye and raised a questioning eyebrow. Leah felt her face grow warm. Self-conscious again, she started collecting the clothes marked for alterations on a standing rack. "Give Poppin' Locks a call, ask for Liz. She'll do a good job with Eli, won't make him freak out too much."

"You noticed the freak-out factor, then?" Jenna asked.

"Kind of hard not to." She hesitated for a moment. "If you don't mind my saying, go easy on him, okay? It's clear that you all care a lot about him and want to make him look good, but he seems kind of fragile. If he gets spooked you'll lose any progress you make."

She didn't dare mention that she knew what had driven Eli to the state he was in. Luckily nobody asked.

"Good point," Gillian murmured. "We'll be careful. *Right*, Jenna?"

"Meh. This is a race against the clock, so I say we push him as hard as we need to." She turned to Leah. "If you think we need an Eli whisperer, I nominate you. Anytime you want to join the makeover team, just say the word."

Chapter 4

The indignities were endless. Just endless. Bad enough Eli's sister and friends were shoving their noses into his love life *and* his closet, but now they were taking charge of his grooming routine. Okay, he would reluctantly agree he was more than ready for a haircut and beard trim . . . which might or might not require the employment of a brush hog by now. But why wouldn't they trust him to take care of it on his own? The whole stinkin' crew had to escort him to the salon instead, as if they were going to have to make sure he stayed in the chair like he was three years old.

Oh God, this place didn't have horsey seats, did it?

No. No, of course not. Good grief, just a few days into this plan and already Eli felt like he was losing his mind.

The little shack his friends nudged him into, around the corner and a couple of blocks inland from the main road, was brightly lit in the gloom of the late afternoon and a fresh round of snow—this batch heavy and gloppy—chucking down. It was a perfect day to stay the hell home, but instead he was committing to phase two of his makeover.

The blast of heat and light as he stepped through the door was downright disorienting, with the wail of hair dryers filling the air and people shouting over them. Eli was busy stamping snow off his boots, so he missed the initial greeting as his sister stepped up to the desk to check him in. Then he heard a very familiar voice.

"The Weedwacker special?"

He looked up to find Leah smiling brightly at him. For the first time he noticed she had a dimple in her right cheek that gave her an even more impish look than her Tinker Bell size and short haircut imparted.

"Brush hog, actually." His voice was raspy, and Jenna, Gillian, and Delia turned to give him a curious look. He ignored them. "Why are you here?"

"Rude," Gillian muttered, elbowing him in the ribs.

"I'm just helping out while Steph's on vacation," Leah said. "Want to step over to the sink, Eli?"

Jenna yanked off his new wool peacoat and scarf and then gave him a shove farther into the salon. He glanced behind him only to give her the stink eye. Of course she was unfazed. His stink eye had never had an effect on his older sister.

Leah settled Eli into the chair, flapped a cape over him, and gently pushed him backward till his neck settled into the groove in the sink's edge.

As she ran the water to warm it up, he said, "Sorry about the outburst. I just wasn't expecting to see you here."

"It's okay."

"But, I mean, how many jobs *do* you have? Am I going to keep seeing you all over town? Because if that's the case, I'm going to start calling you Kirk."

"Kirk?"

"The guy who had all the different jobs on *Gilmore Girls*."

Leah stopped dead, the water nozzle high over his head. "*You* know *Gilmore Girls*?"

"I have a sister, remember?"

Leah smirked. "Oh, is that why you know it?"

"*Yes*," he declared emphatically, fidgeting to settle more comfortably into the seat. "I don't watch much, you know, TV or movies or whatever. Never have . . . uh . . ."

And the rest of his denial disintegrated into a random collection of involuntary noises as the warm water hit his scalp and Leah started running her fingers through his hair. All he could do was close his eyes and work hard not to whimper. Tiny fingers were also magic fingers, apparently. As Leah massaged his scalp, Eli felt the tension in his shoulders dissipate.

"I vote you keep this job," he said, practically purring.

Leah just made a noncommittal noise, but when he cracked one eye open, he saw she was smiling and even blushing a little at the compliment.

"Or," he went on, having to work even harder to form coherent thoughts, "tell me you're also a massage therapist. Please."

He nearly wept when she turned off the water and gently wrung out his hair.

"Not a massage therapist," she said as she wrapped a small towel around his head. "Sorry."

"Not half as sorry as I am." And he meant it, especially when she laid on one more mini-massage through the towel to draw off the excess water.

She led him to a seat in front of a mirror, and a woman named Liz took over. Fortunately there was no brush hog or Weedwacker on the premises.

"So what are we doin' today, hon?" Liz asked, playing with his wet locks.

From the waiting area, his sister bellowed, "Cut it all off, baby!"

Liz met his eye in the mirror. "Shaved head?"

He spotted Leah behind them. Pausing as she swept the floor at another station, she shook her head, mimed a moderate length on top and ran her hands closer to the sides of her head, then passed her hand over her cheek and chin. He grinned at her. Was it his imagination, or did she go pink again?

He returned his attention to Liz. "No, not shaved."

"Don't know if you have a sexy head shape for it?"

"A *what*?" He truly felt like all this makeover talk was a foreign language. "Never mind."

He described to the best of his ability the haircut Leah had mimed, and Liz seemed to understand him.

"What about the beard?" she asked.

In his head, Eli got an instant replay of Leah's hand running over her cheek. "You know what? Let's shave all *that* off."

"Full beards are in," Liz cautioned.

"I want to start fresh."

~

"Much nicer!" Delia sang. She reached up, and he obligingly leaned down the rest of the way to let her ruffle his much shorter hair. "I like the style. Liz is a wizard."

"It was Leah's idea, actually."

"Oh?"

Oh no. Such a small word. Such a loaded word.

As his sister and friends started exchanging raised eyebrows and *oh, really?* looks, he said quickly, "All right, all right, knock it off."

"This one's on me." Jenna shrugged on her coat and pulled out her wallet. "With an extra-large tip for Leah."

Eli's sister was infuriating more often than not, but when she did something like this, she inspired an overabundance of brotherly love. Outwardly, however, all he said was, "Good idea. She works hard. So now are we done?"

"Oh, hell no," Gillian said. "We've only just started, honey."

"What else could you possibly—"

"Facial," Delia stated definitively. "Those pores! Now we can see all of them, and they aren't pretty."

"Manicure," Jenna added as she signed the payment screen with a flourish. "And pedicure. God only knows what's going on inside those insulated boots. I picture toe claws."

And Jenna's sisterly pedestal crumbled immediately, plummeting her back down to earth. Embarrassing brothers—that was what sisters did most of the time. He'd nearly forgotten. A furtive glance at Leah, who was finishing up Jenna's payment, showed that she was taking in every word. He didn't want her to picture him sporting nasty toe claws, but it was too late. He hauled on his coat indignantly. He wasn't *that* much of a hopeless case.

"Don't forget the tattoo," Delia said.

"*What* did I say about tattoos?" Eli demanded. "A big fat no, that's what I said. And Leah agreed."

"Well," Leah said as she rounded the end of the counter and scooped up his scarf, which had fallen to the floor, "the idea's growing on me. Maybe one on your neck, now that it's visible again."

Eli winced. "Please don't encourage them." Leah was holding in her laughter, which made Eli want to laugh as well, even though he covered it with a scowl before his friends took his amusement as a tacit sign he was on board with some painful ink. To deflect, he said to Leah, "Oh, I see. You're probably a tattoo artist on top of all your other jobs. I swear, if I walk by Tattoo-ine and see you in the window holding a needle, I wouldn't be the least surprised."

Leah just handed him his scarf and smiled cryptically.

"And that's just the outer stuff," Gillian said. "We also have to work on the inner."

"*That* is going to be the real challenge," Jenna agreed.

Eli groaned as he held the door open for his friends, who filed out in front of him, squinting into the snow and hunching their shoulders. Without all that insulating hair, the sting of the cold on his face was especially sharp. And he sorely missed his baseball cap. He self-consciously touched his new shortish-on-the-sides-and-long-on-top hairstyle. The styling goo Liz had slathered on his waves stiffened into a crunchy crust in the cold.

Good lord, how was this his life now? He looked back over his shoulder as if to verify he had indeed spent the last hour in a hair salon listening to—okay, and sometimes contributing to—an ongoing conversation that centered around celebrity gossip while a perfumy woman snipped and fluffed his hair. Through the half-steamed-up salon windows, he caught a glimpse of Leah. For a split second it seemed as though she were watching him and his friends with an almost forlorn look on her face, and Eli felt a twinge in the vicinity of his heart. But then she quickly turned her gaze skyward, studying the snow falling in the early-evening gloom. Sure, she was just checking the weather. Which was no different from any other day in the North Country in January: blustery and deathly frigid.

Eli wondered how it was possible that he had gone from never seeing her around town to seeing her everywhere. He realized it probably had something to do with the fact that Leah had been busy as the sole caretaker for her terminally ill foster mother for so long, which Gillian knew all about. He had seen her before, though. Ever since they'd met at the clothing store he'd been racking his brain, trying to remember where he knew her from, but he couldn't figure it out.

Jenna, halfway down the block to her minivan, shouted for Eli to catch up, but he pulled out his phone. "Don't wait for me. I've gotta . . ." He waggled his phone at his sister, who waved him off as a lost cause because she knew he was going to message Victoria. And she was right. He'd felt a sudden need to remind himself who he was doing all this for. As he started to text, his eye was drawn back to the salon windows. They were empty. Leah was gone.

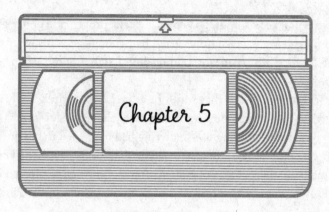

Chapter 5

"I'm going to head out, Liz."

"All right, honey. Hey," the stylist called to Leah as she collected her things from the back room, "you all right? You got kind of . . . I don't know. Quiet there for a second."

"I'm fine."

Leah cursed herself for slipping like that. She thought she'd gotten a handle on her . . . well, back in the mists of time it would have been called melancholy. Every once in a while she just got plain sad, either missing Cathy or wondering where life was going to take her next. Or both. Liz didn't need to know how seeing Eli and his sister and friends together sort of made her heart hurt.

She'd always been alone, ever since her mother, the only family she had, gave Leah up because she wasn't able to take care of her. Leah had been ten, so she remembered absolutely everything, every detail. Although she didn't think so at the time, now she knew her mother had done the right thing. Living with severe bipolar 1, she struggled to regulate her body's chemistry. Finding the right medication was a crapshoot she lost every time. Electroconvulsive therapy only helped for a short while, and she spent the subsequent time after every treatment trying to recover the memories that had been blasted away. Most of the time her mom was unable to hold down a job, keep a house, pay bills . . . take proper care of her only child. Leah knew her mother loved her, enough to want what was best for her, which meant finding her a stable home where she could grow up in peace.

It didn't work out that way, not at first. For a while, Leah was shuttled from foster home to foster home. She refused to think of it as traumatic, as nothing life-shattering had happened to her during that time. She knew the foster parents had been trying their best (some more than others, of course). It had, however, reinforced her realization that she was truly alone in the world, which was damage enough.

When she was fifteen, she'd landed on Cathy's doorstep.

Cathy had two younger fosters at the time, as well as a biological son, Patrick. She seemed to take in Leah reluctantly, but she did it. And if she hadn't exactly been the warm and fuzzy type, Cathy provided stability, structure, a mostly not-leaky roof, and three meals a day. That was good enough to make Leah want to stick around as long as possible. Plus she thought the riverside town of Willow Cove was cute.

To make sure she was allowed to stay, Leah kept her head down, didn't make trouble, and pitched in around the house every minute she wasn't in school or doing homework. It netted her mixed results. Cathy hadn't exactly adored her—but then again, she didn't seem to like people in general—but she couldn't resist a kid who gave more than she got from the system. Leah was grateful she didn't have to pack up and leave almost as soon as she had put her clothes in the battered dresser and narrow closet she shared with her foster sisters, so she put up with Cathy's prickly, moody nature—after her mom's clinical instability, Cathy was a walk in the psychological park—and dug in. And it worked. She stayed with Cathy until she aged out of foster care.

But a close-knit group of friends and years living in the same place? That she'd never had.

～

Leah's rickety Honda squeaked down the road to the small supermarket on the edge of town, fishtailing a bit as she turned into the parking lot. Although the short trip didn't give the car enough time to warm up, Leah dreaded leaving it and getting buffeted by the wind on the way into the store. It was days like these she understood why Cathy said a thousand times she was going to move south, even though she never did. Well, maybe she would have if she hadn't gotten sick. Leah had often tried to draw her out, get her to talk about her life, her hopes and dreams, her plans, but when Cathy was grappling with the worst of her illness, she simply shut down and only lived moment to moment, her entire life telescoping to her next round of meds or her next treatment, and Leah couldn't tease anything more out of her.

The market was a welcome haven of warmth and light. There were very few people shopping, even though it was just about dinnertime. When the options were to go out and get the things you might need for a meal or stay home by the woodstove and make do with what you had, most people would go for the second option every time. Leah would have done the same, but some items were nonnegotiable.

She stopped at the women's hygiene section and flicked a couple of boxes of tampons off the shelf into her cart. Maybe it was her current bout of rampaging hormones making her so wistfully envious at the sight of Eli, Jenna, Gillian, and Delia together. She didn't usually feel that way. In fact, she was so used to being alone, she wasn't sure she'd know how to act if she *did* have a group of friends.

The squeak of her cart's wheels was louder than the nineties pop music permeating the store as she moved on, wondering what cliché she felt like embracing—ice cream, chocolate, something salty, or a combination of all three—when she nearly T-boned another cart going down the main aisle.

"Hey!"

For some reason, Leah's heart leapt at the sight of Jenna. What she was hoping for, she had no idea.

"Haven't seen you in a while," Jenna exclaimed, then rolled her eyes at having spouted the tritest of all greetings.

"What's it been, five minutes? Ten?"

"Just about. But I'm glad I ran into you. I wanted to thank you for helping Eli."

"I didn't do anything."

"Are you kidding? First the clothes, then keeping Liz from shaving his head? That's a lot."

Leah laughed. "Liz can be a little . . . overzealous at times."

"I think Eli would have looked less like a badass and more like a Blofeld."

"Oh, I don't know. I don't think we included any Nehru jackets in his new wardrobe. Does he have a white cat?"

"Oh my God, he does!"

"He seems more the big dopey dog type."

"You'd think so, right? But that ex of his somehow convinced him to take care of her cat while she's away in Italy. Can you believe it? She dumps him, and he still takes the cat because he promised. What do you call that?"

"Being a mensch?"

"I was going to say being an idiot, but, you know—potato, potahto."

"It is a little odd."

"Oh, I could tell stories. As a matter of fact, you know what? We're all going to meet up for some drinks tonight. You should come. I'll tell you stories then."

Leah froze. Go out? Socially? And with Eli's group, no less—the group she'd just been practically licking the salon window over as she watched them leave together? She truly had no words.

"Eight o'clock, okay?"

"The microbrewery?"

"Pfft. Honey, we go to Dickie's. You get more beer for your bucks. Plus you never lose your purse, because it sticks to the floor. So you're coming?"

"Oh . . . I don't know. I have to . . ."

"Wash your hair?"

Leah smiled. The truth was she had to start sorting Cathy's stuff. She'd been putting it off for months. Of course, why she thought she'd get started tonight of all nights was a mystery. No, it was more like an excuse. Leah realized she could keep feeling sorry for herself and stay home alone, or she could take a friendly lifeline when it was tossed to her.

"Come on. Have a drink, relax. We're fun."

Leah definitely knew that. "I . . . okay, sure."

~

But three hours later, she was still in her house, pacing so much she wouldn't have been surprised to see a groove forming in the scraped, pitted wood floor of the tiny foyer. She was getting overheated in her jacket, yet she couldn't seem to take those final steps out the door.

"Come on," Leah muttered to herself. "You've got an invitation to be social, so go out and be social."

She just wasn't used to it, that was all. Socializing was like a muscle, she realized. If you didn't exercise it, it atrophied. Hers had had some sort of wasting disease for years. Make small talk? Was she even capable? Or would she spout uncomfortable non sequiturs until Jenna regretted inviting her? Or, worse, what if she just sat there, unable to join in the conversation at all? She'd spent the past several months having protracted dialogues with the memory of her foster mother. How could she replace that with actual live human interaction?

"Oh, Cathy, what am I gonna do?"

Leah paused mid-pace.

"I'm gonna stop talking to ghosts, that's what I'm gonna do."

She shoved her wallet and her phone in her pocket, crammed a knit hat onto her head, and charged out the door before she could chicken out again.

~

Leah had never been in Dickie's before, but it didn't disappoint. The outside, with its brick half wall topped with smoked-glass windows awash in neon beer signs, promised a dive bar inside, and that's exactly what Leah found. Linoleum floor, metal-frame chairs with cracked vinyl cushions, gloomy booths along the wall, a bar that was probably old enough to be a historic landmark.

It was perfect.

Or maybe her happy feeling came from the group of people beckoning to her from a table in the middle of the room. They wanted her there. They were pleased to see her. Leah liked this a lot.

When she reached the table, a devastatingly handsome muscular guy pulled out the chair next to his. He introduced himself as Gray and offered to get her a drink. Jenna was saying that her husband, Ben, a trucker, was on the road for a few days and her mom had the kids, so they were having a girls' night (Gray's inclusion was honorary) and it was time to make the most of it, which Leah barely caught the gist of because she was glancing around expectantly. Then Jenna's words hit home, and her spirits dipped a little.

She'd cultivated a pretty good poker face over the years, so she didn't worry about giving too much away as she casually asked, "Oh, so no Eli tonight?"

"The recluse?" Gillian rolled her eyes. "It's a miracle we got him out in the light of day for his makeover."

"Twice," Delia put in. "It's unheard of, these days."

"Which just means we can gossip about him all we want," Gray said, setting a beer down in front of Leah. "Want to start us off?" Leah stammered incoherently for a few seconds before he let her off the hook. "I'm just joking," he said with a dazzling smile. "We'll take care of the trash talk. You can just sit back and take it all in until you're ready to join."

"Gray, that's horrible!" Delia exclaimed.

"Fine. We won't trash-talk the mountain man."

"Good."

"We'll trash-talk the ex-girlfriend instead. Jenna? You want to take the lead on this one?"

"You. Are. Awful."

"And you love it."

"You're not wrong, Mr. Powers."

"All right then."

"You're going to make our new friend think we're all evil."

"Well, we kind of are."

Gillian snorted. "Speak for yourself. And while you're at it, mind telling us where you were this afternoon? I thought you wanted in on the makeover, but so far you've been completely AWOL."

Gray stretched, laughed sheepishly, and rubbed his chin. With his every move, Leah realized, Gray telegraphed that he knew darn right well how good-looking he was, and he was going to flaunt it. And nobody was objecting. She could see why.

"I was around," he said. "Just busy."

Jenna narrowed her eyes at him. "You said you weren't working. For once." To Leah, she said, "Gray owns the gym a few blocks down. As you can see." She gestured at her friend's physique. "Would you believe he was a scrawny thing in junior high?"

"I hear it's pretty common for people to change over the years. Like you, in fact." He explained to Leah, "Jenna used to be the biggest troublemaker in school. When she grew up, she didn't just start working for the Man. She *is* the Man. Vice principal of the high school." He shook his head and flashed his blinding smile again. "So back to me and my gym—discounted memberships for friends, if you're interested."

Leah smiled politely but didn't respond to his offer. She didn't have the money for a gym membership, even at a discounted rate. And if she was going to keep her time in Willow Cove short, there was no point in signing an extended contract for anything anyway.

Instead she said, "PowerHouse, right?"

"Yeah. I wanted to name it Gray's Anatomy, but I ran into a little trouble there. Shocking, I know. As for all you judgy individuals," he went on, turning to the others at the table, "I wasn't available today. I do other things on occasion besides work."

"Not today," Delia said into her glass. "You were just too scared of having to make small talk with Brendan."

"Brendan the new stylist?" Leah whispered to Jenna, who was on her right.

"Hookupapalooza," she whispered back.

"Okay, first of all, I'm not *scared* of making small talk with Brendan. I just didn't feel like it today. And, you know . . ." Gray took a swig of his beer before completing his thought. "Not just Brendan."

"Who . . . oh, not *Liz*."

"Maybe."

"Do they *know*?" Gillian asked, a horrified half grin on her face as she processed Gray's latest scandal.

"Beats me. I'm not telling 'em if they don't."

"You abso*lute* man ho."

Amid his friends' shrieks of laughter, Gray protested, also laughing, "All right, all right, you know that's not it. I'm very discerning. That was just . . . an unfortunate coincidence. I met Brendan before he started working at the salon."

Gillian shook her head in amazement. "Where do you find the time? That's what I want to know."

"Apparently he'd rather add to his stable of conquests instead of helping one of his friends," Delia sniffed.

"Stable of—?" Gray looked like he was about to argue, but instead he put on another winning smile and said, "Delia, honey, you seem a little put out that I haven't been able to contribute any time to this project yet."

Delia shrugged, not looking at Gray, until he tucked a finger under her chin and nudged until she met his sultry gaze and blushed.

Well, now. Leah would bet anything it wasn't exactly Gray's absence from the makeover efforts that Delia was pissed about.

"All I'm saying is Leah barely knows Eli, and she's helped him out way more than you have already," Delia grumbled.

Gray turned to Leah again. "So they've dragged you into this, have they?"

"Oh, I wouldn't say dragged, exactly."

"How do you know this mob, anyway? Where did you come from?"

"She works at Thousand Island Dressing. And Stitch, Please," Gillian explained before the conversation drifted into Leah's recent past with Cathy, and Leah was grateful for that. "And Poppin' Locks."

"Damn, you have three jobs, and Delia here doesn't have any."

Delia threw a pretzel at Gray. "I do too." To Leah, she explained, "I'm a jewelry artist."

"Ditched her law practice," Gillian put in. "Just walked away from it."

"I didn't like it. It didn't feed my soul."

"Fed your belly, though," Gillian said.

"Well, now she's independently wealthy, so she can lie around all day and do nothing if she wants," Gray said.

Although she was dying to know the details, Leah was too polite to ask how one achieved that goal.

Delia rolled her eyes. "I don't want to talk about my financial status. I want to hear how Leah got three jobs."

"Are you superhuman?" Gray laughed. "How do you manage that?"

Leah laughed as well. "I'm just making some money. You know, we all do what we can till the tourist season starts."

Her answer seemed to be enough to satisfy everyone. Leah wondered why she didn't tell them the real reason she was trying to make as much money as possible. It wasn't to tide her over till the tourist season started. Her goal was to be long gone by then. But if she told them she was leaving in a matter of months—weeks, if she could swing it—they might not bother to ask her out for drinks again. And she was enjoying herself way too much to say or do anything to prevent that from happening.

"So you're working almost all the time, and in your free time you're helping to make over Eli?" Gray asked.

Leah shrugged gamely.

"He's looking better already," Jenna said. "Way more human. Don't you think so, Leah?"

Leah felt a blush heating her cheeks, and she nodded vigorously while intently picking at the label on her beer bottle. Then she stopped her head from bobbling. She didn't want to look too enthusiastic about Eli, for obvious reasons. But the truth was, once the beard and the excess hair had come off and Leah had gotten a good look at him, something weird had happened in the vicinity of her knees. In addition to those kind blue eyes, which remained her favorite Eli feature, there were full lips she'd caught a glimpse of in the tangle of beard, now finally revealed, and nice cheekbones, as well as a strong chin with a hint of a cleft—not so much that it made him look like a cartoon, but just enough to tip him into the "quite intriguing" category. Not Gaston, thank goodness, but a truly handsome man. As her knees had attested.

Stupid knees.

"Well, thank goodness for that," Gray said, oblivious to her discomfort. "What else is on the list? I volunteer for the manscaping session."

"I'll bet you do. Keep your mitts off my brother."

"You know he's not my type. I prefer someone who isn't so . . . introspective."

"You mean mopey."

"No, I don't. Although he has been that lately. He just takes everything so *seriously*. When it comes to relationships, anyway."

Leah had been witness to that side of Eli last summer, so she couldn't disagree. If she recalled correctly, Victoria had accused him of moving too fast and that they had only dated for four months. And now here it was, months after she'd broken up with him, and Eli was still determined to get her back, even though Victoria had ended things pretty decisively. Which Leah had also witnessed. Leah wondered what this magical Victoria was like, what about her was so amazing that Eli was willing to change so drastically, just so she'd give him a second chance.

She ventured, "Well, I think it's great you're all working so hard to help him. Victoria really must be worth fighting for."

The others all paused, heaved a giant collective sigh, and took swigs of their drinks in unison.

"You . . . don't approve?"

"No, of course we do. She's . . . nice," Delia said.

Ouch. That was damning with faint praise if Leah had ever heard it. "But?"

Jenna answered, "There's absolutely nothing wrong with her. And if Eli is convinced Victoria is the woman for him, then we support him. Obviously, or we wouldn't be working so hard to Pygmalion him."

"But we think his devotion is really nothing more than pants feels," Gillian explained.

Leah struggled not to smile at the woman's earnestness coupled with outdated teenage slang.

"Nothing wrong with pants feels," Gray said.

"It needs to be more than that," Delia snapped. "Pants feels only takes you so far." She plunged a hand into the bowl of pretzels, adding, "Eventually you have to survive on something more long-lasting. Truer. Deeper."

Leah got the feeling she wasn't talking about Eli and Victoria anymore.

Gray, however, failed to notice. "Well, what Jenna said. If Victoria is what he wants, then we make him into Victoria bait. And please, can we put teaching him how to dance on the list? He has got to stop doing those weird moves that make him look like he's trying to shave his own butthole."

"Again with the manscaping." Jenna made a face at Gray.

"Priorities."

Chapter 6

"Hide me."

"Oh lord, what is it now?" Gray slid around the corner of the gym's front desk that Eli had just barreled up to.

"They're after me," Eli hissed with a wild, frantic look.

Gray didn't need to ask who. "And they'd never think of looking for you in my gym, is that it?"

"Dude. Gillian made me dress up in all the new clothes that just came back from the tailor. A personal fashion show. One outfit after another after another—!"

"Okay, I hear you. Do you want some juice?"

"*No*, I do not want some juice! What am I, a four-year-old? That will not erase the memory of my having to parade up and down in my sister's living room like a living Ken doll for an hour, okay?"

"All right, all right. Deep breath. You want to do yoga? Wait, no. No yoga class this afternoon. How about lifting? Get your aggressions out."

Nodding absently, Eli allowed himself to be led farther into the gym.

"So go on," Gray said as he loaded up a barbell. "Lie down and tell me all about the horrors of the costume parade."

"Oh, that was only part of it. Then Jenna sat me down at her dining room table . . . man, what the hell did you put on this bar?"

"Too much?"

"No, I can handle it."

"Attaboy. Breathe."

"What I can't handle . . ." Eli paused to focus on the weights and then continued, "is being plopped in front of a fancy place setting"—*grunt*—"and being quizzed on which utensil was the freakin' fish fork. I mean"—*grunt*—"I'm not a barbarian. I know how to use a knife and fork."

"That doesn't sound so bad."

"She has a buzzer app."

"Oh."

"Smacked that baby whenever I got anything wrong."

"Ouch. Sorry."

"Yeah, and it went off way more than is healthy for anyone's nerves. She started whaling on it even if I only hesitated."

"So you *didn't* know which fork was the fish fork."

"Does *anyone*?"

"Victoria, probably."

Eli let the bar clank back onto the rack. "Yeah," he muttered. "You're right."

"Eli, it's only been, like, a week, and you're already . . . you know . . ."

"Two weeks, actually. And yes, I'm 'already you know.' They're going to kill me before this is all over."

"It can't be that bad."

"May I remind you what my sister, Gilly, and Delia are like when they fixate on something?"

"So just tell 'em you quit and you're going to do it your way. You're good enough, you're smart enough, and doggone it, Victoria should like you just the way you are."

"You know, sometimes I think getting me to quit is Jenna's ulterior motive. I don't think she really wants me to do this. Not just the makeover, but give up Victoria entirely."

"And why would that be?"

"Because deep down she thinks Victoria and I are completely incompatible? Or Victoria isn't worth fighting for? Who knows?"

"Okay, look. Sit up. Hydrate." Gray shoved a water bottle at Eli and dropped next to him on the bench. "Now, no offense to our well-meaning friends, but it's time for you to install me as your main relationship expert."

Eli snorted.

"Hey, hey, who knows more about relationships than I do?"

"You know about *dating*. There's a difference."

"I know plenty. Now, as an outside observer to this soap opera you've got going on, I get to put a question to you, and make of it what you will: Shouldn't this be easier?"

"Shouldn't what be easier? Lifting? Yeah, if you don't start me out with three hundred pounds."

"I won't even tell you that was barely a hundred. But not the weights, this level of drama. Isn't the goal of a perfect relationship to have no stress and no drama? And what I mean is, maybe you shouldn't have to change who you are for her?"

Eli passed the water bottle back to Gray. "Good relationships take work. Not like you'd know."

"Hey. I nurture all my relationships, even the casual ones."

"I'm sure you do. But I'm talking about long term. Like Jenna and Ben. Their marriage seems easy, but it's not. Do you think Ben *likes* line dancing?"

"Actually, I think he does."

"Okay, bad example. But they do stuff for each other they might not really enjoy, solely for the sake of their relationship. This is me doing that for Victoria. Everybody has to bend a little, right?"

"But how much is too much? That's the question." Gray led Eli over to the free weights. "I mean, it just seems like you're changing yourself an awful lot for a woman who might not appreciate it."

Eli bridled at this. "She'll appreciate it. I'll still be me, only better."

"I don't know; it seems kind of weird and unnecessary."

"Whatever I have to do to get Victoria back is necessary. I plan on being the kind of guy who's up to her standards."

"I admire your tenacity. Now tenaciously do three sets of reps with these."

Gray watched Eli's form closely, corrected it, and stood back, arms crossed in front of his impressive chest. "Does she know your favorite movie?"

"She knows I don't have a favorite movie," Eli panted.

"Everyone has a favorite movie. Now, I'm not talking about your *public* favorite movie, which should always be *The Godfather*— and don't say you haven't seen it."

"I've seen movies. I don't live in a cave."

"Like your *secret* favorite movie?"

Eli let the weight thump onto the mat and, with a steely glare, hissed, "We promised never to speak of that again."

"So she doesn't know about *Little Women*? And the tears?"

"I *said* I watched it by accident. I thought it was porn."

"And you didn't bail when you realized those poofy dresses weren't coming off almost immediately?"

Eli switched hands and hoisted the weight again. "Doesn't matter. You're not in a serious relationship, so your opinion is invalid."

"Outside of Jenna and Ben, none of us is."

"Well, Gillian gets a pass, because ever since her divorce she doesn't want to deal with any meatbag with a Y chromosome, and I don't blame her. And Delia . . ." Eli stopped, unsure as always whether to pursue this particular topic with Gray.

Gray decided for him. "You know what? Just lift."

Eli obeyed. Someday he'd broach the subject of Gray and Delia or, rather, Gray-and-anybody-but-Delia-despite-Delia-crushing-so-hard-everyone-could-see-it-except-Gray, but not today. Because—

Gray spun around at the sudden dull thumping noise coming from the front of the gym. "What the . . . ?"

"Crap," Eli hissed. "They found me."

Sure enough, three pairs of fists were banging on the window, and three noses were pressed up against the glass.

"Was the zombie apocalypse today?" Gray asked. "I really need to check my calendar more often."

"Hide me."

"Oh, it's too late for that, my friend. They've breached the perimeter and they're coming for you. Take your fate like a man."

"But they're going to take me to Watertown for a mani-pedi!"

"Gee, I wish I could be there. Wait. No, I don't. Have fun!"

~

"Get in the van," Jenna shouted, climbing into the driver's seat.

"I was busy, if you hadn't noticed. And this is way too cliché even for a kidnapping."

"Move it," Gillian growled, nudging him in his lower back.

"Hey, hey. No pushing."

"Get in the van, Unca Eli!"

As always, Eli's heart lifted at the sight of his nieces. "Ladies. Good to see you. How'd you get roped into this?"

"I love mani-pedis!" Olivia exclaimed, kicking powerfully in her booster seat and leaving slushy smear marks on the back of the front bucket seat.

"I was just an innocent bystander," Zoë intoned somberly.

"Are you *sure* you're nine years old?"

"Uncle Eli, you ask me that all the time."

"Because your multisyllabic vocabulary makes me wonder if you're actually a forty-seven-year-old in a tiny skin suit all the time."

"Seat belt, Uncle Eli."

"Yeah, seat belt!" the more demonstrably five-year-old Olivia echoed. She hugged herself and leaned forward as if she could get to the spa before her mother even put the minivan in gear.

Once they were on the road, Olivia announced that Unca Eli should get hot pink nail polish to match hers, while Zoë went back to her tablet.

"Playing a good game there, Zoë? Or are you watching YouTube videos?" Eli asked.

Zoë gave him a disdainful look she had definitely inherited from her mother. "I'm reading."

"Of course you are. *War and Peace*? *Ulysses*? . . . Never mind."

"Hope you got enough of a dose of testosterone at your gym session, because it's all estrogen for the rest of the day," Jenna crowed.

"Essrogen!" Olivia repeated, one finger up her nose.

"And hot pink nail polish, apparently," he said.

⁓

Which he did indeed go for at the spa. Because there was no disobeying Miss Olivia.

"Hey," Jenna said in a low tone as they sat in their plush chairs, "have you stopped by the house lately?"

"The house" was shorthand for their childhood home.

"A few days ago. Why?"

"Did Mom look tired to you? She looked tired to me."

"No, she seemed fine."

"She looked tired."

"Jenna, do you want me to agree with you that she looked tired?"

"I'm just worried."

"I know. But she's fine. Clean bill of health, free and clear, all of that. She's fine," Eli repeated soothingly.

"Things can happen."

"Or not. Let's go with not, okay?"

"But—"

"Did she say she felt bad?"

"Well, no . . ."

"Was she lying down? Napping? Did the house look untended?"

"No."

"Okay, then. Don't be a pessimistic pouty pants."

That got a wry smile out of his sister. "Did Olivia teach you that?"

"She did, in fact."

Upon hearing her name, the little girl leaned past Jenna and

Gillian in the lineup of chairs. "Unca Eli, you gotta get the fishies to eat your toes."

"Excuse me?"

"She saw a video where some spas have these tubs of fish that eat the dead skin off your feet," Gillian explained. "It's banned in New York, though."

"Thank God. I most certainly do not want to have fishies eat my toes, thank you very much."

"Sorry, honey," Jenna called to Olivia. "It's illegal here. The fishies don't like it. And if you saw Unca Eli's feet, you'd understand why."

Olivia didn't bat an eyelash. "Unca Eli, when are you gonna marry Aunt Delia?"

"Where does she get this stuff?" Eli looked at Jenna and Gillian, who both shrugged. "Why would you think I'm going to marry Aunt Delia?" he asked his niece. "Aunt Delia and I are just friends."

"But she has purple hair. It's the best."

"Oh. Well, you should look for more than purple hair when you want to marry someone."

Olivia looked at him, puzzled. That did not compute. "But . . . *purple hair!*"

"Tell you what, when we're done here, I'll take you to the store for some hair stuff, and we'll put cool purple streaks in yours. It'll look great."

"Uncle Eli," Jenna muttered in a deadly tone over her daughter's exclamations of delight. "Time for your manscaping. Extra-hot wax."

"I'm just trying to be a good uncle."

"You're trying to drive me to drink. Which I will when we're done here."

"While I'm dyeing Olivia's hair? Good idea. It'll keep you busy while we destroy your bathroom."

"Don't forget your facial," Gillian interrupted before things got ugly. "Your cheeks should be as smooth as a baby's bottom.

Victoria won't want to cozy up to something that feels like a rhinoceros's butt."

"Ouch. I didn't think I was that bad off." Eli looked around the salon. "But after my gel polish and my facial, are we done? I mean, the physical stuff is over with, right?"

"Maybe. We reserve the right to amend our plans at any time."

"That's what scares me, Gilly."

"The inside needs as much work as the outside, if not more," Jenna said. "For *that* we need way more time than we've got."

"Whatever happened to sisterly love and support?"

"What do you think your sister and your honorary sisters are doing this for?"

"Torture should not be a display of love."

"It could be. You need to get out more."

"Ew. Stop, Fifty Shades."

Eli was relieved to see Delia and Zoë returning from their facials. Maybe they would change the subject.

"So I was thinking. You should play an instrument," Delia declared, and Eli's spirits plummeted again.

"What? What for?"

"It's the quickest way to a woman's heart," she said, bugging her eyes at him. The "duh" was silent. "Think Lane Meyer."

Immediately, Jenna and Gillian chorused, enraptured, "Lane Meyer!"

"Who?"

"Yeah, but he played the saxophone," Gillian said with a disappointed wince.

"*Who* is Lane Major?"

"Meyer," Jenna corrected him.

"Whatever. Did you go to school with this person or what?"

"Are you kidding?" Delia demanded, hands on her hips. "Didn't you ever see that movie *Better Off Dead*?"

Eli's questioning eyebrows crashed into each other so hard he gave himself a headache.

Gillian sighed at his ignorance. "From the eighties? John Cusack kept trying to die by suicide because his girlfriend dumped him, but then he fell for the French girl and won her over partly by playing the saxophone?"

"Sorry, never saw it."

A collective gasp went up.

"It's a classic!" Jenna exclaimed. "I'm hereby disowning you. You are no longer my brother. Anyway, the point is, women love guys who play a musical instrument."

"But you're forgetting one thing—I *don't* play a musical instrument."

"Oh." Delia brushed him off with a dismissive hand flip. "That's what Liam Neeson said, and Sam learned to play the drums in, like, what was it, a day?"

"Mm, maybe two or three. It was unclear," Jenna said.

Eli felt like he'd slipped into another dimension where everyone else seemed to speak English, but the words were strung together wrong. He officially understood none of what they were saying.

"Wait, what? Drums? I thought we were talking about the saxophone. And . . . Liam Neeson was in this eighties movie?"

"No, of course not!" Gillian said.

"Then *why* are we talking about Liam Neeson?" Eli demanded.

"*Love Actually*?" Delia said, another silent "duh" tacked on.

"That weird Christmas movie?"

Eli almost heard the record scratch as everyone went silent and turned to stare at him.

"Ooh, you'd better not drag *Love Actually*, Uncle Eli," Zoë whispered. "It's their religion."

"Okay, hold up. I have questions. For starters, who the hell is Sam?"

"Liam Neeson's stepson!" Jenna exclaimed, shocked he didn't know this already.

"Well, son, really," Gillian said. "I mean, their relationship was just goals . . ."

"True, true."

"*Why* are we talking about Liam Neeson's stepson?" Eli practically shouted. He was following none of this.

"Well, if you had ever seen the movie, you heathen," Jenna said, "you'd know that if you really want to win a woman's love, you learn to play an instrument. In Sam's case, the drums. Over a couple of days."

"Oh, that's realistic."

"Well," Delia said, "if you don't want to learn to play an instrument, you can always sing, I guess." She turned to Jenna. "*Can* he sing?"

"I doubt it."

"All right, if all else fails, you can just stand outside Victoria's house with a boom box over your head."

"Ah-*hah*! I know that one! *Sixteen Candles*!" And he sat back in his comfy chair with a triumphant wave of his hand.

"*Say Anything!*" they all shouted back. Including his nieces. And the nail technicians.

"I can't believe you've never seen these movies," Gillian tutted.

"Okay, okay," Jenna interrupted. "Forget the instrument, forget singing—"

"Thank God," Eli muttered.

"He needs to brush up on his heroes."

"Say what, now?" Just when he thought he was in the clear, things always got worse.

"He won't listen to us," his sister went on. "So it's the next best way to get all this information through his thick skull."

"Genius!" Delia breathed.

"I mean, we'll still need to teach him other, practical stuff, but the role models in those movies—!"

"They can teach him how to be a romantic hero," Delia filled in.

"Hang on a minute," Eli protested, but Jenna was already digging around in her purse.

Coming up with a pen and paper, she muttered seriously, "We have to make a list."

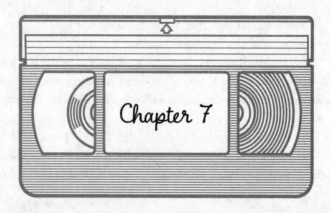

Chapter 7

The trunk of Leah's Honda groaned ominously as she pried it open. Rust flaked off the blister on the edge, dropping into the otherwise pristine interior. Leah flicked away as much as her heavy mittens allowed before leaning in and hauling out two overstuffed garbage bags. How, she wondered for the tenth time, could clothes somehow gather the density of a black hole when more than two pairs of pants and three shirts were packed into straining contractor bags? She was grateful, however, that she didn't have to struggle with the bags while fighting the elements. The wind had died down, the sky was a rare blue, and the temperature was finally out of the teens for the first time in days.

She half carried, half dragged one bag just inside the doors of the thrift store, then went back for the other one. Once she had her load amassed at the donations counter, she pulled off her knit hat and messed with her hair, still contemplating whether she should keep it super short or let it grow. It seemed like a frivolous thing, to let it grow again, as if going back to the way she looked before she shaved her head to help Cathy cope with her chemo side effects was an attempt to wipe out Cathy's memory. Of course that wasn't the case, though she couldn't help but think it all the same.

Kind of like donating all these clothes. Was it an affront to

Cathy's memory, or was it time to clean house? She knew it was the latter, but it still stung a little bit.

"Wow. I was going to ask if you were shopping or donating, but I think those bags say it all." Gillian joined her at the counter. "Not yours, I take it?"

"Just clearing out a few things of Cathy's. She had clothes stashed in the basement, stuff from before . . . well, they certainly were too big for her by the time . . ."

"I get it."

"She was a bit of a hoarder, to be honest."

Cathy was a lot of a hoarder, actually. Leah had tried to clear the house of unnecessary junk more than once since she'd moved back, but her former foster mother wouldn't hear of her removing even one Tupperware container, and Leah didn't want to upset her while she had bigger battles to fight. Now Leah felt like Cathy's ghost was watching her every time she got rid of anything, even the stash of old batteries she'd taken to the disposal center the previous week. Leah wondered what Cathy thought of her donating her old plus-size clothing. She hoped her foster mother understood it was going to people who would appreciate it.

As if Cathy were still around to approve or disapprove.

Determined to drag her nose out of her own navel, Leah asked Gillian, "How about you? Can I interest you in any secondhand way-too-big-for-you clothes?"

"Not today, thanks. I'm on the hunt for something far more elusive, and it looks like I'm going to come up empty."

"What's so rare that you can't find it here?"

Gillian heaved a sigh. "A VCR."

As if she'd said "Bloody Mary" for the third time while looking into a mirror, a pasty gentleman appeared behind the counter.

"I told you," he half said, half wheezed, "there isn't any call for them these days."

"Yes, thank you, Igor," Gillian said. "I got it the first time."

"Dennis," he corrected. "The VHS tapes deteriorate, so there isn't even anything to play on the VCRs anymore. I still don't understand why you want one. You have heard of digital streaming, I take it?"

The blonde woman feigned confusion. "Really? What's that?"

Dennis hesitated, scrutinizing her, then said, "You're messing with me, aren't you?"

"Little bit, Den. Little bit."

"I'm only trying to help."

"Why are you looking for a VCR?" Leah asked Gillian as Dennis started pawing through Cathy's clothes.

"It's part of our Eli makeover."

"You're punishing him with old technology?"

Laughing, Gillian said, "When you're done here, I'll buy you some coffee and tell you all about it."

Another invitation to be social. After her night with the gang at Dickie's, she'd been hoping for this.

"Tell you what, I'll make you some coffee at the house. Because," she glanced furtively at Dennis, "Cathy's hoarder stash . . . includes a working VCR."

"Shut *up!*"

～

"Take it. Consider it my contribution to the makeover project."

"I absolutely have to pay you for it."

"You absolutely do not."

"I wouldn't be able to sleep if I didn't give you something for it. What's the going rate for a vintage VCR these days?"

"Nothing, according to your buddy at the thrift store." Leah didn't want Gillian to think she needed money, but she could tell by the look in her eye that the woman wasn't going to let it go. "Five dollars?" she suggested before Gillian offered her more.

Gillian handed Leah a twenty anyway. "Take it. I don't have anything smaller."

Leah sighed and accepted the bill. "At least let me pour you more coffee."

"That you can do. It's been a long day."

Gillian told her all about their trip to the spa, as well as their plan to refine Eli's mannerisms by making him watch movies, including ones like *Better Off Dead* that the women had on VHS, ones that weren't even available to stream, and they were too impatient to wait for a DVD to show up by mail. Apparently time was of the essence, and Leah soon understood why: they had a list a mile long. Gillian rattled off the titles they had come up with, and Leah caught herself giggling at the thought of Eli taking notes on the traits and mannerisms of fictional romantic heroes.

"Don't forget *The Princess Bride*," she suggested.

"'As you wish!' Eli could use a touch of Westley. I've gotta text that to Jenna. She's got the official list." Gillian pulled out her phone and started typing furiously. "I want to add *Labyrinth*, but do you think Jareth is a bad role model? He's technically evil, after all."

"David Bowie made Jareth sex on a stick. And Jareth is a king. I don't care if it's of goblins."

Gillian typed. "Got any more? We spent way too much time arguing over which James Bond Eli should watch."

"What did you decide?"

"We didn't. We're making him watch all of them."

"That is a *lot* of movies."

"He'll probably tap out way before he gets to the end of our list. We should babysit him to make sure he watches the most important ones, but we're just going to have to give him the list and hope for the best."

"What about Marvel and DC?"

"Leaving them out, unfortunately. We drew the line at expecting him to live up to superhero standards if he doesn't have the powers to go with them. I mean, we have a high enough bar as it is."

"You know . . ." Leah began, then stopped herself.

"What?"

"It's just . . . do you really think Eli is that bad off?"

Gillian put down her phone. "Honestly, hon? I think Eli is a great guy. One of the best. Seriously."

"Then why—?"

"Because Victoria . . . doesn't. But Eli wants to be with her, so . . ."

"You love him enough to make it happen. Even if it means forcing him to watch Cary Grant movies."

"Ooh!" Gillian grabbed her phone again. "Old-school charm, romance, sophistication. Excellent." She studied Leah. "Got any free time to help us out with this project? We could use your input."

"Me? Oh no, absolutely not."

"Why not? I think you have great ideas."

"Because . . ." Leah took a breath. "I really like you and your friends. A lot. And I can tell you believe in helping Eli. But . . . I just think it's silly to turn him into someone else just so he can impress a woman who's . . ." She faltered as her thoughts splintered. "Never mind. I'm sure you know what's best."

Gillian contemplated her in silence for another moment or two, and Leah desperately hoped she wouldn't press her further. Leah wasn't sure what she'd say if she did. If Gillian wanted to know her feelings about Eli—about Eli and Victoria—she might not have an answer. Or at least not one she'd be willing to share.

Leah let out a relieved breath when Gillian said resignedly, "Well, if you change your mind, you're more than welcome. We need as much brain power as we can get."

"You make it sound like a top secret NASA project."

"It's just about as complicated, I swear. I'd better get going." Gillian stood and stretched. "Thanks for the coffee." Leah walked her to the door and handed her the VCR. When Leah opened the door for her, Gillian asked, "What's that sign on your car?"

"It's a magnet I use when I work for Magic Maids."

"*Another* job?"

"Just once in a while, on a case-by-case basis. I'm free on Tuesdays and Thursdays, so when they're busy on those days and they get another call, they toss it to me. It's not too frequent."

"But every little bit helps?"

"Sure does."

"Honey, forgive my asking, but do you have bills you can't pay? I mean, it isn't cheap to pay for heating at this time of year."

"You've got that right." It was nearly impossible, especially without a fireplace or woodstove in the drafty house. "I'm fine. I promise."

"You'd tell me if you had any problems, right? You can, you know."

"Sure, Gilly."

Gillian looked at the Magic Maids sign again, then back to Leah. "You'd never admit it," she said with a sigh, shaking her head as she walked to her car.

Once she was alone again, Leah turned on a lamp to banish the early-evening gloom. These days reminded her of last winter, when she'd first arrived in Willow Cove to help Cathy. She'd stayed in touch with her foster mother in the intervening years, and despite Cathy's gruff demeanor, Leah had always gotten the sense Cathy was pleased that she checked in every few weeks. She never let on overtly, of course; Leah had just learned to identify her slightly warmer tone as they talked. Which was fine. Leah understood. She could be happy with "slightly warm," because it was Cathy's equivalent of anyone else's gushing affection.

It was practically a high honor when the usually taciturn Cathy admitted to Leah she had cancer. She wouldn't, however, admit she was frightened. That was up to Leah to discern from Cathy's tone. There was no question in Leah's mind that she'd come back to Willow Cove to help her out, especially after she called Patrick, who absolutely could not, he said, visit his mother, let alone come back home for any extended period of time to help take care of her. Leah wasn't surprised in the least. So Leah went.

In the late-afternoon twilight of the previous winter, she and Cathy had played cards or watched movies on the laboring VCR or just sat quietly, Leah huddled under the living room lamp, reading, while Cathy dozed. Although they hadn't done much, Leah's mind had been cluttered with a nonstop undercurrent of thoughts and ideas, like the steady hum of a refrigerator that's only noticed by its absence, like in a power outage. As she'd read or watched a movie or talked to Cathy, her mind had also been monitoring Cathy's behavior to determine if she was feeling unwell, keeping tabs on the time and noting when her next dose of medicine was due, trying to decide what to offer Cathy for her next meal that she'd actually find appealing.

Now she had none of that. The hum had been silenced. Leah should have been more at peace, but instead she was fidgety and restless. Good thing she had more housecleaning to do to keep her occupied. What room should she tackle next? Although she'd scrubbed the kitchen, the cupboards and pantry were full to bursting. That would make a good project. Or . . .

She wandered into the small back bedroom that had been hers when she was a teenager and was hers again. She could have moved into the master bedroom on the other side of the living room after Cathy passed, but even with the hospital bed gone and the old regular bed put back, she couldn't imagine taking over Cathy's space. This wasn't her house, and it wasn't her room to make her own.

There were boxes and totes of old papers stacked high on the bunk beds where her foster sisters had slept. Some of Leah's clothes that wouldn't fit in the tiny closet were draped over them. She absently picked up one item, not hers, but something she couldn't bring herself to throw away.

Eli's baseball cap.

Burgundy fabric with a team name, Land Sharks, embroidered in gold, the cap was evidently much loved—the brim was frayed, the back a little discolored, the button on top nearly bare of fabric, displaying the dull aluminum underlayment. No stains, though. Eli had apparently taken good care of it, and the wear was just age. She wondered why it meant so much to him. These weren't Willow Cove High School's colors or team name. She crossed to the dresser and looked in the mirror, then hesitantly placed the cap on her head. The bill curled perfectly—not too much, just enough. It had obviously been gently, patiently trained to curve over time.

Leah imagined Eli settling the cap on his wavy hair, thumbing the bill. She imitated the gesture and wondered what position he played. Was he a pitcher, squinting at the catcher for just the right signal? Or was he a fast-moving shortstop, effortlessly intercepting hits?

Jenna had told him to get rid of the cap because it didn't fit with the look Victoria would like. What look did Victoria like? What was her style? If her face matched the voice she'd heard on the bridge last summer, Leah would guess she was tall, probably almost matching Eli's height if she were in heels, and he was definitely more than six feet tall. She'd bet anything Victoria was always in heels. A long sweep of hair, Leah assumed, dark blonde with brilliant highlights. Or auburn. Definitely high cheekbones and a strong, dramatic jawline. Not like her own face, which peeked out from under the bill of Eli's cap, a pale moon nearly bare of makeup, with chubby cheeks.

Whatever she looked like, Victoria was evidently so special that Eli's friends and family felt he had to change everything about himself just to win her back. It sounded like a stupid plan. She wanted to tell Eli he shouldn't do it, but it was none of her business. She was wasting time even thinking about it.

Leah made a face and threw Eli's cap on the bed, focusing instead on the pile of junk on the bunk beds. She had just carried one of the old boxes into the living room when her phone rang.

"'Lo?"

"Leah?"

"Who's this?"

"You serious?"

"Hanging up now."

"No, wait! It's Patrick!"

Leah immediately wished she'd hung up when she had the chance. "Oh. Hey."

"Nice to talk to you too."

"Sorry. Hi, Patrick. How have you been?"

"I'm great."

Her foster brother offered up no other information, no matter how long Leah waited. She dropped onto the couch and eventually said, "Okay. Good. Happy for you."

"Darn right. So listen. I'm gonna come up next weekend."

Leah noted Patrick didn't ask how she was. She let it go. This was Patrick, after all. "You sure about that?"

"Yeah, okay, okay. I know I said I was coming up before, but things got busy here. I'm getting married!"

That brought Leah up short for a minute. Somebody wanted to marry Patrick? "Oh. Congratulations."

"Yeah, thanks, so I need money. Did you know weddings are expensive? And buying a house?"

"That's the rumor. You're selling this place, then?"

"Well, *yeah*," he said, punctuating his words with an incredulous snort. "What'd you think, I was going to live there or something?"

"I thought maybe you'd keep it as a summer home."

"Nah, I'd rather have the cash."

Leah knew it would come to this eventually. Patrick had dropped hints about the fate of Cathy's house when he was there last, just after Cathy passed. It had sparked Leah's motivation to leave town, to get out before there was no house to live in, but hearing Patrick voicing his plan to sell the only real home she'd known since she'd lived with her biological mother, and relatively soon, still stung.

"So this is what I need you to do . . ."

As Leah half listened to Patrick rattling off plans to spruce up the house, she looked around at the tired little place. What would it take to make it attractive enough to draw a buyer? Some houses in Willow Cove, especially those right on the water, sold practically overnight for astronomical prices. This house would not be one of them.

Leah wasn't sure what Patrick wanted from her. "Are you asking for names of some contractors?" she guessed, interrupting his off-the-cuff brainstorming, which was starting to sound overly ambitious.

"*Shit*, no! That's just a waste of money."

"Then who's going to . . . ?"

"I'll do it. And you can help."

Leah dropped over sideways, the coarse fabric of the couch scratching her cheek. "*How*, Patrick? I'm not handy with tools. Are you?"

She'd added to her handyman skill set already this winter, having taught herself to unfreeze the pipes, which happened way too often, and by now she was very adept at resetting a tripped circuit breaker if she absentmindedly used the toaster and the microwave at the same time. Leah suspected she already knew more about how to fix things in the rickety place than Patrick ever knew in his whole life, but that didn't mean she was willing to take on any more challenges.

Patrick, on the other hand, was oblivious. "How hard can it be?"

Oh lord. "And how long do you think this will take?"

"We could get it done in a weekend, easy."

She turned her head to muffle her laugh in the cushion. That was pure Patrick—completely oblivious to logistics. She knew it would be pointless to try to talk him out of this. All she could do was agree for now and hope he got distracted by some other shiny thing before trying to implement his half-baked plan.

After Patrick hung up, Leah rolled onto her back and stared at the cracked ceiling plaster. "Oh, Cathy," she groaned, "do something with your son."

If only. Cathy had never (mentally) knocked any sense into him when she was alive; Leah couldn't expect her to reach out from beyond the grave to start now.

Chapter 8

Eli should have been enjoying his unexpected day off after the snow-shoeing hike he had been hired to lead was canceled. He could have run some errands, done his taxes . . . or, as he'd ended up choosing, relaxing with a new video game . . . but he couldn't concentrate on anything. Not with *those* objects in his field of vision.

His friends had made good on their threat to make him watch old movies to brush up on how to be a dashing romantic hero. They'd come up with a long, *long* list, and they demanded he start his lessons right away, by delivering a VCR (a VCR? seriously?) and a DVD player. How they got their hands on a VCR was anybody's guess, and why anyone still had VHS tapes—his money was on Jenna—was another mystery. Now the VCR and tapes were squatting threateningly in the corner of his living room, along with an only slightly more modern DVD player and discs, daring him to pick them up.

He'd been ignoring the technological artifacts for a while, but it was getting harder to do with every passing day. Their presence overpowered even the siren song of the video game he was trying to play. Or maybe it was the guilt they inspired. This makeover project was getting annoying, but he knew his friends and family were only trying to help him. The least he could do was cooperate.

Eli heaved a sigh, switched off his gaming console, and examined the VCR. The dusty brick seemed to have all its working parts, even the remote, which was in a ziplock baggie secured to the side with duct tape. The cables dangling from the ports on the back definitely looked alien. But how hard could it be to hook it up, really? A cable was a cable.

He was wedged behind his TV, struggling with the various wires and cursing loudly and creatively enough to fell trees with the power of his voice alone, when someone jiggled the knob on the front door.

Only Jenna was comfortable enough to let herself into his house when he wasn't supposed to be home, so he bellowed, "It's open!"

The shadow on the other side of the shade-covered window in the door remained where it was, and the doorknob kept rattling.

"Jenna! Door's unlocked!"

Still no one came in. With a fresh round of cursing, Eli extricated himself from the cables and cords, tripped over the surge protector, and launched himself into the easy chair next to the TV stand. He brought his swearing to the next level as he limped toward the door and flung it open.

"I *said* it's unlo—Oh."

Eli was brought up short by the sight of a startled Leah, key in hand, earbuds in ears, on his front porch. She jumped a mile and yanked on the wires.

"I'm sorry—"

"What are you doing here?" He wasn't upset at all, but he was definitely surprised. While part of his brain focused on her and why she was letting herself into his house, another part scrambled to gauge how messy his house would seem to a visitor. It did not pass virtual inspection.

"I, uh, Gillian . . . I mean . . ." She stopped, put out her hands, palms down, as if cuing herself to calm down, and let out a breath between pursed lips.

"What about Gillian?"

"She hired me."

"She hired you."

"Well, she found out I worked for Magic Maids, called in a request, and *they* assigned me. I didn't know it was your house. They told me the owner would be at work, and I should let myself in with the key under the mat."

"So this job for Magic Maids, it's job number, what, thirty-four?"

Her lips quirked. "Something like that. Anyway, you're supposed to be at work. You're not sick, are you?"

A little worried crease formed between her eyebrows, and Eli found himself smiling at her concern. It was sweet.

"No. No, *I'm* not sick. The hike got canceled. Because some of the *clients* got sick . . . you know what? It doesn't matter. Come on in out of the cold."

"I don't want to bother you."

"You won't. I'm not doing anything important. I'll stay out of your way."

"I don't know. This monster gets pretty loud."

She indicated the squat vacuum by her side. She also had a bucket, a mop, a broom, and a plastic tote filled with spray bottles and sponges.

"I don't mind."

He reached out the door, grabbed as many of the supplies as he could, and pulled them inside. Once he had her vacuum hostage, she had no choice but to follow it. He closed the door behind her as she stood on the small rag rug, looking around.

"Sorry about the mess," he said, one hand jammed in his jeans pocket, the other awkwardly scratching the back of his head.

Leah smiled. "That's what I'm here for. Anyway, it's not messy," she reassured him as she shook off her jacket. He took it from her and draped it over the nearest chair. "I've seen way worse."

"So you do this a lot, then?"

"No, not really. I just—"

"Fill in."

"You know me."

Eli realized that, aside from all her jobs, he didn't know anything about her at all. All he had was a lot of questions. He got the feeling the answers would be really interesting.

When he didn't say anything, she went on, "This shouldn't take too long. Unless you reserved your rock-star-trashed-hotel-room look for the bedroom."

"Nope, this is pretty much it. And it's, you know, kind of small."

"I like it," Leah said as she took in the knotty pine paneling, worn Indian-pattern rugs, corner woodstove, and caved-in living room furniture. "It's cozy."

"It was my grandfather's. He left it to me and Jenna, and I bought her out. Strangely enough, she didn't put up much of a fight."

"She didn't want to live in the back of beyond?"

"It is a little out of the way," he agreed. Not too far, though, just a ten-minute drive inland from the center of town—enough to give him some breathing room, especially when Willow Cove was thronged with day-trippers and weeks- or months-long vacationers in the summer.

"It's quiet out here. It's nice."

Leah's approval startled him. He'd spent so much time defending his choice of living situation—why such a small place? Why not update this terrible rustic look? Why live so far from where the action was, even as little as what Willow Cove had to offer?

It occurred to him that all those questions had come from Victoria. He shrugged off the thought.

"And who's this?"

Eli snapped back to the present to find his new roommate snaking between Leah's ankles. He scooped up the sweet-faced white feline. "Meet Blanche. She's Victoria's. I'm taking care of her till she gets back."

"Hello, Blanche." Leah got closer to scritch the cat between her ears, eliciting a rumbling purr and a lick on her nose, making Leah giggle. "She's cute."

For some inexplicable reason Eli felt himself break out into a prickly sweat. He eased the cat back to the floor and took a step back. "Well, do what you have to. I'll be over here in the media room if you need anything." He climbed behind the TV and commenced wrestling with the cables again. None of them looked like they fit into any of the TV's ports.

"Oh, you're working on the VCR."

"You sound like you know this contraption."

"It was just sitting on a shelf in Cathy's house, collecting dust. It's nice to know it's going to good use."

Eli popped his head up. "This is *your* fault?"

"Sorry," Leah said with a bright smile. She didn't look sorry in the least.

"So you heard about the movie thing."

"I did. It's an interesting approach to your, uh, education. Oh, this is a good one."

He poked his head out from behind the TV again. She had picked up *Better Off Dead*.

"That's what I keep hearing. But it's not going to get seen if I can't get this VCR hooked up."

"So start with something else."

"They do go on a lot about *Love Actually*."

"You *haven't seen*—?"

"All right, all right. I got that from the rest of them, thank you very much. I've just never been much of a movie person."

"Apparently not. Well, it's good. Don't let the fact that it's not Christmas anymore stop you from watching it."

"I've gotta admit, I am a little curious about this Sam kid, the drumming savant."

"So watch that one first."

Eli only paused for a nanosecond. "Watch it with me."

"What?"

"The only thing worse than having to watch a movie you don't want to watch is being forced to watch it alone."

"I . . ."

"I have popcorn. Also real butter."

"I'm on the clock."

"Oh. Right." Eli thought for a moment, climbed out from behind the TV, and picked up her mop and bucket. "Well, let's get started, then."

"But you're the client."

"And this client wants to help clean his own house and watch a movie afterward with the magic maid."

Leah hesitated. Eli marched toward the back hallway with the mop.

"Think of it this way," he called over his shoulder. "I don't want you to see the grimy depths of my bathroom. You start in the kitchen or the living room and let me hide my own mess from you, okay?"

After another second, Leah laughed. Eli quickly decided it was one of the best sounds he'd ever heard.

~

"Now . . . see . . ." Eli paused to stuff another handful of popcorn into his mouth, dropped a few kernels, and picked them up. "Wait. Can't have any food land on my nice, clean furniture."

He and Leah had worked in companionable silence for several hours, scrubbing and decluttering until every surface was clear, every floor shone, and every pillow was plumped and dust-free. He could eat off his kitchen floor now. He wouldn't want to, but he *could*. He hadn't even minded cleaning his own toilet, as long as he heard the sounds of Leah somewhere else in the house, vacuuming or spraying something or scouring something else. It was comfortable. Felt good.

Now they were slumped side by side on the well-worn leather couch, sock-clad feet propped up on the coffee table and Blanche curled against Leah's hip, studying the heroics of Sam striving to get the attention of his one true love, among other plotlines. Eli had initially been pretty standoffish about the whole movie, but he'd gotten sucked in somewhere along the way.

"Okay, now, Snape—how is he a role model?"

"You know Alan Rickman was in the Harry Potter movies, but you've never seen him in this?" Leah shook her head as she leaned over and took some popcorn. "Okay. Alan Rickman's character, the one cheating on his wife, is *not* a role model. He's an example of how *not* to act."

"This is very confusing."

"It's not . . . *actually*."

"Hurr."

"Your role models are Jamie, the guy who fell in love with the girl who helped out at his writing cabin even though they didn't speak the same language; Sam, the kid drummer; and the prime minister. They're heroic. They put it all on the line for love. Oh, also Karl, the hot guy, if you want to be generous, because he ends up being sort of understanding when Sarah's brother needs her. Cheating Harry, however, is a cautionary tale."

"What about the one going to America to get laid?"

"We'll just pretend Colin doesn't exist. And Mark—the guy in love with his best friend's wife—is problematic at best, but we're supposed to understand that he can't help it, and he's trying to get a grip and move on. Now hush and watch the movie."

Which they did, for the longest time, and Eli was torn between falling into the movie and being keenly aware of the warmth of Leah's arm all but touching his own. He jumped and nearly sent the popcorn flying when they both stuck their hands in the bowl at the same time. To remedy the situation, he handed it over to her and paid attention to the movie. And that turned out to be a mistake.

"Are you okay?" she whispered.

"I'm fine," he rasped. "Shh."

"But—"

"Watch the movie."

"I've *seen* the movie. I'm worried about you."

"Well, don't be." Then, after a few minutes, Eli burst out, "How could he *do* that? You don't make Emma Thompson cry like that—you just don't!"

"Eli."

"What?"

"Don't knock over the TV or whatever you're thinking of doing. It's only a movie."

Uncomfortable pause.

"I know."

"Okay, then."

"But what's it all for?" he burst out again. "Does Emma get to punch Snape in the nuts by the end?"

"Figuratively. Mostly this is to show how not everybody gets a happy ending in life. You know, some people don't get a romance, but there are different kinds of love instead."

"I don't like that answer," Eli grumbled.

When the movie was over, Leah faced him squarely. "You all right?"

"I'm fine."

"Want a tissue?"

"No!" he snapped petulantly, then surreptitiously wiped his eyes on his sleeve when she turned to put the popcorn bowl on the table. "But what the hell was this supposed to teach me? I already know not to be a douche."

"I told you, the whole Harry story is not your focus. The fools for love are. Be a fool for love like Sam and those guys."

"I already was," he muttered, half to himself.

"I mean pay attention to their heroic, courageous gestures. The prime minister didn't give up until he found the woman he let go. Sam learned the drums for his one true love—and almost got arrested just to see her one last time. Jamie learned a foreign language to communicate with the woman he loved. That's why the movie was on your list."

Eli said nothing, just raised one eyebrow as he studied her.

Leah sighed. "I'm not getting through to you, am I? Maybe you need a comedy next. What else is on your list?" She picked up the paper Jenna had given him. "*Pretty Woman, Bull Durham* . . . ooh, the kiss speech is really good . . . *Hitch* . . . very nice, James Bond . . . can't go wrong there . . . Cary Grant movies . . . *The*

Notebook? Um . . . the nineties *Emma* . . . yep, Jeremy Northam is smooth. Oh, *Pride and Prejudice*—the movie *and* the miniseries! Mr. Darcy! Yes!"

"Miniseries?"

"Six episodes."

"I don't have time for that!"

"What else have you got going on in your life?"

"Uh . . ." His eyes strayed to his frequently used gaming console. "Plenty," he lied.

"Okay." She gave him a sidelong knowing glance and a smirk before continuing. "*Love Actually* we just did, *Better Off Dead* . . . we've got to figure out how to get the VCR working. *The Princess Bride, Labyrinth* . . . ooh, *Dirty Dancing, Say Anything* . . . there are a lot of movies on here, I grant you. You might have to get selective."

"I draw the line at the Fifty Shades movies. And *Twilight*."

"Same thing." At Eli's puzzled look, she went on, "*Fifty Shades*? Fanfic of *Twilight*?"

"*How?*"

"I never could figure that out. But I do support your decision. You know what? Even though this is a long list, we should add *The Empire Strikes Back*."

"Now you're talkin'!"

"But just the Han and Leia scenes."

"What? Why?"

"Because! Han wooing Leia was . . . oh!" And Leah started fanning herself.

"Were you named after her?"

"What?" Startled, she looked up from scribbling on the list. "No. Wait. Are you telling me you finally know a popular movie, but you don't know the princess's name?"

Eli had no idea what she was talking about. "Leia," he said, pronouncing it like Leah's: Lee-uh.

"*Lay*-uh," she enunciated. "Tch. My name is spelled differently too, by the way. L-E-A-H. Anyway, my mom said she just liked it. I'm not named after anybody at all."

"So you knew your mom?"

Leah hesitated. "Uh . . . yeah, I did." She carefully set the list and pen on the coffee table. "I should go."

And in a flash she was on her feet and pulling on her jacket. *Shit.*

"Hey." Eli reached her just as she was trying to open the door while corralling all of her cleaning equipment. She stopped, mainly because the vacuum and the mop were fighting back. "I'm sorry."

Leah took a breath but didn't meet his eye. "It's okay."

"Apparently it's not." He kept his voice low and even and waited until she looked up at him. "I didn't mean to pry."

"I know. Everybody's just naturally curious. I get questions all the time."

"Well, not from me. Not anymore. It's your business." Once she nodded in acknowledgment, he said, "I'll help you take this stuff to your car."

Eli held open the door for her, and she picked up the tote of cleaning sprays, walking ahead of him to her car while he scooped up the rest. Before he went down the porch steps, he squinted into the distance, spotting something where his driveway twisted through a small clump of trees.

He loaded up Leah's car and waved her off. Once she was gone, he marched down the drive. The familiar car he'd seen through the pines surrounding his house had started its engine but was having trouble getting traction in the snow. It was still in the same spot when he knocked on the driver's-side window.

Delia eased it down, and he leaned in, glaring at her and Gillian. "Really?"

"We were just—"

"Just what, Delia?"

"Making sure Leah came to do the job?" she offered.

"And what job was that?"

"Cleaning, of course!" Gillian said, a little too heartily.

"And the binoculars on the seat there?"

Gillian shoved them into her bag at her feet. "Just . . . making sure she was cleaning . . . properly."

"You don't trust her?"

"No, no, of course we do."

"Or maybe, when you found out from Jenna I was going to be home today, you wanted to see what would happen when Leah and I were thrown into a room together?"

"What?" Delia exclaimed. "Wh—why—what would make you think that?"

"Look, guys. You haven't exactly been subtle about Leah before this. So I'm telling you right now, if you have some ulterior motive, you can give it up right now, okay?"

"Don't you *like* Leah?" Gillian asked.

"Of *course* I like Leah! What's that got to do with anything?"

"How *much* do you like Leah?"

"See? Exactly what I'm talking about. You're pushing it, both of you. Now get your minds out of the gutter and get out of here."

"No."

"What do you mean, no?"

"We're stuck," Delia said timidly. "Can you give us a push?"

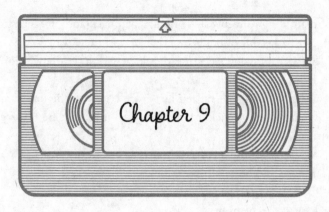

Chapter 9

Knock.

Knock.

Knock knock knock.

Leah poked her head out of the kitchen. Was someone at the door? No one was ever at the door. Not even when Cathy was still alive. That's what came from being overly independent and antisocial. She'd had no friends dropping by to bring her a casserole or some pot brownies after her chemo treatments. That was why Leah had come back to help her out. Cathy had had no one else in her life.

Neither did Leah, when it came to that. She'd always kept to herself—when she was in the foster system, when she was on her own after she'd aged out of foster care, and recently, when she came back after Cathy got sick. The few recent instances when she'd spent time with Gillian and her crew felt like a social whirlwind in comparison.

Knockknockknockknockknockknock—

Growling impatiently, Leah charged across the room and hauled the door open, then jumped at the sight of Eli on her doorstep.

"Hey, whoa," he said, hands up. "This is Willow Cove. There are no serial killers here."

Scrambling to recover, she took a step back and oh-so-casually blew her bangs out of her eyes. "I never said there were."

"So why are you answering the door with a deadly weapon in your hand?"

"What?" Then she realized he was referring to the pretty massive wrench she was wielding. She lowered it to her side. "Sorry. It wasn't meant for you."

"My deep condolences to whoever it *was* meant for."

"That would be my frozen pipes."

"Ooh, that's too bad."

"It sucks, to be honest."

The only thing those frozen pipes would have been good for was to prove to Patrick the house needed more work than he assumed. But of course Patrick had to be his predictable old self and flake out on her. He'd texted only that morning that he wasn't going to be able to come up and check out the state of the house after all. And he'd reschedule. Probably at the last minute, knowing him, and then he'd really expect all the repairs to be done the night before a real estate agent hammered a FOR SALE sign into the front yard.

"Yep, sure has been pretty darn cold these past couple of days," Eli said. "Like right now, in fact. *Pret*-ty darn cold."

Leah took the hint. "Would you like to come in?"

"Thought you'd never ask."

Eli stomped in on a wave of frigid air, and even after she'd shut the door behind him, the cold seemed to keep radiating off his jacket.

"I, uh, brought you something." He held out a plastic bag, but when she reached for it, he raised it out of her reach, drawling in a weird accent, "Okay, we're gonna do this nice and slow, see? I hand you the bag, and you give up the wrench."

"Nobody told you to watch old James Cagney movies."

"It's the only imitation I can do well."

"Sure you do."

"So are we making a fair trade?"

Leah rolled her eyes. "Yes."

When she was in possession of the bag and he had the wrench, he waved it around in a small circle. "Were you going to shut off the main?"

"I got the wrench out just in case, but I don't think I need to. I'm pretty sure it's just one pipe."

"Bathroom or kitchen?"

"Oh, you don't have to—"

"Bathroom or kitchen?"

Dwarfed by him in the small space of the entryway, she stepped back as he started to make himself at home. He leaned the wrench against the wall and toed off his insulated boots, each likely able to accommodate the proverbial old woman and about thirty of her kids, then windmilled his long arms to remove his jacket.

"Kitchen," she finally answered. "You know, you really don't have to."

But he was already finding his way through the house, apparently more than ready to do battle with the offending pipe, and she had to admit she was grateful he was willing to take over the unpleasant task.

Leah peeked into the bag and called, "Hey, this is Cathy's VCR. That's not a fair trade."

"Sure it is. You get a useless piece of junk, and I unfreeze your pipes." He stuck his head back out of the kitchen doorway. "That wasn't suggestive at all, was it?"

She ignored his last comment. "This isn't useless. I'm pretty sure it works."

"Well, it didn't work for me," he shouted over the groaning plumbing. "Hey, your pipes are frozen."

"Just couldn't take my word for it, huh? There isn't enough insulation in the outside walls. Cathy always talked about getting the blown-in stuff, but she never did."

Leah set the VCR on the table, pulled a cardboard box out of the bag, and lifted the lid. Donuts.

"Hair dryer?"

"Bathroom, down the hall."

Eli brushed past her while she leaned in the kitchen doorway with a chocolate-frosted donut in hand. "What's the occasion for the goodies?"

"Extension cord?" he asked as he came back through.

"Junk drawer, to the left of the fridge."

"The donuts are an apology."

"For what?"

Eli paused in his bustling and unwound the extension cord slowly. "What I said the other day. Being nosy about your . . . you know, your past."

"I said it was okay."

"I wanted to make sure."

"So you hunted me down at home?"

"Well, that wasn't hard. I know where Cathy lives. Lived. Sorry." He sighed. "I keep sticking my foot in my mouth, so I'm going to stop talking now."

She couldn't help but smile. "You're fine. The donuts weren't necessary, but I never turn down a dose of sugar, so thank you. I also wouldn't turn down help unfreezing my pipes. Not to sound suggestive or anything."

"Happy to. Eat, lounge. This shouldn't take long."

Leah did eat, but she didn't lounge. By the time the sound of freely running water roared from the kitchen and Eli came out winding up the cord to the hair dryer, she'd downed a second donut (Boston cream) while hooking up the VCR to the ancient TV in the living room.

"How did you *do* that?" Eli exclaimed.

"It's easy when both appliances are from the same century."

"Impressive." Eli looked at the scene playing on the TV. "Is that an old episode of *Wide World of Sports*?"

"There was a tape in the machine. Cathy liked to watch figure skating. Too bad you don't have your movie with you."

He pulled the tape from his jacket pocket and waved it at her. "I was going to give up and return it to Jenna today. Risking her wrath, I might add."

"Well, now you don't have to." Leah made room for him on

the couch. "Watch it here. And eat. Some nice person brought me donuts."

Eli cocked his head, a half smile on his face. "Really?"

"What, 'really'? Of course."

When Eli continued to hesitate, Leah realized why. Watching *Love Actually* with him was an isolated incident, a happy accident that didn't imply the event would be repeated. Inviting him to watch a second movie with her could be construed as making a habit of it. Was he okay with that? Of course he was, who was she kidding?

But was she?

She could be. He was just a person, Leah told herself. It wouldn't be "a thing" unless she made it one. And she wasn't about to do that.

"Of course," she repeated, more firmly. "Sit."

Eli seemed more than willing. He launched himself onto the sofa and rooted around in the donut box. She pointed the remote at the VCR, but he put his hand in front of the beam. "Wait a second. I just want to make sure we're good."

"You brought me donuts. Of course we're good."

"No, seriously—"

"Eli." Leah found herself automatically adopting the low, measured tone she had learned to use on Cathy whenever she'd gotten agitated in her last few months. It always seemed to calm Cathy, and she hoped it would have the same effect on Eli. She wanted very much to shut down this discussion once and for all. "I swear, you're fine. I'm fine. Everything's fine."

He still looked at her dubiously. "It's been bothering me."

"I can see that. But don't let it. Just enjoy the best eighties teen movie you've never heard of. Oh!" She stopped herself just before hitting the play button. "I have a great idea—a John Cusack double feature."

"Er . . ."

"No, wait, hear me out. This character of his you're about to see in *Better Off Dead*, Lane Meyer, is like the little brother to his iconic role in *Say Anything*, Lloyd Dobler. If we watch both back to back, you could see how an everyguy character can evolve from mopey and insecure to confident and independent."

"And this helps me how?"

"It's the evolution of a hero."

"An eighties hero."

"Heroes are timeless."

"And where does Cusack's iconic role in *Hot Tub Time Machine* fit into this timeless hero archetype?"

"Shut up and watch the movies." Then she realized. "Unless . . ."

"What?"

"I didn't even ask if you have anything to do this afternoon."

"Yeah, actually, I do have something to do."

Leah tried to ignore the sinking feeling in her stomach. "Oh."

Eli grinned and took the remote from her. "I have to do my homework and knock two of these movies off my list. So do you have *Say Anything* on VHS, in keeping with this eighties party?"

"No! DVD, of course."

"You know, we *can* do twenty-first-century streaming at some point."

"Not in this house. There's no such thing as Wi-Fi around here."

"You and the Amish, huh?"

Leah didn't tell him it wasn't by choice. She wasn't about to spend her hard-earned money on frivolous luxuries like Wi-Fi while she was saving up to leave town. She definitely wasn't going to show him the flip phone she had for a cell.

~

"*What* are you showing me? I just sat through two movies with a hangdog hero who's all sensitive and shit. I don't need sensitive. I have sensitive coming out my butt."

"A very sensitive thing to say."

"I thought I was supposed to be learning how to be cool and tough or whatever you ladies say I need to be to be a better person."

"'You ladies'?" She arched an eyebrow at him, and Eli started to backpedal immediately.

"No, no, that's not what I meant. Don't get it twisted. My point is I'm doing all this because my sister and my friends keep telling me I need to be different, and they yell at me because I'm too sensitive already."

"Okay." Leah sighed and prepared to break it down for him, but Eli would not be deterred from his rant.

"You've gotta admit this list is kind of random." He pulled the paper, now worn and creased, out of his back pocket and flapped it in the air until it unfolded. "On the one hand there are all these suave, manly men who can take or leave women, like Bond and everything—*all* the Bonds, I might add, and thanks for that—but then there are all kinds of sensitive guys, like Lane Dobler."

"It's—"

"I know who it is. I'm making a point."

"Lane Meyer and Lloyd Dobler aren't the same guy, though. Lane was dopey about his ex-girlfriend who didn't deserve him, but he becomes more confident in the end." She bit her tongue so she didn't point out any parallels between Eli and Lane. "Lloyd is every woman's hero, because he's so self-assured and exudes this . . . calm, authoritative vibe, so much so that Diane trusts him enough to put her faith in him after her dad goes to prison, even to travel to another country with him. This list"—and Leah twitched it out of his fingers—"is less about manly men and more about what makes women swoon."

"Keeping us men confused is what gets you guys off?"

"Hey, we contain multitudes. We can swoon over a he-man *or* a sensitive guy. It's all the better when they're the *same* guy."

"You seem to know an awful lot about it," he murmured, studying her.

Leah quickly looked down at the list. Oh, that voice. She'd never understood what people meant when they used the word "honey" to describe the sound of someone's voice, but now she did. Dark honey, this one. Over thick, sweet corn bread. She tried to shrug it off but noticed her own voice was a little shaky when she retorted, "Well, I *am* a woman."

"I *know*."

Oh God.

"I mean," Eli continued, "you sound like you have your own Lloyd Dobler to rely on. Is that how you know? Oh, wait." He ran a hand over his face and sighed. "Crap. Too personal? Did I mess up again?"

She smiled and shook her head. He was cute when he was nervous. Wait. Not cute. No. Not thinking that.

"I figure we're friends, right?" he went on. "So we can talk about . . . things? I mean, after all, you saw me, you know, *not* cry."

"You were chopping onions when you were watching *Love Actually*. You had the cutting board on your lap. I saw it all."

"Exactly. How did onions get into my house? I'm still not sure. Anyway . . . ?"

"Yes," she answered warmly. "We're friends."

Eli went quiet, studying her again. She forced herself to look him in the eye. She would not get flustered around this guy. Not going down that road. Not today, not any day.

"I believe," he said, "it may be my life goal to get that dimple to appear." Leah looked away again. She couldn't maintain eye contact when he said things like that. "And getting you to blush, apparently."

OH GOD NO.

"So, friend to friend, who's your Lloyd Dobler?"

She wanted to run, just like she'd dashed out of his house the other day when he started asking intimate questions. Too bad she lived here and couldn't escape. But she had just agreed they were friends, and friends talked about this kind of thing. She'd heard, anyway. It had been a long time since she'd had someone she could talk to about such trivial matters as boyfriends, yet here was Eli, looking at her earnestly, exactly the sort of person she would be able to trust with her personal details.

So she admitted, "I don't have a Lloyd Dobler. Currently. In fact, I don't think I've ever met anyone as heroic as Lloyd Dobler." She quashed her next thought—that maybe there was one right in front of her. "Can I ask you something?"

"Of course. I've been asking you all kinds of things I probably shouldn't, so it's only fair."

"Is . . . is all this worth it? This whole transformation thing?"

Leah expected Eli to start protesting immediately, but instead he sighed heavily, slouched against the couch cushion, and tipped his head back to stare at the ceiling. "That's what Gray asked me."

"And what did you tell him?"

"That I'll do whatever is necessary to get Victoria back."

Leah's stomach clenched.

"Which is why I look like I'm dressed for a book-club meeting, when the weather calls for fleece and Carhartts instead."

He plucked at the shawl-collar sweater Jenna had forced on him as Leah said, "You do look very dapper."

"Yeah, well, my sister snuck into my house and stole most of my clothes! She just left me the new stuff."

"Hardcore. She knew you'd never wear it unless you had to."

"And don't get me started on the fish-fork lessons and everything."

"Fish fork?"

"You don't want to know, trust me. Anyway, I'd like to think Victoria isn't that shallow, but then I have to wonder . . . is it shallow? Or necessary? When everybody around you tells you you need fixing, how can you not take it to heart?"

"So you believe your sister and your friends when they say you have to change."

"I figure they must know something I don't."

"Well, even if they're right—and I'm not sure they are—do you need to change *everything*?"

"It's not everything. I'm still me."

"Well, that's good. But you seem to have changed things you don't want to."

"I made some . . . alterations . . . already, when I was with Victoria. That's just part of being in a relationship."

"What did you change?"

"Uh . . ." He studied the ceiling again, running his fingers roughly through his hair. "Okay, you know the baseball cap my sister made you throw away? I coached a kids' softball team. The Land Sharks. When my kayak tours business started to pick up, it was a little more challenging to coach, but I was managing okay for a couple of years. Then I met Victoria, and she . . . she didn't want to spend our time together sitting in the stands cheering on a bunch of little kids. You know. So I gave it up."

Leah nodded slowly. "Make sure you watch *Bull Durham*. But not *Field of Dreams*."

"Now, that last one I *have* seen. Lots of chopping onions."

"True."

"Especially because I got my love of baseball from my dad, and he's been gone awhile now."

"Oh, I'm so sorry."

"People pass."

"They do."

There was a silence for a few moments, which Eli broke by asking, "Do you play? Softball?"

That made Leah laugh. "I play nothing. I think I'd suck if I did."

"Why do you say that?"

"I've just never been the sporty sort."

The joiner sort. The team-member sort. Because when she was a kid, she couldn't commit to something like a season of playing a team sport if she was going to be moved from a foster home unexpectedly.

"I consider myself Team Books and Movies," she said.

"Which explains your Cusack expertise. But you should try a sport. You might surprise yourself."

"You mean when leagues form in the spring?"

And although she was intrigued, Leah shut it down almost immediately, because just like when she was younger, by the time team sports ramped up in the spring and summer, she was going to be gone again, this time by her own choice.

"No, right now," Eli said.

"Wh . . . right *now*?" Leah pointedly looked out the window. "Uh, you know what season it is, right?"

"Have you no imagination?"

"Look, I might not play any type of sportsball, but I do know softball is totally incompatible with snow."

"Get your coat."

⁓

"Why do you have an orange baseball in your Jeep?"

"This," Eli said eagerly, holding the neon-hued ball under her nose, "is a softball, first of all, but also it's orange because that's what you use to play . . . *snow softball*."

"You're making this up."

"Don't you know about the town tournament in March?"

"Oh." She started to recall signs for it all over town last year around this time. Of course she hadn't attended, what with taking care of Cathy and all, but she vaguely remembered the town being abuzz about the event. March in the North Country did not promise spring in the traditional sense. It only meant more frigid temperatures, broken up by a day or two of false spring here and there to give rise to just-as-false hope, amid a long slog to an actual thaw. But there was so little going on in the dead of winter that a softball tournament—sometimes played on snowshoes to great comic effect, she'd heard—and some hot chocolate and hamburgers were the height of the town social scene in the dead of winter.

"Is it that time of year again?" Leah asked. "Where *does* the time go?"

"Don't mock. We take this tournament very seriously around here. Anyway, it's in about a month. And you can be on my winning team."

"Oh . . . no."

"Why not?"

March . . . could she manage to leave town by March? Possibly, if she kept working and was careful with the money she'd already saved. So once again, it was wiser not to commit, not to get involved, because she straight up might not be there. She couldn't tell Eli that, however, because he might just try to convince her to stay. And, she'd learned, he could be pretty persuasive.

Instead, Leah said, "I'd just drag you down. I'd hate to be the reason your winning team lost this year."

"Well, then, we'll just have to make sure that doesn't happen."

"What part?"

"The dragging-us-down part. There's a way to avoid that."

"Right. By my not playing on your team."

"Or by becoming an exceptional member of the team. Come on, get in the car."

The next thing she knew, she was several blocks away, knee-deep in the snow in the town park, a baseball glove over her winter glove, trying to catch a neon-orange projectile . . . and failing miserably.

"Put the glove in front of your face!" Eli was shouting from several dozen paces away. "Hold it up high, not low."

"But if I hold it up in front of my face," she shouted back, "you'll aim at my face, and if my glove doesn't catch it, my face will!"

"Have more faith in your skills than that!"

"I have no skills! Haven't you been listening?"

"All right. Underhand, here it comes. Get ready!"

And then he was gone, toppled sideways into a snowdrift by two small projectiles and flailing and roaring. The orange softball popped up, glowed briefly in the dusk, and disappeared in the snow.

Leah plowed across the open expanse till she got to the writhing bundle, which consisted of a tiny human in pink and a slightly larger human in yellow, wrestling with the snow-covered Eli and squealing.

"Pah!" Eli spat some snow out as he pushed himself out of the snowdrift and pulled the girls to their feet. "Where did you two come from?"

"We were walking home with Mommy," the smaller girl said, pushing at Eli again. Naturally this did nothing, now that he was alert to ambushes.

"What are you doing?" the older girl asked.

"Playing catch. Find the ball and I'll throw it to you too. But first come meet my friend." He gently turned the two kids to face Leah. "Leah, these are my nieces, Jenna's girls, Olivia and Zoë. Girls, this is Leah." With a wink at Leah, he pronounced it *Lay-uh*.

While Zoë said a polite hello, Olivia burst out, "You're a princess?"

"Oh, uh—"

"No, she's not," Eli said for her. "You know, I thought so too at first, but I was wrong." As Olivia peeped out a little disappointed noise, Eli went on, "Don't you remember what happened to the princess in *Star Wars*? Something way better." That got his little niece's attention again. "She's a *general*."

"Wooowww," Olivia breathed, swinging her arms until her mittens came close to flying off. Even Zoë lit up at the news.

Leah just covered her face with her baseball-gloved hand. When she peeked over the top she saw Eli smiling at her as he adjusted Olivia's mittens.

"I was wondering if the girls were thwarting a mugging," Jenna said, catching up to them. "Which they're totally capable of. Now I see they just found my weird baby brother and his orange ball. That's what she said."

"That's not how that works."

"Also what she said." Jenna turned to Leah. "Good to see you. So my brother has you out in the park in nearly subzero temperatures why?"

"Playing softball."

"As one does when one is trying to give a friend frostbite."

"Oh, I'm all right. It was fun."

"Mmkay," Jenna said skeptically, but she was smiling. Then she whacked her brother on the arm. "You coming or what? The pizza's not going to order itself."

"Right, yeah, of course."

Eli's upcoming family time was Leah's cue. "I should get home. Thanks for the softball lesson."

"Wait—I'll drive you."

That got his nieces clamoring for a ride in Unca Eli's Jeep, so Leah said, "No, it's okay. You go ahead. Drive the girls home. I like to walk."

"I can do both."

"Here." She handed him his glove back.

Eli didn't accept it. "Keep it. You'll need it for the tournament."

With a massive eyeroll, she said, "Not playing in your tournament." She walked backward a few steps. "Nice to meet you, Olivia and Zoë. Stay warm. I'll see you around, I'm sure, Jenna."

As she turned toward home, Eli called after her, "I'll convince you!"

Chapter 10

"Well?"

It took Eli a second to realize Jenna was talking to him. "Hm? 'Well' what?"

His sister shook her head slowly. "Go on."

"Go where? I thought we were going to your house for dinner."

"Apparently not without the orphan, sad-face boy. So go on, go get her."

"You think?"

"Quick, before she gets away."

There was no chance of that. Eli could close the gap between them in a few strides. The question was, would she accept an invitation to spend an evening with the raucous and messy Masterson-Page clan? Plus they'd already spent hours together; she certainly could have had enough of him by now. Then again, maybe she'd welcome a chance to have dinner with friends instead of alone, in a warm and welcoming atmosphere instead of—he hated to think it, but it was the truth—the chilly and, frankly, sad little house—

"Eli!" Jenna's admonition snapped him out of his reverie.

"Right, right."

And he put his long legs in motion to catch up to Leah before she disappeared into the darkness.

An hour and a half later, wine had been opened, salad had been ig-nored, two pieces of pizza had already landed sauce-side down—one on the linoleum, one on the carpet—and the dog had stolen a third, tears (Olivia's) had been shed as the stolen piece of pizza had been hers, and two baths had been forced upon two unwilling children.

Despite the pandemonium, the Masterson-Page clan was noth-ing if not welcoming, and as long as Leah didn't mind being en-listed to help in the kitchen and then being a lap for Olivia, she was definitely welcome. Jenna had made sure she'd gotten the seat on the end of the sofa closest to the woodstove and Ben had topped up her wine without asking, probably to ensure Leah stayed mellow.

But Leah didn't seem to need any liquid courage. After the girls' baths—at which, of course, they demanded Leah's attendance but were vetoed by Jenna, prompting much whining—Olivia settled back on Leah's lap with one of her dolls, and Zoë offered to read her a bit of whichever Harry Potter volume she was on. She was, ef-fectively, trapped by cuteness and completely malleable when Jenna announced . . .

"Chapter whatever in Unca Eli's makeover. Time for a movie."

Eli, however, still had all his faculties. "Oh, no. Nope, not gonna happen. I already watched two today. I have limits."

"Would you rather go over the art history stuff I sent you the other day?"

Eli groaned. "Who's got the remote?"

"A movie! A movie!" Olivia exclaimed. "I want *Tangled*!"

"No cartoons, honey. This is for Unca Eli."

"Well," Leah ventured, "Flynn Rider, though . . ."

"You make a good point."

"No!" Eli protested. "No kid stuff. I've had it up to here with teen movies too. Why can't I learn something from grown-ups? And another thing," he added. "No more sensitive, squishy guys. You want me to be tough, give me a tough guy."

"A man's man, huh? I can get on board with that," Ben said.

"If the next words out of your mouth are 'Eastwood' or 'The Rock,' you can leave the room right now," his wife said, pointing the remote at him.

"Time for some Bond, then?"

Jenna shook her head. "It's not even close to the girls' bedtime. They'll mutiny if I try to get them upstairs now." She thought for a second, then her eyes lit up. "I've got it."

Minutes later they were all watching Baby carry a watermelon.

"Is *Dirty Dancing* appropriate for small children?" Eli ventured.

"Mostly," Ben grunted while said small children bounced around to the soundtrack.

"They're not even paying attention to anything but the music," Jenna said. "This'll wear them out, and they'll fall asleep way before the serious stuff."

"You know, I said show me a movie with a tough guy. Would someone mind telling me what I'm supposed to be learning from this dude in tight pants on a dance floor?"

"Please say it's not learning how to dance like this," Ben said, wincing at the complicated gyrating happening on-screen and eliciting a fist bump from his brother-in-law.

"You did *not* start without me."

Gray burst in on a gust of cold air and indignation, halted only by the body slams of Zoë and Olivia. He tossed them around a bit, making them scream with delight, then set them aside, dropped his jacket, and climbed over the back of the couch to land between Eli and Jenna.

"So, what, you just have *Dirty Dancing* radar and let yourself into any house that has it on?" Eli asked.

"Or Jenna texted me." He leaned past Eli to flash his winning smile at Leah. "They got you too, I see."

"They lured me in with pizza and wine, and sealed the deal with Patrick Swayze."

"Deadly." He turned back to Eli. "Welcome to more of your education. Now, let's start with the dancing."

"Let's not."

Moving like that? Patently ridiculous. Eli broke out in a cold sweat at the mere thought of Gray trying to make him attempt that sort of dancing. Well, dancing at all, period.

"It's a skill you need to have if you want Victoria back. Or any woman, for that matter."

Eli shook his head as vehemently as a toddler faced with a spoonful of creamed spinach.

"Okay, look," Gray said, squaring his shoulders. "I saw your list of movies, and I said nothing, even though it's about as cishet as they come—"

"Cis-what?" Ben interrupted.

"Cisgender and heterosexual," Gray answered patiently.

"Okay, not helping."

"Let's just say Eli's lessons are all coming from a super traditional view of gender identity and heteronormativity, not to mention they're totally binary, and don't even get me started on how white it all is. But"—he sighed—"I'll allow it, because our boy here *is* cisgender and heterosexual, as is Victoria. Unless there's something about your intended you're not telling us," he directed at Eli.

"Nope, Victoria and I are, sadly, a cisgender, heteronormative couple."

"What a shame. Well, I'll give *Dirty Dancing* a pass because it's a classic. And Swayze's ass always could stop traffic. But if you're not interested in his ass or his dance moves, why are we watching this?"

"That's what I want to know!"

"Integrity."

The soft word came from his left. Everyone turned to Leah, who was still and small in the corner of the couch. She had been relatively quiet all evening except with the kids, so this came as a surprise to not only Eli but the rest of the group as well. All eyes on Leah, she colored a bit, and not for the first time, Eli felt a little tug in his gut.

"What?" he asked, hoping he was sounding encouraging.

But she just shook her head. "No, never mind."

Eli remembered how lively and vocal and opinionated she'd been at their other movie sessions, how he'd learned so much from her not only about the movies, but about the characters' behavior. He knew whatever she had to say would be valuable, so he gave her his full attention.

"No, seriously, go on. You said integrity?"

"Well . . . Johnny's rough around the edges, sure, but he would do anything for the people he cares about. I mean, for his dance partner, Penny, and then for Baby."

"Why? What happens with them?"

"Well, you'll just have to watch the rest of the movie to find out, won't you?"

"I intend to."

"So you *are* interested."

Eli burrowed deeper into the couch and downed a glug of wine, then murmured in her ear, "I have a mom-crush on Kelly Bishop."

"How do you even . . . oh. Because she was on *Gilmore Girls*. Which you know all about—"

"Because I have a sister. I told you."

"Mm-hmm," she muttered skeptically, but with a smile.

"What's the conversation over there?" Jenna demanded, pausing the movie. "Are we watching this or aren't we?"

Eli, rudely torn from his study of Leah's dimple, waved his hand, and Jenna started it up again. He tried to take mental notes on Johnny's personality, carriage, dress sense (the movie made him wonder if he could pull off a leather jacket like that), and of course his moves, but the plot kept distracting him. Until Johnny and Baby were finally completely in love and pawing each other in the dance studio.

"I can't take it anymore," Gray declared. "If this song doesn't get you to move, I don't know what will."

And maybe it was the music, or maybe it was the copious amount of wine, but when Gray got up to dance to "Love Is Strange," Jenna did too, pulling Ben with her.

"What is happening right now?" Eli murmured, agog at the impromptu dance party that started up between him and the TV screen.

"Masterson, if you don't get your atrophied ass of the couch right now, I'll lift you off myself," Gray snapped. "And you know I can do it."

"I don't dance. I can't dance!"

"I know. I've seen you."

"Hey."

Gray turned to Leah and held out his hand. "Don't leave me hanging, sugarplum. This song won't last forever."

Leah laughed and stood up, and Eli stiffened.

"You're falling for this?"

"You heard the man," she said, brushing down her flannel shirt. "Women love a man who can dance."

Gray swept Leah up, grinning goofily at Eli over her shoulder, and Eli rolled his eyes. All the dancing going on left Eli the only one in the room still sitting down, lost in a thicket of legs. Jenna and Ben, in a world of their own, held each other close, laughing loudly at a private joke. This woke Olivia, who had fallen asleep in the dog bed with Zoë about ten minutes earlier. Drowsily scrambling to her feet, she tottered over to Eli and clung to his knee.

"I wanna dance too."

"You're still asleep," Eli said, fondly brushing down the snarl of tight curls that had clumped up on one side of her head.

"Nuh-uh."

She tugged on his hand, leaning back with her whole body, until Eli stood up.

"I got you, booger," Gray said, scooping Olivia up in the crook of his arm. "You can dance with me." To Leah, he said, "Do something with this one, would you?" And he spun away, leaving Eli and Leah staring at each other.

"Well, uh . . . ?"

Eli held out his hand awkwardly, and Leah stepped forward, placing her right hand in his left. "It is for educational purposes, after all."

And then the minute he was about to put his arm around her, the song stopped.

They both dropped their hands. Leah tucked hers into the back pockets of her jeans. Eli pressed his lips together and his eyebrows crept upward. "So."

"Yeah."

"That was a pretty narrow escape. For you, I mean," he babbled. "Who knows how many of your toes I would have stepped on, you know?"

Leah just nodded slowly. The color was high in her cheeks, which did strange things to Eli's insides. Eli could feel everyone's eyes on him, and he had the sudden need to pop the balloon of whatever this feeling was that was growing in his chest. He spun around and plopped back into his spot on the couch. "So what happens next?" he asked, forcing a light tone and hoping his voice didn't crack from the strain of it. "Do Baby and Johnny get their happy ending, or what?"

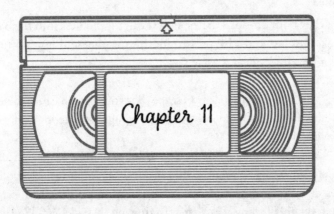

Chapter 11

"Don't even bother."

Leah was afraid Mr. Lehman would say that. As a matter of fact, she really didn't even need to call him to know she shouldn't attempt to go to work at Thousand Island Dressing, because she wouldn't be able to find it. Sure, it was still on Main Street as far as anyone knew, but neither it nor anything else in the vicinity was visible. When she looked out her window, white was all she could see, all that was out there. An endless monochrome expanse turned cars, trees, and bushes into shapeless lumps. More white stuff was falling out of the sky, peacefully vertical one minute, and the next, when a gust of wind kicked up, swirling around like van Gogh's stars.

"Are you sure? I could walk. It wouldn't be so bad."

The store wasn't far away. She could make it.

"Absolutely not," Mr. Lehman shot back immediately. "I won't be party to your death in the Arctic tundra."

"Don't you think that's a little exaggerated?"

"We haven't seen snow like this in decades. Those drifts are going to be higher than you are tall. I wouldn't be able to live with myself if you disappeared and they found you curled up in a snow-bank at the spring thaw. Don't think it can't happen."

Leah was certain it was highly unlikely, but she also knew better than to argue. She promised not to venture out and ended the call just as another gust of wind sent what seemed like buckets of snow pelting down and up and around the house. She knew she should have been grateful she had a (mostly) secure roof over her head and a furnace that wasn't misbehaving, as well as a fair amount of food in the fridge and pantry. If there was going to be a snowstorm, there were worse places to hole up. But the last thing she wanted to do was hole up alone, with a head full of thoughts she'd rather not be having.

Not that anything going on in her head was detrimental to her health, as long as she kept those thoughts in there under lock and key. But she couldn't seem to evict them, either, and her headspace was getting crowded.

With, you know, those thoughts she'd rather not be having.

She pressed her nose harder against the frigid window in the living room and turned her head, trying to see something, anything, up and down the street. Any sign of life. But there was nothing. Well, except for old Roy Westerhoffer, across the street and three doors down, who loved his noisy yard toys so much he couldn't wait for the snow to stop falling before trotting out his snowblower. She could just about make him out, a bundled-up lump walking glacially slowly behind a clear plastic shield while the roaring machine spewed its own small snowstorm out of its chute. Behind him, the snow started filling in the path he'd cleared.

Leah slid away from the window with a heavy sigh. There was plenty to do inside—all of Cathy's grunge to clean and possessions to sort. She should be able to keep her mind from wandering to those places she didn't want them to go. Like remembering Jenna's impromptu get-together a few nights ago. And all that entailed.

Well. Nothing had happened, not really. Nothing overtly monumental. But there had been a shift inside Leah on several fronts—an alarming shift. Sometime between the moment Eli had run up behind her in the park and put a hand on her shoulder to ask her to join his family for dinner and the awkwardly muted ride home in his Jeep at the end of the night, Leah had slipped into downright dangerous territory.

Around the time she'd been full up on pizza, wine, and Patrick Swayze, she'd blinked and realized she was surrounded by a normal, happy family, and they were including her. It had made her tumble headfirst into a warm, fuzzy feeling she hadn't been able to shake. Although Leah normally had no problem being alone, having had lots of practice, apparently all it took was a couple of hours in a family's friendly embrace for her to lower her guard and start wishing they'd adopt her. Even after she'd accepted, well over a decade ago, that nobody would ever adopt her.

And then there was Eli. When he'd turned to her and held out his hand for a dance—even though the dance never did happen— she'd tumbled headfirst into something else entirely. No, not tumbled. Slipped down some scree as she tried desperately to scrabble for a handhold to keep herself from plummeting into a sarlacc pit of emotions she had no business having.

"Cathy?" she whispered. "I have a crush on a boy."

It was just because he was part of a normal, happy family, she told herself. It was because he was part of that warm, friendly evening. It had nothing to do with him as a person. Not those kind eyes or his broad shoulders or his conspiratorial winks he seemed to dish out solely to lift her spirits. Or the way he adored his nieces, his gentle nature, his innate courtesy to her and everyone else. Or the bright, broad smile that lit up his whole face and occurred far too infrequently, so when he did bust one out, it was blinding and all-consuming. At least to her.

"I feel stupid."

She certainly did. For crushing on Eli, for pining after a family that wasn't hers, and for talking to the walls as if Cathy were still around, when she most certainly was not. For a while after she died, Leah had sort of been on the alert for any ethereal shenanigans, but nothing had happened. Of course it hadn't. Cathy was too practical for that. She'd probably just arrived on the Other Side, thought,

"Thank goodness *that's* over with," adjusted her wings and halo, and flown off.

So why was Leah still talking to her?

Because it made her feel better. Less alone.

"I *can't* like him."

Wasn't that the truth. Eli was in love with someone else, for better or worse, wisely or foolishly. Everything he did, every waking moment of his day, was for Victoria. Eli's devotion to her meant there was no room in his life for Leah. And there certainly was no room in Leah's life for some ridiculous, unwelcome emotions about *him*. She should just take a step or two or twelve back, view Eli impartially, maybe consider him as a guideline for the type of man she should be looking out for someday—*someday*—and let the nonsense go.

Why should she be wishing for ties of any kind? Well, she knew why. That normal, happy family she got to be a part of for a little while, for one night of pizza and wine and laughter and warmth and kids and a movie.

And Eli's smile.

Stop.

Leah wasn't a part of the Masterson-Page clan, and she should just stop pretending she was. What was real in her life right now was that she had about three months to wrap things up here, which wasn't much time at all. If she was going to be housebound today, she might as well make the most of it. Clear a path, clean, separate the junk from the valued items of Cathy's life.

So far it looked like everything in the house was straight-up junk.

Leah decided to sort through a cabinet under the built-in bookshelves along one wall in the living room. The dust was thick on the generic knickknacks on the shelves, and she didn't have the strength to tackle those just yet.

She yanked on the cabinet doors, which stuck to each other and put up quite the fight. They finally popped open, the metal clips giving up their hold on the securing pegs with a musical little *ding*. Out slid VHS and DVD cases. That made sense. Leah and Cathy had watched a lot of movies together. Reading had been too taxing for Cathy—and she had never been much of a reader anyway—but movies were fine. She could watch or not watch movies. She could nod off, and when she woke up, she could rewind to the spot she remembered last if she felt like it. Movies kept both of them busy in the endless hours of her illness.

Leah sifted through the cases. Funny how Cathy's movie collection staved off the dark hours and darker thoughts of her months with cancer, while Eli's required movie watching was intended to propel him into a bright, shiny future with Victoria.

Nope.

She would not automatically think of Eli every time she picked up a movie . . . oh crap.

She didn't remember Cathy owning *Dirty Dancing*, but there it was. Leah smiled in spite of her intended self-imposed ban on thinking about Eli, remembering his baffled look when the rest of them were dancing.

A massive roar outside, sounding like a T. rex was trying to pull the house down, broke through her reverie. She jumped up and looked out the window to find a giant pickup truck with a plow blade affixed to its front charging into the driveway, scraping snow, the blade clanging on the newly unearthed blacktop.

"Oh shit," she muttered, racing for the front door, pausing only long enough to shove her feet into her boots and pull her jacket from the coat rack. She didn't know who this person was or why they thought they could plow before asking if she had the money for it, but whoever it was, they were going to be sorely disappointed.

She gasped at the iciness of the wind and the amount of snow piled up on the stoop. There was a *lot* more than she thought. She felt around blindly for the step, which was somewhere in that knee-high white mass. Her heel caught it while her toes dipped into the gap beyond, and she grabbed the railing to avoid twisting her ankle and pitching face-first into the drift. By the time she got to the driveway, the plow was almost finished.

When it paused for a second, Leah ran up to the cab and knocked on the window. It slid down to reveal an older woman looking at her inquisitively. Her cheeks were ruddy—understandably—and she had a cloud of curly, coarse blonde hair sticking up in all directions. Leah decided being frank was the best approach. It was too damn cold to beat around the bush.

"I'm sorry, I didn't order a plow. I mean, I appreciate it, but—"

"No, honey, your friends did."

"I'm sorry, what?" Leah pushed her hood away from one ear.

"Ben and Jenna sent me. All paid for. Now, you'd better get yourself back inside. You're so tiny you might get swallowed up by a snowbank."

"Yeah, I get that a lot."

Leah didn't know what else to say, so she just thanked the woman and backed away from the chugging diesel-powered pickup. The woman waved and raised her window again. After one last swipe of the outer edge of the drive, she took off down the street, the giant truck charging through the unplowed drifts as if they were vapor.

Leah pushed through the snow on the front walk, telling herself she'd shovel later, once the snowpocalypse had exhausted itself, and went back inside. Jenna and Ben had hired a plow to come out to her house. They'd thought of her beyond last Saturday night, no matter what she'd told herself.

She did have friends.

Well, that sucked.

After all, it was easier to leave town when she thought nobody cared about her. It was easier to believe people were ultimately selfish—no, not selfish, but too wrapped up in their own lives to open their door to a lone orphan like her. She didn't want to have to change her outlook.

So this was a onetime thing, she told herself. Maybe because she'd hung out with them a few days ago, they were—oh God—feeling sorry for her, and they just happened to tell their plow person to hit up her house. Wouldn't happen a second time. She was certain of that. Still, she should give Jenna a call and thank her. It was the polite thing to do.

As if on cue, her phone started ringing. But it wasn't Jenna's number showing on the screen. She didn't recognize it at all.

"Hello?" she said tentatively.

"Leah?"

"Yeah?"

"It's Eli. I got your number from my sister. I hope you don't mind."

Leah's heart surged at the same time her stomach dropped. She had so much going on with her insides, it was like a car crash in her torso. She sat in the nearest chair, felt too restless, and immediately jumped up and started pacing.

"No, it's fine. What's up?"

"There's a snowstorm."

"You don't say." Playful sarcasm was her best defense at this point, she was sure of it.

"Ha. I mean, are you okay? Do you need anything?"

And now her core temperature was getting in on the act. She felt her cheeks flame. He was checking up on her. "N-no, no, I'm good. Shut up tight against the storm."

"Yeah, I've seen your house. It's anything but shut up tight."

"Well, it's not like there are snowdrifts in the living room."

"You sure? Better check the corners."

A smile fought its way out, no matter how hard she tried to suppress it. "I am very sure. And your sister and brother-in-law sent over a plow, so I don't even have to shovel the driveway."

"They did? Good. If you went out there—"

"Don't tell me. I'd disappear into a snowdrift?"

"You get that a lot, do you?"

Now her giddy smile broke free completely, and a pleasant warmth spread through her, making her fingers and toes tingle. "Are *you* okay out there in the wilderness?"

"I'm always okay out here in the wilderness. It's really peaceful, actually."

Leah pictured the cabin in the trees, the snow piling up on the branches of the pines and woodsmoke curling from the chimney, and she had to admit he was probably right. She also nearly admitted to herself—nearly—that she would have rather been there with him than here in this drafty house without even Cathy's ghost to keep her company.

"So what are you doing on this dark day?" she asked. "Skinning a bear or something?"

"I have all the bearskins I need right now, so no."

Leah plopped onto the couch, thoroughly enjoying the conversation. "Are you doing your homework, by any chance?"

"Why yes, I am."

It came out "Woy yiz, oy em."

Now she laughed outright. "What in the world was *that*?"

"My Cary Grant impression. Pretty good, huh?"

"Uh . . ."

"*Pretty good*, huh?" he demanded.

"It's . . . something. What have you watched?"

"*His Girl Friday* and *Charade*."

Damn. Leah wished she'd been with him for those. They were two of her favorites.

"And what have you learned?"

"I've learned Audrey Hepburn is perfection, double-breasted suits should come back into fashion, and I'll never be as slick as that guy. Like, never."

"Well, Cary Grant is more of a state of mind. You can get there if you want to. I agree about Audrey."

"And . . ."

"And?"

"I watched *The Notebook*."

Leah tried to keep the laughter out of her voice. "Go on."

"I would like to kill myself now, please. Can you point me in the direction of the nearest Ferris wheel?"

She couldn't keep it in any longer and started laughing again.

Eli harrumphed down the line. "I'm glad my pain amuses you." He waited while she dialed it down to a giggle, then said, "It'd be more fun if you were here for these."

Leah quieted immediately.

In the silence, he blurted out, "I mean, I don't think I'm getting as much out of these movies without someone to point out what I should be paying attention to."

"Oh. I . . . I'm sure you can figure it out."

"It's not as much fun, though."

He had to stop saying things like that. Her heart couldn't take it. She had a pretty good barbed-wire barricade up, but he'd brought wire cutters, and that wasn't fair. He didn't even know what he was doing to her. But talking with Eli couldn't do any harm, could it? She could separate simple friendship from anything that would get her heart into trouble, couldn't she?

Her options were to end this call right now, and not allow any others in the future, or get a grip on her emotions and just enjoy Eli's company. Leah stared out at the snow swirling around as the daylight dimmed. The storm was bringing on an early twilight. She sighed to herself. She was such a sucker.

"Do you have *When Harry Met Sally*?" she asked him.

"I can find it on demand. Why?"

"Well, it's not on your list for a he-man lesson—I mean, Billy Crystal is anything but suave and smooth—but it's a classic. I'm sure Victoria would love that you'd seen it."

Now it was time for Eli to be silent on the other end of the line. Had she said something wrong? She hadn't bad-mouthed Victoria. Maybe just bringing up her name was painful for him?

Before she could ask, he said, "I don't know . . ."

"Okay, hang on a minute. There might be a way to make this work for you."

Leah crossed the room and pawed through Cathy's collection of movies, apparently making quite the ruckus, because Eli said, "You know, whatever you're doing would make more sense if we were video chatting so I could see what you're up to."

"Not happening, boyo."

"You're not wearing pants, are you?"

"Like I'd even tell you if I weren't." Finally she fished out the

DVD she knew she'd seen earlier. "All right, here's the deal. We stay on the phone. When I say hit play, start your movie. I've got mine here."

"Watch the same movie while talking on the phone?"

"You bet. And you'll see why in about half an hour."

Eli might not appreciate it, but Leah was pretty smug about how meta their movie watching was about to get, what with Harry and Sally watching *Casablanca* together by phone. And this way she got to spend time with Eli, just not in person, which would feed her addiction in a safe way. If they were in the same room together, she'd feel compelled to lean against him or stare at him all dopey-like or do something else entirely inappropriate. No, this was much, much safer.

Which wasn't true in the least. But she was willing to lie to herself for a little while longer.

Chapter 12

"This is the life."

"Shh. No talking."

"Dude, what? That wasn't part of the deal."

"If you're going to go for a walk in nature, pay attention to the nature," Eli admonished Gray.

The massive snowstorm had paralyzed the area only briefly—it was nothing they couldn't handle—and the resulting volume of fresh snow in the mountains had Eli itching to go on a hike for days. Cabin fever was not his friend. No clients had stepped up to hire him, so he dragged the guys out of doors, to mixed reactions.

"I *said* 'This is the life,' which is appreciating nature."

"Some silence would be even better."

"Can you both shut up?" Ben demanded. "My house is filled with nonstop yammering from morning till night. I'm all in favor of some tranquility. So can we have some, please?"

All three men fell silent as they stepped carefully, single file, on the crust of the otherwise knee-deep snow on the Adirondack Mountain trail, the only sounds the crunch of their snowshoes and their panting breaths as they headed up a rise. The quiet didn't last long, however.

"I feel like we should be doing more than walking," Gray muttered. "Like running, at least."

"Okay, *you*," Eli said, stopping dead on the trail and twisting to face his friend with an instructive index finger raised, "need to slow the hell down sometimes. Not everything is an opportunity for an over-the-top workout."

"But it should be," Gray said with a grin.

"You are a sick, sick individual."

"And you are a lazy slob."

"Ugghh," Ben suddenly burst out. "I can't take much more of this. My legs are going to fall off. Can we take a break?"

"What was that about lazy slobs?" Eli asked Gray.

"That'd be me. Recliner Olympics gold medalist, ten years running, and damn proud of it. This outdoor stuff sucks." Ben plopped onto a stump just off the trail, breathing heavily. "What does a heart attack feel like, by the way? I'm just seeking information at this point. I'll let you know when it becomes relevant."

"You're not having a heart attack," Eli muttered, pulling out his phone and removing one glove.

"So why are you dialing nine-one and waiting to hit the final one, then?"

"I'm not. I'm just . . . checking my messages."

Gray chugged from his water bottle, then snuck up behind Eli and looked over his shoulder. "Bullshit. Are you on Victoria's Insta?"

Eli immediately clutched the phone to his chest. "Ye—no. Maybe. What's it to you?"

Gray made a grab for it, but Eli was too fast. He held it high out of the shorter man's reach and kept him at a distance with his other hand to Gray's chest.

"I don't know how you got a cell signal out here," Gray grunted as he made another swipe at the phone, "but it is entirely disrespectful to these here great outdoors. Plus, why are you torturing yourself, man?"

"It's not torture," Eli protested, returning his attention to the phone once he was satisfied Gray was standing down. "She's in Europe, doing research for a book. I'm interested in what she's doing."

"Not worried about *who* she might be doing?"

"Whom," Ben corrected.

"Dude. Seriously?"

Ben shrugged. "I'm married to an educator. So sue me."

Without glancing up from his phone, Eli muttered, "My sister is more of a ball-breaker, junior division."

"What I said. She *educates* the delinquents at the school not to act like dipshits or they'll end up in detention. She provides a much-needed service."

"Hey," Gray said, "is my artwork still on the desks in the detention room?"

"Strangely enough, these are not the things the vice principal and I discuss at the dinner table."

"Well, why *not*?"

"It's all about you, G, isn't . . ." Eli trailed off, his good-natured grin disappearing as his voice faded away.

"What?" Gray asked, concerned about Eli's change of mood.

He pocketed his phone. "Nothing. Let's keep going."

"Oh, like I'm buying that. Spill."

"I said it's nothing!"

"What's on her Insta, man?" Ben asked.

"A lot of stuff, okay? She looks like she's having a great time in Italy, and I'm happy for her."

"But?"

"No buts. No anything. That's it."

But while Eli's head was turned, Gray reached into the pocket of his ski jacket and grabbed the phone.

"Hey!"

"You really should lock this. You're way too trusting."

"Gray . . ."

"Ah, ah, ah, just hold on there, son. Let's see what's got you all tied up in knots." He flicked through Victoria's posted images. "Mmkay, we've got the usual here. Landmarks . . . touristy stuff . . .

absolutely delicious-looking food, good grief . . . a nice composition with a cup of espresso, open laptop, and some papers—at least she's working sometimes . . . and . . . oh. Sha-zay-um."

"Yeah." Eli sighed, his mouth a grim, taut line.

"What is it?" Ben asked.

Gray winced. "A guy. A *hot* guy. In a couple of shots. Which makes that one too many."

"We don't know who it is. Could be a . . . a colleague, right?" Eli suggested, sort of desperately. "Someone at the university there?"

"Sure. Maybe," Ben said, eager to talk his brother-in-law down.

"I mean, that one picture—it's at a restaurant and there are obviously other people at the table."

"Obviously."

"If they're out in a group, and they just *happen* to be sitting next to each other, and somebody goes to take a picture, they both face the camera. No big deal. Right?"

"Tags," Gray said. "If she's tagged him, we are gonna be *all* over this boy's Insta account."

After a few moments watching Gray squint at the screen, Eli burst out, "Well?"

Gray sighed. "No tag. And really, there's nothing in these photos showing they're, you know, *together*."

"Exactly. Exactly!" Eli agreed a bit too eagerly. "It's probably nothing."

"He's one hot dude, though, with the olive skin and the white teeth and the smoldery eyes."

"Whose side are you on?" Eli demanded.

Gray held up his hands in surrender and gave Eli his phone back. "Yours, man. Always. Sorry."

"Okay, then. I'll just like a couple of her posts, and we'll get back to the hike."

"Not too many," Gray cautioned. "Don't look desperate."

"Right."

Eli doled out his likes sparingly but made sure to tap the heart on one of the photos with the mystery man in it. It was ridiculous to think she wouldn't make new friends while she was in Italy.

Eli, Gray, and Ben made their way up the rest of the rise to a crest. They broke out of the slight tree cover into a wide-open area, the sun glinting off the unbroken snowfield nearly blinding.

Eli sighed. He'd wanted to show Victoria the Adirondacks, maybe climb one or two of the High Peaks, especially in the fall amid all the striking colors, but they'd never gotten here. Damn, the relationship should have made it beyond one season.

"That's pathetic, dude."

Shit. "Did I say that out loud?"

"You are absolutely losing your mind," Gray said.

"Never mind me. Just . . . take in the scenery. Beautiful, right?" Eli prompted his friends.

Gray muttered an agreement, while Ben said, "Yep, great. Hang on, gotta take a whiz."

"Sheer poetry there, bro," Eli called after him as his brother-in-law went back into the tree line for a bit of privacy.

"Hey," Gray said while they waited.

"I'm fine. Victoria can do what she wants."

"No, I wanted to ask if you and I were good. You know, after last weekend. I was wondering if I'd pissed you off."

Eli had no idea what his friend was talking about, and it must have shown on his face, because Gray prompted him, "Movie night?"

"Refresh my memory."

"Uh, Leah?"

Something in Eli's abdomen seized at the sound of her name, but outwardly he made sure not a muscle twitched and his face stayed neutral. "What about her?"

"I was wondering if maybe you thought I was coming on to her."

"Of course not. And so what if you were? I mean, what's that got to do with me?"

"I just wanted you to know I would never do that to you."

"To *me*? Why . . . why to me?" Eli's lips suddenly got all flappy and his brain disengaged. "I don't . . . Why would you . . ."

"All right, all right. I just thought you looked a mite jealous when we were dancing, is all."

"Me? Jealous?" Wow, his voice hadn't hit that octave since fifth grade. "No way. Of course not."

"I mean, I know you've always wanted me, so if you're gonna thumb-wrestle Leah for me, go easy on her."

The penny dropped, and Eli muttered, "You son of a bitch."

Gray burst out laughing. "Why? What did you think I meant?"

"Shut up." Eli grinned. "But . . . I mean, *do* you like Leah?"

"Of course I do! She's great!"

"Who's great?" Ben asked, coming back out of the trees and absently checking his fly.

Eli said, "Nobody—" just as Gray said, louder than Eli, "Leah."

"Oh yeah, she is great. You should hit that," he said to Eli.

"Did you whack your head on a low-hanging branch while you were desecrating our pristine preserved wilderness? What were we just talking about?"

"Leah?"

"Victoria!"

"The woman who broke up with you and is now tooling around Rome with the hot Italian guy?" Gray said.

"We don't *know* that!" Eli burst out, frustrated.

"We know she broke up with you," Ben said. "You're single. No harm, no foul. You should bring Leah as your date. You know, to our anniversary party."

Eli blinked. "Anniversary party?"

"You forgot?"

"No, I didn't!" he scoffed.

Yes, he did.

"I mean," Eli went on, "I know you have an anniversary coming up. This is just the first I've heard of a party. But come on, even Jenna's not weird enough to want to throw a party for your *thirteenth* anniversary. Why now, instead of the usual landmarks like fifteenth or twentieth?"

Ben shifted, obviously uncomfortable. "For . . . you know, for your mom."

"Oh no." Eli groaned loud enough to risk starting an avalanche. "She isn't."

"I know, I know, it sounds kind of morbid. But Jenna . . . she worries."

"That Mom's not going to make it to your fifteenth?"

"I guess."

"But she's fine!"

"Things happen, Jenna says."

"My sister is a paranoid, doom-and-gloom fatalist of epic proportions—"

"And yet we love her," Ben interrupted in a warning tone. "So we will celebrate at a thirteenth anniversary party, and we will all smile as we do so. Maybe we can have a luck theme, good and bad— you know, upturned horseshoes and four-leaf clovers and black cats and broken mirrors and stuff."

"That's a really great idea, actually," Gray chimed in.

"Thank you, my man. Bring a date. But let Eli bring Leah."

"I am *not* bringing Leah as my date to your party."

"You seem kind of defensive, friend. Why is that?" Gray teased.

"I'm *not* . . ." Eli sputtered for a few seconds, then gave up with a growl. "You're both giving me a headache."

"But you *have* been spending time with her lately, right?" Ben asked.

"Before stuff gets all blown out of proportion, yes, we've been . . . hanging out a bit. She's dragging me through that ridiculous list of movies the ladies came up with."

"Mm," Ben nodded, looking thoughtful.

"What does *that* mean?"

"It means," Gray said, "you're halfway to dating status already. Just appear in public and you're all set."

"I'm not dating Leah! I'm watching those movies and doing

all this other nonsense like getting manscaped and learning about formal place settings for *Victoria*."

He may have been emphatic about this point for Gray and Ben. Then again, he may have been emphatic about this point for himself. Because yesterday, when Leah had mentioned how much Victoria would appreciate his having seen *When Harry Met Sally*, it was like someone had dumped a bucket of snow from the storm down the back of his shirt. He'd been looking forward to spending time with Leah so much, he'd forgotten the point of the makeover project. He'd forgotten Victoria.

Chapter 13

"Welcome to Thousand Island Dressing. May I help you?"

"Why, yes. Yes, I think you might. I have a return."

"Sorry, sir, no returns."

"This sign on the counter here says otherwise."

"We employees are allowed some discretion. And I'm afraid your item doesn't qualify for a return."

"You don't even know what it is yet."

"I'll bet I do." Leah plucked the dreaded trilby off Eli's head and held it out to him. "Would it be this item, perhaps?"

"Can you blame me?"

"No returns for you."

"But it's a stupid hat. Which makes me look stupid."

"No returns."

Eli rested his elbows on the counter and leaned forward. "What if I asked to speak to your manager?"

"You're looking at her. Mainly because I'm the only employee in the place. And this manager says no returns without a receipt, and I know you don't have one of those. Do you dare get it from your sister?"

"Not on your life. Or, actually, not on mine."

"Thought so." Leah pretended to consider the situation. "Well, because you seem like an honest sort of person, I'll allow an exchange."

Eli made a face. "I'm full up on men's clothes these days. Thanks, anyway."

"We have a nice selection of other hats."

"I'm not really a hat guy."

"You don't say. Because I was thinking . . . well, you wouldn't be interested in this old secondhand thing, would you?"

Eli actually gasped when Leah brought out his baseball cap from behind the counter, and his face lit up so much she had to bite the inside of her cheek to keep from beaming back. The look on his face made her happy she'd decided to get it out of her house and into the store just in case an opportunity like this presented itself. Oh, she'd wanted to keep it, she wasn't going to lie to herself about that, but she just couldn't, knowing how much Eli missed it.

"Where did you . . . you kept . . . ?" He gave up on trying to use words and lifted the hat from her fingers almost reverently, settling it carefully on his head. "Ahh." He sighed, closing his eyes blissfully. "I feel like myself again."

Now Leah allowed herself a small smile. "You're an idiot."

"I can't believe you defied my sister and rescued it."

"All I did was not throw it in the trash."

"Well, thank you."

Eli was looking at her so openly, so warmly, that a buzzing started behind Leah's knees. What this guy did to her . . . it was criminal.

Just as Leah started to think the silence between them was going on a bit too long, Eli said, "I almost forgot to tell you—I kind of went rogue with the whole movie thing."

Leah fought hard to find her voice again and match his lighthearted tone. "Sounds dangerous."

"Well, Zoë recommended one, and I trust her taste implicitly."

"Good call. What was it?"

"*Pretty in Pink?*"

Leah gaped. "You. Have never. Seen *Pretty in Pink* before. You're incredible."

"Why, thank you."

"Not like that. *How* have you gone for, what, thirty years—?"

"Thirty-one."

"Thirty-one. And never seen these classics?"

"I was never a movie kind of guy. I like to be outdoors, doing things. Anyway, I watched it, I liked it, but damn—"

"Andie should have ended up with Duckie," Leah chorused with him.

Now it was Eli's turn to gape. "You know this?"

"*Everyone* knows this!"

"Well, what the hell! Why didn't she? They were perfect for each other. Duckie was her best friend. He was nice, and he was funny, and . . . and . . ."

"He wasn't afraid to wear a stylish hat."

"Touché. But unlike me, he could pull it off. And he even made the old lady swoon."

"What old lady?"

"The one who owned the record store."

"Annie Potts's character? You realize she was only a couple of years older than you are now, right?"

"Don't do that to me."

"Anyway, there's a theory Duckie was gay."

Eli paused to process this. Then he blurted out, "*Naaahhh*. Not the way he looked at Andie. But she ends up with *Blane*? The rich guy?"

"Hey, not every guy looks good in white pants—you gotta grab one when you find him."

"But she was totally out of his league—I mean *she* was too good for *him*. Who needs a rich guy when Duckie would have laid down his life for her? Plus Blane was a wimp—just because they were so different and their relationship got too difficult, he ran. What kind of person . . . *what?*" he demanded.

Leah was giving him a significant look, which he caught but obviously didn't understand. It figured.

She considered pointing out his hypocrisy, but she wasn't sure he'd be able to see it even then. Swap the pronouns and he could star in his own *Pretty in Pink*.

She got the feeling Eli would never figure out that, from what she'd heard so far, he and Victoria were so different in every way, he'd be better off with his own Duckie. And who would that be?

Well. *Quack.*

She'd have to work on that too, darn it. For all she knew, Victoria was a wonderful person, and she and Eli deserved a second chance like the one Andie and Blane got.

Leah rounded the end of the counter and walked over to a table full of accessories in the middle of the shop. She'd straightened them all already during the long, dull hours without a customer, but she did it again, just to have something to keep her hands busy when she said, "Tell me about Victoria."

"Well, that's a change of subject."

Not really.

"Why do you ask?" Eli stayed where he was, leaning one elbow on the counter in a grand attempt to look casual, but he suddenly looked awkward as hell. Why did her request make him uncomfortable?

She shrugged. "Just curious. You know, she must be an amazing person if you're working so hard to get her back."

"Oh, she is."

"Go on."

"Well . . ." Eli cleared his throat and shifted his baseball cap. "She's really beautiful. Just gorgeous."

Inside, Leah thought. *Talk about what she's like inside.* But she just kept straightening socks and refolding ties that were already folded perfectly and waited for him to go there by himself. Eli wouldn't be so superficial as to just describe her physically, she was sure. Although a part of her wanted him to stop there so she could believe there was nothing else to admire about her.

"I don't know where to start."

"Start anywhere. How did you two meet?"

"I led her college art department faculty on a team-building kayaking trip."

"And?"

Was it love at first sight? She didn't think she could handle love at first sight.

Eli shrugged one shoulder. "I thought she was nice. And beautiful. She said I made her laugh. We just clicked, you know?"

Leah was surprised at how unremarkable their meeting had been. With all the weight Eli had been putting on his and Victoria's relationship, she had somehow expected something much more dramatic, something that showed that these two were meant to be, a love for the ages. Or, at the very least, that they'd had a rom-com-worthy meet-cute.

In any case, it gave her the courage to press on. "College professor, huh? She's smart, then."

"*So* smart."

"And she's nice?"

"Unbelievably nice."

Leah ignored the churning in her gut. She needed details, even though deep down she knew better than to poke at what amounted to an open wound. It wouldn't help her head, or her heart, to know what Victoria was like, but she really wanted to know. Poke, poke, poke.

"What kind of nice are we talking, here? Does she volunteer at a homeless shelter? Fundraise for charities? Does she rescue animals?"

"Sure does. Blanche was a rescue cat. She runs," he added in a rush, proud he was able to contribute something else. "For charity."

"Well, then. That's great."

Yeah, she sounded patronizing even to herself.

"And?" she prompted. "What else?"

"What else what?"

"What made you ask her out? You clicked and . . . ?"

"Well," Eli cleared his throat, "she said I made her laugh—"

"Yeah, you said that already."

Eli looked confused and slightly wounded, and Leah felt bad for being so petty. She needed to do better.

"Sorry. I mean, what happened after that?"

"After the kayaking trip? She went home to Potsdam, but then she came back. She said she was enchanted with Willow Cove."

"And you."

"And me, if you can believe it. I couldn't. I mean, just when I was looking for a serious relationship and everything, there she was."

"What made you decide it was time for a serious relationship?"

"Well, I'd had girlfriends before, of course, a few, but they all felt too casual. When I met Victoria I was thirty, which felt . . . major somehow. Like I needed to get my shit together and settle down. I mean, my parents were completely settled by the time they were thirty—owned the house, had Jenna and me already, and I was thinking time was sort of slipping away from me. It sounds dumb, I know, but my parents . . . they were so great together. I always admired their relationship, and I kind of wanted to model my life the same way. When I didn't . . ."

"Have it all?"

"Have it all by thirty, I started to worry. And then I didn't have to."

"Victoria fit right into your plans."

"I thought so."

"But she didn't."

"Apparently not."

Leah studied Eli as he stared at the parquet floor, and she found herself feeling sympathy for him. She still thought he was misguided, sure, but his heart had been in the right place. Right place, wrong woman? It wasn't for her to say.

"Leah?"

"Yeah?" she responded quietly.

Still without looking up, he murmured, "Did you ever feel so sure about something, so absolutely certain, that nothing could change your mind? But then some time goes by and you start to wonder if maybe you . . . I don't know . . . got it . . . wrong, some-how?"

"All the time. You too?"

He shrugged and sighed. "I don't know. Sometimes I wonder if maybe . . ."

Eli drifted off as his phone chimed and he pulled it out of his pocket distractedly, looked at it with a confused frown.

Then, "Oh." A split-second pause. Then, louder, "Oh!" He came to life, looking entirely shocked but pleased as he tapped the screen. "Hey!" he exclaimed, grinning at the phone.

Leah heard a tinny female voice say, "*Ciao, bello!*"

"Victoria! I was . . . I was just talking about you! Oh my God, it's so good to see you!"

"I know it's been a while," Victoria's thin, faint voice continued. "It's just been nonstop here, you know?"

"Yeah, yeah, no problem. It hasn't been *that* long, and I know you're busy."

Six months, Leah noted, could be considered a long time. But it was none of her business. However, Eli and Victoria having a conversation in front of her, that was her business. Something she did not want. He was going to have to take this outside, never mind that it was about ten degrees. That was his problem. He could let his love keep him warm. She cleared her throat. No reaction. She did it again, louder.

Eli looked up, startled. Had he *forgotten* she was there?

"What's going on?" Victoria asked.

"Oh, that's, uh, that's—"

"Leah," she supplied, her voice clipped.

She wasn't sure she wanted to hear how he was going to label her. A friend? An acquaintance? Nobody you'd know? *The retail clerk?* It remained a mystery, because Eli never finished his sentence.

Instead he eagerly edged over to Leah, holding the phone at arm's length so the camera could capture them both in the frame. "Say hi!"

Out of the corner of her eye, Leah could see herself in the small inset, staring at him incredulously. She quickly turned her attention to the phone. The larger part of the screen held . . . well, exactly what she expected. A beautiful woman with long waves of rich brown hair, dramatically arched eyebrows, full red lips, the works.

"Hi," Victoria replied with a bright smile. "It's so nice to meet you!"

Okay, Leah hadn't been expecting that. After all the sighing, head shaking, and eye rolling she'd witnessed from Eli's group of friends, it was easy to demonize this woman in her head. To have her be friendly and cheerful sort of trashed that image she'd invented.

Obviously intrigued at the implication of a woman hanging around with her ex, Victoria cocked an eyebrow at him. "Eli," she said in an amusedly accusatory tone, "is there something you're not telling me?"

"What do you mean?"

"Oh my God." Laughing, she rolled her eyes dramatically.

"How's Rome?" Eli asked her, oblivious, as Leah stepped out of view of the phone's camera. He didn't seem to notice.

"It's *amazing*!"

Leah decided to start dropping heavier hints to get Eli to move along. Maybe closing up would do the trick. She pulled out the cash drawer and took it into the back room. There was no need to count it, as she hadn't made a sale all day. She put it in the safe, got her coat, and turned out the lights. Eli, of course, didn't notice.

"Tell me everything!" he said to Victoria.

"Oh, I wish I could, but I have to go in a minute. The reason I called—I was wondering if you could do me a favor."

"Sure! You name it. What do you need?"

"You know how I had a friend who was subletting my apartment? Well, she got a job out of state and my apartment is going to be empty in a week. Could you stop by there, make sure the heat's turned down, maybe water my plants?"

"We're closed," Leah said, her voice cold and impersonal.

"Yeah, no problem! I could . . ." He glanced up to see the store was dark. *Sorry*, he mouthed to Leah.

She flicked her hand to usher him out onto the street. He obeyed, frowning with concern.

"I really am sorry," he whispered.

"Nothing to be sorry about," she whispered back. She winced at her own tone, but again, Eli didn't seem to notice. "Better get back to your call."

She locked the door and hurried away, working hard not to look back. She'd just closed an hour early. Not that anyone would notice. If her boss asked her about it later, she'd come up with some excuse. Right now she was focused on burning off her excess ire by power walking down the street. She knew her anger wasn't logical, but it was there all the same. No, not anger. Jealousy, pure and simple.

She was being ridiculous. She knew Eli was completely devoted to Victoria. She'd been witness to it last summer on the bridge, and it obviously hadn't abated since, judging by his reaction to her video call. Which meant there was no room in Eli's heart for Leah. Any connection they seemed to have—and they sure did seem to have one—was solidly classified as friendship. Anything more was all in her head. All the time they'd spent together had been to help him work on getting Victoria back, after all.

God, she was so stupid.

No, not stupid. She'd just let her guard down, was all. She was vulnerable after Cathy's death and thought she could risk some sort of connection with other people. And look where it got her—friends in a place she was going to leave and a crush on an unavailable guy.

Good grief, she was more like Duckie than she thought.

As she passed Dickie's bar, she caught a distorted, shadowy glimpse of her own face in the blanked-out smoked-glass windows. She stopped and really looked at herself: small and pale, with round cheeks, a turned-up nose, and a super short haircut that wasn't really attractive on her, no matter what she thought in her more confident moments when she was feeling cute. She thought back to the sight of Victoria on Eli's phone, all billowy hair and makeup and femininity, and it made her regret looking like an elf.

No, she didn't regret what she looked like. She never had before, and she wasn't about to start now. She was who she was, and that was fine. It wasn't her looks that were the problem, it was that she was mired in a hopeless crush, resenting the perfectly pleasant Victoria, devoted Eli, and . . . herself. There was only one solution: forget about Eli and stick to her plan to get out of town as soon as the snow melted.

Now she just had to get the last of the money she'd calculated she'd need to move on. She doubted Mr. Lehman could give her more hours at the shop, not at this time of year. She glanced up and down the street and only saw dark storefronts. Restaurants, breweries, art galleries, wine shops. Most of them, plus the B&Bs and inns up the side streets, were closed till tourist season started. The town wouldn't come to life for three more months at least.

She muttered to her reflection in the window, "Think, Keegan. You're usually smart. Where did your brains go?"

Turned to mush by her infatuation with Eli, probably.

Then she noticed the sign in the window, beside her reflection. She pulled open the heavy door of Dickie's and went inside.

Chapter 14

The brilliant lights in the drugstore were blinding after the dark of the early evening outside. Eli and Ben blinked and looked around a little confusedly as the automatic doors swooshed closed behind them.

"You're okay with this, right?" Ben asked Eli as they walked the length of the main aisle.

"Yeah, yeah. Absolutely. I . . . look, you and Jenna and everybody have worked so hard to help me out, and I've been giving you nothing but grief. I apologize for that. It's just this . . . this . . ."

"Makeover?"

"I hate that word, but yeah. It's important. I know it now, after talking to Victoria the other day. I need to focus, keep trying to become the best version of me, right?" Eli stopped in front of a rack with bouquets of flowers wrapped in cellophane. He reached for one, then hesitated. "This is weird, though. A practice date. And on Valentine's Day—did you plan that?"

"Nope," Ben said. "Had the idea, set it up, then realized we'd picked the most loaded date in the romantic calendar. We're kinda magical that way."

"So I get flowers."

"And candy."

"And candy. I'm all dressed up, I'm ready. Who's my date, and where are we going?"

Ben flinched. "Well . . ."

"Oh no."

"Just keep an open mind."

"Tell me it's not Gray."

"No, Jenna said your date had to be a woman. For, you know, a realistic experience."

"Realistic? So it's not a blow-up doll either."

"No." His brother-in-law laughed, scratching under his chin.

"Okay, grab a box of candy and meet me up front, then we'll pry Gillian loose from the pharmacy. Where did you say we were going?"

"I didn't. I said to keep an open mind."

"Not your kitchen. Please, not your kitchen."

"I wouldn't wish that on you."

Eli stepped into the checkout line while Ben inspected the candy aisle. A teenager was in front of him, in a dress shirt and tie, looking just as uncomfortable as Eli. Eli wanted to tell this kindred spirit the whole dressing-up thing, not to mention the dating thing, didn't get any easier with age, but he didn't want to kill the kid's mood. He too had flowers and candy—a bigger bouquet by far, which made Eli second-guess his choice, and a two-layer box of chocolates—as well as a small teddy bear.

"Cute," Eli muttered. "Shoulda . . . Ben!"

The boy looked over his shoulder at Eli, and Eli gave him a somber nod. Brothers in arms, off to divine the mystery of the feminine wiles. The kid didn't nod back, just looked at him nervously. Whether he was uneasy about his upcoming date or Eli's scrutiny, Eli couldn't tell. Ben trotted up with a small box of chocolates, and Eli sent him back for a bigger one.

Once they paid for their loot and collected Gillian, they headed down Main Street. Eli spotted his comrade across the road and shouted, "Good luck, man!"

"Who is that?" Gillian asked.

"No clue. But I share his pain."

"Oh, it won't be so bad. Do your best to be a great date—"

"I'm already a great date."

"Do your best to be a better one. You said Victoria likes elaborate dates and fancy restaurants and you came up short in both areas before, right?"

"I don't think she minded."

"Oh, she minded. Work on your skills tonight. At least there's no pressure with a practice date."

"So where is this Valentine's Day extravaganza, anyway? Are we leaving town, or . . . ?" And then they stopped walking. "Wh—*Dickie's*? Are you serious?"

"Desperate times, desperate measures, darling," Gillian said. "There isn't a lot to choose from in town, and by the time we thought of this, we were too late to make reservations someplace nice. But Dickie said he was pulling out all the stops for Valentine's Day."

Eli heaved a sigh as he held the door open for his friends. "Well, now I feel stupid. All dressed up and everything and we end up at *Dickie's*."

"Well, don't say it like *that*," the owner in question shouted from behind the bar. "Appreciate the ambience."

"Is that what you call it?"

In honor of the holiday, Dickie had taped a few shiny red cardboard hearts here and there on the paneled walls, and the fireplace channel was on all the TVs. The trouble was, all the TVs were hanging above the bar, so it just looked like the place was burning down.

"Hey, I put new votive candles on all the tables. Do you know what that cost me?"

"No, no, it's . . . nice," Eli amended.

Gillian murmured, "Don't focus on the surroundings. Just stay in your date bubble and pay attention to every step of it. We're in the corner booth. There's Jenna."

"Wait. You're going to be here the whole time?"

"Well, how else will we be able to score your performance?"

"Do what to my *what*, now?"

"We'll be watching and taking notes, so we can critique you afterward. We need to get the big-picture view, so we won't be right on top of you, but we'll be close enough."

"And who's the lucky lady who's going to stand in for Victoria?"

"She's on her way. Delia's picking her up."

"I need a drink," Eli muttered.

"Nope, no drinking before your actual date. You need to be firing on all cylinders. That's a Dating 101 tip right there."

Eli heaved another sigh and looked around. It seemed Dickie's Valentine's Day extravaganza was a bust. Only two or three tables were occupied, by what looked like long-married couples treating it like any other night—dressed casually, barely talking, and digging into cheeseburgers, nachos, and baskets of wings. If Eli was going to pretend he was at a fancy French restaurant having a gourmet dinner with Victoria, he wasn't going to need a drink, he was going to need hallucinogens.

Gillian led him over to a small table done up nicer than the others, with a white tablecloth, taper candles, and two full place settings that almost didn't fit on the tiny square surface. "Sit. Your date should be here any minute. When she gets here, don't forget to stand up, take her coat, compliment her appearance, and pull out her chair. Got it?"

"I know that."

"But have you ever *done* it before?"

"Of course I have!"

Eli had only been sitting at the table a few minutes, randomly poking different forks and spoons, when Delia slunk into the bar. Alone. She sidled up to Jenna and Gillian and whispered something furiously.

"Oh, *seriously?*" Jenna burst out.

"What's going on?" Eli called to them.

His sister made a face and came over. "Your date's not coming. She said she got a real date for tonight."

"Who was it?"

"Liz."

"The woman at Poppin' Locks who wanted to shave my head?" When Eli had been in Liz's chair they'd chatted a bit, as one did at a salon, but he certainly hadn't detected any spark between them.

"She thought you were cute."

"We are talking about Gray's sometime date, right?"

"So what?"

"That gets messy. I'm actually grateful she blew me off. Let's just take the L here and have some wings, okay?"

"Oh no you don't." Jenna pushed him back as he tried to drag his chair over to their booth. "You're supposed to have a practice date, and dammit, you're going to have one."

"With whom, exactly, Jenna?"

"I don't know. I'll do it, I guess."

Everyone recoiled at the same time.

"What, too creepy?"

"By half," her brother confirmed.

"Don't look at me," Gillian said, holding up her hands in protest when Jenna zeroed in on her. "I don't even do practice dates anymore. If you want to sour the kid on relationships completely, I'm your girl. But I don't think you want that. Besides, I *really* want to get judgy, so I'm hanging onto my scorecard and staying right here with my cheap-ass wine."

She settled back into the booth with a thud, daring anyone to try to budge her.

"I'll be your date, honey," Delia said with a watery smile.

"Aw." Eli gave his friend a warm hug. "I appreciate that, I do. But I don't think your heart's in it, is it?"

"It shows?"

"It always shows. How about you spend tonight having a serious talk with someone you *really* need to communicate with, hm?"

"Uh," Delia said, pausing to take a wavering breath, "not tonight."

"Honey, when are the two of you—"

"Just . . . not tonight. I think the reason Liz blew you off was because she was going to hook up with Gray."

Eli winced. "Oh."

"All right, all right," Ben burst out. "I'll do it."

"Dude."

"What?"

Jenna glanced across the room and her eyes widened. "Yeeeess," she exclaimed.

Eli turned around to see what she was looking at. "Oh my God."

Leah froze under the weight of their stares, her brown eyes as big as the dinner plates she was carrying.

"Perfect," Jenna whispered, delighted.

"What's going on?" Leah asked, her wary glance darting to each of them in turn.

"You do *not* work here too, Kirk."

"No reason why not," Leah said flatly, bustling over to some patrons and setting the plates down in front of them. "Dickie said he was expecting to be busy for Valentine's Day and was going to need extra help," she said when she came back to face the group.

"I don't know why my ad in the PennySaver weekly didn't get more traction," Dickie grumbled. "I spent fifteen bucks on it." To Leah, who joined him behind the bar, he said, "You can probably knock off. I don't think it's gonna get any busier. These guys were the only reservation I got."

Leah looked disappointed. "Are you sure, Dickie?"

"I'm sure. I don't want to waste your time," he muttered, truly despondent.

"Oh, hey," she said in a soothing tone, patting his arm. "Don't be upset. You did your best. Maybe you can try again next year, get a tradition going."

"Yeah, I guess."

As Leah came around the end of the bar, Jenna stepped in front of her. "Dollface, I've got a great idea. Be Eli's date tonight."

"Wh . . . what?"

"He must have told you about his practice date, right?"

"Actually, he didn't."

"Doesn't matter. Liz blew us off, and you'd be perfect. All you have to do is sit across from him, eat a meal, and let him lavish you with attention. What do you say?"

"Oh, I—I don't think that's a good idea."

Jenna ignored her. "Dickie!" she roared. "Keep the girl on the clock while she eats dinner with Eli, wouldja? It's the least you can do, if she can't get a full night's pay for serving."

"I'll do it. Because I like you. Not you," he said to Jenna. "You," he said to Leah.

"Like I care," Jenna spat back. "You and your stupid vendetta."

"I'm still hurt!"

"Get over it." Then she turned to Leah. "Okay? You in? Cash and a free meal. Can't argue with that."

Eli watched this exchange with interest. He hadn't seen or talked to Leah since he'd stopped by Thousand Island Dressing days ago. There was something about their last conversation . . . she hadn't seemed like herself. Maybe if she was his practice date, they could talk about it.

Or, wait, was that a bad thing to do on a practice date? Was he just supposed to be superficial and charming instead? Would this dinner be like an Olympic sport? Would his friends and relatives hold up their scores on big cardboard squares? Would he get a 4.5 if he forgot to keep his elbows off the table? Why didn't anybody explain the rules to him before this whole thing started?

"I . . . uh . . ." Leah stammered, "I smell like fryer grease."

"You say that like it's a bad thing." He stood up and pulled out the other chair before she could change her mind. "Please, sit. Be my date." After she was settled and he'd taken the seat opposite her, he leaned in and murmured, "I'm really glad you're here."

"This is nuts," she whispered back.

"I know. Thank you for participating anyway. It makes it more bearable."

Leah visibly softened at that. "Okay."

"Oh, here." He handed her the flowers, candy, and teddy bear. "For you."

"Or someone like me."

But she sniffed the flowers and caressed the bear's ear, and Eli got the feeling she was pleased with his offering to the love gods.

"So I haven't seen you in a while," he said, flicking his cloth napkin into his lap.

"I've been, you know, busy."

"Oh, I do know. Adding Dickie's to your work roster is pretty ambitious."

"It's not so bad."

"All the wings you can eat?"

She wrinkled her nose, and Eli was captivated. Such a small gesture, but cute enough to stop his thoughts cold.

"What?" she asked, her voice accusing.

Oh God, had he been staring? He'd been staring. Dammit. "Nothing. We should order, right? Let's order." He picked up a piece of paper that was lying on his plate. "Oh."

"What is it?"

"So we've got a special menu, apparently. This is not Dickie's normal stuff. Do you have one?" She shook her head. "Here, take a look at this, then."

"You're supposed to order for her!" Jenna shouted from the corner. "Minus five points."

"Do you want me to order for you?" Eli asked Leah.

"Hell, no."

"Yeah, it seems kind of . . . condescending, doesn't it?"

"At the very least."

"The lady does not wish me to order for her," he shouted back at his sister. "Mind your own business. And please enter the twenty-first century with your dating rules."

"Get the chicken," Dickie advised from behind the bar. "I don't trust Chip with the other stuff on that menu your sister came up with."

"Yeah, I'm pretty sure lobster thermidor is not in Chip the fry cook's repertoire," Eli said to Leah. "You okay with the chicken? Or are you a vegetarian or vegan or anything?"

"Nope. Chicken's fine."

"May I shout the order for you?"

Ah, that was better. Leah was almost smiling. There was something odd about her tonight; she wasn't her usual playful self. And why would she be, after being ambushed into taking part in this bizarre scenario? But he'd get her to loosen up.

"Garçon," Eli bellowed in Dickie's general direction, "we shall have two of your finest lobster thermidor dinners, my good man."

"Aw, come on, Eli—"

"Just kidding. Two chicken parms." He turned to Leah. "And some potato skins?"

She nodded.

"Make it happen, Richard."

"Lobster . . ." Dickie grunted, whapping the kitchen door open to deliver the order to his cook. "Practically gave me a heart attack . . ."

"Potato skins are not a fancy French restaurant staple!" Gillian scolded from behind her wineglass.

"Well, they should be. If we've gotta go through this, we're gonna need potato skins. Now leave us alone. I have a date to lavish with attention."

Even in the low light, he could tell Leah was blushing as she looked down at the tabletop and fiddled with her water glass.

"Hey," he said in a low voice, "everything okay?"

She looked up, and again, when her huge eyes met his, Eli felt some strange bottoming-out feeling around the area of his navel.

"Yeah, fine."

"Pour the champagne," Ben hissed loudly.

"Best idea I've heard all night," Eli said to Leah. "May I?"

Chapter 15

Okay, this whole thing was absolutely bananas. What was she doing here? It was true that when Leah lost control of her emotions she fantasized about what it would be like going out on a romantic date with Eli. Those fantasies, however, didn't involve Dickie's. Or subbing in for Liz subbing in for Victoria. Or dating coaches. Very vocal dating coaches. Ben's outburst about the champagne had made Eli jump. Apparently he was concentrating hard as well. On what? Likely trying to imagine Victoria in her place, on a real date in a real upscale restaurant. Which Dickie's absolutely wasn't. And Leah was hardly Victoria. She wasn't kidding when she said she smelled like fryer grease. The stains on her Dickie's ring-neck T-shirt, spotless merely an hour ago, were all gained from carrying food too close to her torso (rookie mistake). There was no way the smell of french fries could be passed off as French perfume.

Eli pulled the bottle out of its nest of ice in a bucket normally used to hold Dickie's signature mega-jumbo serving of wings. "Okay, first a toast. Come on, let's do this," he prompted as Leah hung back.

She reluctantly lifted her glass. "What are we toasting to?"

"Well, if this were a real date, I'd say . . . to us."

"But it's not a real date."

"Hush with that and get with the program."

"To us," she muttered.

"There ya go."

Leah didn't much like champagne, but she wasn't going to complain right about now. It was alcohol and it was in her hand. Plus Eli was wearing one of his new suits, which looked damn good on him.

"So did you get a look at the getup?" Eli asked, as if he could read her mind. Had she been staring? He gestured to said suit with a flourish. "Not bad, right?"

"Your fashion consultant is a genius."

"She is. So what have you been up to, genius? I mean, I haven't seen you or talked to you in a while. Since the, you know, the . . ." He lowered his voice to the barest of whispers. "*Hat rescue.* Thanks again, by the way. I've hidden it so Jenna can't throw it away again."

"Good plan."

He waited. She didn't say anything else. His eyes flicked over to his friends' table, just once, but he didn't seek their help. He craned his neck to see if Dickie was coming out of the kitchen with their potato skins.

He wasn't.

Eli cleared his throat. Leah took a sip of champagne.

This was too weird in general, and worse because of their last encounter in Thousand Island Dressing. Leah felt a little bad about it. Normally they could talk up a storm, like in their movie-watching sessions—even the one on the phone, when they'd talked for an extra hour after *When Harry Met Sally* ended, just yammering about anything and everything. But now? Leah was silent and Eli was fidgeting.

"How's Blanche?"

Eli let out an obviously relieved breath. "She's good. She's really made herself at home."

"So . . . is she your cat now?"

"I'm just keeping her till Victoria gets back."

"Don't tell me you're going to use Blanche as leverage to make sure you see Victoria again."

"*No*," he snorted, then coughed as some champagne bubbles went up his nose. "Of course not. She asked me to take care of Blanche, I'm taking care of Blanche. I think I can get together with Victoria when she gets back without holding her cat hostage."

Leah sighed and raked her fingers through her short hair. "You're right. Sorry. Anyway, I'm not sure we should be talking about your ex-girlfriend on a Valentine's Day fake date. Kind of ruins the vibe, doesn't it?"

"We're supposed to have a vibe?"

"Of course you are!" Gillian exclaimed.

"How many glasses of wine has she had?" Eli asked the others. They all held up a different number of fingers.

At first Leah laughed, but then reality came crashing down. She couldn't do this. No matter how much she liked spending time with Eli, she liked spending time with Eli a little *too* much. Add his friends in the mix—who, she reminded herself, were definitely his friends and not hers—and it just made it worse. All on a fake date, no less. Where she was Victoria's stand-in.

Before she even knew what she was doing, Leah pushed back her chair. "You know what? This was a bad idea."

She started to rise, but Eli quickly stood as well and put out a hand to stop her.

"No, sit, please. I'm sorry. This is weird, I know, but can we just . . . have a nice dinner?"

"With your friends' commentary?"

He gestured for her to sit, then crossed the room, placed his hands flat on the group's table, and leaned in.

"What's going on?" Delia hissed, apparently thinking she was whispering, but failing. "Do you need some backup?"

"I need you to leave. All of you. This is ridiculous."

"But—" Jenna started.

"Nope," he cut her off. "No buts. I have decided I would like to have a nice, quiet, relaxing dinner with Leah. I can't do that if I know you're over here scoring my performance. So please leave. I've got this. Jenna, Ben, it's Valentine's Day. Go have some alone time at home while Mom's got the girls. Gillian, go fire up a movie. I could recommend some romantic ones with strapping heroes, but you probably want a true crime documentary where the wife gets away with murdering her husband, so I'll leave that to you. Delia . . ." Eli faltered, but then charged ahead. "Go find Gray, kick Liz out into the snow, and *tell him how you feel, for God's sake.*"

"Oh, Eli—"

"I know," he said gently. "But you can do it. You'll never have a moment's peace if you don't. Think about it, okay? Now, get out, all of you. Right now, please."

He stepped back and waited. They scooched out of the booth with much grumbling and sorting of coats and hats, Gillian scooping up the sheets of paper she'd brought for everyone to take notes on his dinner performance. Only once the door had closed soundly behind them did Eli turn back to his dinner date.

"Better?" he asked Leah.

She didn't answer right away. What he'd just done was admirable, and it started up a whole host of butterflies in her stomach, but . . . "You're still on a pretend date with the wrong person."

"You know," he said, sitting back down and adjusting his suit coat, "I don't think I am."

That was the kind of comment she could definitely take the wrong way, which would get her heart into a whole lot of trouble. Leah decided to err on the side of the impersonal. "I can prep you for Victoria? I don't see how."

"No, I mean I like hanging out with you. No qualifiers, no other reason than I just . . . like you."

Oh God, he was making it worse with every utterance.

"But the only time we 'hang out' is when we're working on your . . ."

"Makeover project?"

"Which is absolutely . . . dumb."

"What is? Us hanging out?"

"No!" she burst out. "The whole makeover thing. It's nuts."

"Why?"

"It just . . . it shouldn't be necessary."

"I *am* trying to win Victoria back, remember?"

"And you think *this* is going to do it?" Leah gestured at the fancy dishes and the candles, the flames reflected in the depths of his eyes, dark in the dimmed light. "Look," she said with a sigh, "it shouldn't be this complicated. You shouldn't have to change who you are for someone else. Not that much, anyway, and not if it makes you unhappy."

"I'm happy. I'm ecstatic!"

She leveled a glare at him and said, simply, "Trilby."

"Most of the time," he muttered, taking a gulp of champagne.

Leah sat back, crossed her arms, and studied him. Finally she asked, "Why?"

"Why what?"

"Why do this? What keeps you going with all this? Is she really worth it?"

"Yes."

"Why?"

"I . . . I don't know how to explain it. She's just . . ."

"The one?"

"Yeah."

"Impressively vague. That's only acceptable from Sam in *Love Actually*. How is she 'the one'? Why is she 'the one'? Can she hit that high note in 'All I Want for Christmas Is You'?"

Leah paused as Dickie finally brought over a platter of potato skins. Eli, ever the gentleman, put some of the skins on Leah's small plate.

She didn't protest; in fact, she lunged for one. "Sorry, I'm starving." After she downed a huge bite, she said, "Anyway, I take it back. You're not Sam. You're Romeo."

"That's good, right? The OG romantic hero?"

"No, that's bad."

"What? Why?"

"Romeo was not the OG romantic hero. He was nothing more than a horny teenager who wanted to be in love, no matter who the object of his affection was. He was just lucky enough that for once a girl liked him back. Or unlucky, considering how it ended."

"So I'm going to die for love?"

"Let's not be so melodramatic. Dying for love makes good theater, but in real life it's not as impressive as carrying on afterward."

Eli helped himself to some potato skins as well. "So you're saying I'm stupid for doing this."

"Misguided, I'd say. Your judgment has been clouded by infatuation."

Eli plopped the potato skin he was holding onto his plate. "How do you know it's infatuation? What if I'm in love with Victoria?"

"You should get over it, because she's obviously not in love with you."

Eli's expression darkened and it looked like his bile was rising. "You only met her by video call for ten seconds. How do you know?"

"I know you only went out for a few months, which is barely enough time to get to know anybody, let alone the person you say you love."

It was like she couldn't stop herself. Everything she'd kept silent about for months, ever since she was clued in to this ridiculous plan, was coming to the surface.

"I know that she hasn't contacted you for six months. You told me so. And then she video calls you when she needs a favor. Coincidence? I think not. I also know she's not that into you. Now, *there's* a movie for your list."

"You don't know she's not."

"She turned down your proposal, broke up with you entirely, and couldn't wait to leave the country! I mean, read the room, Eli!"

Leah looked away and felt herself flush. The heavy food curdled in her stomach, the bacon grease and butter slimy on her fingers.

"How . . . ?" he began, then froze. "You were there," he said, his voice low. "Last summer. That's where I know you from. We were on the bridge, you were in the boathouse."

"I didn't want to hear your conversation, but I did. The whole thing. I know what I saw and I know what I heard." She forced herself to look at him and said quietly, "She broke your heart and didn't care, Eli. And I don't understand why you're chasing someone who would do that to you and leave without a second thought."

Eli slowly wiped his hands on his napkin and stared at the dark lump of leftover potato skin in front of him. Leah tried to surreptitiously swipe at her cheek, but he zeroed in on the motion.

"Are you crying?" he whispered.

"You piss me off, Masterson. And sometimes I angry cry. Deal with it."

"What can I do?"

Leah sighed heavily. Why did he have to be so . . . so . . . *nice*? She tucked her hands between her crossed knees and tried to close off her heart.

"You can take me home, I think. Please," she added belatedly.

Chapter 16

After Eli dropped Leah off, he stayed parked in her driveway for a minute and massaged his forehead. This night had given him a raging headache. The fact that the practice date was a bust wasn't really surprising, although he knew his sister and friends had meant well. Having dinner with Leah added a whole new level of preposterousness to it, though. She had been right when she'd said it was a bad idea.

No, wait, she'd said the entire makeover project was a bad idea. Which was far worse. A stupid dinner they could have laughed about together, but for Leah to lose it on him, attacking the whole plan, was entirely unexpected and more than a little off-putting, because she was forcing him to look at his choices in a new light, when he'd thought he was doing fine and on the right track for his future.

Was it pointless trying to get Victoria back? Did he even want Victoria herself, or was it just a Romeo-like desire to have someone, anyone, even if it wasn't the perfect person for him, like Leah had said?

Well, hold on just a minute. Even if Leah had been there when Victoria broke up with him, even if she knew more than he thought she did, it didn't necessarily mean she was right. She'd just managed to *sound* right, with her absolute statements and sharp insight that made sense if he thought about it . . . and, he had to admit, even before she pointed out the weak spots in all this, he had *occasionally* wondered if he was doing the right thing. In fact, he'd almost confessed as much, to Leah no less, the other evening in Thousand Island Dressing. Until he was interrupted by Victoria's video call.

And hey, Victoria had called him, and they'd talked, and it had felt like old times. That video call had reassured him that yes, he was doing the right thing. Crisis averted. Still on track.

Except . . . Leah had pointed out that this was the first time Victoria had called him, and only because she needed a favor.

Dammit.

No. Only he and Victoria knew what was between them, and he still thought it was something worth saving. No matter what Leah's strong opinion was. Her very, very strong, presumptuous, overbearing opinion. That may have had a kernel of truth in it. But she was still wrong.

He needed some time, that's what he needed. He needed to lock himself in his cabin and just think this through. But he wasn't going to be able to analyze anything while his head was pounding. He rifled through his glove compartment and found nothing but some old cough drops. He was pretty sure he was out of painkillers at home too, so he headed back to the pharmacy.

When he got there, he had a hit of déjà vu, because once again the teenager was standing at the checkout counter with his Valentine's gifts. Were they caught in a time loop? Or did the kid have a second date? It was only eight o'clock, after all. But as Eli went in search of drugs, he heard the boy say in a weak, dejected tone, "Can I return these? It turned out I didn't need them after all."

Ouch.

Valentine's Day was the work of the devil, no doubt about it.

He got in line behind the teen, who was fidgeting as the cashier contemplated whether to allow him to return the gifts. It seemed the stuffed bear and candy were acceptable returns, but the flowers were in question for some reason.

"Rough night, huh?" Eli ventured.

This time the kid was too depressed to be wary. "You have no idea."

"Oh, I think I do. Want to talk about it?"

"Nope." Then the kid loosened his tie and said in a broken voice, "She didn't want me, I guess."

"There's a lot of that going around." Eli sighed. "Look, I want to say it gets easier, but you know what? It doesn't."

The kid smirked. "Rough night?"

"You have no idea. But I did learn something. A friend once told me—about ten minutes ago, actually—not to waste your time chasing after someone who's not interested. And I hate to admit it, but she might have a point."

"But—"

"I know. The heart wants what it wants. I get it. I guess we just have to . . . oh."

"What?"

Eli understood now. "Let our heads convince our hearts to let it go and move on. Here, give me those," Eli said, gesturing to the bouquet. "I'll buy 'em off you."

He handed the kid a too-large bill, and the boy lit up a little bit over the profit he'd just made off his misery. Eli hurriedly paid for the painkillers, scooped up the flowers, and jumped back in his Jeep.

∽

"These are for you."

Leah leaned wearily on the open door. "Eli . . ."

"Please. Take them."

She rubbed one hand, buried in the cuff of an oversized sweatshirt, across her eyes. Makeupless and in sweats and bulky socks, she was definitely in for the night and likely a few minutes from bed, and here he was bothering her again. But it couldn't wait.

"You already gave me flowers, candy, a stupid little teddy bear . . . isn't that enough?" She sighed.

"You were going to wedge in 'and a miserable night' after the 'stupid little teddy bear,' weren't you?" She didn't deny it. "Anyway, those gifts were for my practice date. *These* are specifically for you. As an apology. You were right about everything, and I'm sorry."

"And you're a dope."

"And I'm a dope. I understand what you're saying about Victoria. I do. It's just . . ."

"She's still under your skin? Like a tick?"

Eli smiled. "Something like that. I'm working on it, okay? It's just . . . really confusing right now. So . . . ?" He waggled the flowers again, rattling the cellophane hopefully. Or maybe he was shaking from the cold.

Leah noticed. The way she noticed everything. "Do you want to come in?"

"Do you mind? These dress shoes are murder in this weather. I can't feel anything from my ankles on down."

Leah could have simply been following North Country protocol: it was common courtesy to invite someone in to avoid frostbite, no matter how you felt about the sufferer. Eli didn't care at that point, though. He really was freezing in his too-thin dress clothes and shoes. Leah opened the door wider and relieved him of the bouquet as he entered. Eli took it as a good sign.

"Thank you," he said, shucking his camel-hair coat.

"Stop being nice," she groused, but her nose was in the bouquet when she said it, and he spotted a small smile behind the blossoms.

Eli hopped awkwardly as he yanked off first one brogue, then another, and nearly fell into Leah. Her free hand shot out to steady him.

"How much champagne did you have, anyway?"

"Numb feet, remember?"

"Are you hungry?"

"No," he lied. They hadn't gotten past the appetizer stage of the dinner. He followed her farther into the house and looked around. "I like what you've done with the place."

"Shut up." She wasn't snappish—Leah hardly ever was that—but instead there was a hint of amusement in her voice, lifting Eli's spirits.

She'd been busy. Where there had been clutter, there were now stacks of boxes of every size and condition, most liberated from the supermarket and the liquor store, judging by their labels. Without all of Cathy's stuff on display, the house should have looked neater, but instead it just looked . . . sadder. More bare areas meant it was easier to see the discolored paint, gouges in the walls and floor, smudges on the switchplates . . . the place hadn't been spruced up in years, likely long before Cathy got sick and didn't have the strength to keep the place up.

"My foster mom was never a big fan of housecleaning," Leah explained. "I did what I could, but . . ."

"You were a little preoccupied."

"I guess you could say that."

"It must have been tough packing up all her stuff. I mean, emotionally as well as physically."

Leah just shrugged.

Eli wanted more than a shrug. He wanted to know everything. He wished she would open up completely and tell him what it was like being a foster child, what it was like living with Cathy and her son and the other foster kids. And to tell him where she came from, what happened in her life that landed her in foster care, how she ended up here in Willow Cove.

She didn't owe him anything, of course. He knew that. No matter how curious he was, no matter how much he wanted to know what went on inside her head—and her heart—they weren't anywhere near close enough for her to trust him with her past or even her present. Maybe someday. Soon, he hoped.

He asked a question he hoped wasn't too intrusive. "So how come all this is on you? What about Patrick?"

Although she didn't answer right away, Leah must have been able to tell that the silent treatment wasn't going to work on Eli because she finally said, "When Cathy died, Patrick told me he was going to take care of everything, but he didn't. He called a while back and said he was going to come fix the house up because he wants to sell it, but he didn't. That's Patrick, though—lots of promises, no follow-through. I don't know when he's actually going to show up, *if* he ever does, so I figured I'd better do something with all this stuff in the meantime. Before—" She stopped abruptly, and Eli wondered what she almost said. "Anyway, it's all junk. I'm sure Patrick is just going to want to throw it out. I've already thrown out or donated a lot."

"Well, there has to be some personal stuff he'll want."

"Actually, there isn't."

"Mementos? Letters and postcards? *Photos?*"

Leah shook her head. "Nothing."

"How could Cathy not have kept anything personal?"

"She wasn't very sentimental. She was . . ." Again Leah stopped herself, this time drifting off instead of clamping her lips shut. "She wasn't very touchy-feely, let's say."

"Was it hard to take care of her?"

"No, not really. She was grouchy, sure, but she was in a lot of pain. You kind of make allowances for that. And then later she . . . changed, I guess."

Eli didn't move, didn't speak. He got the feeling he was going to get a tiny piece of the Leah puzzle if he just stayed still. Like waiting for a wild animal to approach.

After a moment she went on, "When she was really bad . . . on a lot of medication, sleeping a lot, pretty helpless, and hospice started their regular visits . . ." Leah stared blankly at the wall, obviously reliving that time. "If I did something simple for her, like if I got her to eat a spoonful of vanilla ice cream, or arranged her pillows just the way she wanted, little things like that, she'd put her hand on my arm and call me her angel."

"That's sweet."

"I hated it," Leah spat.

Eli started. "Why? Didn't she mean it?"

"Oh, she meant it. That was the problem. It wasn't the Cathy

I knew, talking like that, openly grateful. It scared me, because I knew she was looking at life differently, because she was so close to the end."

"It sounds like she loved you very much, though," Eli murmured.

As if she didn't hear him, Leah went on harshly, "Do you know why else I hated when she said that?" Eli shook his head even though she wasn't looking at him. "Because it wasn't true." Her voice broke on the last word. "I wasn't her angel. Angels work miracles. Angels help people. I couldn't fix her, couldn't save her. I could only try to make her comfortable. And I barely managed that."

Eli's heart broke. She was so hard on herself. Keenly aware that he was running the risk of Leah coldcocking him, he came up behind her and put a hand on her shoulder. She didn't push him away, but she didn't turn to him either. Instead, she rubbed her eyes tiredly again.

"You did more than most people would do," he said softly. "You were there for her, and you did your best. Cathy was grateful because she knew it."

Leah nodded, and a shudder went through her. Eli could feel it, just as he could feel the warmth of her body, only an inch or so in front of him. He had an overwhelming urge to wrap his arms around her, but there was a good chance that kind of contact would send her flying to the opposite side of the room. The last thing he wanted to do was spook her, so he remained still and, to his surprise, Leah leaned back against him as if already accepting the support he didn't dare offer her. Every part of him went loose, and it was as though his insides melted and pooled at his feet.

"Anyway, if Cathy's penchant for clutter has taught me anything," she said, staring at the stack of boxes in the corner of the alcove that housed the dining room table, "it's that not much is worth keeping. The *stuff*, there's no point in hanging on to it. You know?"

She looked over her shoulder at him, her eyes large and glistening with unshed tears, and Eli's breath caught. "Yeah," he rasped. "I do."

"No, you don't."

"I know you're not talking about photos and letters anymore."

"I am." She took a ragged breath. "But not much else is worth hanging on to either."

"People?"

"If you don't leave them, they leave you."

Eli froze, stunned at her cold assessment of life. Did she really believe that? It didn't seem like her. Then again, he reminded himself, he didn't know her well enough to tell.

"You make it sound like Cathy chose to die."

"Who said I was talking about Cathy?" In the heavy silence that followed, Leah studied the bouquet as if she'd just discovered it was still in her hand. "These need water." She pulled away and hurried into the kitchen.

Eli stayed in the living room, figuring she needed a minute. He did too. Had she been talking about her biological family? Her other foster families? How many homes had she been placed in before she turned eighteen and was on her own?

After a few minutes, Eli edged over to the kitchen and leaned in the doorway. A box was open on the floor, its packing tape ripped off and curling on the edge, a wad of bubble wrap on the counter. She'd unpacked a vase and had put the bouquet from their "date" in it; now she was adding the new flowers. It wasn't lost on him that while Leah was talking about not being sentimental and not hanging on to things, she was still prolonging the life of the flowers he gave her.

Eli watched her as she carefully tucked each stem into the arrangement. With her delicate features in profile, her longish bangs dipping close to her left eye, she looked every inch a fairy, the way he'd pictured them when his sister had read him fairy tales when they were little. In the dim light of the kitchen, he could imagine giant wings shimmering at Leah's back.

How much champagne had he had, anyway?

The spell was broken when she turned her head and hit him with a sly look that made him doubt she'd shown him any vulnerability whatsoever a few minutes earlier. "You still here?"

"Yeah. I was robbed tonight."

"Robbed?"

"I lost an entire night to someone's stupid idea of a fake date."

"That *was* a crime."

He took a chance on her throwing him out into the snow by demanding, "Now I want some retribution. I want . . . I want a movie, and I want popcorn, and I want to break into the giant box of candy you stole from me."

Leah smiled, seemingly in spite of herself. "You gave it to me, remember?"

"As part of the fake date. Which didn't happen."

"Keep it up, and I'll make you eat the teddy bear instead." She wiped some stray water droplets off the counter with a tea towel, picked up the vase of flowers, and walked past him, back into the living room. "Well, come on," she called over her shoulder while she set the flowers on a side table with chipped veneer. "I've got the perfect movie for you."

There was a sudden lightness in the vicinity of Eli's heart as he followed her to the couch. "Please, not another lesson in how to be a ladykiller."

"Oh, it most certainly is."

He groaned and dropped onto the sofa. "I'm tired of taking notes on fake male behavior."

"No notes." She held up a battered cardboard VHS case.

"What is that?"

"Classic camp eighties horror/sci-fi/I don't even know what. All you need to know is there's a heroine in a skimpy buckskin mini-dress, complete with fringe, and low-budget aliens who are basically humans in cheap scuba gear."

"I'm in. Wait—not that I'm against it, but why is the heroine wearing buckskin?"

"She shoots things with old revolvers, I think."

"Like the aliens in scuba gear?"

"Ah, for the answer to that, you have to watch the movie."

"You don't *know* the answer to that, do you?"

She plopped the box of candy into his lap and nudged the tape out of its cardboard case. "I haven't seen this in years. I can't remember every detail. Only that it's one of the worst movies you'll ever see in your life. It'll be good for your soul."

~

The movie was indeed surreal and awful. The one thing Leah hadn't mentioned was it wasn't surreal and awful enough not to be boring as hell. Despite the sugar rush from gorging on Valentine's chocolates while they watched it, halfway through the movie they both nodded off. Eli woke first, to a silent, chilly room and a blue screen on the TV. He wondered briefly how the story ended, then realized he didn't much care. But the part of the movie they did see had worked the right amount of magic—by heckling the celluloid trainwreck, he and Leah had buried the tension from earlier in the evening and were comfortable with each other again.

Eli stole a glance to his left. Leah's head was resting on his arm, just below his shoulder, and she was breathing softly and evenly. In the light of the TV and a dim table lamp, he could see the blush high on her cheeks and a smudge of chocolate on her lower lip. He was getting a cramp and sorely needed to use the bathroom, but Eli didn't budge an inch. He couldn't disturb her.

He kind of just wanted to keep looking at her, if he was going to be honest with himself.

No, that wasn't true, not quite. He thought back to the day at the salon when he'd asked Liz to shave his beard off, how Leah had silently made the suggestion by running her hand over her own smooth cheek. Despite the fact that he'd ignored the connection that day, he realized he'd said he wanted to shave off his beard because if he didn't, he wouldn't be able to feel the softness of a woman's cheek against his own. Leah's skin looked luminous, smooth, and soft. And with her full cheeks, maybe she did resemble her non-namesake in *Star Wars* a bit. But it was the softness he was drawn to, so much so that he didn't even realize his hand was drifting to her face before his thumb was already brushing her cheek, lightly, so lightly, so he didn't disturb her. And it was softer than he'd been able to imagine.

Despite his care, she shifted a little and made a small, sleepy sound in her throat. Eli was surprised he didn't immediately draw back and jump off the couch. He couldn't. He was willing to take his chances if she woke up and saw him there, so close.

Which she did.

She stared at him with those enormous brown eyes while her brain caught up to their present status—movie over, middle of the night, both of them physically closer than they'd ever been before. If she'd looked alarmed, Eli would have begged her forgiveness a thousand times and hustled out to his car as fast as those slippery brogues could carry him in the snow. But she didn't look alarmed. Instead, she studied him calmly while his thumb caressed her cheek.

He moved it to her bottom lip. "You've got some . . . chocolate . . ." he whispered.

She let him wipe it off, still staring at him. He couldn't look away. It was as if she'd trapped him, physically trapped him, with her gaze alone.

When he pulled his thumb away, she ran her tongue over her lower lip as if checking for the chocolate.

"It's gone," he said, his voice rough, as he fixated on the red of her lips, the pink of the tip of her tongue.

"Okay." Leah's voice was quieter but as rough as his.

Unable to resist, Eli caressed her cheek again, and a sigh escaped him. Still, Leah didn't move, and she kept looking at him, into him, through him. Eli saw her color rise under his touch, and her breath grew ragged.

The pools of her eyes, the warmth of her skin—that was all there was in the world. Nothing else. Not before this exact moment in time, and not after. If there was a God, there would be no after. They would just stay there, in this exact moment, for eternity.

Except Leah edged up slightly, and suddenly her lips were closer to his. He didn't know anything anymore, except that he wanted his lips on hers. To feel that softness the best way he could imagine.

Touch.

Lips to lips.

Eli hesitated for a fraction of a second before the action he knew would decimate him. Her soft breath on his face nearly did him in. There was no protest, no change of intent, and his racing heart sped up even more. And then someone—whether it was him or Leah, he would never know—closed the infinitesimal gap.

The electric shock was not something Eli expected. It wasn't from static in a dry winter room, but from Leah herself. Well, from the two of them. Together. He'd never experienced anything like it. He started, but he didn't pull back. He wasn't capable. Their lips had met, and the only way was forward. More.

And more.

What began as a tentative soft touch escalated gradually, lips caressing lips, to a hungry urgency expressed with mouth, tongue, teeth. Leah rose up to meet him, and the shock became a surge. He pulled her to him, desperate for the feel of her hands on him, arms wrapped around his neck, her hands in his hair. He wanted all that and more. This soft, sweet, beautiful, smart, funny puzzle of a woman had occupied his thoughts for weeks. Had he known it would come to this? He didn't know, couldn't answer, didn't care.

More.

Now.

Until—

As if they telepathically shared the same thought, Eli and Leah pulled away at the same time. Leah, swollen lips parted and eyes wide, looked as shocked as he felt.

"I . . . I . . ."

"I'm sorry," he said in a rush, cutting her off. "I didn't—"

"It's my fault—"

"What? No! How could it be your fault? It's not your fault. It's my fault." With every utterance, his voice was getting higher, wilder, his words tumbling out faster. "It's absolutely my fault. It was . . . I mean, I shouldn't have . . . I'm rambling." He slapped a hand over his mouth. "I'm rambling," he said between his fingers. "I'm sorry."

Eyes still wide with shock, she said simply, almost congenially, "You should go."

"I should go," he said at the same time.

Chapter 17

"Okay, fella, let's chat. Are you friendly?"

The pale-gray cockatiel looked at Leah with bright, attentive eyes while it chewed on its foot.

"More important, do you need to have your cage cleaned? Speak up, now, I've got a serious time constraint."

But the bird did not, in fact, speak up. Instead, it tucked its head under its wing as if sniffing for pit stank and picked at its feathers. Leah studied the perky critter and debated whether or not to text Jenna to ask if cage cleaning was supposed to be part of the housecleaning service. Jenna had called Magic Maids and specifically asked for her, which Leah appreciated. She also appreciated that it was Jenna doing the calling and not Eli. Not after . . .

She shook herself. No time to dwell on what had happened on Valentine's Day. She had a house to clean. She knew she couldn't avoid thinking about the . . . *incident* . . . for much longer, though. It had already been a few days.

Eli, on the other hand, seemed eager to talk. He'd been texting her and calling her, but coward that she was, she'd been letting all his calls go to voicemail and deleting his texts without reading them. Her clunky, basic phone only showed her the first word or two of any text, so she couldn't even read them if her resolve failed her.

The first few began with "hey," "hi there," and the like, then eventually devolved from friendly greetings into a string of question marks. Leah felt bad for avoiding him, but really, what could they say about the other night? Sure, it had turned her into a shocked, lovesick zombie, and she was in that state all that night and the next day as well. But then she forced herself to snap out of it by seeing sense. Eli was still going full tilt after Victoria, and if she wanted to retain her sanity and keep hold of her heart, she'd best keep that in mind. One accidental lip collision in the middle of the night when they were both strung out on chocolate didn't change anything.

No matter how she felt about him. And those kisses. Which were . . . bone-dissolvingly great.

Didn't matter. A guy like Eli didn't just turn on a dime and fall for someone else just because she happened to be nearby and therefore more convenient. He was more loyal and had more integrity than that. There was only one logical conclusion, one sane course of action, that he'd figure out soon enough, if he hadn't already: they needed to put a whole lot of distance between them. Eventually, when he'd apologize and ask to forget what had happened and stay friends, she'd be capable of smiling and nodding and agreeing, but she didn't want to go there just yet. If she was going to be honest with herself, she wanted to stay in her little if-only bubble for a while longer. To do that, she ended up avoiding Eli. Not the most mature course of action, but kissing Eli had scrambled her brain. She needed to sort herself out before she could be sensible again.

When Jenna had phoned, Leah had worried she was calling about her brother. But Jenna had innocently asked her how the rest of the Valentine's Day dinner went (a simple reply of "fine" seemed to suffice, thank goodness), saying nothing more about Eli. It was clear Jenna had no idea what had happened between Leah and Eli—and, really, why should she? He didn't seem like a kiss-and-tell kind of guy, especially not to his sister. Leah wasn't about to tell her, that was for sure. The less said about the rest of that night, the better, as far as she was concerned.

Jenna had actually called to let her know that the assignment she'd just received from Magic Maids was her request, to clean their mother's house as a birthday present. Leah's first impulse was to back out. Then she reconsidered. So it was Jenna and Eli's mom's house. So what? Why turn down some ready cash just because the client was Eli-adjacent? According to Jenna, she and Ben and Eli were going to take Alyce out to lunch in Alexandria Bay that day, giving Leah more than enough time to give the place a good scrub-down and straightening and be long gone before they got back.

At the house, which was indeed vacant except for the bird, Leah stayed professional and perfunctory, waylaid only by some photos of Eli and Jenna as kids. Okay, more than a few. They were everywhere: on the bookshelves in the den, on the dresser in Alyce's bedroom, and of course in the place all parents put photos of their kids, on the wall along the stairs to the second floor.

There was nothing remarkable about the pictures—candids from what looked like vacations in warmer climates, including the requisite Disney photos with everyone in mouse ears; the usual school photos; Jenna and Ben's wedding photos; pictures of Zoë and Olivia from birth to the present day—but Leah found them charming just the same. She particularly enjoyed the ones of Eli at around nine or ten years old, with freckles, a dark cowlick, and his trademark bright smile, recognizable even then, dominated by huge front teeth.

Leah ignored the small ache in the pit of her stomach, not just because of the cute photos of Eli, but because the house was heavy with memories. It was clear this was a family homestead where the kids had grown up, and they had left home when they were ready. It wasn't yanked out from under them.

Leah had only one picture of her mother, a small, blurry, creased photo taken before Leah was born. Her mom was slouched on a chair in what looked like someone's rec room (there was a preponderance of paneling on the wall behind her). She was holding a drink and laughing. Looking at it always made Leah happy, helped her remember that her mother's true nature was fun loving and optimistic, no matter what happened after that.

Well.

Never mind.

Different people had different childhoods. She was long past feeling sorry for herself for not having a traditional family life. What was done was done, and she refused to compare her own experience to other people's.

She could, however, be a tad envious, just for a second.

The bird squawked from the kitchen, and she almost dropped the picture she was dusting.

"Sure, now you decide to get vocal," she called to it from the den.

The bird replied, in a jaunty tone, "Bite me!"

"Oh, it's gonna be like that, is it?"

The bird started clattering around in its cage.

"Ignoring you!" she shouted as she straightened a pile of magazines. She loved that senior citizens still subscribed to print periodicals.

Leah checked the time; she had about half an hour to finish up. She collected all her cleaning implements and wrapped up the vacuum cord, then lugged everything to the back door in the kitchen.

"All right, my feathered friend," she said. "I'm done here, and you're on your own for a little while longer. If I was supposed to clean your cage, it's too bad. I couldn't risk"—she turned to the cage—"losing you."

The door to the cage was open, and the bird was gone.

"Oh no."

~

Leah didn't realize she knew so many swear words, but she employed one after another, and they just kept coming as she combed the house for the fugitive cockatiel. She was grateful she hadn't opened any windows or doors—the frigid weather ensured that—but where in the world could the bird have gone?

She called to it while wondering if birds answered to humans calling them. She waved around a cracker while wondering if birds actually ate crackers. She tried to whistle and failed. She stood still in each room and waited to catch a glimpse of movement out of the corner of her eye.

No bird.

"Where did you go, you little shit?" she muttered, fearing all the while it had done something drastic and tragic, like . . . flying up the chimney flue?

She dashed into the den and stuck her head up the chimney, but she couldn't see anything—not even whether the flue was open and large enough for Alyce's pet to escape anyway. She pulled her head out, stood up, and forced herself to take a steadying breath. Okay, she'd start over, basement to attic. Even though the basement and attic doors had been closed the whole time.

She was in the guest bedroom, still birdless, when she heard voices. The family was back.

Hiding was pointless; her car was in the driveway. She forced herself to go back down to the first floor, all the while praying fervently that the group that had just entered didn't include Eli.

Of course the first face she saw at the foot of the stairs was his.

What made it worse was that he lit up when he saw her.

"Hey!"

". . . Hi."

"Where have you been? I've been trying to get in touch with you. Did you lose your phone or something?" She winced involuntarily, and he blinked, his smile fading. "Of course you didn't. You just didn't want to talk to me."

"Eli—" she started, but was interrupted by the rest of the family entering from the kitchen.

"Wow, this place looks great!" Jenna enthused. "Thanks, Leah. Happy birthday, Mom!"

Alyce Masterson was a tall, rangy woman with a gray bob and the same blue eyes as Eli. She looked around with a sharp gaze. "What have you done to my house?"

Leah's stomach dropped.

Then the woman broke out a bright smile that also reminded

her of Eli's. "It looks incredible. Thank you, honey," she said, embracing her daughter and planting a loud kiss on her cheek. She turned to Eli. "Did you go in on this?"

"Uh, no, actually," Eli stammered, coloring a bit. "I just gave you the sweater."

"Which I love. So you get a kiss anyway." And she planted another loud one, this time on her son's cheek. "Now, who's this?" And she turned her eagle eye on Leah, who swallowed with difficulty. "You're the person I really have to thank for this, aren't you?"

Oh, she wouldn't be so grateful when she heard about the bird, Leah was certain.

"This is Leah, Mom," Jenna said. "She's our friend, and she's a really good cleaner. She got to the bottom of Eli's cabin a while back."

"Ooh, a mighty warrior," Alyce said with a twinkle. "Very brave, very brave. Well, if you're done here, have some cake with us."

"Oh, I—I—no—"

"Great idea," Jenna agreed. "You can stay, can't you, Leah?"

"I lost your bird!" Leah blurted out.

Alyce blinked, a quizzical look on her face. "What?"

"Your bird. I'm sorry. I lost him. Her. It. First he was in the cage, and then I heard a noise, and then the cage door was open, and he was gone, and I haven't been able to find him, and I'm so sorry."

Alyce rolled her eyes. "That idiot."

"Ex . . . excuse me?"

"Bryce is always escaping," Jenna explained. "Mom should have named him Houdini."

"Eli," Alyce said with a sigh, "go get him, please. Leah, go with him. He'll show you what that birdbrain gets up to."

Leah took a breath. Bryce the bird did this all the time? Her remorse was slowly being edged out by irritation. How long had she spent looking for him, thinking he'd flown away or gotten trapped in some hidden spot? Long enough that she was still here when the Masterson clan returned, when she was supposed to be long gone.

Now she was in the same room as Eli—the absolute last thing she wanted. For that, she would never forgive the feathered escape artist.

Eli squeezed past her and climbed the stairs. She didn't want to go with him, but Alyce was standing there, shooing her upward, with Jenna beside her. It would be worse to make a big deal out of this, so she followed Eli.

He led her around the hairpin banister, through Alyce's bedroom, and into the en suite bathroom, where he gestured with a big wave.

Leah glanced around. "I don't see him. And I've looked in here, like, five times."

Eli pulled open the shower door.

Still nothing.

"Come on, Bryce," Eli called resignedly. "The jig is up."

Leah almost missed it, but then there it was—a slight movement behind some shampoo bottles on the corner shelves. She ducked involuntarily when Bryce shot out, wings spread wide, and he glided across the shower stall to land on Eli's head.

"The idiot loves the water droplets," Eli explained. "Plus I think he thinks the loofah is his girlfriend. Don't ask." The bird proceeded to groom Eli, plucking at his hair. "Ow. Quit it, Bryce."

"Well, I'm glad Bryce is safe," she said simply, ducking out of the bathroom.

"Hey, hang on a minute."

Oh. Leah knew she wasn't going to get away that easily. She stopped and waited, although she didn't want to. But she knew she couldn't dodge this issue forever. They had to deal with it, so it might as well be now. With Eli's family one floor below . . . and his mother's cockatiel perched on his head.

"Can we talk about this, please?" Eli said, following her into the bedroom.

"I don't think we have to."

"I disagree."

"Look, Eli, just forget it. It's fine."

"No, it's not. How can you say that?"

"What I mean is, it's not worth talking about. We're both adults, so we can skip the angst, okay? Here, I'll cut to the chase for you. It was a mistake, just a freak thing, let's pretend it never happened and stay friends. How's that? Good? Good."

"No, not good. Because it *did* happen, and we can't just pretend it didn't."

"If I can pretend you don't have a bird on your head, you can pretend what happened didn't happen."

Eli rolled his eyes upward. He reached up with both hands, but Bryce pecked him pretty sharply.

"Ow!" he yelped, sucking on the spot between his thumb and forefinger, then shouted, "Mom! Can you call your bird, please?" They both waited for a response from downstairs. "Mom!" he bellowed, giving Leah a glimpse of what he was like as a teen. Maybe not with the bird on his head back then, though. "Come on, Bryce, move it."

"Bite me," Bryce chirped cheerfully.

Resigned to being Bryce's temporary perch, Eli turned back to Leah. "Can I just speak my piece, please?"

Leah shrugged and gave him a *go ahead* wave.

"Okay. That thing you just said? It's probably what we should do. Even though you forgot the part about how we should give each other some space."

"Oh, right. Yes, we should do that too."

"But even though that seems like the logical course of action, I can't say I agree to any of it." Leah started to protest, but he rushed on, "Yes, the . . . thing . . . happened. But does that mean it's the end of . . . of us?" He waited for a moment, then said, "I don't think so," at the same time Leah said, "Yes."

"What?"

"What?" Leah shook her head. "Eli, we really should stay away from each other."

"I don't want to. Stay away from you, I mean."

He had to stop talking like that, stop staring like that, stop giving her false hope. She didn't even know how to respond, so she just . . . didn't.

Eli went on, "I don't want to stop hanging out with you, because I like you. We like each other. We get along. Right? You make me laugh, you make me think, you . . . you make me happy. I think I do the same for you too. Honestly, I . . . I'm at my best when I'm with you. So please tell me things don't have to change. I don't think they have to."

"I so want to believe you," Leah whispered. "But . . ."

"But what?"

"But it's hard to take you seriously when you have a bird on your head."

"*Mom!*"

Finally, from the foot of the stairs, they heard Alyce call, "Bryce! Snacks!"

And Bryce was in flight, heading for the food.

"That was all it took?" Leah marveled.

Finally bird-free, Eli took a step toward her, a hopeful half smile on his lips. "So? Can we stay friends? I don't want to lose you."

"Are you still doing your makeover?"

"What does that have to do with it?"

"It's to get Victoria back. Don't forget. She's 'the one.'" Leah took a deep, steadying breath and forced herself to say, "There really isn't anything more to discuss. Excuse me."

And she pushed past Eli and ran down the stairs.

Chapter 18

"What did you do?"

Jenna punctuated her last word with a dope slap on the back of Eli's head.

"Ow! Nothing!"

"You expect me to believe that, when Leah ran out of here like her Honda was going to turn back into a pumpkin any minute? What did you *do*?"

"No hitting!" Eli said, seeing Jenna's hand come up again.

"Jenna, stop hitting your brother," Alyce said with a sigh as she passed through the living room. "Coffee'll be ready in a minute."

"Mom, I'll do it," Jenna offered.

"No, I don't like you messing around in my kitchen. Stay in there," their mother called over her shoulder. "When are the girls getting back from their play date?"

"Not till after dinner. They're social butterflies who want nothing to do with us. We've barely seen them all winter break. Sleepovers and skating and any other chance to get out of the house. Plus they keep insisting on a day with Unca Eli, of all people. I'm penciling you in for tomorrow, by the way," Jenna said to her brother. "Does this mean we're boring?" she asked Ben, who just shrugged. "Guess

I have my answer there." Just when Eli thought he was in the clear, his sister rounded on him again. "Spill."

"Better do it, man." Ben sighed. "She's not gonna let go of this till you do."

"Does it have something to do with Valentine's Day? What happened?" She turned to her husband again. "I knew we shouldn't have left them alone at Dickie's."

"They're adults; they didn't need chaperones," Ben said. "Did you?" he asked Eli.

Eli winced. Maybe a chaperone or two would have been a good idea. He exhaled heavily. Ben was right; Jenna was never going to let this go, so he might as well confess.

"Okay, we may have . . . sort of . . . kissed."

The word was the equivalent of a ball of lightning shooting through the room. Ben jumped in his chair and Jenna lit up. They double high-fived, and she whipped out her phone.

"What the hell, Jenna? Did you guys have a bet or something?" His stomach clenched. "Don't tell me you planned this whole thing. Did you drag me to Dickie's just to set me up with Leah?"

"Oh, please," Jenna scoffed as she started texting to spread the news to their friends. "Do you really think we're that organized? Can't say we weren't hoping, though, once we spotted Leah there and she agreed to have dinner with you."

"Don't," Eli said, putting his hand over the screen. "Please."

Jenna obeyed, lowering her phone. "What happened?"

"It didn't end well. Obviously. I tried to talk to her just now, upstairs, but . . . I don't know. I screwed up. She doesn't want anything to do with me."

"Well, what did you say? And you do realize the only correct answer is you told her you want to be with her, and Victoria is only a distant memory, right?"

"What? No. Why would I do that?"

Jenna flopped back in her chair. "Well, there's your problem, dummy."

"What problem?" Alyce asked as she entered the room. She knocked Eli's feet off the coffee table and sat beside him on the couch. "And don't call your brother names."

"But he is a dummy. Eli's got the hots for Leah."

"I do not!"

Jenna shot him the stink eye.

"Okay, maybe a little. I mean, she's . . . you know."

"*Oh* yeah," Ben agreed heartily, which got the stink eye turned on him.

"Honestly," Jenna muttered, then said to Alyce, "But he's still being stupid about Victoria."

"I see," she murmured.

"Mom, tell him to stop being stupid about Victoria."

"Oh, I don't like to interfere in my children's love lives."

"Since when?"

"Jenna, your brother is a grown man. If he wants to throw his life away chasing after a woman halfway around the world who isn't the least bit interested in being caught, that's his prerogative."

Jenna snorted. "*There* it is."

"Mom!" Eli protested.

Shrugging, Alyce said, unapologetic, "This is why I don't get involved. All I'll say is Leah seems very sweet. Don't rule her out."

"I'm not! No, wait. That's not what I . . . just . . . please, everybody stop." Eli dropped his head and clutched at his hair with tense fingers. "I am in love with Victoria. I'm going through this ridiculous makeover thing *for Victoria*. She will come back from Italy, and we'll get back together, and we'll get married and give you so many grandchildren you won't know what to do with them all. Okay? Everybody got that? Meanwhile, Leah is a friend. An attractive friend, but just a friend."

"That you kiss," Jenna muttered.

"That was *one time*! It was a mistake!"

"Was it, though?" his sister mused with a wicked glint in her eye.

"Augh!" Eli grabbed his hair again, then froze. "Did . . . did Bryce poop on my head?"

⌒

"Okay. Okay," Eli muttered to himself, mashing an in-progress grilled cheese a little too forcefully with his spatula. "No big deal. Leah and I are just friends."

He turned down the heat under the pan and dug around in his fridge for something healthy to balance out the butter and cheese. He came up with a bag of raw cauliflower and immediately threw it back. There was no way his nieces would eat the hard tasteless chunks of "raw brain," as they'd called it in the past, no matter how resolutely Ben and Jenna tried to get them to broaden their nutritional palates. He opted for a side of grapes instead.

"I don't know why nobody gets it," he muttered, straightening up and slamming the fridge door.

"It's because," piped up a voice, "you're not really believable."

Eli jumped a mile and spun around to find Zoë staring at him from the other side of the kitchen island. He narrowed his eyes at her. "Eavesdropping is uncool, you know."

"You're talking to yourself at full volume in the kitchen, so technically it wasn't eavesdropping."

"Yeah, well . . . whatever you want to call it, forget what you heard."

"You can't *unhear* something. Logically, that doesn't work."

"Okay, Spock."

"Grilled cheese is burning," she commented casually as she climbed onto a stool.

"Dammit!" Eli yanked the pan off the burner. "Uh . . . forget you heard that too."

"You're a terrible babysitter, Uncle Eli."

"Yeah, well, four rounds of Minecraft says different, in my opinion."

"Mm, but your heart wasn't in it. I could tell."

Eli sighed. Even though he normally loved playing video games with his nieces, Zoë was right—he hadn't been into it. He hadn't been into much the past couple of days. Ever since the debacle with Leah and his subsequent efforts to make sense of it, he'd been flailing, searching for a way out of his mental morass. Nothing was working, not even overexplaining to anyone who would listen. Including himself.

To save face with Zoë, he countered, "Shows how much you know. Maybe I lost on purpose."

The little girl considered and immediately dismissed his argument. "You never lose on purpose. Obviously you're too messed up about Victoria and Leah to focus on the game."

"What? Where are you getting—"

Zoë held up a hand like a traffic cop. "Uncle Eli, please."

"I'm hungry!" Olivia announced, barreling into the kitchen and doing a pull-up of sorts to bring her chin up to counter level. "And what about Gen'r'l Leah?"

"Uncle Eli is in a love triangle."

"I am *not*—"

"I like Gen'r'l Leah," Olivia declared.

"Yeah, but what about Victoria?" Eli offered hopefully. "You remember her, right? She was nice, right?"

Olivia made a face as if he had force-fed her raw cauliflower. "Gen'r'l Leah," she insisted.

"Leah has my vote too," Zoë said.

"This is not a democracy! This is . . . this . . . you . . . you fill your opinion holes with the lunch your long-suffering uncle has made you with his own two hands, and never mind about my love life, all right?"

Shaking her head, Zoë sighed and picked up half of the grilled cheese Eli plopped in front of her. "Pretty sad, Uncle Eli."

"The sandwich?"

The girl eyed him balefully. "Whatever you need to believe."

~

An hour or so later, after Ben picked up the girls, Eli wandered around his empty cabin, cleaning up the little-girl detritus that got scattered around his place whenever his nieces visited. At a loss for what to do and sick of his own drama, he dug out his sister's movie list from a pile of clutter on his coffee table. He'd tried to get back to his "homework" over the past few days, but he had to admit that he just wasn't interested. Watching his assigned movies alone was nowhere near as much fun as with Leah.

No doubt about it, he'd really screwed up this time. One moment of weakness, hypnotized by the blush in her cheeks and the chocolate smear on her lips, and the one good thing in his life was gone for good.

One good thing?

One?

Hardly. He had his family and his friends and his business, even if jobs were occasional at this time of year, and his home, and his health, and Victoria. Eventually.

Which was who all these movies were for.

An hour went by, in which he'd started, and abandoned, *The Princess Bride*, *Pretty Woman*, and *Hitch*. Nothing was holding his attention.

He picked up his phone and scrolled through his list of recent calls. Jenna, Leah. Gillian, Leah. Gray, Ben, Leah, Leah, Leah. His text record was similar.

He thought about contacting Victoria. It was early evening in Rome; she should be around, maybe getting dinner. Maybe getting ready to go out to dinner. Maybe with that guy.

Just as he was scrolling through his list of contacts, Victoria's cat jumped up on the couch. He scritched behind her ear with his free hand while his thumb hovered over Victoria's name.

Blanche bonked his hand holding his phone, breaking the spell, and he didn't call. Well, he could blame it on the cat, but deep down he knew he changed his mind mainly because . . . why? Was he afraid Victoria wouldn't pick up, or was he afraid she would?

He decided to check her Instagram instead. She hadn't posted much lately—maybe she was too busy, or having too much fun, to take time out to share it all—but the photos she had added were more of the same: the classic artwork she was studying, street scenes, the group of new friends.

"Okay, this is not helping," Eli muttered to Blanche, who stared at him, issuing a silent command. He knew what it meant. "Yes, master." Eli stretched out on the couch and tipped his head back against the arm, an extremely uncomfortable position, but one Blanche demanded, and he couldn't deny her. If he did, it was highly likely her retaliation would involve a large hairball and the inside of one of his favorite shoes. Definitely not worth it. He shoved a mashed-down throw pillow behind his neck and pretended he was fine. She assumed the kitty-loaf position, settling on his chest like a furry anvil, and blinked at him with inscrutable green eyes.

"So, Blanche," he muttered, "tell me about your owner. All her dirty little secrets. Leah asked me what Victoria does for charity, and I was a little . . . uninformed, let's say. Made me realize there might be other stuff I should know but didn't bother to find out while I was in love with her for four months. Which doesn't seem like much time, now that I think about it. Do you know she's going to be gone more than twice as long as she and I were together?" He paused. "Do you think that's weird? I mean, *I* don't think so, but everybody else does. My sister . . . yeah, she's let me know her opinion about it. Everybody has."

Especially after Jenna broke the moratorium on sharing the gossip about him and Leah. Then the rest of his friends had come for him in a big way.

"Even Leah has thoughts on the matter, and she doesn't have to say much to get her point across. She'll just look at me sideways with those huge eyes, and . . . her eyes are brown, by the way. A really nice warm, dark brown. And then I'll know exactly what she's thinking, whether I want to or not. She's so smart, Blanche, and somehow I get the feeling she's always right about pretty much everything . . . Am I talking about Leah too much?"

Blanche just yawned wide, displaying every one of her tiny

sharp white teeth, then got up and stalked off, pausing only to stretch one leg out behind her.

"Sorry if I'm boring you!" Eli called after her.

Great. Even the cat had deserted him. Eli considered doing some work. He had to create a calendar and update his website before his busy season started.

He rubbed his leftover-pizza-laden belly. He was going soft with all this inactivity. That was also part of his business—being in shape enough to put his clients through their paces without getting winded himself—and he hadn't paid enough attention to that part of it either.

Eli heaved himself into a sitting position. Enough. He had spent enough time freaking out about Victoria, enough time worrying about Leah. There were other things in life besides women, and he had to get to them. He picked up his phone.

"Hey."

"My man," Gray said. "Where've you been?"

This. This was what was important. Friends. And work. Living life without worrying about what some woman thought, what some woman was going to say, whether he was ever going to see huge brown eyes looking at him warmly ever again.

Hazel. Victoria's eyes were hazel.

What had he just told himself? Enough.

"Got a question for you," he said to Gray. "Did you ever get that rowing machine fixed?"

"Oh, better than fixed."

"What do you mean?"

"Come on down and find out. I've got an idea, and it involves you."

~

"Are you kidding me?"

"Right?" Gray agreed, proudly surveying his new acquisitions: nine brand-new, gleaming rowing machines lined up in three rows, filling one of the gym's workout rooms.

"Okay, this is amazing. I'm impressed. Really. But won't the yoga fans be pissed off?"

"Ah, I got rid of those candy-ass namaste jokers. Who needs 'em?"

Eli just raised an eyebrow.

"Okay, okay, the classes got so full I finally moved 'em over to the big studio next door. They're sharing space with the barre classes."

"You're a success in spite of yourself."

"Doesn't anybody want just cardio anymore?" Gray lamented.

"So why'd you get so many machines and put them in their own room?"

"Are you kidding? With so much boating and outdoorsy stuff around here, there are tons of people who want to get in shape for it. I want in on the action. And that," Gray said, clapping him on the shoulder, "is where you come in."

"How do you mean?"

"Teach my rowing classes. You get in shape, you do the thing in the off-season, you make money, I make money."

"You're always thinking, aren't you?"

"How to make money? Ya damn right."

"I don't know, though . . ." Eli paused, scratching the back of his neck.

"What else have you got going on? Are you just gonna sit around till Victoria gets back, taking notes on movies and talking to the cat and . . . you know . . . avoiding Leah?"

"She's avoiding me," Eli corrected with a wince.

"And this, son, is why you don't go around kissing your friends."

"Hey, don't use my mess to justify your life choices."

"When are you going to get off this Delia nonsense?" Gray snapped.

"Not till you two are together, where you belong."

Gray just leveled a deadly stare at him.

"My situation is completely different!" Eli protested.

"You're being intentionally obtuse."

"Gym rats shouldn't use large vocabulary words like that."

"I'm a *complex* gym rat. And I'm right. Shut up," Gray said quickly, as Eli started to protest again, "and tell me you'll take the job. Before you bore me to death with your weak arguments."

Chapter 19

"I'm sure you're wondering why I called you all here."

"There's been a murrrrder?" Ben offered archly, tenting his fingers.

"Only of my spirit, Ben, only of my spirit. No," Alyce went on, addressing the crowd in her kitchen, which consisted of her children and their friends, as well as her grandchildren. "I've heard what you're all up to with my baby boy here, with this makeover plan, and I have a few issues with it."

"Thank you, Mom!" Eli said from across the room—as far as he could get from where Bryce's cage stood, as he no longer trusted the bird.

"Don't thank me yet, dear. I'm hashtag Team Makeover. I just don't think you're going far enough."

Eli groaned while everyone else cheered. Well, almost everyone, as Leah was busy trying to make herself as small as possible in the corner. She found herself desperately wishing she had asked more questions before saying yes to Alyce's invitation to her house for "a little lunch, and don't worry about Eli." Alyce had implied it would just be her and Jenna, to thank her for cleaning her house, and Leah had been enchanted with the idea of spending time with nice people who weren't handsome, sexy men who made her knees knock.

To be fair, Alyce hadn't actually said Eli *wouldn't* be there, but she sure hadn't said he *would*, either. And there he was, right over there. Leah smelled a conspiracy, although she couldn't prove it. So much for trusting sweet older ladies. Now she was stuck, and there was nowhere to hide in the kitchen, nowhere he wasn't in her sights and she in his. Unless she crawled into a cupboard and shut the door. Which she was seriously considering. The only thing that kept her in her current spot and happy to be there was Olivia, who was clutching her hand and grinning up at "Gen'r'l Leah" joyously.

The Masterson matriarch went on, "Now, I'm not fond of the notion of changing Eli too drastically, although I have to admit he's much more fashionable, which is a vast improvement."

Gillian waggled her fingers at Leah, and Alyce gave her an acknowledging nod.

"You've all contributed your time and effort to this project, so I think it's time for me to do my bit. I've decided we need to make sure Eli knows how to cook."

Cheers again, from everyone except Eli.

"Now, I'm no great chef, but I'm a damn sight better than both my children."

"Hear, hear," Ben said, immediately ducking behind his hand to dodge his wife's laser glare.

"And these days, men should be just as capable in the kitchen as women . . . *Ben.*"

"Yes, ma'am," her son-in-law replied. "Smash the patriarchy."

"Naturally Eli hasn't had much motivation to learn to cook before, but now he does, because being able to make a meal is a great weapon in a man's arsenal when it comes to winning a woman's heart. Everyone should have at least one go-to dish they can make without a recipe, and boxed mac and cheese doesn't count. I think Eli can handle lasagna, don't you?" Alyce looked around at the group, reserved a reassuring wink for Leah, and said, "Let's get to it, then."

"Why is everybody here for this?" Eli asked as Alyce tied a

pink-and-yellow apron around his waist. "Are they all going to sit there and yell instructions at me?"

"Of course not. I've got plenty of pans and pasta, and a mountain of cheese, so we're all going to make smallish lasagnas. Even the girls."

This news made Zoë and Olivia jump up and down excitedly.

"Just keep the sauce off the ceiling, is all I ask. And remember, you're going to be eating the food you make, so try not to poison one another."

Alyce set to separating everyone into smaller groups, deftly steering Leah away from the kids and toward Eli with a whisper in her ear to help him out. Leah didn't have the heart to tell Alyce she wasn't any better a cook than her son was . . . or that she was highly uncomfortable spending time next to him these days.

"Traditional, pesto, veggie, chicken—take your pick," Alyce was saying. "I've got ingredients for all different kinds. Eli, stick with traditional for now."

"Yeah, noob," Ben called from across the room. "This is virgin territory for you."

"That'd be a first—" Gray started, but Alyce cut him off.

"May I remind you there are children and your target's mother present, gentlemen?"

"Yes, ma'am," they chorused, focusing on their workstations.

"Well, hello there," Eli murmured in Leah's ear as she pulled the pasta sheets out of the box.

"I . . . I didn't realize it was going to be this whole big thing," she stammered. "Your mom—"

"Let me guess. She invited you over for lunch? 'Small and quiet' or some line like that?"

"I fell for it. I'm so sorry."

"I'm not," Eli said immediately. "I'm so glad you're here."

He was, she realized. He truly wanted her around. And she was glad to see him too. She'd missed him more than she wanted to admit to herself. The past couple of weeks had been long, dark, and dull without his cheerful smiles, his goofy texts, his full attention whenever they were together. When they talked, it was as though there was no one more important to him than Leah, nothing more important than what she had to say. And yet he devoted the same time and attention to his friends and family, especially his nieces, and she definitely enjoyed seeing that. In her opinion, people could have their hot men acting tough and aloof; she'd take a caring, nurturing guy any day. Like Eli.

Only *not* Eli.

No matter what had happened between them, he still had his plan to get Victoria back, and she respected that. So while this situation was definitely not good for her heart, Leah had come to realize not having Eli in her life at all was far worse. Her heart would adapt eventually. It had gone through quite a bit already, after all, and it had developed a pretty good resiliency.

"Okay, look," Leah said to Eli, trying to keep her voice even. "Whether this was a setup or not—"

"Oh, it was a setup all right."

"Yeah, your mom does seem pretty devious. Anyway, maybe this is a good thing. I've been thinking a lot lately about what you said, and you're right. We shouldn't lose our friendship over one accidental . . . *incident*."

Eli brightened. "Really?"

She nodded firmly. "Really. I like you, and I miss you, and I'm sorry for freaking out. Do you think we can put it behind us?"

"Yes!" He breathed, smiling broadly, and it made her heart leap. "Yeah, of course. I'm . . ." He looked like he wanted to grab her and hug her, but instead he only bumped her shoulder with his arm. "I'm so glad you said that. So we're good?"

Leah bumped him back. "Absolutely."

The next couple of hours devolved into culinary chaos, with spattering sauce, sizzling chicken and hamburger on the stovetop, bloopings of ricotta on the floor, and drifts of shredded mozzarella everywhere. Leah loved every minute of it, now that she was with

Eli again. While they did their best to stay focused—this was a lesson Eli had to take seriously, after all—the rest of their friends were more casual about the assignment.

"Big mistake. Huge," Jenna admonished her husband when he screwed up the layers in the lasagna pan. "Speaking of which, *Eli*, I cannot believe you haven't watched *Pretty Woman* yet."

"I started it. I'll get back to it. It's just not high on my list, considering Victoria isn't a prostitute."

"You are *so* missing the point."

"Which is Richard Gere," Gillian said. "In very natty suits."

"Amen," Jenna agreed.

Olivia broke away from the usual strict control her grandmother had over her and her sister, especially where foodstuffs were involved, to run over to Eli and hang on his leg.

"I love you, Unca Eli," she cooed, smiling up at him.

"How sweet, honey. Did you come over here to say that or to wipe your sauce-hands on my jeans?"

"Uh-huh."

"Thank you," he sang, rolling his eyes at Leah.

"Olivia, there's a towel right here!" Alyce exclaimed. "Unhinge from your uncle, or I'm teaching you how to do laundry next."

"Who put me with this guy?" Gillian complained. She was wedged into a corner with Gray, who was studying his phone instead of cooking. She elbowed him. "Hey. Are you going to help or not?"

Gray continued typing as he muttered, "Sure thing, hon. Just gotta settle on the details for tonight. Seeing Brendan again," he added, flicking his eyebrows, which elicited an irritated grunt from Delia, who was working with Zoë at the kitchen island.

Eli cleared his throat loudly and significantly. Then he cleared it again, even louder and more significantly.

"Are you sick, bro?" Ben asked.

"Sick of something, yeah," Eli answered, openly glaring at Gray, who didn't even notice, as he was still staring at his phone and grinning delightedly at whatever text he'd received from Brendan.

"I'll be right back," Gray said, scooting into the living room.

Eli muttered, "Idiot," and aggressively slopped a bit more sauce than was necessary onto the layer of pasta.

"What's going on?" Leah whispered.

"Ah . . . nothing. I just hate it when he hurts Delia like that."

Leah glanced over her shoulder at the woman in question. She certainly did seem less lively since Gray's giddy revelation about his date with Brendan. "What's their story, anyway?"

"Datingus interruptus, several times over the years, mainly because of Dingus dudicus."

"Gray?"

"Yeah."

Eli started to explain but was interrupted by Gillian, who called to Gray, "Screw you. This is now officially my lasagna and youse can't have any."

"Gillian, your Philly's showing," Eli said. To Leah, he explained, "It comes out when she gets mad."

"Gilly, you're not from around here?" Leah asked, surprised.

"Moved here as a teen, but originally, nope. West Philadelphia born and raised."

Which, of course, got the response she intended—a full-throated chorus of the *Fresh Prince* theme song from everyone in the immediate vicinity, eliciting bewildered looks from the little girls.

"Is this really how you wanted to spend a Sunday afternoon?" Eli asked Leah.

Leah just smiled broadly. Her answer, of course, was an unequivocal yes. And not just because she was pressed against Eli's side in the normally generous but currently crowded kitchen. It was everything—the noise, the chaos, the cooking, the joking, the bickering. She loved every minute of it. She was so grateful to be included, and if she ever felt disappointed that Eli was only another one of those platonic friends instead of something more . . . well, she'd just have to adjust her attitude.

Leah did have second thoughts about the group dynamic, however, when everyone decided to fill the time while the lasagnas were cooking by having snow softball practice in the backyard in preparation for the upcoming tournament. Alyce was the only one who got a pass to stay inside and watch over the lasagnas; Leah was dragged out into the snow with everyone else.

"But I told you, I don't know what I'm doing!" Leah wailed as Eli stuffed a baseball mitt onto her gloved hand for the second time.

"It's not rocket science. Here, I'll help you."

"How—" Her question became a shriek as he got behind her, picked her up by sticking his forearms under her armpits, and carried her to a position in the outfield.

His hands were over hers as he lifted her arms to catch the ball. His entire body wrapped around hers to help her swing the bat. And when she actually hit the orange softball, he picked her up and carried her around the bases.

"I *know* how to run!" she laughed, breathless.

"Nope, you can't be trusted. Gotta make sure you know which direction to go in."

"I'm not that hopeless!"

"No, you're not," he said, panting, as he planted her feet on home plate again. "Not at all. It's just fun to toss you around."

"Thanks a bunch."

She had to admit, if only to herself, it was pretty fun *being* tossed around as well.

⁓

"Are you ready?"

Leah raised one eyebrow. "Oh, I think the bigger question is are *you* ready?"

Eli's mouth quirked; he was obviously trying to look serious and failing. Leah squinted back at him. Her serious face was probably as big a fail as his. She stared. Eli stared. She tried to ignore the tingling in her belly that inspired. They sat cross-legged on the floor, knees touching, staring at each other, their faces inches apart. Very *Sixteen*

Candles. If there had been a cake between them. And if Eli had seen the movie. Leah doubted he had, the weirdo.

"Go on, then," she prompted. "I'm waiting."

"Maybe this was a bad idea."

"Too late. You promised. 'Fess up. I want to hear it all."

He heaved a sigh, sat up straighter, rubbed his palms on his knees. Was he nervous?

"Okay." Eli cleared his throat, tilted his head first to one side, then to the other, to crack his neck.

"Quit stalling."

"Shh. I'm preparing myself."

It was Leah's turn to sigh. "You know, if you can't manage—"

"I love you," Eli blurted out, so suddenly that Leah blinked and froze, her spine so straight she could have been a meerkat sighting something on the horizon.

"G-go on," she stammered, her voice breaking a little.

"I love you, and . . . and I know we've wasted a lot of time, and I'm sorry about that. I don't want to waste another minute. We're meant for each other."

"Reasons," she said. "Details."

"Okay, uh . . ."

"If you can't come up with any reasons, why should—"

"Just a second. There are so many reasons, I'm not sure where to start."

"You're losing me."

"Hang on! Sheesh, the pressure."

"Oh, you have no idea."

"Hush, you. Stop distracting me."

"You should be *so* focused, have *so* much conviction, nothing should distract you."

"Well, you're beautiful."

She rolled her eyes. "Looks? Really? You're leading with *looks*?"

"All right, all right. I . . . I love how you challenge me, how we can have serious conversations . . . and not so serious."

"Like?"

"What do you mean, 'like'?"

"Examples. No woman is going to fall for vague generalities. Not just 'beautiful'—you have to point out some *detail* of her beauty, like an adorable mole. Not some hairy, nasty thing nobody would believe you think is cute, though. Not just 'conversations'— you have to recall some obscure *detail* of a conversation to show it stuck with you. Remember Harry's speech to Sally at the New Year's Eve party? He talked about how she ordered her food. He mentioned the crinkle between her eyebrows. Stuff like that. Honestly, with this approach of yours . . . I wouldn't get back together with you if I were Victoria. F minus."

"Damn, you are harsh."

"I'm helping you."

"You're ruining me."

"Try again."

"I need a break." Eli turned and stretched his long legs, feet toward the fireplace, and leaned back against an ottoman.

"We've barely started," she scolded.

When Eli didn't answer, Leah turned toward the fire too, elbows on her crossed knees, chin in her hands. They sat that way for a while, both quiet, until Leah felt Eli's eyes on her.

"Stop looking at me."

She didn't dare imagine what sort of image she presented, full up on four different kinds of lasagna and a couple of glasses of wine; wearing an old, pilled sweater, now with sauce splatters; her jeans, damp from the knee down after the group's impromptu snow softball practice, drying to stiffness in the heat of the fire; her hair likely matted from being mashed under a knit hat for an hour or so—or, more likely, sticking straight up at the crown, as it tended to do if she didn't tame it with some product—and her makeup long gone.

But there was Eli beside her on the rug in front of the fireplace, on strike after her attempt at talking him through his speech to get Victoria back, staring at her, smiling delightedly.

"I mean it." She gave him a half-hearted shove, which didn't budge him an inch. Of course.

"Fine," he muttered, sliding down to a prone position, resting his head against the ottoman, and closing his eyes. The house was nearly silent, everyone else having left an hour or so before. Somehow Eli had convinced Leah to stay a while longer to help clean up. Well. She didn't need much convincing. Now Leah could hear Alyce puttering around in the kitchen, putting away the dishes and pots and pans they'd washed after dinner while Bryce chirped at her occasionally. Whenever he did, Alyce answered him in complete sentences, which made Leah smile. She was at peace. Well, she would be, except Eli lying so close to her made her vibrate with tension.

"Why don't you have a boyfriend?"

She jumped. "Excuse me?"

"Why don't you have somebody saying these sappy things to you?"

"You just did."

"You know what I mean."

"Oh, you mean to *me*, instead of me-as-a-Victoria-stand-in?"

"Right."

She shook her head and let out a little huff of a laugh. "Well, it *might* have something to do with the fact that I just spent the past year locked in a house with a cancer patient who then died. Since then I've been a little busy taking as many jobs as I can to get some money together so I can leave town."

In a subdued voice, he murmured, "Oh."

In that one small word from Eli she heard sympathy, which she accepted, and pity, which she didn't. She had to nip that in the bud.

"So yeah, I haven't exactly had much free time to hop on Tinder and see what the North Country has to offer in terms of potential boyfriends."

"You know, not every guy would appreciate the elite, professional level of sarcasm you achieve like I do."

She patted his leg, relieved they were on safer ground. "That's why I like you."

They fell quiet again, the only sounds in the room the crackle of the flames and the hiss of a damp log.

After a few minutes, Leah asked, "Are you asleep?"

"No. I'm looking at you."

"With your eyes closed. Okay."

"You think I need to look *at* you to look at you?"

"You're making no sense. Are you halfway to a food coma or something? I know I am."

"I'm quite alert. And I can see you very clearly. Right here." He tapped his temple.

"Oh really?"

"Yep. I could paint you right now. If I could paint. But I can't. Maybe an ice sculpture."

"You're no Phil Connors."

He opened his eyes again, rolled onto his side to face her, and propped his head on his hand. "Now, *Groundhog Day* I have seen. Why wasn't it on my list?"

"Because Phil was an ass for most of the movie."

"It was still a good story." He paused, then said, "I wouldn't mind being trapped in a single day over and over again with you."

Leah took a shaky breath. She could take his comment seriously and freak out, or she could defuse the situation right now. She chose the latter. As a matter of self-preservation. She smirked and knocked his arm out from under him. "You couldn't handle me. I would destroy you by day three."

"Oh, you think so, do you?"

He bounced up immediately, coming for her, and she let out a little shriek as he wrapped one arm around her, pinned her to him, and moved in for a noogie maneuver.

"Who wants cocoa?"

Eli and Leah flew apart as though someone had set off a cartoon bomb between them.

"I put Baileys in it."

If Alyce had seen anything, she didn't let on. Not that there had been anything to see. Just two *friends* talking . . . and laughing . . . and wrestling. Nothing to see here; move along. Alyce focused on carrying the tray she was holding so the giant mugs of hot chocolate didn't spill. By the time she set it down on the side table, Leah and Eli were miles apart, she nervously smoothing down the back of her hair, he knocking down the logs in the fireplace with the poker as they frantically combusted with heat from the inside out, crumbling to brilliant red and orange pieces.

Chapter 20

"Hey."

Eli fidgeted, unsure how to behave around Leah, especially after the last time they were together. Oh, nothing had happened, but he'd realized that all it took was a roaring fire, a couple of glasses of wine, and some time alone with a beautiful woman to make him lose his damn mind. He could lie to himself all he wanted, but he had definitely been flirting with her. If his mother hadn't come in, he didn't know what would have happened.

Well. Leah wouldn't have let anything happen—probably—but on his part? He wasn't so sure. Eli knew he had been spending far too much time thinking about Leah lately. He couldn't seem to help it. When he was with her, he couldn't get enough of her. When he wasn't with her, he wanted to be. If he had a quiet moment here or there, he was recalling something kind she'd done or something funny she'd said. Whenever he realized his thoughts were drifting, he'd forcibly wrench his fickle mind and heart back to Victoria, concentrating on composing his next friendly text to her, remembering the good times they'd had together and planning for more of the same when she got back from Rome, anything that would get his mind off Leah. But the minute he let his guard down, Victoria vanished and Leah was in her place again.

None of that was fair to him. Worse, it wasn't fair to either Victoria or Leah. He'd decided ages ago it was Victoria he wanted, and he'd made his plans quite clear to Leah. He needed to stick to those plans and not hurt Leah in the meantime.

"Ready?" she asked.

"I was born ready, thank you very much," he said, as flippantly as he could manage.

And just like that, they were walking side by side toward the high school, lit up brightly in the dusk. Eli instinctively reached out and grasped Leah's elbow when she slipped a little on the icy sidewalk, and neither of them flinched at the contact.

"I really do appreciate this, you know. I need the support."

"You'll be fine," she reassured him. "You've done your homework, right?"

"Oh, sure." Eli kept hold of her arm even though she was on firmer footing. Just in case. There could be more ice, no matter how generous the custodians were with the salt. Sure, that was the reason. Not that it simply felt good to touch her, even through coats and gloves.

When they entered the main hallway, propelled by the crowds of people pushing through the doors on their way to the annual Willow Cove Student Art Show, Leah took off her knit hat and shook out her bangs. "God, I haven't been here in years, but the place looks exactly the same."

Her school years. That was another thing Eli didn't know about her. "I don't remember you. Were we at school at the same time?"

"You must have graduated before I transferred in. If you were here, I would have remembered you."

"Oh really?"

"Don't get all conceited. You're just . . . really tall."

She would have remembered him. That made him feel lighter all of a sudden. A grin crept up on him. Funny how that happened every time he was with Leah.

He was so preoccupied with her he didn't notice the arm that shot out, barring his way. "Just where do you think you're going, mister?"

"Mr. Jimenez! Come on, are you still checking hall passes?"

The teacher laughed and shook Eli's hand. "How have you been?"

"Great, thanks. How's the social studies game?"

"The students get dumber every year. Or maybe I get more curmudgeonly every year I get closer to retirement. Your sister tells me you're doing really well. Camping gear, is it?"

"Adventure tours, actually. Kayaking, camping, hiking."

"Well, good for you. But you know . . . I've gotta say, I always thought you'd be a teacher."

"What?" Eli laughed, surprised. "Why would you think that?"

"You did so well with the outreach program at the elementary school. Are you still coaching softball, at least?"

"Ah, not anymore." Eli glanced over at Leah, who was standing beside him quietly, people watching as families streamed into the school. "Do you remember Leah Keegan?"

"Leah . . ." Mr. Jimenez murmured, thinking.

"I don't think I had any classes with you," Leah said. "But I remember you moderating the class officer debates. You were great at those."

"Leah Keegan," the teacher muttered in a singsong voice, still trying to place her. "Do your parents live out on Barton Road?"

"Oh . . . no . . . I lived with Cathy Carter."

"Oh, of course." The social studies teacher nodded sagely. "I'm so sorry to hear about Cathy."

"Thank you."

"Hey, how about that rascal Patrick? What's he up to these days, still playing football?"

"Selling used cars. Gained quite a bit of weight. I think he's pretty dedicated to his fantasy league, though." Leah hooked Eli's arm and tugged a little. "We really should get going. It was nice to see you, Mr. Jimenez."

Eli held in his laughter till they were far enough away from the teacher. "What was that all about?"

"I used to get a lot of that garbage when I was in school. 'Hey, you lived with Patrick. Is he playing for the NFL yet? Tell us everything!' Ugh."

"Not a fan, huh?"

"You never really get the true measure of a person until you live with them. I lived with Patrick for a year, and a year was more than enough, thank you very much. If I never hear one more word about the Willow Cove High football team, it'll be too soon."

"So what was your thing?" he asked as they trooped down the crowded hall toward the gym.

"My thing?"

"Yeah. Doesn't seem to be sports."

"You've seen me fail to catch a ball. You know it wasn't."

"Theater?" Eli couldn't imagine Leah in a play. She didn't seem to like being in the spotlight. "Math club? Quiz team? Debate? You would have been good at that." He stopped in his tracks and snapped his fingers. "Yearbook."

She laughed. "No, no, no, no, and no."

"Then what?"

Leah started walking again. "Nothing. I just kept my head down and did my schoolwork. There wasn't time for extracurriculars. I had to help Cathy with the house and the younger foster kids."

"How many were there?"

"Two more girls. Little ones."

It figured they'd be in a huge crowd on the way to an art show when she felt comfortable enough to talk about her time in foster care.

"What about Patrick?"

Leah rolled her eyes, but she was smiling when she said, "Oh, he didn't have to contribute his time. He was a *boy*. And Cathy's cherished biological son, who was busy being a football star."

"But you're not bitter."

"Not in the least."

"You're filling this hallway with so much sarcasm it's seeping into my boots. What was your best subject?" he asked.

She leveled her gaze at him. "Psychology."

"Not even a little surprised. Did you have Mrs. Russo? She was great. She's still teaching, in fact. Maybe she'll be here tonight. Oh, do you remember that awful lunch lady? The one who always seemed to have a cigarette hanging out of her mouth even when she didn't?"

Leah laughed again. "Mrs. Wix. 'Whaddya want?'" she tacked on, in a startlingly accurate imitation of the rough-around-the-edges cafeteria worker.

"I swear, I thought she could use her tuna scooper to gut a student at ten paces."

"She may very well have. Please tell me *she's* not still working."

"No, she finally retired after she took a five-gallon drum of chili to the back of the head."

"Oh no!"

"No worries. *She* dented *it*, not the other way around."

They reached the gym and went in search of Jenna and Ben and the girls in the part of the room set aside for the elementary school artists. First, however, Eli had to run a gauntlet of kids, all of them from past softball teams, who stopped him to say hi. He fielded questions, high fives, and hugs, one after another. When he looked over at Leah, she mouthed something that may or may not have been "rock star." The way she was smiling at him, eyes dancing, that arresting dimple of hers on full display . . . Eli's body responded, heat rushing through him as he was overcome with the urge to go to her, pull her out of the crowded school, get her alone, and—

"Unca Eli! Unca Eli!" Olivia bombed toward them and clung to Eli's leg like a nettle on a wool sock. "Come see my art!"

Oh. Right. There was an art show on.

"Say hi to General Leah first."

Olivia tipped her head back and swung from her uncle's leg. "Hi, Gen'r'l Leah."

"At ease, soldier."

The little girl giggled and grabbed both of them by the hand, dragging them over to the kindergarten display of warped, curling watercolors and yarn art, where the rest of the family stood.

"Well, you might as well start," Jenna said to Eli.

"Do we really have to do this?"

"Yes, *you* really have to. It's part of your—"

"Don't say makeover."

"Makeover. So get to it."

"Art isn't really my thing."

"Doesn't matter, because it's Victoria's thing. Sorry we couldn't take a road trip to a real art gallery to test your knowledge, but with school back in session, it just isn't in the cards right now. And you're running out of time—Victoria will be back in a couple of months. So this will have to do. Consider it a low-rent version of the real thing." Jenna didn't wait long before she prompted, "So? Start analyzing."

"What, *now*?"

"This one's mine, Unca Eli."

Olivia directed him to a large watercolor hanging on a black fabric backdrop alongside works by the rest of her classmates.

"Oh, wow," he murmured. "This is really something. Is this a picture of your mom and dad?"

"No, *silly*." Olivia punctuated her word with a gentle swipe at his arm. "It's Fredo."

"Right, right. Stop laughing." Eli directed this at Leah, who was fighting a grin. "Now I see the resemblance. *Silly*," he said accusingly to Leah, as if she'd been the one misidentifying the subject of the painting. "That's the dog, *obviously*."

Leah clamped her lips together. "Obviously," she fought out.

"Chasing the bunnies in the backyard," Ben supplied. "Clear as day. Those are trees, you said, Olivia?"

The little girl nodded vigorously.

"I see. Well, it's very . . ." Eli glanced at his sister, who raised one eyebrow expectantly. "It's very, uh, impressionistic. Reminiscent of Degas. If, you know, Fredo, uh, took ballet lessons. With the bunnies."

Leah snickered. Eli elbowed her. She elbowed him back. Jenna scrutinized them both. Eli ignored his sister's suspicious look.

Jenna considered his assessment of the painting. "Fail," she declared. "Olivia's work is obviously abstract expressionism. Try again."

Eli steeled himself and expounded on select works in the kindergarten section, pointing out the shades of Pollock in a spatter painting and the echoes of Picasso in a skewed portrait.

"Better," his sister said. "Let's visit Zoë's class exhibit."

Eli's other niece's work showed quite a bit of talent, and he was pleased to note that her very serious self-portrait reminded him of Frida Kahlo. Jenna made the rounds of the rest of the show, partly as her duty demanded as vice principal, partly to shepherd Eli through various exhibits to get him to display the rudimentary knowledge of art he'd managed to collect over the past couple of months.

This makeover stuff, he thought, not for the first time, was exhausting.

The only thing that kept him going was the amused look on Leah's face and her encouraging nods whenever Jenna stopped by yet another work of art and waited for him to come up with an astute analysis of it. At one point he really got into assessing a high-schooler's sculpture, comparing it to Rodin, so much so he didn't even notice Jenna had turned away to chat with a parent.

He only stopped when Leah burst out laughing and said, "Oh my God."

"What?" he demanded, laughing along because, honestly, he couldn't *not*. "I have no clue what I'm saying, but it sounds damn good, doesn't it?"

"The art teacher is over there, and she's about to eat you alive."

"Oh great, that's all I need—someone hating on me for screwing up culture."

Leah gaped at him. "You honestly have no idea, do you?"

"I have no idea about most things," he admitted. "What are we talking about, exactly? I already said I didn't have a clue about art."

"She's following you all over this gym, hanging on your every word. And it's *not* because of your astute observations, trust me. You really don't know the effect you have on women?"

"Yes, I do. I know it well. I send them running to Europe."

Shaking her head, Leah said in amazement, "You dummy."

"Are you going to explain, or are you going to keep calling me names?"

"The art teacher is checking you out, and you don't even know."

Eli didn't blush much, but now he felt heat creep up his neck.

"And before you protest, yes, I'm serious. You there, with the . . . the . . ." She flapped her hand at him, indicating everything to do with him. "The tall and the charming and the looks and the twinkle and all the other nonsense. It's . . . you pull people in. And you don't even notice. You could have *any* woman in this room right now."

Eli blinked and, completely flustered, said the first thing that came into his head. "I don't want just any woman."

There was a silence, a heavy, weighted thing, dropped like a stone in the middle of the chattering crowd as their eyes met in a long, steady gaze.

And then Leah looked away—at the art, at the wall, at the floor. She couldn't seem to settle on one thing, but she made certain she didn't look back to Eli. It was her turn to flush, and Eli watched the pink rise in her cheeks.

Finally she said softly, "Then Victoria is very lucky."

There it was again—that hollow feeling in his middle. As though he were hungry, starving for something he couldn't quite identify. Leah made him ache, made him want. And Leah uttering Victoria's name in the middle of their happy evening was like a wasp's sting. All this . . . he needed to sort it out once and for all.

"Leah—"

"Eli, we've got an issue," Jenna interrupted, phone in hand.

Never taking his eyes off Leah, he said, "Can it wait, please? I'm kind of in the middle of something."

"Mom called. She's sick."

He took a breath and forced himself to focus on his sister. "I know. She told me yesterday she wasn't sure she was going to make it tonight. It's okay. She just has a cold."

"It sounds worse than that."

"Oh, I don't—okay, hey, don't get that look," he said.

"Well, what do you expect me to think, Eli?" Jenna snapped. "She has a sore throat, she can't swallow, and she thinks her lymph nodes are swollen. You know what the doctor said."

"I do," he answered in a quieter tone, hoping it would calm her as well. "But those are also the symptoms of a virus. Let's not assume it's anything worse."

"I'm going."

"Jenna. You should be here—for the event, for the girls." He gently took hold of her shoulders and looked past her to Ben, who hitched his head in support. "I'll go." He glanced over at Leah. "We'll go." Leah nodded. "All right? We'll check on Mom, make sure everything's okay, while you do your vice principal thing here."

Jenna didn't seem to like this decision, but she gave in. "Take her to urgent care or the hospital if—"

"I know, I know. I'm not taking this lightly, I promise. We'll see what's going on and I'll call you. Okay?"

"What *is* going on?" Leah whispered as they made their way out of the gym.

Eli sighed. "My sister can be a little . . . overprotective of our mom. She was sick a while back . . ." His voice faltered. What if Jenna was right? "Overprotective" was an understatement. She was downright paranoid about Alyce's health these days.

And Eli was always the voice of reason. But he'd be lying to himself if he didn't acknowledge he'd felt more than a slight stab of fear at Jenna's news just now.

"Anyway, we're kind of on the alert for any secondary problems."

Leah seemed to accept his explanation and didn't press for details. He would have provided them if she'd asked, but he was more preoccupied with navigating his Jeep out of the crowded parking lot and through town to Alyce's house.

Chapter 21

When Eli and Leah entered through the back door of the Masterson home, they found Alyce puttering in the kitchen in her pajamas, robe, and slippers, not on her deathbed as Jenna had implied.

"Mom, what is it?" Eli demanded immediately.

"Oh, stop."

"Jenna said—"

"I regret giving your sister any details of my impending demise. I have a cold. My throat hurts. Throats do that when you have a cold. Hello, Leah, dear. How are you?"

"She's fine. Don't patronize me, Mom. Jenna said your lymph nodes are swollen."

"Elias, light of my life, my darling son consumed by paranoia, lymph nodes also happen to swell when you have a *cold*. I know Jenna wants me to rush to the hospital or some such nonsense, but it's late at night, it's cold out there, and I'm already ready for bed. I'd just as soon the good lord take me in my own home instead of getting out of my warmest bathrobe and traveling an hour to sit in a giant, chilly room with a bunch of other sick people coughing up a lung or bleeding out on the linoleum."

Eli turned to Leah. "My mother watches too many medical dramas. Also, my mother is overly dramatic in general."

Leah barely heard him; instead she was staring at Alyce, who nodded and touched the skin above her collarbone, where there was a long horizontal, shiny pale scar.

She said in a matter-of-fact way, "Thyroid cancer. Last year. They removed it, I went through treatment, I'll have to take medication daily for the rest of my life. The point is I survived, I was fortunate, but my children can't seem to get over it. All I have to do is clear my throat, and they're convinced the cancer has come back."

"Mom, we're supposed to watch out for certain symptoms."

"You think I don't know? I'm well aware. But a cold is a cold, which is what this is. If you have any good drugs, I'll take them. Otherwise, I'll thank you to just let it go. Now, I'm making some tea with honey and lemon, and you're welcome to have some with me. If you don't want any tea, both of you go do something enjoyable instead of sitting here listening to me cough."

"But—"

"Not another word, or I'll sic Bryce on you."

At the sound of his name, the bird squawk-chirped and chewed on one of the bars of his cage. Leah didn't even glance toward his corner. She felt frozen and a bit terrified. Out of the corner of her eye, she saw Eli and his mother exchange alarmed glances.

"Leah?" Alyce said gently, taking both of the young woman's hands in hers. "Why don't you sit down for a minute?" It was more of an order than a suggestion.

"What—" Eli began, but a look from his mother silenced him.

The older woman led Leah the few steps to the kitchen table and waited while she sank into one of the chairs; when she landed, she blinked and came around a little.

"I'm sorry," she said.

"Never mind apologizing," Alyce cut her off, taking the seat beside Leah and turning the chair to face her. "Eli, would you put the kettle on, please?" While her son turned on the faucet, she continued, "Eyes up here now, okay?"

Alyce waited until Leah focused on her face.

"That's better."

"I'm . . . so sorry . . ." Leah rasped. "I'm being rude."

"Not at all." Alyce paused for a moment and then said, "I know what you went through, being Cathy's caregiver, and the effect it had on you. Even if," she rushed to speak over Leah, who opened her mouth to protest, "even if you swear on all that's holy you're fine now. It gets to you. It gets under your skin. It can take a long time to process. I knew your foster mom, of course; we both lived in Willow Cove all our lives. I tried to help her when she got sick, but naturally she refused. That was Cathy for you. You should be proud she let you take care of her. She certainly wouldn't let anybody else near her."

Leah smiled weakly and nodded.

"You went through a lot, and don't let anybody tell you any different. It takes away your perspective. The painfully obvious, like the fact that not all people who suffer a serious illness die . . . well, that kind of gets away from you. You stop thinking rationally or optimistically. It takes all you've got to stop being on high alert for the next death. Caregiver PTSD, if you will. But think of me as a reminder that a lot of the time people who get sick actually stick around and even get better. Like me, for example . . . much to the dismay of my offspring."

"Mom!" Eli exclaimed, offended.

"Hush, I'm talking to Leah. Make the tea, please. And Eli . . ." When her son turned back to her, she sighed and said, "If this illness doesn't ease up in a day or two, you can take me to the doctor. Happy? Now," she said, turning back to Leah, "should we take this into the den to talk more, or just drink our tea?"

At Alyce's mention of caregiver PTSD, she felt herself bristle, ready with the usual protest of "I'm fine," but . . . maybe she wasn't. Maybe she was still processing Cathy's death. After all, she was still talking to her, still living with her memory in her house. Did she just need time to recover from a year at Cathy's bedside? Or would her plan of leaving Willow Cove for good banish her ghosts?

She looked at Eli, bustling about with the kettle and mugs and tea bags and honey, and then at kind, no-nonsense, caring Alyce, and she started to question her longstanding plans to move on.

"Tea, please," she said softly, dredging up a smile.

"Tea it is," Alyce said. "Just remember we can talk about this anytime you need to, all right? Now tell me about this art show I missed. And don't leave out any details of Eli demonstrating his newly discovered knowledge of the visual medium."

~

"So," Eli said quietly as he turned off the ceiling light, leaving only the small fluorescent over the sink to illuminate the kitchen in its cold half-light. "Do I get to ask what all that was between you and my mom?"

They'd spent about an hour with Alyce, until the older woman said she wanted to knock herself out with cold medication and sleep off her illness. Eli and Leah had seen her upstairs, washed the mugs, covered Bryce's cage, and promised to lock up behind them.

"I'm sorry," she said. "It's . . ."

"Please don't say it's nothing."

"That is my go-to response, isn't it? I'm sorry," she said again, lifting her jacket off the back of the kitchen chair.

Eli took it from her and held it out so she could slip her arms into the sleeves. From behind her he asked quietly, "How about if I walk you home? Seems like this kind of conversation deserves a little more than three minutes in the car. If you want to talk about it, that is."

She considered, but it really didn't take long for her to decide. This was Eli, after all—someone, she'd come to realize, she could trust not to make light of her fears. And she felt like she owed him an explanation for her reaction to the news of his mom's illness.

Once they were out on the street Eli kept a close eye on Leah so she didn't slip on any icy patches on the sidewalk and said softly, "Whenever you feel like talking."

Leah shoved her mittened hands into her jacket pockets and sighed. "Your mom's cancer. It kind of got to me. I know it's not rational, but your mom was right. After Cathy, when I hear the word 'cancer,' I tend to think the worst."

"It was rough? Taking care of your foster mom? I mean, obviously it was. Don't mind me."

"It wasn't exactly a walk in the park," she murmured.

"I can't even imagine what you went through. A year?"

Leah nodded again.

"My mom's cancer was treatable and contained and . . . and over with pretty quickly. I mean, it wasn't easy. It never is. She had the surgery and treatment, Jenna and I spent all our time imagining all sorts of awful possibilities, but we were lucky. She was lucky." They walked a few more yards without speaking, the only sound the squeak of their boots on the snow. "Did . . . did what she said to you help at all?"

"It did, actually. Your mom's pretty great."

Eli smiled fondly. "She is, even when she's being a pain in the ass. She likes you too, you know." He hesitated, stole a look at her, and ventured, "And all this after your . . . parents?"

It was time. And, Leah realized, she didn't mind talking about her past. Again, solely because it was Eli, who always listened. "My mom. I never knew my dad. He died in a car accident when I was around three. I barely remember him."

She paused; Eli waited. She appreciated that. Eventually she shared the basic facts—her mother's struggle with being bipolar 1, how hard it was to regulate. Her eventual acknowledgment that she should enter a psych center. Which sent Leah, who had no other relatives, into the foster system.

The entire time, she could tell Eli wanted to say something soothing or maybe hug her. She was glad he held back. Even if some part of her wished he would pull her into his arms, his reserve made it easier for her to talk.

Leah didn't cry—she was beyond that at this point in her life—and after a few quiet moments she decided it was time to end the drama of the evening. She gave Eli a reassuring smile and said, making sure her voice was lighter, "Other than my weird freakout, tonight was fun, Mr. Art Critic."

Eli went along with her abrupt change of subject.

"It was," he agreed. "I'm so glad you came along."

"I'm all about the moral support."

"Well, you're very good at it."

They walked on in silence for another half block. They were getting closer to Leah's home, and Leah forced herself to ignore the kernel of disappointment rattling around inside her at the thought of saying goodbye to Eli again.

Eventually he said, "You know, the last time we were at my mom's . . ."

"The night of the dozen lasagnas?"

"It shall forever be known as that now. Thank you."

"What about it?"

"That night you said you were leaving town."

She shrugged, working harder than she ever had in her life to keep up a noncommittal facade. "I did."

"Why? I mean, it would suck without you around. Why do you have to go?"

"Well, I can't stay here."

"Why not? Willow Cove is a nice place. With nice people. Work'll pick up in a couple of months, and then you probably will only have to work one job instead of forty. And the weather does get warmer eventually."

Leah wrinkled her nose and, almost buying into her own casual bravado, said, "Okay, let me break it down for you. I'm living in a house that isn't mine. I have no claim on it, no right to be there, ever since Cathy died. Patrick, who was AWOL almost the entire time his mother was suffering and dying, is going to show up at any minute to yank the house out from under me and render me homeless. Get it? Besides," she added, "with Cathy gone, I don't have any attachments here."

"You've got us. I mean, the crowd I run with is weird, I admit, but they're good people. They all like you."

Leah stayed silent, because suddenly there was a lump in her throat, and she couldn't guarantee that if she tried to speak she wouldn't end up in tears.

When she didn't reply, Eli added, "You've got me."

Oh God, that was worse. She toughened up by imagining hanging out with him and Victoria. That'd be fun.

"Well, where are you planning to go?" he asked, sounding truly concerned. "What, you know, what'll you do?"

"I'll figure it out. I've been on my own most of my life, one way or another. This is no different."

"Well, yeah, I know, but—"

"No, you don't know." It didn't come out mean, just weary.

"You're right, I don't. But if you wanted to explain it to me, I would do my best to understand."

It sounded like he meant it, and that was deadly. She couldn't do this. She couldn't fall into the trap of Eli caring about her. She'd open up to him, she'd lap up his care and concern, want it to be more, and then . . .

"Okay, I'll try." She stopped walking and held out her hand. "Let me borrow your phone?"

He handed it over without question.

"You really should lock this thing, you know," she said as she pulled off one of her mittens and woke it up.

"Yeah, I've heard."

Swallowing hard, she held up the phone so he could see his background picture—him and Victoria, both in sunglasses, laughing in the bright summer sunshine, the river in the background. The image shone brightly in the dark.

"There's nothing for me here," she said simply, an ache in her voice she couldn't quite manage to hide.

Eli moved closer and took the phone out of her hand, his eyes never leaving hers until he looked down at the screen and started tapping. He was so close she could feel his breath on her cheek when his head dipped closer to hers. This time, he turned the phone to her as he looked into her eyes again, his own expression earnest and pleading. She almost couldn't look away to see what he was showing her.

When she did, her throat tightened. It was a selfie of the two of them in the snow. When had they taken that? She couldn't remember. He took the phone back and swiped, turned it toward her again. Another selfie, this one from their cooking session. Leah had a smear of ricotta on her cheek. Eli was laughing so hard his eyes crinkled at the corners. She couldn't remember what joke had made him laugh like that, because there had been so many. Another swipe, and it was a group photo, again in the kitchen, taken by Alyce. Another swipe, and it was a picture of just her, this time outside, during their impromptu softball practice that day. One more swipe, and it was another selfie he'd taken of the two of them. Leah was looking at the camera; Eli was staring at her.

Kind of like the way he was staring at her now.

"Eli," she whispered, fully intending to protest even as they drew closer to each other.

Lightheaded, Leah wavered as though her knees were giving out. If she swooned, she was going to blame it on the cold. She refused to give Eli the credit for having so much of an effect on her that he could turn her into a cliché character in a gothic novel. But she couldn't deny the pull he had; she was drifting toward him, almost imperceptibly, her breathing shallow, then quickening when Eli nuzzled her temple. Her eyes drifted closed. He was barely touching her, and she was ready to go up in flames.

"Please," he whispered back, "don't go."

If she had been doing anything besides staying still, Leah would have been certain she'd broken a bone. Maybe cracked a rib. Because something snapped somewhere in the vicinity of her heart, and it hurt like hell.

Eli let out a breath of a sigh that warmed her cheek, and she wobbled a little. At her side, his fingers pressed into her waist and steadied her, then he brought his hand up to cradle the side of her neck, lightly, as lightly as the kiss he placed high on her cheekbone. Leah wavered again, trying desperately not to fall into him, physically and emotionally. It would be the worst thing she could do. It was the only thing she wanted to do. More than anything in her entire life.

Leah turned her head toward him, her lips seeking his. She had no resistance, no willpower . . . no choice.

As frenzied as their first kiss had been, this one was its opposite—slow, soft, lighter than air, tentative but not fearful. They tasted each other, just a bit, and Eli's lips were the sweetest thing Leah had ever encountered, as sweet as his nature, his kiss as gentle as his demeanor. It wasn't just her attraction to Eli that was the problem; it was that she loved him with all her—

Leah wrenched herself away, her hand covering her mouth as she realized. Well. She'd always known. But she never thought she'd admit it, not even to herself.

Leah shook her head. "Eli . . ."

He rubbed his eyes. "I know."

"We can't."

"I *know*."

"Then why does this keep happening?"

But Eli said nothing, just stared at her helplessly. Of course he couldn't respond. He didn't have an answer. Neither did she.

Chapter 22

"Only a few more—you can do it. Let's bring it home!"

"I hate you and I should have smothered you in your crib when I first had the thought."

Jenna almost couldn't complete her sentence because it took all her strength to pull on the rowing machine handles one more time.

Eli looked out at his first class in Gray's gym with a sense of pride. Granted, it only consisted of his family members and friends and a couple of random fitness buffs who would try just about anything PowerHouse offered if it could generate the endorphins they craved so much. But it was a start. And this was good. This was healthy. This was the perfect way to channel all the energy he suddenly had.

"Deal with it. This is what you signed up for. And it's good for you! Don't you want to come on a kayaking trip with your little brother in a few months? You need that endurance, you need those muscles."

"You need . . . to . . . shut up . . . now," Jenna panted, pulling slower and slower with each breath.

"Well, I have a microphone, and you don't."

"Don't say it," Ben warned.

"So you will listen to every damn word I have to say."

"Who let him watch *The Wedding Singer*?" Ben grunted.

"That'd be me," Gillian said casually as she lounged on her own rowing machine and examined her manicure. "I figured we were on a roll, so why stop now?"

"And it just renewed my Drew Barrymore crush," Eli said, "so thanks for that."

"How are you not gasping for air?" Jenna demanded. Her ability to form full sentences returned after she gave up trying to match the pace Eli had set.

"This is great!" Gray crowed, yanking away on the handles so enthusiastically it looked like he was about to pull the cables right out of the machine and launch himself backward through the plate-glass windows. "Best new hire I've made in ages."

"Don't act too happy," Eli warned him. "Once the thaw comes, walls can't contain me. I'll be traveling on real water soon enough. All right, time for the cooldown."

"*Ohthankgod*," Jenna heaved, abandoning the machine altogether. She stumbled to her feet, flung her towel around her neck, and started chugging from her water bottle. "I absolutely hate you."

"That's not a cooldown," Eli warned.

"Don't care," Jenna tossed over her shoulder as she walked away.

"Your muscles will cramp."

"Still don't care."

"What's gotten into him?" Gillian asked Jenna when she joined her at the windows.

"Spring fever? A good night's sleep? Sexual frustration?"

"I can hear you," Eli called to them. "The room's not that big."

Gillian called back, "Is it sexual frustration?"

"A little louder, there, honey. I don't think the barflies at Dickie's heard you."

Jenna and Gillian looked at each other. "Sexual frustration," they deadpanned in unison.

"He's missing Victoria that much?" Gillian asked.

"What's wrong with the simple explanation?" Eli protested as the class finished up and stopped rowing. "I'm leaning into my workout to excel at my career."

His sister snorted. "That's not what I heard you were leaning into Sunday night."

Ben started laughing, turned it into a cough, and buried his face in his towel.

Jenna explained to Gillian, "After the cooking lesson, Mom caught him getting a little too up close and personal with our favorite pixie. *Again.*"

The other woman gasped. "Did he really?"

"I was *not* kissing Leah!"

Not that night, anyway.

Jenna snorted. "Now who's sharing personal information with the patrons of Dickie's?"

Dammit. His mic was still on and everyone was staring at him. One rower who had left the room came back in to hear more. Eli pulled off his headset and hung it on the rowing machine. Well, hell, if you couldn't trust your mother not to rat you out, who could you trust? But he'd spoken the truth—he hadn't kissed Leah Sunday night.

He'd kissed her Tuesday night.

Dammit. Now he was back to dwelling on the one thing he thought leading this class would drive out of his head for at least a little while.

On Sunday night, he and Leah had drunk their cocoa in the presence of his allegedly unsuspecting mother, and he'd been grateful for the Baileys kicker she'd added. On Tuesday night, all bets were off. Until Leah at least came to her senses. The "before doing something we'll both regret" was implied. So he'd walked her the rest of the way home, stood there on the stoop as she'd stepped inside as he'd done a dozen times before. But this time she'd given him a searing look before shutting the door, those huge, dark eyes of hers seeing straight into his soul, a knowing look tinged with enough sadness to twist his heart as the lock clicked into place between them.

He'd never regretted going home alone so much in his entire life.

But then reality kicked in, and he knew he had to get Leah out of his head somehow. Working out seemed to be the best, fastest solution, so he leaned into planning the rowing routine. Today's successful class was the result of his desperation to focus on something other than Leah. It had pretty much worked, at least temporarily. Gray and his gym patrons were happy, anyway. Eli's friends, not so much.

"Can we get cheeseburgers now?" Ben groaned as he scooped up his sweatshirt and water bottle from the floor next to his machine.

"Defeats the purpose," Gray said.

"Yeah, but I want to hear more about this incident with Leah," Jenna said. "So I think a trip to Dickie's is in order."

Gillian nodded. "I agree."

"Nope," Eli declared. "I'm not talking about Leah anymore. So if you want to completely undo any progress you made in my rowing class with beer and cheeseburgers, have fun at Dickie's. But I'm not going with you."

"Fine. Be that way. Deny all you want. But we'll find out the truth eventually. In the meantime, *you*," Jenna said, patting her brother's cheek a little too forcefully, "figure it out."

Figure it out, Eli mouthed sourly to his sister's and friends' retreating backs, fully aware he was acting like a child. Like figuring it out was so simple. Well. It *should* have been simple: focus on Victoria and forget Leah. It was what he kept trying to do. So why had he given in to his attraction to Leah again? He should know better. He was an adult, and he should keep his head straight.

Except . . . he still couldn't seem to help himself when Leah was around. She had some sort of magnetic pull he'd never experienced before, not from anyone. It was something he should have been ascribing to Victoria, he knew, which made it even weirder. Victoria was bewitching in her own way, of course. She'd certainly captivated Eli last summer. But Leah was altogether unique. It went well beyond her warm eyes and sweet smile. There was something about her quiet watchfulness, her sharp insight, even her independence to the point of stubbornness. Everything about her. She dug right into his soul. Eli hadn't been lying or exaggerating when he'd told Leah he was at his best when he was with her. He liked who he was when he was around her. And it was easy, so very easy, to be with her.

He knew which way his friends and family were leaning as well. It was obvious the gang wanted to keep Leah around. Eli wondered if they'd feel the same way if they'd ever really had a chance to get to know Victoria. She was great too, after all. But they hadn't spent any time with her. Whenever she'd visited Willow Cove, Eli had suggested they attend cookouts and other get-togethers with his friends and family, but Victoria had always had an excuse. Or she'd do that cute thing to get him to cave, raising one eyebrow and smiling wickedly, head tilted flirtatiously, promising they'd have more fun if it was just the two of them. It had worked every time.

Then again . . . maybe his friends and family weren't that enchanted with Victoria *because* she had been so intent on keeping Eli all to herself and never bothered to get to know the important people in his life.

Huh.

As Eli pulled on his sweatshirt, his phone chimed from the depths of his gym bag. Leah? He pulled it out only to find a text from his sister: a photo of the gang at Dickie's, unapologetically displaying the beers and burgers he'd warned them against. It figured.

While he had his phone open, he decided to check Victoria's Instagram. It dawned on him that he hadn't looked for any new posts from her in quite a while. A quick scan showed only one recent item, a meme from a couple of days ago. The stark white letters on a black background were practically accusatory: *I NEVER COUNTED ON YOU.*

Eli puzzled over the cryptic post. All of Victoria's other photos were bright and colorful like-magnets: classical sculptures, nights out with her new international friends, plates of pasta or pizza or arancini or tiramisu. This post looked morose in comparison, and he got a distinct bad feeling about it.

Almost before he knew what he was doing, he found himself video calling Victoria.

He was startled when she appeared on his screen right away.

"Eli? Oh my God, how are you?"

He skipped the pleasantries. "What's wrong?"

He watched Victoria stammer a bit before she fought out a dismissive, "What?"

"I saw your cryptic Insta meme."

"Are you stalking my 'gram?" she asked with a suggestive smile.

"What? No! Just . . ." He sighed. "Staying in touch. So what's going on? Don't say nothing."

Still keeping his eyes on his phone, he went back into the room with the rowing machines, now empty of gym patrons, and shut the door.

Victoria ran her fingers through her hair, disturbing a mass of waves that filled the screen as they rippled and cascaded before settling, making her look like one of the portraits she was studying. It occurred to Eli that as distressed as she seemed, she still made sure her beauty was carefully curated, every dramatic movement choreographed.

"I don't know if I should be telling this to you, of all people, but . . ."

"Go on."

"I met someone."

Oh.

Well, that was a complication.

Except . . . hadn't he, as well? He ignored the thought to focus on Victoria.

"And you love him?" he guessed, judging by how agitated she seemed.

"I do," she whispered. "Please don't be angry."

"Why would I be angry?"

"Because of what happened with us, how we ended it."

How she ended it, he thought, but all right.

"And I got the feeling that, you know, you were hoping we could reconnect when I got back."

"Oh, well . . ." He shrugged noncommittally. He had. But did he *now*? The best answer, he decided, was no answer, at least while he figured out what his heart was up to. He definitely had some questions for that pesky organ of his. "Look, I just want you to be happy. Does this guy make you happy?"

She laughed, tipping her head back and rolling her eyes dramatically, her long neck curving white against the deep green of her silk blouse. "Yeah. Most of the time."

"Just *most* of the time?"

Eli realized he was talking to Victoria the way he used to talk to Jenna about guys. Was he treating Victoria like a sister now?

"He's wonderful, really. His name's Fabrizio."

"And?"

"He's . . . Eli, come on, do you really want to hear this?"

"If it's important to you, then of course I do."

She turned her dramatic eyes full on the camera. "It was love at first sight," she whispered. "We've been inseparable since we met, the second night I was here."

The hot dude in the photos. Eli was certain of it. Not that it mattered. Fabrizio could have been a short, fat, bald sixtysomething and it wouldn't have mattered, because it was obvious Victoria was head over heels.

"So why are you upset?" he asked. "What was the Insta meme all about?"

"Eli, I'm in love with an Italian artist. I'm a cliché!"

"A very romantic one."

"Don't make fun of me." But she was smiling again, and blushing a little too.

"I would never. You know that. So he's an artist?"

She nodded. "A sculptor."

She was worried about being in love with a penniless artist? Was that it?

"Of course, he doesn't *have* to work. He comes from old money. His uncle is a *count*."

So much for the penniless artist angle. "And the problem is?"

Victoria let out a little incredulous laugh. "I have a life in the States. I have classes starting in the fall. I have a book to write. I can't just . . . run off to be with some unexpected . . . love of my life."

That only stung a little bit. In all honesty, the longer Eli stared at Victoria on his phone, the more she felt like a complete stranger. Or at least someone far removed from his own life, and not just physically. He couldn't help but compare her dramatic, detached beauty on-screen with the people he loved who were all around him, every day. Especially one lively pixie he couldn't seem to get enough of.

"Victoria, you need to follow your heart. Only you can say if your heart's with Fabrizio."

"You're being very deep."

"Hey, I've always been brilliant and insightful. Maybe you just didn't notice."

"Then I was wrong, and I apologize. I hope someone else notices. Or . . . maybe someone else already has?"

"What are you talking about?"

"Come on. I confessed; now it's your turn. Why don't you tell me about the cutie pie who was with you the last time we chatted?"

"Who, Leah?"

"Let it out. You know you want to."

Eli groaned and scrubbed his cheek with his free hand. "It's complicated." He didn't want to tell Victoria *why* it was complicated, because, well, *Victoria* was the complication. Or had been. Now, however, the way seemed almost clear.

"Well, why don't you *un*complicate it?" Victoria said. "I wasn't the right girl for you, but maybe she is. You need to follow your heart."

"Very funny."

"You're the best, Eli," Victoria said, her voice warm with affection. "You deserve to be happy too."

It occurred to Eli that this was better than talking to his sister. Where Jenna would just give him shit, Victoria took him seriously and boosted his confidence.

"I appreciate that. You're a good friend, Victoria."

"So are you, Eli," she murmured. "I'm glad you're not mad at me for, you know, what happened before I left."

He really wasn't, Eli realized. Not anymore.

"Don't give it another thought. But hey, keep me posted on this Fabrizio guy, okay? You'd better let me know if he gives you any trouble, because he'll have to answer to me."

Finally Victoria let out a truly genuine laugh. "I'll keep that in mind."

Chapter 23

"Hello, ma'am, this is Za Za Zoom, the local pizzeria that doesn't play games with your order. Sorry—they make me say that. Anyway, your delivery is approximately three minutes away. We'll be there shortly."

"Why didn't you just text me?" Delia asked.

"We don't text and drive, ma'am. Oh, now I'm in your driveway."

When Delia opened the door, her morose expression morphed into one of almost delight. "Leah?"

"Hi, Delia."

"Another part-time job?"

"You bet. Free unclaimed pizza at the end of the night, too. What's not to love?"

"Well, come on in."

Leah clumsily fought her way through the front door with the insulated bag and slipped the extra-large pizza box out, taking care not to drop either the food or the bag. Or both. It had happened once. Okay, twice. It was only her third night making deliveries, after all, so she was still working on her technique. If she dropped one more order, Ty, the manager, was going to bench her, maybe make her work the deep fryer. She wasn't afraid of hot oil, but she preferred the freedom of zipping around town from dusk till the wee hours of the morning when the streets were deserted, making people happy by handing over pizzas, calzones, and subs while they stayed snug and warm in their pajamas. Like Delia was.

"How have you been?" Leah asked.

"I'm about to consume an entire extra-large pizza at ten o'clock at night. So, you know, I've been better."

Delia sighed in a way that worried Leah.

"Delia? Are you okay?"

At first she looked like she was going to brush off Leah's question, but then she took the cardboard box from her and said, "Want some pizza? Otherwise I *will* eat this entire thing by myself. I'm entirely capable and, more important, willing. Oh, I'm sorry. You're working. Never mind."

Leah immediately set down the insulated bag and pulled out her phone. "Ty? Yeah, it's Leah. I'm taking my lunch break now, okay?"

Ty didn't seem to care, especially because nobody was ordering takeout. It was a Wednesday night and above freezing, so people had been out and about, even digging their gas grills out of snowdrifts. With a promise to have her phone at the ready in case someone needed a delivery, Leah ended the call and followed Delia through the small foyer into the living room.

"You have such a cute home."

When she'd pulled into the driveway, her first thought was that Delia's house belonged in the Swiss Alps. It was covered in scrollwork, sporting wooden shutters, and each part of the exterior was painted a different brilliant color. The screened-in wraparound porch, the early twentieth century's version of air-conditioning, would be a dream once summer truly arrived and breezes drifted across the river several hundred yards away across the pancake-flat yard. Inside, the fairy-tale theme continued, with decidedly feminine décor—dotted Swiss curtains, ruffled slipcovers—set off by contrasting paint colors on walls and trim. Very, very Delia.

Except for this Delia in front of Leah, who was decidedly not colorful despite her purple hair, green sweatshirt, unicorn slippers, and hot-pink flannel pajama bottoms with cartoony Eiffel Towers and poodles in berets all over them. There was a definite cloud of gloom over her head, Leah decided, that muted her sparkle.

"Thanks," Delia said as she grabbed a roll of paper towels from the kitchen counter. "It was my prize purchase, my summer home, when I was earning my *quite* nice estate-planner attorney salary in Albany."

"The one you gave up?"

Delia ushered her over to a very eighties giant-cabbage-rose-print sofa. "I did. Because I hated it. I had to watch family members fight one another over money, or property, or a ceramic cow-shaped creamer that had 'sentimental value' or some such nonsense. It got ugly way too often. So I gave it up and came back here as fast as my Louboutin-clad feet could carry me, promptly threw the Louboutins in the river . . . okay, not literally . . . and decided to live the life I was born to live."

"As a woman of leisure?"

"As an artist. My workshop's through there." She gestured with the hand that was free of pizza to the other side of the house.

Leah jumped up from the couch and peeked into a small room covered in knotty pine paneling that had obviously been some gentleman's man cave at one point. Now there were tables filled with compartmented boxes holding jewelry findings and beads, a large illuminated magnifier on a stand, tools scattered about, and even a blowtorch.

"Impressive. And intimidating," she said when she returned to the living room. "Have you been selling your jewelry at the festivals and souvenir shops?"

"Not yet. I'm building up my inventory so I'll have enough to sell in one sitting, like at a craft fair, this summer. I'll make you something nice, if you don't mind being a guinea pig."

Although Leah's first thought was she wouldn't be around when Delia completed "something nice" for her, her second thought was of Eli, pleading with her not to leave. She shook it off and distracted herself with the intention of eating her body weight in pizza.

As if Delia could pick up on what she was thinking, she said, "So. Let's fail the Bechdel Test and talk about men."

"This is about Gray, I take it?"

"Not this time," Delia said, giving her a sly look over her slice.

"Then what . . ." Leah nearly dropped her food as realization hit. "You lured me here under false pretenses—and pizza—just to pump me for information about me and Eli! I walked into a trap!"

Delia burst out laughing. "I swear I didn't know you worked for Za Za Zoom. However, one of the perks of my law education is I've become really good at thinking on my feet, so when you showed up at the door . . . it sort of turned into a spur-of-the-moment trap?"

Leah groaned. "Because of course you heard. It's like you're all one organism or something."

"Horrifying description. But accurate."

"So you know everything."

"Plus Jenna's take on the situation, and Gilly's take on the situation, and—"

"Oh, fabulous."

"I'm not a creeper who wants the gory details about you and Eli—okay, maybe I do, a little—my bigger question is, what's all this he mentioned about you leaving town? And some weak excuse that you don't have anything to keep you here? I'm offended. You've got us, and that's major. We're selective. You think we let just *anyone* into our group? You think we let Victoria in? Hell, no! And to this day Eli thinks it's because the two of them spent too much time off by themselves for Victoria to bond with us. Nuh-uh. We blocked her overprivileged ass."

"I thought you all liked her."

"Well, she's not a *demon* or anything. But she doesn't fit in with us. You do." Delia hesitated. "I'm not sure if that's a compliment or not. But it's meant to be."

Leah smiled warmly. "It is a compliment. But it's not going to change my mind."

"Because of Eli?" Delia waited, but Leah couldn't quite form an answer. "Honey, you can tell me the truth. If anybody's going to understand, I am."

Suddenly the food stuck in Leah's throat. Yes, her plan to leave had been in play for months, but the sudden urgency damn sure was because of Eli. Yet she could barely admit it to herself, let alone another person, even if that person was super nice and feeding her pizza.

"I can barely stand to be around him now, Delia."

"Are you mad at him?"

"No!" she rasped, unshed tears constricting her throat. "Just the opposite. I want to be with him all the time. Being around him makes me happier than anything that's happened to me in so, so long, I can't even remember . . . and . . . and I can't tell him, or show him, and to know in a little while he's going to be back with Victoria—"

"You *don't* know that."

"It's what he's been planning for months. He can be very . . . single-minded."

"He is a sweetheart. But he's wasted on Victoria. She doesn't appreciate him. Not like you do, not like I do. Or any of the rest of us. If you ask me, I'd rather see him with you. Everybody else agrees with me too, you know."

"Too bad Eli doesn't," Leah muttered bitterly, picking at her crust.

"Oh, what does he know? If he was still obsessed with Victoria, he wouldn't be kissing you, now, would he?"

Leah laughed despite her misery. "You're so great, Delia. Gray's an idiot."

"Thank you for that. I happen to agree."

"Look . . . I never want to pry, but . . ."

"You want details about me and Gray, huh? Well, it's only fair, I guess, since I heard all about you and Eli. I suppose I owe you my tale of woe."

"Only if you want to share."

"If I don't, Jenna or Gilly will be happy to fill you in."

"That's true."

Delia crammed a hunk of crust into her cheeks like a chipmunk foraging for winter. When she had swallowed the overlarge mouthful, she said, "Well . . . to start, who else but an idiot like me would crush on a guy like Gray? For *years*, mind you. And the whole time, he was totally not interested."

"Are you sure he wasn't interested? And you're *not* an idiot."

"Let's put it this way—he knew, he did nothing."

"It doesn't necessarily mean he wasn't interested. Maybe he was—is—interested, and he just doesn't know how to . . . proceed?" It sounded weak to her even as she heard herself say it, but she believed the thought was worth pursuing.

"That's the thing, though." Delia reached for another piece of pizza and didn't meet Leah's eye. "He did. We did. Once upon a time."

"Oh *really!*"

"Oh yes. We were quite the thing for all of, oh, five minutes, about a year ago. But of course *some*body had to get spooked."

"And it sure wasn't you."

"Oh, it was totally me."

"What!" Leah yelped.

"Yeah, I freaked out a little."

"But . . . why?"

"Think about it—have you *seen* the guy? I kept wondering what he was doing with, you know, me."

"Oh no, that's not fair. You're fabulous."

"I know, I know, but I thought it anyway. Plus I don't mind admitting his dating history was a little—a lot—intimidating. So many beautiful people . . ." She closed her eyes and shuddered.

"You don't have to feel intimidated by anybody," Leah corrected her. "You're Miss Delia Dupree, dammit."

"Yeah, well, there I was, second-guessing everything, but I figured I could overcome it in time. He was the one who jumped to conclusions, suggested we take a break, and the next thing I knew . . . poof. Over. I had to wonder if he was looking for an excuse and used my moment of weakness to pull the trigger."

"I still don't understand why you got spooked. I mean, you got what you wished for."

"*Exactly*: I actually got *everything* I wished for. I didn't quite trust it."

Both women paused to process this.

Then Delia went on, "Of course, we're *completely* incompatible anyway. I mean, I like to go dancing. He likes to work out. I like to go to movies. You know what he likes to do? Work out. I like to go out to eat—"

"And he likes to work out?"

"No, he likes to drink green smoothies. And *then* work out. Yeah, I had to go and fall in love with a musclehead."

Leah paused, startled. "You did?"

"Did what?" Delia asked, distracted by rogue drips of mozzarella she was swinging back onto the surface of her slice.

"You fell in love with Gray?"

Delia whimpered and plopped the pizza onto the paper towel she was using as a plate so she could cradle her head in both hands. "I don't know! I guess I did. It was a short plummet. I'd been most of the way there for years, after all."

"Wow. That's . . . huge."

"Too huge, apparently. Men."

"Men," Leah agreed, and they toasted one another with their pizza. "So . . . do you think you two will ever try again?"

"Honey, I have no idea. I get excited every time I'm around him—how pathetic is that?"

"It's too familiar for me to consider it pathetic. If you know what I mean."

"That means we're going to be like silly teenagers chasing their first crushes when we get to see the men in their element on Saturday. Wait. You *are* going to the softball tournament, right?"

"I *was* going to, but now . . ."

"No, please go! We'll show up looking fabulous—"

"Under twelve layers of clothes?"

"Honey, we can look fabulous wrapped in sleeping bags."

"That's about the same look, actually."

"And we'll laugh and have a good time and make those men eat their hearts out."

~

When Leah arrived at the town park, she wasn't sure there would be much laughing or having a good time, let alone any men eating their hearts out at how fabulous she and Delia looked, because she couldn't see a damn thing and neither could anybody else. She'd finally made peace with the concept of playing softball in winter, but was it even possible in yet another snowstorm?

About thirty people were milling around by the baseball diamond or, rather, where the baseball diamond normally would be, its location identified only by the chainlink backstop looming up out of the snow. Some confused individuals were hovering by the white mounds that hid the small built-in barbecue grills, clutching bags of charcoal, spatulas, and grocery bags full of food. One person was carrying a cooler, which was likely the most redundant thing possible to tote to this event; someone else, who was smarter, had jammed bottles of beer into a pile of snow so it looked like a giant hedgehog.

Leah squinted against the whirling flakes to find any animated bundles of clothing that looked familiar. Fortunately Delia was easy to spot, because she was wearing the pinkest of hot-pink ski jackets. Leah headed toward that beacon, leaning into the squall.

"Is it supposed to be like this?" she shouted through her scarf when she reached the group.

"Not usually this bad." The voice, which she recognized as Ben's, came from behind a sturdy balaclava. "Did you summon this?"

"I came here from Florida. This is the last thing I'd wish for." To Delia, she asked, "Do we look hot yet?"

"Don't you see the snow melting?"

"Is Gray here to appreciate your fabulousness?"

"He's over there having a serious discussion with Eli."

At the mention of Eli's name, Leah's stomach leapt. She hadn't seen him in nearly a week, and it had felt like a year. Not for the first time, Leah wondered how she was going to get over him once she was gone.

As though she could feel her anguish through their multiple layers, Delia jogged her arm. "I'm so glad you came."

"I am too?"

The bundled form that resembled Jenna laughed. "Not even a little convincing."

"Where's Gilly?"

"Working, the lucky bitch."

Leah had to ask. "Seriously, how do you guys play softball in this?"

"I don't think we're going to," a voice rumbled close beside her. Again, her insides seized. Leave town? Not likely, because she was going to die of a heart attack first.

"Hey, stranger." Eli smiled down at her—well, he was wearing a balaclava too, so all she could see were his eyes, but the corners were crinkling, which always meant he was smiling. She breathed a little easier. "I wasn't sure you were going to make it."

"Wouldn't miss it for the world."

"Again, not even a little convincing," Jenna said. "Eli, please say the snow softball tournament is snowed out. The only ones enjoying this so far are the kids."

Sure enough, while the adults were standing around fidgeting as they tried to figure out whether to give up and go home, their children were having a blast running around, falling into the drifts, having snowball fights.

"I never thought I'd say this, but it might come to that."

"It's your call, so you'd better make it."

It was his call? Eli was in charge of this? Leah was only a little surprised. It did seem to be his kind of thing—outdoor sports in the snow—but trust him to be modest enough not to mention this was his baby.

"I think we can tough it out," Gray said, popping up on Eli's other side.

Leah felt Delia flinch, just as she had a moment ago. She squeezed Delia's mittened hand in solidarity.

"'I don't think the heavy stuff is gonna come down for a while,'" Eli said, with a roguish raised eyebrow directed at her.

Oh God, a *Groundhog Day* quote. Which sent Leah's mind reeling back to the last time they discussed the movie, in front of Alyce's fireplace. *I wouldn't mind being trapped in a single day over and over again with you.* He was reminding her of that night on purpose. This time it was Leah's turn to grasp Delia's hand in search of solidarity. Delia squeezed back.

"Knock it off and call it," Jenna ordered. "I have a hot toddy with my name on it back home."

"Or . . ." Eli ventured.

Jenna heaved a sigh. "What?"

"We could move this indoors?"

"What are you talking about?"

"You can open up the school."

"Oh, you stinker." Jenna laughed ruefully and shook her head. "Is that a yes?"

"You can't play softball indoors."

~

But they could play Wiffle ball.

In almost no time at all, the crowd was filling the high school gym. Jenna was policing everyone with the energy of a prison warden to make sure they left their wet boots in the foyer instead of creating a slip-and-fall hazard on the lacquered floor, as well as threatening death to anyone who even thought about firing up a hibachi in the hallway. The softball teams turned in their metal and wood bats for plastic and checked the roster to find out which teams played each other in the first round.

Meanwhile, the kids who had unwillingly been dragged out of the snowbanks were at a loss, so they resorted to running laps around the gym and up and down the bleachers, their screams echoing in the high-ceilinged space.

"Somebody's gonna break a neck," Jenna muttered, the fear of lawsuits floating around her head like a halo again.

Eli watched his sister fret; Leah hovered on the periphery and watched Eli think. Jenna narrowed her eyes at her brother.

"*Where* did you get that *hat*?"

Once he was out of the snow, he had put on his favorite baseball cap, the one Leah had rescued. Eli's beautiful blue eyes cut to Leah immediately, as if he'd known where she was in the crowd the entire time. He flashed her a conspiratorial smile. But he didn't give his sister an answer.

Instead, he said, "Okay, don't worry. I've got it handled."

He called Gray over and they had another conversation, Eli pointing this way and that around the room and then at the roster. He took a silver whistle from around his neck and handed it to Gray, then marched into the thick of the kid-swarm. One sharp whistle blown between his teeth, and all the youngsters froze in their tracks.

"All right, anybody younger than thirteen, follow me!" he shouted.

The Pied Piper couldn't have done any better. He spun about without checking to see if any kids were following him, but they all fell into line and trailed Eli diagonally across the gym, one of them shouting, "Coach Eli! Are we gonna play?" And they disappeared through a door in the dividing wall separating the two halves of the gym.

Leah couldn't help but follow. While everyone else was organizing their teams, she crossed the gym as well and pulled on the metal ring in the door. On the other side, Eli had already divided up the kids into two large teams and had pulled a kickball out of the gear closet.

To hell with Wiffle ball, Leah thought. The only thing she wanted to do was to stay right there and watch Eli in action.

She wasn't disappointed. Within minutes, Eli got a game under-
way with himself as pitcher. Once they got a groove going and one
of the girls clamored to be allowed to pitch, he handed her the big
red ball and took over as catcher/cheerleader, shouting encourage-
ment to both teams, giving advice to uncertain-looking kids who
came up to bat, and high-fiving the ones who rounded the bases
and crossed home plate.

It was mesmerizing. Where anyone else would have seen a goofy
guy running a victory lap with five kids hanging off him like
chimps dangling from a tree, Leah saw magic—the most amazing
man she'd had the honor to know. He was sweet, funny, handsome,
selfless, thoughtful, and so, so kind.

And she just hoped Victoria appreciated all his wonderful
qualities.

Of course, she reasoned, if Eli wasn't supposed to be with Victoria and was supposed to be with her instead, she'd be fine with
that. All she needed was a sign.

Doof.

And her head was knocked sideways into the door as the kickball ricocheted off her temple.

Chapter 24

Eli was across the gym in a split second, crouching where Leah had slid down to sit on the floor, a dazed look on her face.

"Ow."

She said it calmly and quietly, but Eli's heart was rabbiting as though she'd screamed and blood was gushing from her head. There was nothing of the sort going on in front of him, but it didn't seem to matter to his insides.

"Are you okay? Are you hurt? Are you bleeding? Let me see."

"Eli . . ."

"I'm just going to turn your head really carefully for a second, all right? Let me know if I hurt you."

"Eli, I'm fine. Just . . . surprised."

He didn't listen. Of course he didn't. He'd watched her get whomped with the ball and go down. Like he was going to believe her protests that she was fine without checking for himself. All the kids had gathered around, most of them fidgeting nervously, sliding their socks on the shiny floor or chewing on their nails. Eli zeroed in on the most distraught boy, Jase, the one who had kicked the ball with such force. Poor kid. It wasn't his fault his powerful kick had fouled out to left field.

"Jase, buddy, do me a favor?"

The boy's worried eyes focused on Eli.

"Go get an ice pack, okay? Find Mrs. Masterson-Page in the other gym. She'll know where to get one."

The boy squeezed around him and scooted through the little door, and Eli turned his attention back to Leah. Placing his hands on her cheeks, he gently turned her head so he could see her left temple. There was no blood and he couldn't see a bruise forming, but still, he feared the worst. Because it was Leah, and he never wanted to see her suffer so much as a paper cut.

"I think you might need to have a CT scan or something. You could have a concussion."

That was a bridge too far for Leah. She cupped her hands over his, which were still cradling her face, and pulled them down.

"Eli, listen to me. I do not have a concussion. The ball was soft. The door, I admit, was hard, but my head is harder."

"But—"

"Stop, okay? I'm fine."

Her soft, warm hands hadn't let go of his, a fact he was keenly aware of. Her fingers found their way through his and they locked there.

"I appreciate that you're so concerned, though," she said.

"Well, Jenna's in a constant state of panic somebody's going to get injured during this unauthorized event on school property and sue the district for millions, so . . ."

"Oh, so you're checking to see if I'm a litigious liability?"

"What? No—" He broke off when he saw her eyes had refocused and were twinkling at him. His smile bloomed, matching hers.

"Okay, fine," he said reluctantly. "Apparently you're still capable of using fifty-cent vocabulary words, and alliterative ones at that, so I'll believe you for now. But I swear, if you act sleepy or dopey—"

"Or any of the other dwarfs?"

"You are about the same size."

"How about grumpy, if you don't knock it off?" She smiled brighter, though, as she moved to get up. Eli brushed the kids back and took her arm. "Eli, come on."

"Sorry." He held his hands up in surrender. "But from now on, I'm watching you." And he pointed two fingers first at his eyes and then at her.

"I'm fine with that."

Her simple words flipped his stomach, set his nerve endings on fire.

"Now . . . how about putting me on a team, coach? And don't you dare say I can't play because I'm injured."

Leah hadn't said anything out of the ordinary, so why did he feel like he was about to levitate? Well. Again, because it was Leah. Obviously. "All right, all right. Outfield? No, wait. How about catcher? It's mostly low impact with this bunch, catching rolling balls they've missed. Just remember, though . . ." And he did the *I'm watching you* thing with his fingers again.

"Okay, okay. Sheesh."

Leah batted at his hand and walked over to home plate, giving him a significant look over her shoulder that nearly brought him to his knees. Jase returned with the ice pack Eli had forgotten he'd told the boy to fetch. Eli took it from him, but with Leah on her feet and ready to play kickball, he was at a loss for what to do with it. No, that wasn't entirely true. He punched it to get the cooling agent flowing and held it to the back of his neck. He needed it all of a sudden.

～

"You're really good at this, you know?"

"Eating two meals at the same time? Yeah, I've been training all my life." Sitting cross-legged on the floor in the school hallway, he did a couple of curls with each arm, brandishing a hot dog in his left hand and a hamburger in his right.

"No, not that." Leah laughed and took a sip of her soda. The locker behind her rattled as she leaned against it. "I mean organizing the kickball game and keeping the kids busy. You're great with them."

Eli shrugged nonchalantly even though her words sent a

warmth and energy through him that made him want to run one of those marathons Gray was always on his back about. "They're good kids. A lot of them were on my softball teams. And, ahem, we won the league trophy two years ago," he said, pointing at his Land Sharks cap.

"It's more than that. I mean, it's not just getting the most out of the kids, sportsball-wise."

"Is that a technical term?"

"Absolutely. Try to keep up. Anyway, I'm talking about how you interact with them. Have you ever considered doing more of that?"

"You mean going back to coaching?"

"Or more."

Could she read his mind? "Well, I did have this plan . . . I mean, just a vague idea . . ."

"What?" she prompted.

"I've always wanted to teach kids' paddling lessons—kayak, canoe. Maybe crew for the older kids. Or . . . my house is on a lot of land. It would be perfect for a ropes course or something. I don't know," he rushed on. "I'm just talking out my ass, really."

"No, no, it sounds amazing." Leah turned to face him, leaning forward eagerly. "You could have a summer camp. Or just different lessons. It could give the local kids something to do in the off-season, and then you could ramp up the attendance with the kids who come here for the summer. Eli, it's a fabulous idea."

"It is?"

She let out a breath of a laugh, incredulous. "Yes! Why are you acting like you just said you invented a bicycle made of bubbles that you could pedal to Mars?"

"Well, I was going to tell you about that next."

She gave his knee a gentle shove. "It's a great idea, and if anybody can do it, you can. These kids follow you everywhere as it is. If you offered them something like an outdoor course, whether it's ropes or rowing or . . . anything, really, they'd all sign up like a shot."

"You think so, huh?"

"I do."

There was that levitating feeling again. It definitely hit anytime he made eye contact with this wonderful woman. He felt himself blushing—blushing!—as he looked down at the floor. "Well, thanks. I . . . I haven't told anybody about that idea in a long time. I started to do the initial stuff—checking the marketability of it, looking into liability insurance—but when I told Victoria, she didn't think it was very practical. Kind of talked me out of it." Leah didn't say anything. When he glanced up, she just looked sympathetic. "Anyway." He brushed aside the subject. "You haven't told me what you're thinking about doing in the future. Are you going to turn pro with the fifty-four-jobs thing, or . . . ?"

Leah laughed. "God, I hope not. It's exhausting!"

"You make it look easy."

"Yeah, well, I still don't want to make a habit of it. Just a few months of it has been quite enough, thank you. I was thinking of going back to school, actually."

"Really?" Now it was Eli's turn to lean forward with interest. "Studying what?"

"Well, I had been going to a community college in Florida, just taking different courses to figure that out. I really enjoyed being in school, you know? Then Cathy called, and . . ." She shrugged. "I gave it up. I mean, I put it on hold. And that was fine. Helping Cathy was more important. That year gave me time to think, to make a clearer plan for when I would be able to get back to school."

"What's the plan?"

"I want to go into social work. Helping foster kids."

"That's perfect," he said.

"Mm, we'll see."

"Does that mean you're going back to Florida?"

"I . . . I don't know."

Something heavy suddenly hung between them—the memory of Leah saying there was nothing for her here and Eli begging her not to go. And what had happened after that.

"There are a lot of good schools in New York State," Eli reminded her.

And now it was Leah's turn to blush, smile, and train her eyes on the floor.

"Hey, do you want to get out of here?" he asked. "Maybe watch a movie?"

~

They went back to Eli's house, traveling at a near-crawl despite the Jeep's four-wheel drive and massive snow tires, because the snowstorm wasn't abating in the least. When they finally fought their way into the cabin, Eli stoked the woodstove while Leah scrolled through his on-demand options. He was glad the power was still on. Then again . . . his mind took off on flights of fancy about what could happen if the two of them were trapped there without movies as a distraction.

"So I was thinking," Leah began when he dropped onto the couch next to her. "You've pretty much covered every aspect of your makeover, haven't you?"

Eli groaned. "I hope so. I'm exhausted."

"Learning how to dress nicely and have cultured conversations is exhausting?"

"Damn right it is. Plus that stupid manscaping *itches* when it starts growing in again. Jeez!"

"*Any*way," she went on, turning her attention back to the TV, "there is one part of this plan you've neglected so far, and movies are your best teacher for it."

"And that is?"

"The grand gesture."

She still wasn't looking at him, just staring straight ahead at the TV screen, but her eyes seemed unfocused and her smile looked a bit forced.

"What grand gesture?"

"To get Victoria back. Every romantic hero—okay, sometimes the heroine, but let's stay with the heteronormative clichés for now—"

"Have you been talking to Gray lately?"

"Hey, he's not wrong. Anyway, you know, at the end of the movie there's the huge, over-the-top grand gesture as a declaration of love. Most often the guy has realized the girl is his one true love and is running to tell her before it's too late. Like in *When Harry Met Sally* when Harry runs through Manhattan to find Sally at the New Year's Eve party. Or in *Love Actually* when Sam runs through the airport. Or Lloyd Dobler with his boom box—"

"I get it, I get it. And I know about the grand gesture, in theory; I haven't lived under a rock for thirty-one years, no matter what you might think."

"Well, when Victoria comes back, what are you going to do, just text her and say hey? Or casually invite her to meet up at Mc-Donald's or something? If you want to win her back, you have to hit her hard and fast with the romantic grand gesture—an act she can't miss and can't refuse."

"And women like this kind of thing?"

Leah just rolled her eyes and mouthed what looked to Eli like "men."

"I'm kidding," he rushed to say, nudging her shoulder with his. "All women are into it, I get it—"

"No." Suddenly she was dead serious and looking right at him. "Some women don't need a huge production like a marching band or skywriting or . . ." She looked away again. "The *right* gesture . . . it just has to be sincere and honest, not massive. But we'll assume, for argument's sake, Victoria wants something huge."

Eli didn't respond. He was thinking about all those fantasies he'd concocted where he'd meet up with Victoria again, in his new polished look and his best new clothes, and she'd get off the plane looking beautiful but tired and glad to be home, and she'd spot him, and her eyes would light up. Then there would be some pala-ver about how wrong she was and how she'd missed him. It varied every time he imagined it, but it all came out the same in the end, when she'd say she'd been wrong to break up with him and she desperately wanted him back. In some versions Eli would get down on one knee right there and produce a ring—a proper diamond this time, big as one of her knuckles (or, if he was really letting his imagination go wild, big as one of his)—and she wouldn't even hesitate to accept.

He'd imagined so many of those scenarios one should have been easy to recall now, but nothing came to mind. He was too distracted by Leah's profile as she read through the movie menu on the screen. He'd stared at her face hundreds of times over the past several months, and he'd never gotten tired of it. She seemed to only grow more luminous every time he studied her. He'd spent hours with her and never been bored. Sure, they'd had their times when they'd disagreed, but nothing, nothing had ever been a deal breaker. He thought about what Willow Cove would be like if she actually left, and his heart ached. He couldn't imagine his life without her in it.

When had this happened? When had he fallen so completely for this lively little dark-eyed woman? Well. When he wasn't paying attention. When he was chasing after some other fantasy that, he knew now, was nothing more than a figment of his imagination. Leah had been right again: he was a modern-day Romeo, in love with love, plugging Victoria into the "object of desire" spot when, really, she had no interest being there. Now he had no interest in keeping her there either.

What he really wanted was this beautiful, kind, patient, and funny woman sitting here, still trying to help him achieve his unreasonable goal, even if she didn't approve of it, even if she had feelings for him herself. He hoped.

Eli reached out and gently took the remote from her. "I have a question."

She turned to him again. "Okay."

He swallowed, his throat tight, and he wondered if the strangled noise was as loud to her as it was to him. "What's . . . what's the movie where the guy is so stupid and so blind he doesn't see that the best thing that's ever happened to him is the woman who's been right in front of him the whole time?"

Leah froze, her full lips slightly parted in surprise. After a moment she stammered, "That . . . that'd be most of them."

Although Eli's heart was slamming against his ribs, blood rushing in his ears, he forced himself to hold her gaze, silently communicating he had come to a realization about who he wanted in his life. He was certain. The only thing he didn't know was why it had taken him this long to figure it out.

"Then I don't need to see any of those either. Because I'm living it."

"Eli." It came out on a shallow breath, more like a question. For the first time, he noticed, it wasn't a warning.

"I'm an idiot."

"I *know*." Leah smiled playfully, her dimple appeared, and the tension abated, just a little.

"You're not making this any easier," he said.

"Not my job."

"Can I continue, please?"

"Sorry. Please, do go on."

"Thank you." He hesitated. "Well, now I don't know what I'm supposed to say."

"Maybe you do need more movie lessons."

She started to take the remote back, but he held it high out of her reach.

"Oh sure," she groused, "pick on the short person."

"What if I didn't do one?" he blurted out. At her confused look he went on, "A grand gesture, I mean. What if I didn't run to the airport or sing or play a romantic song on a boom box or run through the streets of . . . of . . . Willow Cove, I guess? What if I didn't do any of it to get back together with Victoria at all because . . . I don't want to?"

If his words shocked Leah, she didn't show it. She just batted back, "Then you've wasted nearly four months preparing for it."

"No. I didn't. Because I've spent those months with you. And they've been the best months of my life."

That silenced her.

"Look"—he settled himself, making sure his eyes were trained on hers—"you were right. About everything." He paused. "Here's where you say 'naturally.'"

"N-naturally."

"Thank you. I couldn't continue without that." He reached out, tentatively, and cupped her face, his thumb caressing her cheek. "You're amazing. And beautiful. And—"

Leah put one small hand over his mouth, gently. "I don't need a speech."

And she leaned closer, took away her hand, and touched her lips to his. The electric jolt went through him again, and all his nerve endings crackled. The magnetic pull was beyond anything he'd ever felt. He was grateful that when he deepened the kiss, so did Leah. He wasn't sure his heart could take it if she pushed him away this time. He drew her to him, and she went willingly, wrapping her arms around his neck, rising up on her knees and ducking her head down, taking over.

He let her.

Everything about her was so soft—her lips, her skin, her tongue, the curves of her body—and he wanted to drown in that softness. But it was what was behind the kiss that wrecked him. This wasn't a simple gesture of lips on lips, skin on skin, although that would have been enough to knock him sideways. There was more. A message. *Finally.* And *I've wanted this forever.* And *I need you like I need air.* He could feel the emotion radiating from her, knew exactly what it was, because he gave the same right back.

Eli picked Leah up and eased her back to lean over her, breaking their kiss only to explore her neck, her earlobe, her throat. The helpless sounds she was making were gratifying, were permission to continue. Which he did.

"So," she whispered as he pushed aside her sweater to kiss her shoulder, "no movie?"

"I told you, I'm done with makeover stuff."

"Hey."

She sounded serious, so he reluctantly lifted his head.

Running her fingertips through the short hair at his temple, she said softly, "You know you never needed a makeover, right? You've always been perfect just the way you are."

"Does that mean everybody's going to stop chasing me with the damn trilby hat?"

"How about no hat?" She reached over to the coffee table where he'd set his Land Sharks cap and waved it at him. "We'll just save this for later."

"Later?"

"I kind of want to see you in it."

"You have."

"Wearing just that. Nothing else."

"You're going to kill me, you know that? But I definitely will die happy."

Chapter 25

"Now you have to tell me everything."

Leah felt an uncontrollable giggle rising in her as Eli's voice vibrated in a low rumble against her bare back, even as she thrilled to the feel of his hand, large and warm, on her stomach. Trying to sound stern but failing, she said, "I don't have to tell you diddly."

"Oh yes, you do." He rolled her toward him, and she went willingly. She'd go anywhere with this man, but she really hoped they'd stay right there, cocooned in his bed, warm under the blankets, as the snow kept falling. Rolled over was about as far as she wanted to travel. "I want to know everything in there"—he gently tapped her temple—"now that I know everything . . . here." And he ran his hand the length of her body.

Leah shivered at his touch and promptly lost whatever train of thought she had. She barely knew her own name at this point. She certainly didn't know what time it was, whether it was still Saturday night or early Sunday morning. She didn't much care, either.

"You can't just be satisfied with what you already know?"

"Oh, I'm satisfied there. For now." He gave her a wicked look. "But I said everything, woman. Start from the beginning. What breakfast cereal you ate as a kid. Who your favorite cartoon character was. Or is. No judgment. Who you crushed on in middle school. How long you believed in Santa."

"Okay, okay, I get it." She laughed. "Everything."

"Everything."

Leah looked up into Eli's wide-open face, marveled for the hundredth time how his blue eyes drank her in, every breath, every movement. She had never felt more seen or cared for. So she really didn't want to start lying to him now.

"I . . . ate whatever breakfast cereal was in the cupboard. When my mom wasn't on a health kick and made me eat unflavored yogurt for breakfast. Sometimes, when she wasn't . . . doing well . . . there was nothing, and I ate hot dogs or leftover pizza." His giddy look faded a bit at a time, and she hated doing this to him, but he had asked for everything, so here it was. "I had a thing for *Tiny Toons* reruns and *SpongeBob*, of course. I watched *The Simpsons* because nobody stopped me. I never crushed on anyone in middle school, because I missed a lot of it until I went into foster care. I was taking care of my mom, and sometimes—a lot of the time—she needed me at home. Then, when I went into foster care, I was a little too preoccupied with my new . . . situation . . . to notice boys in school. As for Santa—"

"I'm sorry," Eli murmured, stroking her shoulder. "I wasn't thinking."

"Don't be sorry." She shrugged. "This is me. I'm okay. My past wasn't always great, but I'm okay now. I could have just rattled off a bunch of platitudes, but I'd rather tell you the truth."

"Of course." He took his hand away and kissed her shoulder instead. "Always."

"Foster care isn't always hellish. I was pretty lucky; my life could have been a lot worse."

"And you left Cathy's when you were eighteen?"

"I could have stayed in foster care till I was twenty-one, but yeah, I left. We'd talked about my staying, getting a job, helping to take care of the younger foster kids, but I just decided it was time.

My mom was out of the psych center and she swore she was better. So I moved back in with her in Syracuse."

"And how was that?" Eli nearly whispered.

"It was . . . pretty good. I got . . . closure, I guess?"

"Closure? Why?"

"Mentally she was in a good place. Physically . . . not so much. We had two years before she died. Heart failure. Eli . . . Eli . . ."

"What is it?"

"I can't breathe."

He loosened the vise grip he had on her, which had tightened gradually the more of her history she shared. God, his arms were huge. They felt wonderful wrapped around her, making her feel safe and warm and cared for. But she didn't do pity. Never had.

"Thanks." She snuggled into the crook of his arm and stroked his hard, broad chest. Yes, his manscaping was growing back. She wondered if he was going to refresh it or let it go. She was fine with either option. "My past is just that—my past. It affected me, it shaped me, but that doesn't mean it damaged me for life. I'm not fragile, and I'm not broken."

"You're tiny but super strong."

Leah laughed softly, and a thrill went through her as she recalled their first conversation in Thousand Island Dressing. It seemed like forever ago. "Anyway, I don't want you to worry or pity me or anything. I've made peace with everything. And my mom passed a long time ago. I'm not actively grieving for her anymore. I remember her with love."

"What about Cathy?"

"I'm glad I came back to help her. Even if she made it a challenge."

Leah fell silent. God, she was talking a lot, about stuff she never thought she'd discuss with anybody, stuff she didn't think she *wanted* to talk about. Huh. Now here they were not talking, and that was fine too. More than fine, in fact. Leah realized she was happy lying there without saying a word, Eli's arm draped over her, his finger lightly tracing a circle on her bare shoulder. So she stayed very still, eyes wide with wonder, letting the quiet wash over her.

"Frosted Flakes," she said eventually.

Eli's chest shook under her cheek as he laughed, confused. "What?"

"My favorite cereal. If we had that in the house, and there was actually fresh milk in the fridge, I'd eat the entire box."

Eli slid down in the bed until they were face to face, and he studied her in the dim light of the lamp in the far corner of the room. Again, Leah was stunned by his open gaze, his rapt attention, the wonder in his expression as he drank her in. It thrilled her and terrified her in equal measure.

He drew her closer and kissed her slowly, his entire being focused only on her. Leah's bones liquefied as she molded herself to him. When Eli had gotten her well and truly malleable through his kisses alone, he drew back a little and with a small smile said, "You hungry?"

"Meaning?"

One dark eyebrow arched. "Well, now. I do believe we've unleashed a monster. I was talking about, you know, food."

"Oh, that. Sure, I could eat."

"I'll be right back."

"Take your time," she said, happy to watch his retreating bare ass for as long as he wanted to display it.

When he was gone—with a little butt wiggle on the way out, just for her entertainment—Leah closed her eyes and stretched until her joints popped. She couldn't seem to get this smile off her face. She was *happy*. For the first time in who knew how long. A warmth had taken up residence in every inch of her skin. And it wasn't just the kisses. Or the sex. Although both of those things were *exceptional*. It was the kisses and the sex and the conversations and the laughter and the feelings of contentment and safety . . . with Eli. All of it with Eli. And he—

Leah's thoughts were promptly derailed when there was a light *flump* on the bed beside her. She cracked one eye to see Blanche sitting there squinting at her.

"Hey, cat," Leah said conversationally, desperately trying to ignore the accusing stare the feline was giving her. But that was impossible. "Okay, I'm *sorry* we locked you out of the bedroom before."

The stare continued.

"We were, you know, busy. Party of two. And you around, with the claws? Hard pass."

Blanche was unimpressed.

"It's because of the whole Victoria thing, isn't it?"

The cat didn't say yes, but she didn't say no, either. Because she was a cat.

"Look, can we be reasonable about this? I mean, your owner broke up with Eli ages ago. So there's no real moral dilemma here."

Blanche licked her paw and used it to clean her ear, her studied indifference the feline version of *I'm not mad; I'm just disappointed.*

"I mean, I know it seems kind of sudden, Eli and me. Is that what's bothering you?"

Blanche switched to the other paw, other ear.

"Okay, Eli did sound pretty devoted for a while, what with the whole makeover thing for Victoria, but he's over her now. He said so, and I believe him."

Blanche moved on to folding herself in half, pointing a leg toward the ceiling, and licking her private parts.

"Yeah, fair enough—he knew Victoria for four months, and that's as long as he and I have known each other. But it's really not the same thing at all, is it? The thing with Victoria, it was . . . it was misguided. No offense against her or anything. Yeah, let's call it that—misguided. Because saying it was *wrong* is really judgy. Kind of like the vibe I'm getting off you, furball."

Blanche continued her campaign to assiduously ignore Leah while simultaneously messing with her head by staying put and looking through the transgressing human female. It worked. The longer Blanche sat there, the more unsettled Leah became, and not just because of the pissy vibes emanating from the animal. Which, of course, were all in Leah's head. Probably.

She had told Eli she was completely unscathed by her time in foster care, but that was a lie, much as she had tried not to keep any of the truth from him. She *had* been affected and still was, whether she wanted to admit it or not. Trust issues—she had them, and with good reason. She was perpetually braced for the moment something would be taken away from her—a home, a place in the world. Someone she hoped to love. This was no different.

But it *was* different. This was Eli. Loving, affectionate, trusting, trustworthy Eli. And she wanted to believe he was over Victoria. She wanted to believe he had seen something so worthwhile in Leah that he'd happily kicked over the shrine he'd built to his ex-girlfriend and chosen her instead. She had to stop doubting him, stop doubting the possibility of the two of them together, and trust him with her heart. Now the question was . . . could she trust herself to give it?

Eli backed into the room, nudging the half-closed door wider with his unfortunately now-boxer-brief-clad buttocks. He must have unearthed them from wherever they'd thrown them earlier.

Leah sat up, self-consciously holding the blanket to her chest as he turned around, carrying an upturned cover of a cardboard file box as a tray.

"Blanche, dammit," he muttered, spotting the judgy kitty loaf in the middle of the bed. "Sorry," he said to Leah, "for the very nosy cat. And for the box top. I don't have a serving tray. I do, however, have a kitchen full of matching dishware, glassware, and silverware, because Jenna said real men don't eat out of Tupperware containers, nor do they try to wash disposable plates. I even have a mandoline slicer thing. I'm not sure what to *do* with a mandoline, but I have one in case of . . . uh . . . slicing emergencies."

Eli placed the makeshift tray on her lap. "I learned things," he said, proudly indicating the properly arranged full place setting of gray-blue pottery, a cloth napkin, and sleek silverware. In the center was a heaping bowl of Frosted Flakes.

"Well, shit," Leah whispered, awestruck.

"You didn't really want that?"

"No, I . . ." She tore her eyes away from the bowl to meet Eli's worried gaze.

Careful not to upset the bowl, she reached out, tucked one hand behind Eli's neck, and drew his head down so she could kiss him. There may or may not have been little pricks of tears at the corners of her eyes.

"I cannot believe you," she whispered.

"I just want you to have everything you never had in your life."

"What did I say about pity, mister? That includes feeding me Frosted Flakes."

"Frosted Flakes are not pity. Frosted Flakes represent an overwhelming urge to make you happy. Because I want to see that dimple as often as possible."

Which, of course, made her smile.

"There it is," he whispered, kissing her again. "Tiny but super strong. I couldn't possibly forget." He paused, thinking. "You know, I had a thing for you from that very second."

"You did not."

"Excuse me? You're going to tell me what I felt when I felt it?"

"I'm saying you were still all about Victoria then."

"No, I . . . okay, maybe."

"Mm-hmm."

"Oh, so smug. You think you know everything, don't you?"

"Pretty much."

"Well, what you don't know is you broke through my fog that day. You were the only one to do that in months."

"Maybe you were just ready to move on by then, but you wouldn't admit it to yourself."

"Or you could take some freakin' credit for changing my life. How about that? Uh-huh." Now it was Eli's turn to be smug as Leah stared at him, stunned. "The tea should be ready. I'll be right back. Eat before the cereal gets soggy."

Eli left her there, gaping like an idiot. When she recovered, she dug deep into the bowl but paused with the spoon at her lips. She raised her eyes. Blanche had her judgy stare turned up to eleven.

"All right." Leah sighed. "Let's settle this right now, cat. Your mom gave up a perfect guy. Willingly. She's okay with it, he's okay with it, and now you're going to have to get used it too. Because I've never wanted anyone as bad as I want that goofy guy right there. So here. Let's grease the skids a bit."

She dipped her finger into the milk and held it out to the cat. Blanche's eyes went from Leah's face to her finger, but she didn't accept the offering. Leah shrugged.

"Your loss, cat." And she licked the milk, sweetened from the cereal, off her finger.

As Leah ate, Blanche inched closer, excruciatingly slowly, which amused Leah no end. She pretended not to notice. Just to annoy the cat. If Blanche could do it, she could do it right back.

Eli walked in with a mug in each hand. "Making friends?"

"You're going to have to ask Blanche," she said, setting down the cereal spoon and reaching up to accept one of the mugs.

"I think she's spoken."

Leah turned to find Blanche whiskers-deep in her cereal bowl.

"Hope you were finished with that," he said.

"I am now."

"Come on, feline." Eli set down his mug and scooped her up. "No milk for you—I don't want to clean up any ugly accidents later." He poured her out on the threshold and closed the door firmly behind her.

Trying hard to sound nonchalant, Leah said, "Victoria's cat."

Eli took the tray off her lap and set it on his desk under the window, then settled back onto the bed next to her. "True."

"Are you keeping her, or will Victoria want her back?"

"Are you asking me if I'm going to see Victoria again?"

"Maybe."

"Sounds like we need to talk about some important stuff."

"That might be a good idea."

Eli sighed and rubbed his eyes. "Okay, let's see if I can boil this down for you." He took a sip of his tea, then put his mug on the nightstand and turned to face her fully. "Yes, I was all about Victoria . . . which turned out to be a bad choice all the way around. No, I was not right in thinking I was in love with her and she was my destiny. Yes, I am over her. No, I am not secretly plotting to win her back anymore. Yes, I am fully and completely into you. No, I'm not substituting you for her. Yes, I'll probably see Victoria again if she wants her cat back. No, I won't fight her for custody. Yes, I'd be happy to keep Blanche if she doesn't want her back. No, it won't establish a permanent tie between me and Victoria, since it's not a joint custody kind of thing and we're not coparenting. What else do you want to know?"

So many thoughts were tumbling through Leah's muddled mind, but one stood out. "What did I ever do to deserve you?"

And she kissed him again, her emotions surging. Try as she might, she was helpless to resist him. She decided to stop trying.

Chapter 26

"Did we have to do this now?"

Eli had to shout to be heard over the chaos of the high school main hallway between classes. He was buffeted from all sides like a sailboat in a hurricane as the students surged around him. In the middle of it all stood his sister, unmoved.

Until she whipped around suddenly, pointed down the hall, and bellowed, "Flaherty! Paine! Kerrigan!" Three gangly boys turned, startled. One pointed at himself questioningly. "All of you, in my office at second lunch."

Although Eli couldn't hear them, the teens were obviously groaning, irritated.

Jenna was unbowed. "And bring Lynch with you too!"

The boys stomped away down the hall, pushing other students out of their way in frustration. Jenna snickered.

"What did they do?" Eli asked his sister, following her to her office through the thinning crowd.

"Nothing," she said simply. "I just like to fuck with the little shits every once in a while. Keeps 'em on their toes."

"You're the devil."

"That's the idea."

Once they were in the startling peace of her office, Jenna

dropped into her chair, and Eli leaned against the wide window ledge. "Why was I summoned, Mrs. Masterson-Page? Am I in trouble too?"

"Maybe. I haven't seen or heard from you in forever. Weeks, anyway. You all right?"

Oh, he was all right. He was more than all right. He had been spending every moment he could with Leah, after all. For a few of those moments they were even vertical. And clothed. But only a few.

"Why are you grinning like a moron?" Jenna demanded, squinting at him.

"I'm not."

"You absolutely are."

Eli shrugged. "Must be spring coming on. Don't you feel it?"

"No," Jenna said with a snort. "It snowed another four inches yesterday."

"Temps are in the double digits, the sun even came out. I'd say those are pretty good signs."

"You *are* a moron. We don't get anything but false spring until May, equinox or no. But it's April, and you know what that means."

"Practical jokes?"

"Of a sort. Our anniversary party is in less than two weeks."

"Already?"

"Yes, already. And it's a great time for you to work on another skill: party planning."

"Are you kidding me?"

"A guy who wants to win Victoria's heart should be able to plan an event, bring together all the elements effortlessly, and be a good host. That isn't 'women's work' anymore."

Eli opened his mouth, shut it again. He didn't know where to start. Jenna didn't know he'd abandoned his makeover. She didn't know he no longer wanted to get Victoria back. She didn't know he and Leah were together. Actually, nobody did, just because they hadn't bothered to socialize with anyone since after the Wiffle ball tournament. If he were the crass sort, he'd say they had been busy gettin' busy. But he wasn't, so he didn't. In any case, there were going to be a lot of questions. There likely would be a lot of gloating from folks who had predicted it. There would definitely be a lot of squealing on Delia's part. Maybe Gillian's too. Or maybe Gilly would just grunt in approval. If she approved.

Nah, who was he kidding? Everyone would approve, because everyone loved Leah and, apparently, loved him and Leah together. He happened to agree with them, and he was prepared to shout it from the rooftops. He knew, however, that he was going to take a lot of shit for this sudden development, so he wasn't prepared to share just yet. He decided to focus on the party planning instead.

"This doesn't really have anything to do with the whole make-over thing, does it?" he asked.

"Not even a little. I just wanted to push some of the party prep onto someone else."

"I did mention you were the devil, didn't I?"

"Here. I made a list." Jenna pulled a slip of paper out of a drawer and slid it across the desk.

"You're the only person I know who can't manage to text this kind of thing."

Eli scanned it quickly. The list was made up of the usual duties—fetching balloons and decorations, compiling a playlist, confirming the menu. It wasn't anything he couldn't handle.

"Most of the stuff you're going to have to get in Watertown. Take Leah with you. She'll make sure you make good choices."

"Okay."

"And you should bring her to the party so she's not wandering in on her own."

"Okay."

There was a silence, punctuated only by the dripping of icicles on the eaves, melting ever so gradually in the stronger spring sun. Eli went from placidly checking the to-do list to staring intently at it while still attempting to look casual, hoping Jenna's silence only meant she was distracted by something on her computer.

He should have known better.

"Leah." His sister said it in a flat, neutral tone, implying nothing.

"Yep."

Another pause. Then, "Leah."

"Mm?"

"Leah."

"What?" Eli demanded, finally looking up at her.

"I knew it," his sister hissed. "You're fidgeting, and your pupils are blown. Either you're high as shit or something happened between you two."

"All right!" he burst out. "Yes! Fine! It did. Happy now?"

"Wh . . . *really?*"

"You were *guessing?*"

"Amazing superpower, isn't it? It's how I get the truth out of these teenage delinquents. And your nieces. Apparently it works on adults—or adult children—too." She leaned forward, her tone changing from casual to concerned. "So . . . is this a good thing? Or was it a onetime deal and now there are regrets and you have to cross the street to avoid each other from now on?"

Eli's smile returned. "It's a good thing. For real."

"And Victoria?" It was almost as though Jenna didn't want to say the woman's name, in case it retriggered the spell Eli had been under for months.

"Victoria who?"

"Be serious."

Eli wanted to explain, clearly and succinctly, how he had felt about relationships before he fell for Leah and how he felt now. It was true that he had thought Victoria was his soul mate. Until he met Leah. He wouldn't have thought relationships could be so easy when he was with Victoria. That was a struggle all the way. Like paddling against the current. But with Leah . . . this was like coasting downstream on a brilliant, sunny summer's day. He had a flash of Sam, the little kid from *Love Actually*, holding up his index finger. *She's the one.* Now he understood. Not to be sappy or anything, but he had to admit he had a penchant for sappy, especially these days. He had Leah to blame—no, thank—for that. He was going to embrace his sappiness from now on.

All he said to his sister was, "I *am* serious. Victoria's my past. Leah's my present."

"And your future?"

"I sure hope so."

Eli expected the usual dope slap, scowl, and "dumbass" epithet thrown in for good measure. Instead, his sister lit up.

"I hope so too. I'm really happy for you."

"Really?"

"Really. I love Leah."

"I do too."

"You *do*?"

"I shouldn't use that word, should I? That's bad. I mean, with my history."

The old Jenna returned in a flash. "*No.* Dumbass. It's great, because I can tell you really mean it this time. I don't want to speak for Leah, but I think she *might* just feel the same way about your weird ass. Lord knows why. So don't screw it up. Now, I am done discussing my little brother's love life. I need a few minutes to prepare, so I can effectively scare the living shit out of the delinquents who are coming to see me. If they don't figuratively crap their pants in my presence, I'll have failed as a vice principal. So take the to-do list, get out of my sight, and do not—*do not*—blow it with Leah, you hear me?"

Grinning, Eli stood, pocketed the paper, and rounded the desk to plant a kiss on top of his sister's head. "You're the best sibling a moron could ever have."

"You're damn right. I'm so great, I'm not even going to say I told you so about Leah *or* you should have listened to me about Victoria ages ago."

"Can I get my old clothes back now?"

"Absolutely not. Now scram."

"Come on. I want to show you something." Eli tugged on Leah's hand to stop her from going up the front steps of his cabin. "Not inside."

Leah hesitated. "Uh, we usually head inside when you say something like that."

Laughing, Eli tugged a little harder, until she did a little free fall off the bottom step and into his arms.

"Where, then?" she asked. Eli gestured at the trees surrounding the little house, and Leah's eyebrow quirked. "Out there? Isn't that where monsters are?"

"A few trees means 'here be monsters' to you? Seriously?"

"I've never really been all that comfortable with the great outdoors."

"And you want to hang out with me, huh?" he mused, feigning concern. "With all the kayaking and the camping and stuff? This could be a problem."

"Oh, well then . . ."

Leah made a move to go around him, pretending to leave, but slowly enough that Eli could hook her around the waist and drag her back in front of him. "Do you think you might be able to give the great outdoors a try, though? If you had, you know, a wilderness guide?"

Leah did the thing she often did, studying him with a sharp eye that would have made lesser men quail. "Can you recommend one?"

"I can recommend an excellent one." He placed her back up on the step and, before she could protest, he turned around, hooked his hands behind her knees, and hoisted her onto his back. Leah wrapped her arms around his neck as he set out across the driveway and around the back of the house. "I promise to go easy on you," he added.

"Why? I can handle whatever you dish out."

"Tiny but super strong."

"Damn right."

"Okay, Tiny, you're on."

"Not if you take to calling me that on the regular."

"If I keep carrying you like this, can I call you Yoda instead?"

"Walking stick, I wish I had. Beat you with it, I would."

Eli laughed and kept walking until they left the shelter of the trees and came out at the edge of a clearing. "This is it," he said softly. "Grandpa's legacy."

Leah nudged him to loosen his grip and she slid smoothly to the ground. "It's beautiful."

"You should see it in summertime." Right now it was a vast white expanse, unbroken except for a few bent tops of tall grasses poking up through the snow here and there.

"This is all yours?"

"Yep. It's around fifty acres. The property line is a few hundred yards into the trees on the other side of the field. My grandfather loved this area and always wanted to keep a piece of it undeveloped."

"It sounds like Grandpa was a good man."

"He was. You would have liked him. I'm sure he would have loved you." Eli took a deep breath and went on, "I was thinking this could be the site of the ropes course. It could straddle the tree line—some of it in the trees and some of it out here."

Leah tucked an arm around his waist. "It's perfect."

"Yeah? Really?"

She laughed up at him, likely because he was sounding like a dork. "Yeah, really."

"It'll take a while to build. And there are a lot of details to iron out. I'm excited about it, though."

"You should be." Her other arm came up and she enveloped him in a tight hug.

"Thank you," he murmured, squeezing back.

"For what?"

"Are you serious right now?"

"I didn't do anything."

"Yes, you did. You let me tell you about my stupid plan, and you said it wasn't stupid."

"Wow, you're easily impressed," she said, and he could hear the smile in her voice even though she was looking out at the view.

"Hush, you. I mean it. So . . . thank you." He wanted to say more, to shout, to have his cry bounce off the trees and come back to him as an echo, *I'm in love with you.* He wasn't going to make the same mistake twice, though.

Instead he said, "I guess we should get started on Jenna's party-chores list, if you're still willing to help."

Leah let out a small groan. "I do want to help, but I can't right now. I'm picking up another shift at Dickie's."

"I thought you hated smelling like fryer grease."

"I do. But the place isn't crowded at this time of year, so it's easy. Plus he's got the best trait for being a good boss—he's pretty easygoing. Except with your sister. Why does he give her so much grief, anyway? Did she criticize his wing sauce once or something?"

"Oh, that. They have a history. A *long* history. All of it ridiculous. It went from dating to hating. Lifelong enemies. Jenna can tell you about it sometime. It's a cautionary tale for the ages."

Eli threw his arm over Leah's shoulders and they started walking back through the woods. "I'm a little surprised you're still working all your jobs."

"Money makes the world go 'round, my friend. I don't have it; I need it; today Dickie is willing to give me some in exchange for several hours' hard labor."

"I know how capitalism works, thanks."

She poked him in the ribs, the jab softened by his jacket and the mitten on her hand. "Don't worry about me, okay? I do what I have to do. I'll be fine."

"I hate to stand by and watch my girl exhaust herself working so much."

Leah's steps stuttered, but she gave no other indication he had just called her his girl. Eli risked a glance over at her. When he saw she was blushing, her eyes downcast shyly, the back of his neck started tingling and a burst of emotion bloomed in his chest. Maybe his sister was right. Maybe Leah's feelings for him were as strong as his for her. He desperately hoped so.

Unable to hide a wide smile of his own, he simply said, "I'll drop you at Dickie's, then."

Chapter 27

"Okay, we're going to try this *one* more time."

Leah leaned over an openly confounded Eli, who was fidgeting in his seat at Jenna and Ben's kitchen table.

"Laughing at someone else's distress is not okay, you know," he groused.

"You're cute when you're frustrated."

"What's the big deal? You take a piece of ribbon, you tie it, done. Am I right?"

Leah exchanged a long-suffering look with Jenna.

"My brother can't tie a bow." Jenna sighed. "Sad."

"Hey, I've been able to tie my shoelaces since I was five."

On a cough, Jenna muttered, "Ten." To Leah, she explained, "Relied a little too heavily on Velcro, this one."

"My *point* is," Eli cut in, "how is this any different?"

"Don't you want your sister and brother-in-law's party favors to look nice?" Leah demanded.

Eli listed sideways to eyeball her. "I can't say I care all that much, no."

"Well, you should, and it's time you learned. So we do this . . ." With one arm on either side of him, Leah stretched forward and took up the ribbon on the table. Which had a more detrimental effect than she'd planned, as Eli relaxed against her instead of leaning in to the bow-tying lesson.

"This is all right," he murmured in her ear, sending shivers down her spine and launching her nervous system into overdrive. For the thousandth time since she'd met Eli, she felt her cheeks flush.

"Pay attention."

"Oh, I'm paying attention."

She could not handle this. Could not. She had to retreat, but not before gently nipping the top of his ear. "Hopeless. Put the ribbon down. You'll be more useful picking the dead leaves off the bamboo centerpieces."

As Leah walked away on unsteady legs, pretending to be annoyed, a strong hand grabbed hers, and the next moment she found herself sitting on the washer in the laundry room, with Eli kissing her senseless. Which was a very nice predicament to be in, all things considered.

"Can we leave soon?" he murmured against the curve of her jaw, and her shivers showed up for an encore performance.

Her voice was embarrassingly breathy when she answered, "Not yet. There's still a lot to . . . um . . ."

What were words, again?

"Do?" he filled in for her, and suddenly that tiny word was loaded with innuendo, with suggestion, with promise.

"Yeah. That," was all she could manage in response.

"I refuse to tie any more ribbons," Eli growled, and she melted into him a little more. She'd never been with anyone who could make her laugh and want to tear his clothes off at the same time.

"Just put the stuff in the bags and I'll tie them," she said.

Jenna and Ben had decided to go all in on the luck theme for their thirteenth anniversary party. Leah had helped Eli select the charms for the guests' gift bags: a tiny horseshoe, a four-leaf clover encased in resin, a rhinestone ladybug lapel pin, a new penny, an acorn, and a blue glass evil-eye charm. They'd picked up the bamboo plants at an Asian imports store, where they'd also found a giant maneki neko, a waving good-luck cat, that Eli thought looked like Blanche. It would take pride of place in the restaurant in ten days.

Leah felt good about being able to help Jenna and Ben flesh out the theme of their party, but nowhere near as good as she was feeling with Eli's lips skimming her neck.

So when he said, "Okay . . ." (kiss) ". . . but after we do that . . ." (kiss with a tickle of tongue) ". . . you're coming home with me, right?" all Leah wanted to do was say yes.

Hell, all she wanted to do was say "Forget the party prep" and run out the door with him right now. She was so grateful her own luck was finally turning, and she and Eli were growing closer and happier together every day.

Then those warm feelings curdled in her stomach as she forced herself to say, "I can't."

"What? Why not?"

"Patrick, remember? He's finally coming into town, and I promised I'd meet him at the house."

"Oh. Well, that sucks," Eli said, stepping back so she could hop off the washer.

"Tell me about it. I can't think of anything that would suck more."

"What sucks?" Ben asked, pulling beers from the fridge as they reentered the kitchen. "Party planning?"

"Let me tell you, Ben," Leah said, politely declining one of the bottles he held out to them, "I would rather stay here all night tying up those mesh bags if it would get me out of this weekend with my foster brother."

Jenna made a face. "So the dick is back in town, huh?"

"Coming in hot any minute."

Ben popped the cap off his beer. "To put the house on the market? Now?"

"Not yet. First we have to fix it up. No problem, Patrick says. Simple."

"Who are you using? Because I know a guy."

"Oh no, that's the thing," Leah said, all sarcasm, "apparently we're going to whip the whole house into shape in a matter of days. Just the two of us. Because he's a cheapass, apparently. And delusional. On second thought . . . may I?" She stole Eli's beer and took a healthy swig. "Somehow I get the feeling that isn't quite how it's going to play out."

"What kind of work are we talking about here?"

"I don't even know. I mean, cosmetic stuff, sure, but I think there are problems with the wiring, and the pipes keep freezing because there isn't enough insulation in the walls, and I'm pretty sure there's a large mouse colony that's claimed the basement as their own. One more generation, and they're going to have enough mousepower to storm the kitchen, take me hostage, and liberate the contents of the refrigerator. So I think Patrick's in for a bit of a surprise." She sighed. "I'd better go. He hasn't texted me, but I'm sure he'll be here soon. I need to go gird my loins before he shows up."

"Do you want me to go with you?"

Leah's heart warmed at Eli's earnest offer. "No, it's fine. Stay. Your nieces told me they want you to help them make some of their own decorations for the party, which I'm *pretty* sure means you and everything around you in a ten-foot radius will be covered in glitter. And that's more important, right?" She directed her question at the two small Masterson-Pages who had careened into the kitchen, flying superhero action figures over their heads, while Jenna bellowed at them to stay away from the party goods.

"Right!" Olivia answered immediately, ditching Supergirl in a mostly empty bowl of pasta left over from lunch. "Unca Eli, you get the markers, and I'll get the glitter!"

"That's my cue, I think," Leah said, laughing at Eli's stricken face. "Have fun, now."

⌒

If Leah was never very fond of Cathy's house, it seriously came up lacking after the warmth and comfort of Ben and Jenna's home.

The front yard was mostly mud with random lumps of icy grayish slush at the street, now that the area had finally gotten a protracted period of fairly warm weather. Without the snow cover, the crumbling concrete of the front steps and the rust on the wrought-iron railing were robbing the little ranch of whatever curb appeal it might have had. Leah wondered if Patrick was going to put those items on their list of things to fix.

The front door stuck as well, having expanded in the above-freezing temperatures. She twisted the tarnished, pitted knob and hip-checked it, nearly falling into the foyer when it finally gave.

"Oh, Cathy," she muttered, "I've been trying with this place. Really, I have. But it's been fighting me every step of the way."

As she dropped her keys onto the small side table and wrestled her way out of her coat, she went on, "Maybe I should have tried harder, earlier, but you've gotta admit you refined and perfected this filth over decades. There's no way anybody can make it all pretty in a couple of days. Or a week. Or . . . how long have I been at this? Months? Even that long."

Leah stopped short. Something was weird. Then she realized. She hadn't "talked" to Cathy in quite a while. Since she'd started spending time with Eli.

"You talkin' to me?"

If Leah were a cat, she'd have done one of those freestanding jumps where all four paws left the floor at the same time. As it was, she gasped and clutched at her heart, which was suddenly hammering double-time.

"Patrick! What the hell?"

"Hey. Good to see you too. I will accept compliments on my De Niro impression now, thanks."

Her foster brother was lounging at the dining room table, half-hidden by a stack of boxes, one of the few remaining mugs—of the dozens of free ones Cathy had had stuffed in the kitchen cupboard, almost all of which Leah had recently bestowed upon Dennis at the thrift store—in his hand. He'd opted for the thick, curved, midnight-blue one with the white anchor advertising Spencer's

Marina and Boat Repair. Her favorite mug. Although Patrick had no way of knowing it was her favorite, she found herself getting irritated all the same, as though he'd used it on purpose.

"What are you doing here?" she asked, her tone sharper than she intended.

"You forgot I was coming already? I said I was."

Yeah, he'd said that four times since Cathy died, and he'd bailed on her three times. Whatever made him think she'd believe him for promise number four?

"Hey," he went on, in his usual awed-at-everything tone, his full, almost puffy lips slightly parted, "do you have problems remembering what day it is too? Man, they should invent something that'd tell you that, like, every day."

". . . A calendar?"

Patrick seemed not to hear her, just stretched his legs and grinned. "You should have seen the look on your face just now. It was like you forgot me or something."

Same old Patrick. Well, almost. He was as good-looking as ever, although definitely softer around the middle, having lost the football-player hardness he'd had back in high school. He still sported some muscles and the thick neck she remembered, now emphasized by how short his dirty blond hair was, clipped with geometrical precision around his ears and across the back of his neck. He was more put together and better dressed, but deep down he hadn't changed a bit, she knew.

"Well, I didn't know you were in town already, or that you were going to let yourself into the house."

His blue-gray eyes, smallish to begin with, got smaller as he studied her in confusion. "It's my house."

"I know. It just . . . hasn't been your *home* for a long time."

"And it won't be again pretty soon."

Leah squinted back at him. None of that sentence made any sense.

"Selling it," he explained impatiently. "I'm selling it, so it won't be again."

"No, I know. It's just that the way you put it . . . You know what? Never mind."

She looked around at the stacks of boxes she'd worked so diligently to pack. Several of them were open again, the flaps sticking up and the packing material on the floor.

"I know you're here to clear the house, Patrick, but it looks like you're doing the opposite already. What's up with this?"

"I was wondering what was in all the boxes."

"Your mom's stuff," she said, not even bothering to hide her incredulity. What else did he think was in there, Christmas presents from Santa? "I was getting a head start. And there was a *lot* to pack up." She hastened to add, "I didn't throw out anything but junk, don't worry. You can take all this back home with you."

Patrick paused again. When he took the time to process something, Leah thought she could hear the echo of gears actually turning somewhere under his poof of hair. After a minute he said slowly, "*I* don't want it."

Leah shrugged. "It's your house, like you said. And therefore so is all the stuff in it. Congratulations."

The pout Patrick produced clearly telegraphed he didn't like that answer. Well, too bad. If he was going to swoop in at the last minute and evict her, then he was going to have full possession of all the stuff that had to be dealt with.

Wait. Evict? He wasn't evicting her, and it wasn't on short notice, not really. She'd been preparing for this eventuality ever since Cathy passed last summer. It was why she was working all her jobs and scrounging as much money as she could. It was why she hadn't settled in and made the house more of a home.

It was why she had had every intention of keeping to herself and not forming attachments in Willow Cove.

Which had gone really swimmingly, what with a new circle of friends and a bona fide boyfriend to boot. Now here she was, breaking all her promises to herself, clinging to all of it—Eli, her new friends, the town, even the house. The weirdest thing was, she didn't regret it. Not one bit. Except for the house, of course, because it was about to be yanked out from under her. But first things first.

"What were you looking for, exactly, Patrick? Some memento? Because I really didn't find anything like that."

Patrick listlessly rifled through the nearest open box. He pulled out a melon baller, the paint on its wooden handle chipped and peeling, and studied it intently. Leah was ninety-nine percent sure he had no idea what it was. Suddenly he pointed it at her and asked, "Did my mom tell you she was leaving you anything? I mean, pacifically?"

Leah ignored his malaprop—also typical Patrick—to puzzle over his near-accusation. Where was this coming from? He of all people should know his mom didn't have anything to give away even if she wanted to. Nothing of value, anyway. Maybe he did know what the melon baller was and was hoping it wasn't bequeathed to Leah. She sure hoped it wasn't anything more complicated than that.

Sliding into one of the chairs at the table, she said carefully, in her best soothing tone, "Of course not. Patrick, your mother never gave me anything or promised me anything. You and I both know she had nothing to give away. It's why she didn't even bother with a will. And if she *had* tried to give me something, I wouldn't have accepted it."

"Yeah." Patrick turned the kitchen gadget over in his hand. "So this is mine too?"

"Without a will, everything goes to the nearest blood relative, and that's you." She shouldn't have had to add the last part, but this was Patrick, after all.

"Yeah, but my mom liked you. Better than me, I think."

Leah was stunned. All she could do was watch Patrick as he dropped the melon baller back into the box with a thunk. He rummaged around in the kitchenware again, coming up with a pair of tongs next. This time his eyes lit up and he nodded—apparently he recognized these.

When she found her voice, she said, "I don't believe that for a second. You were her *son*. She loved you more than anything." Even if Cathy had never uttered the L word in her life, she'd obviously adored her only biological child. "You were the golden boy, with your football career and everything. She was so proud of you."

Patrick nodded reluctantly, his head down. "I guess."

Leah hesitated, then dared to ask, "Patrick, do you think your mom was mad at you because you didn't come around much when she was sick?"

He was all aggression again. "Did she tell you that?"

"No," Leah nearly whispered. What she didn't say was that at the end, when Cathy had been under the influence of heavy doses of morphine, she'd kept asking when Patrick was going to arrive, as if she'd gotten word he was on his way. But he hadn't been. If Leah had lied to the woman occasionally and said her son would be there soon to get her to relax and sleep, well, she had no regrets about it. Leah hadn't wanted Cathy to be mad at Patrick.

"Yeah, well . . ." It looked like Patrick was going to toss the tongs into the box, but at the last minute he changed his mind and tucked them into his back pocket. "I just always got the feeling she wished you were her kid, not me."

Leah's breath caught. Where was this coming from, all these thoughtful, introspective statements from the king of superficiality? As long as she'd known him, Patrick had been all about Patrick, and that consisted of sports, working out, and having a good time. Not like Gray, who was smart and thoughtful and genuinely cared about his friends. Patrick was just a walking id and always had been. But maybe she was wrong about him now. Maybe he'd changed.

"Hey," he said again, his mood changing abruptly as a new thought tickled him, "wouldn't it have been hilarious if you and me had gotten married?"

"*No*, Patrick, it would *not* have been 'hilarious,'" Leah retorted. "You were my foster brother."

Balancing a four-sided cheese grater on his head and bobbing and weaving to keep it there, he said, "I wasn't your brother. You were just somebody living in my house."

Leah blinked and looked away. Patrick's comment stung more than she ever would have admitted to him or anyone else. He was right, though. He wasn't her brother. Cathy wasn't her mother. Just because Cathy opened her house to Leah when she was a teenager, and no matter how much bonding the foster system tried to encourage, Cathy and Patrick were not her family. Not really.

Hiding behind her frustration, which unfortunately was always in large supply when Patrick was around, she snapped, "Don't make me explain the foster system to you again. I did that way too many times when we were teenagers."

Patrick had never hidden his disdain for those "other kids" living in his house, eating his food, putting demands on his mother's time. There was no reason for Patrick to feel threatened, as Leah had done her best not to be a bother and had worked hard to help her younger foster sisters with anything they needed as well. Cathy had always lavished plenty of attention on Patrick. Yet it seemed Patrick never caught on, and even to this day his outlook hadn't changed in the slightest.

Leah's had, however. Now she didn't have to appease her foster brother. She didn't have to be accommodating, to tiptoe around him and make herself invisible. She didn't have to be nice. There was a sense of freedom in that. This had been her house for more than a year, and Patrick had been gone far longer. She was going to use that leverage.

"Put your stuff in your mom's room," she said brusquely, standing up and brushing imaginary fuzz off her jeans. "You'll be more comfortable there. Your old room is cleared out anyway. We'll start dealing with everything tomorrow."

Patrick seemed to respond to decisive, direct orders—he would have done well in the military, she thought—and went out to the car to get his bag. Leah ducked into the larger bedroom, ignoring the shadows of Cathy that seemed to lurk in every corner, and checked the dresser and nightstand drawers to make sure everything was empty for Patrick's stuff in case he stayed long enough to unpack.

The dresser drawers were clear, but there were a few things in the nightstand. Leah scooped them up and dumped them in her bedroom on the way to the linen closet to get some sheets. She had no idea how long Patrick was staying, but whether it was the weekend, as he'd said, or more realistically a week (or more), it was going to be a tedious slog.

Chapter 28

"Jealous?"

"What? *No*." Eli smirked and took a swig from the bottle in his hand. At the last minute he added a dismissive snort for good measure and nearly sent beer shooting out of his nostrils.

"I don't know, man, Patrick was one good-looking, popular dude back in the day."

Eli studied Gray as he wrapped up his minor coughing fit. "Why are you even here?" he rasped.

His friend waved a ribbon in his face. "Jenna needed reinforcements, since *some* people were sorely lacking ribbon-tying skills."

Gillian bustled in, two full shopping bags preceding her as she entered the kitchen. "Okay, I've got the supplies to bling up the fabric swag, including three different kinds of glue, because I wasn't sure . . . what?" she faltered, once she got a glimpse of everyone else's expressions.

"That's what I keep asking," Eli muttered, putting down his beer and relieving Gillian of the bags.

"Patrick's back," Jenna said simply.

"Oh."

"Okay, what are we talking, here?" Eli demanded. "Is he dangerous?"

"No, nothing like that," Jenna said.

"He's just never been what you'd call a great guy," Gillian added.

"I mean," Jenna went on, "he was always a dick in school."

"Loved getting into fights," Gillian said.

"Brought up on vandalism charges for trashing that big old abandoned house on the island," Jenna went on.

"Didn't everybody vandalize that place?" Ben asked.

His wife shook her head slowly, dismayed. "It's like I don't even know you anymore."

"I didn't say *I* did."

"And he got out of trouble every time," Gray cut in. "Magnetic as hell. If you like narcissists."

"Oh God, the football uniform."

At Jenna's comment, everyone around the table started laughing.

"Wait." Eli started putting the pieces together. "Not *that* guy."

"Yep," his sister confirmed.

"The one who used to strut around town in his gear like he just walked off the practice field?"

"Helmet to cleats," Ben said, roaring with laughter.

"Never figured out he could simply let his team jersey do the talking," Gillian added, giggling uncontrollably. "Let's just say he may have been the victim of one too many sacks on the field."

"Such a tool. Definitely not bright." Gray shook his head ruefully. "Damn good-looking guy, though."

"Did you . . . uh . . . ?" Eli ventured.

"Of course not!" Gray snapped. "I prefer my love interests' IQ to be a higher number than their shoe size." A pause, then, "Plus he was hopelessly straight. Believe me."

"So the guy wasn't the greatest back in high school. That was a long time ago. No big deal, right?" Eli asked.

"Sure," Ben muttered curtly, focusing on dropping items into the row of open gift bags in front of him.

"What does that mean?"

With a sigh, his brother-in-law explained, "Well, you heard

Leah. All the stuff Patrick wants to do to fix up the house has got her worked up, and for good reason. Hasn't she dealt with enough lately, taking care of Cathy? And now this . . . this . . ."

"Tool," Jenna supplied.

"Thank you, hon. This tool comes charging in, ordering her around, putting more stress on her? I wouldn't let her go through that alone if I were you."

"But she said she was fine. She wants to deal with this on her own."

Ben folded his hands, fixed his brother-in-law with a look.

"I'm honoring her wishes and respecting her independence," Eli protested.

Ben waited till he figured it out.

After a moment Eli lurched to his feet. "I've gotta—"

"Feed the cat?"

"Wash your hair?"

"Darn your socks?"

~

In no time, Eli was parked on the street across from Leah's house. This wasn't caveman "ug-ug" logic, was it? Was he overstepping, getting possessive or overprotective? Leah said she was fine. She was hardly a damsel in distress even on her worst days. Patrick, for all Eli knew, could have changed since high school. It was a long time ago, after all. He could have become a great guy. He and Leah might very well be hanging out right now, laughing and reminiscing like best friends.

He tried to see inside the house through the big, blank picture window, but he couldn't make anything out. The drapes were flung aside, which wasn't always the case. There were no lights on in the house. Leah's car was in the driveway, although that didn't mean she was home; a lot of Main Street was within walking distance.

Screw it.

Leah was his girlfriend, and he had every right to stop by her house and provide any moral support she might need. He didn't need an excuse.

Eli flung himself out of his Jeep and marched halfway across the street before he stopped abruptly, spun on his heel, went back, and reached into his vehicle. He didn't need an excuse, but he had one handy anyway.

"Hey!" Leah lit up when she answered the door, which made Eli feel a whole lot better about checking up on her. Which he absolutely wasn't doing. "What's up, stranger?"

"I, uh, you forgot your scarf."

Was it his imagination, or was Leah fighting back a laugh?

"Want to come in?"

"Oh. No. I don't want to disturb you."

"Okay."

But Eli's foot was in the door before she could start to close it. "Now that you mention it, I could use a glass of water."

"You don't say." She backed inside, making room for him, tugging on the scarf he still held like she had him on a leash. Which she pretty much did, in all the best ways. Because he would follow her anywhere. She drew him closer with the scarf, until she could reach up and wrap her arms around him. "Missed me that much, huh?"

"You bet."

"You didn't just leave to get away from the ribbon tying?"

"Nope."

Leah drew his head down to hers as she rose up on her toes, meeting him halfway to place a sweet kiss on his lips.

Much as he would have loved to kiss Leah back, Eli couldn't help but pull away slightly and ask, "Did Patrick show up?"

"Surprisingly, yes. Fourth time's the charm."

"Is he here right now?"

"If I say no, will you kiss me again?"

"Absolutely." But Eli couldn't quite fall into Leah the way he usually did. Breaking the kiss again, he asked, "So where *is* Patrick, exactly?"

Leah heaved a sigh. "Out. With his football buddies at Dickie's. They have some major reminiscing to do. Why, did you want to say hi?"

"Not to him, no."

"So you're here why?"

"Can't a guy miss his girlfriend and want to see her again?"

"And the real reason?"

Eli fidgeted. "Look, I know you said you could handle all this stuff with Patrick on your own, but everybody was saying he was kind of a . . . a . . ."

"Tool?"

"That seems to be the consensus. So even though I know you're independent and fierce and all, I just thought maybe you wouldn't mind having someone else in your corner to knock heads if need be." He hesitated. "I hope that's more woke than possessive."

"It's a fair balance. It helps that you're cute when you're possessive and woke at the same time."

"Is it possessive or woke to politely ask you to shut up and kiss me?"

Leah pretended to consider. "The command would be possessive, but the fact that it's a polite request is woke. It's messy overall, but I'll allow it."

Eli stopped any more words from either of them with a passionate kiss. Leah's arms grew tighter around him and she fluidly melded her body to his, weakening his knees. He couldn't get enough of this beautiful woman, couldn't ever be close enough. He easily scooped her up, and she wrapped her legs around his waist. A primal need took over in Eli, to carry her off somewhere and—

Eli's head was so clouded that although he dimly registered a sound coming from behind him, his brain couldn't process what it was, or didn't care. Probably the latter. Definitely the latter. When Leah was in his arms, everything else was secondary.

It was only when a decidedly male voice boomed, awfully close to them, "Well, hey!" that they reacted, Leah first, as she reluctantly drew her lips away from Eli's.

"Patrick," she grumbled.

Eli awkwardly turned his head as Leah slid down until her feet rested on the floor. Now he could place the infamous Patrick. He remembered the puff of light hair, the square jawline, the thick neck.

"You've got a boyfriend!" Patrick exclaimed delightedly, hands on hips. "Good for you!"

"Don't patronize me," Leah said. "What are you doing back?"

"Forgot my wallet."

"You mean you left your wallet home and hoped the guys would pay for your drinks but they're making you buy the next round?"

"Potato, potato." Patrick pronounced the word as "po-tay-to" both times.

Eli thrust out his hand. "Hey, Patrick. Eli Masterson."

"Masterson?" Then the light dawned in Patrick's small eyes as he pumped Eli's hand. "Oh, you're Jenna's little brother. Damn, she was hot. Is she still hot?"

"I . . . don't know how to answer that."

"She was totally wild too, back in the day. Hey, is she single?"

Eli opened his mouth to answer, but nothing came out. Leah was quicker on the draw.

"Seriously, Patrick? Didn't you say you had to sell the house to help pay for your wedding?"

"Oh, right!" He slapped his forehead and laughed. "Duh."

Eli risked a *WTF* look at Leah, who merely rolled her eyes and shook her head, the very picture of suffering and forbearance.

"So, Patrick," Eli said, all forced cheerfulness. "I hear you're going to be fixing the house up before you sell it. Do you need any help? I'm pretty handy with a hammer."

"Oh, no, dude, but thanks. Leah and I are gonna do it. Make her work off all that free rent she's been getting, you know what I mean?"

Eli bristled. Leah, sensing him tensing up, put her hand on his arm in warning, tightening into a stronger squeeze than he thought she was capable of. Eli pressed his lips together, focused on forcing a smile, and said nothing.

Patrick disappeared into the master bedroom in search of his wallet, and Eli took the opportunity to mutter to Leah, "What a douche. And the two of you can't fix this house up in forty-eight hours. That's nuts."

"Plus if he gets drunk with his old football buddies, we'll lose half of tomorrow to his hangover."

Eli thought a moment. "We'll help you. All of us. Ben and Jenna are good with renovations, Gray knows his way around a breaker box, Delia's artistic. And you know Gillian isn't afraid of tackling anything."

"No," Leah said definitively. "I can't ask you all to do that."

"But—"

"And who knows if Patrick would welcome the help? He sure didn't want to hire a contractor."

"Well, 'hire' is the operative word. We'll be just a bunch of goons doing our best not to burn the house down while we spruce it up."

"Really not helping your case, there."

"Trust me," Eli said in a rush as Patrick breezed back through the house.

"Later," he said, stuffing his wallet into his back pocket. "And if you're gonna get freaky, put a sock on the doorknob, okay?"

Eli winced as Leah quietly murmured, "Ew."

"On top of everything else," Eli said, "he's a buzzkill."

Chapter 29

"I. Am. So. Sorry!"

Leah leaned her forehead against the kitchen door frame and closed her eyes. "It's okay. It's not your fault."

"I should have canceled. I will. I'll cancel."

"What? No! People booked the trip, this is your livelihood, the weather is perfect. You have to go."

Eli's sigh hissed through her phone. She wished he were beside her so she could feel his breath on her ear, but a paying gig came first.

"I still don't like it," he muttered.

"Nothing to like or not like. Now go rafting."

"But I promised I'd help with the house."

"Don't worry about the house. Go lead, Daniel Boone."

Eli hesitated.

"Davy Crockett? Whatever. Just go," she insisted. "Be careful, be brilliant, make the wilderness freaks happy."

"Hey, now."

"And hurry back."

"I will definitely do that."

Leah ended the call and heaved a sigh of her own. She didn't blame Eli for how disappointed and alone she felt. But she sure blamed Patrick. Who, no surprise, had come back from his bonding session with his old high school buddies in the wee hours of Saturday night/Sunday morning, apparently having drunk every drop of alcohol in Dickie's inventory, slept through most of Sunday, and left town on Monday, already having forgotten the projects he said would only take the weekend to accomplish. Needless to say, not one thing had been completed. Or even started.

Even though Leah had told him not to, Eli had intended to corral their friends to help, but the work week would not be denied. Ben was on a trucking run, Gray had his gym, Gillian her job at the pharmacy, Jenna her spiritual calling terrorizing high school students. Even Leah had to work two days at Thousand Island Dressing and in between do a deep-cleaning job of a B&B owned by some of Alyce's friends before they opened for the season. And now Eli was off on his spring rafting trip. Delia, whose time was her own, offered to help with any redecorating she had in mind, but it would mean Leah had to spend some of her hard-earned money on supplies since, true to form, Patrick hadn't left her a dime to work with.

~

The first thing that hit Leah when she set foot in the old hardware store was the sledgehammer scent of contractor-grade coffee drifting from the ancient drip machine on a tiny table just inside the door. It was oddly soothing.

She bypassed the racks up front filled with candy bars, toy cars, tchotchkes, and souvenirs meant to entice tourists in warmer months and headed for the hardcore renovation materials toward the back. Stopping in front of the wallpaper display, she stared longingly at the rolls of patterned paper, one above the other, on a rack stretching from knee level to nearly the height of the ten-foot ceiling. She would have loved to renovate Cathy's house. She'd often dreamed of how she'd make the place beautiful. It hadn't happened, however, because she'd had her hands full taking care of

Cathy, and they'd had no money. Then, after Cathy passed, she still had no money. It wasn't her place anyway, so how could she make changes, even if they were necessary?

Now the house was a dreary mess, and it seemed the task of fixing it up was squarely on her shoulders, since Patrick had disappeared again with only an off-the-cuff reminder to get started because she "owed" him, and he'd be back . . . sometime . . . to help. She didn't feel beholden to Patrick to spruce up the house, but she did want to do it for Cathy's sake, in honor of her memory, before she moved out of the house for the last time.

Leah checked the wallpaper prices. Bad idea. Her breath hitched, and she regretfully patted one of the pretty rolls and turned to the paint display instead. Those prices were just as bad.

Depressed over the cost of even one gallon of paint, let alone several, she gave up. Never mind the soothing colors, or the eye-catching patterned wallpaper, or even what she'd come in for in the first place, which was to buy some tools she thought she might need to work on the house. Never mind anything.

"Leah?"

She jumped and turned around to find Ben looking at her quizzically. She hadn't been saying any of that out loud, had she?

"Hey, I didn't know you were back."

"Just got in last night." Ben pulled her into a tight bear hug. "So. Abandoned by the dickhead, huh?" he asked as he set her back on her feet. "Yeah, we heard."

"I thought you might have." Leah shrugged. "I can handle it."

What? No! She couldn't believe the garbage that came out of her mouth sometimes. She most certainly could not handle any of this. But her go-to response, her usual reaction to any challenge life threw at her, was to refuse any help and just handle it.

Good thing Ben saw right through her. "Really?"

She knew she could hold the line, stick to her usual story, and send him on his way . . . or she could tell the truth.

"No," she said on a shaky breath. "Not even a little bit."

"And Patrick expects you to remedy all these problems before he puts the house on the market? When he skipped town again?"

"Apparently." Leah shrugged.

Ben regarded her sympathetically. "I get it. You're a good daughter even now."

Those simple words made Leah's throat close up and tears prick the corners of her eyes. All she could do was nod and try to get her emotions under control.

"So what are you getting here?" Ben asked.

"Tools?"

Ben raised an eyebrow. Yeah, she wasn't sounding very authoritative at all.

"Cathy had a lot of stuff, but oddly enough she was a little short on those, so here I am. Of course, first I have to figure out the difference between a wrench and a chainsaw."

"Kind of an important distinction."

"Okay, I'm not *that* bad, but . . ." She pulled off her knit hat and scratched her head in frustration. "This is nuts, Ben. I don't know where to start."

"Look, don't buy anything. I've got a garage full of tools you can borrow. *Not* my chainsaw," he added hurriedly. "You don't get to come near it if you don't know you can't use it on a water pipe. Why don't you bring over a list of repairs, and we'll figure out what you need?"

The wave of relief that washed over her nearly knocked her off her feet. "I will. You're the best, Ben."

He patted her shoulder affectionately, and Leah turned back to the paint options with a renewed sense of purpose.

⁓

Leah spent that night and the following day devising a plan of attack. She drew up a list of projects in descending order of importance, made a corresponding cross-referenced list of supplies and tools she thought she'd need to borrow from Ben, and spent some time at the library watching home-repair YouTube videos that simultaneously energized and terrified her. Patrick called, but she ignored it, and he didn't leave a voicemail. She knew he just would have yammered about why he disappeared and come up with some promise about returning to Willow Cove to knock out these repair jobs in record time. She didn't want to hear it. She was going to tackle these jobs by herself, to the best of her ability . . . or lack thereof.

On Saturday morning, however, Leah had strong second thoughts. The list of repairs was long, and she was only one person. Her stubborn independence was going to get her into trouble before this was all over. But tools were at least a start. She tossed on a jacket and hunted down her car keys, looking forward to meeting with the patient and generous Ben, and perhaps getting to visit with Jenna and the girls if she was lucky. But when she pulled open the front door, Leah knew that luck had deserted her.

"Hey, why aren't you answering your phone? I thought you died or something."

"Really bad taste there, Patrick," Leah muttered.

It took Leah a moment to realize she wasn't stepping back to let Patrick into the house. She wondered how long she could get away with keeping him on the front steps instead. Because the only thing worse than Patrick on the front steps was Patrick in the house again, draining her of whatever energy she had left. Unless he had arrived in Willow Cove again with the sole purpose of finally completing this cleanup project. If she didn't let him into the house, she'd never find out. Hoping her optimism wasn't unfounded, she stepped back, opening the door wider.

"I'm not seeing anything happening here," he said, hands on hips as he looked around. "You spending too much time with your boyfriend and not enough time fixing stuff?"

"Me?" Leah gaped. "Since when is it my responsibility?"

"Okay, get your boyfriend to do it."

"That's sexist. Also not his job. That's your job, in case you've forgotten."

"Because I'm a guy?"

"Because it's your house, as you constantly remind me."

Leah wasn't sure what had gotten into her. Usually she was more patient with Patrick, even if it was just on the outside, while her insides were busy hating him. She really shouldn't hate him, though, she knew. Patrick was just Patrick.

"Well," she said, "you're here now, and I guess that's what matters. I'm going out. Why don't you get settled—assuming you're staying for a while this time—and I'll be back in a bit."

"You can't go *out*."

Bristling again, Leah said, "I'm pretty sure I can do what I want."

"I mean, you've gotta help me with the house."

Good lord. After months of empty promises, Patrick expected her to drop everything now? Leah could barely form words. All that came out was, "You hypocrite."

"I think I'm more of a crocodile. Way cooler."

"Hypo*crite*, not hipp . . . you know"—she exhaled—"if I had the time or the inclination, I'd find out once and for all whether you're genuinely dumb or if it's all an act. But I don't have the time, and quite frankly, I don't really care enough."

Patrick wasn't listening. "Anyway, so you're not going out, right?"

"Oh, I definitely am, and you're going to have to deal with it the way I've had to deal with you ghosting me a dozen times and repeatedly breaking your promise to get the house ready for sale. You can wait for me for once."

"Can't stay away from your boyfriend that bad?" Patrick snickered, wandering over to the boxes in the dining room, pulled there again by some magnetic force even he probably couldn't explain.

"That's none of your business," Leah snapped, her irritation increasing. Yes, with Patrick, but also—possibly more so—because she realized, deep down, that Patrick was right. In a way. She desperately wished she were with Eli right now, because she hated dealing with Patrick on her own. If Eli had her back she'd feel much more secure. When had she become so dependent on Eli? Or on anyone, for that matter? She'd lost her edge. Her independence had collapsed. Damnation.

Somehow she liked her new reality and hated it at the same time. Or maybe that hatred was actually fear. She'd opened up to new friends for the first time in ages, put her trust in other people. It was terrifying, as though she were on a sky-high platform, her toes hanging over the edge. She had a bungee cord; now she had to convince herself that it wouldn't break.

"Stop obsessing over my love life. And don't you dare touch those boxes again," Leah ordered Patrick, seeing his hand drifting to the nearest stack. "I'm not hiding a thing from you, so get over yourself and start working on something, anything, that will make this house more presentable. If you're not going to fix anything, then just go home, Patrick, and take the loss when you sell it. Or don't sell it. I don't really care."

This got Patrick's small eyes trained on her. "You can't live here anymore."

There was more fear bubbling up, and she had to acknowledge it. She knew she couldn't live in Cathy's house any longer, and she didn't want to, but where was she going to go? Was she really going to leave town when now she desperately wanted a reason to stay? Not for the first time, she thought about her small stash of money and her standing plan to leave as soon as Patrick took over the house. And not for the first time, especially recently, she longed for that plan to change. But aside from the moment in Alyce's house when Eli had begged her not to go, they hadn't spoken about their future. Could she stay in Willow Cove? She and Eli were so new, she didn't know whether it would be a reach or not. She was going to have to make some big decisions pretty soon, however, because the house was about to be sold out from under her. She and Eli needed to have a serious talk about . . . well, about how serious they really were.

Leah laughed to herself. After all the crap she'd given Eli for moving too fast with Victoria, here she was, ready to ask him where they stood after dating for about five minutes. Who was the hypocrite now?

"You know what, Patrick? You're totally right."

"I am?" He blinked. "Okay then." He abandoned the pull of the boxes, brushed past her, and returned to the front door. Grasping the doorknob, he said, "You need to get out. For good."

Chapter 30

Eli blinked and vigorously rubbed his face as he sped down Route 81. The last thing he'd expected to do was drive to Syracuse so early on a Saturday morning, especially since he'd just gotten home. He'd dragged himself into his cabin at one in the morning, longing for his bed. He hadn't even called Leah—although he'd wanted to—in favor of letting her sleep. He'd just fed Blanche and dropped face-first onto his mattress when his phone had pinged with a text. He'd lunged at it, hoping Leah was up late, checking to see if he'd returned from his rafting trip. What he'd seen startled him even more: a message from Victoria.

Hi.

Hey, he'd typed back. *How are you?*

I'm doing all right. What's going on back home?

The usual. Snow's finally melting. Ben and Jenna are having a thirteenth anniversary party tomorrow. Mom's doing great. How's your research?

Instead of answering his question, she'd texted, *I'm coming back early. On the way right now, actually. I'd love to see you.*

Is everything okay?

The three dots on Victoria's end had pulsed for so long, Eli had started nodding off. Then her response had come through: *Would you mind picking me up at the airport?* After a few seconds she'd added, *Please.*

A little zing of alarm had shot through him. *What's wrong?*

Nothing, she'd replied, but Eli hadn't bought it for a second.

Victoria, come on. Give me a little bit of credit. I know something's up, or you wouldn't bail on your dream trip and your new guy.

We can talk on the ride home. My plane arrives at noon.

Now he was driving a couple of hours on very little sleep to have a heart-to-heart with his ex. Someone he hadn't seen and had barely spoken to in eight months.

His thoughts were interrupted by plaintive yowling from the crate on the passenger seat.

And he was going to return Blanche.

"Just hold on a little while longer," he said to the cat. "We'll be there soon, and then you can be reunited with your owner."

Blanche peeped pathetically.

This made his heart hurt just a little bit. Not because of any bittersweet emotion about seeing his ex again, but because he felt like Blanche was his pet now, and he didn't want to give her up.

∼

Eli checked the arrivals board for what felt like the fiftieth time in twenty minutes. Victoria's connecting flight from JFK had been delayed. Here it was going on two additional hours, and there was no sign of the flight's status changing. This was seriously messing with his schedule. He'd have to hustle to get her home to Potsdam and still have enough time to get back to Willow Cove to supervise the last-minute preparations for Ben and Jenna's party. He'd texted Jenna about his change of plans and she was fine with it—at least, that was what she'd said—but if he was delayed too long Leah was going to have to handle the party supervising duties on her own.

In the meantime, he felt like a complete schmo, standing in the middle of the busy airport with a mewling cat raising a ruckus in the pet carrier at his feet. He hadn't seen Victoria in ages. She was coming back early for some reason she didn't want to talk about via text. Should he buy her flowers? A balloon? Both? What did someone do in this kind of situation? His manners and comportment lessons didn't cover this. Maybe there was a pamphlet at the gift shop: "So You're Seeing Your Ex-Girlfriend for the First Time in Months Even Though That's the Last Thing You Want to Do," with advice on how to act. Was the reunion supposed to include a yowling cat? Because he definitely had one of those.

Eli tugged at the collar of his dress shirt. Despite all the times he'd fantasized about winning Victoria back with his new look and new mannerisms, ideally the minute she stepped off the plane, he wasn't dressed to impress her now, but to go straight to the anniversary party after he got her home. And to look nice for Leah.

He should call Leah, he realized. She wouldn't know where he was and might worry.

He pulled out his phone but nearly dropped it as he was swarmed by a glut of kids in matching windbreakers, a marching band from a nearby school, all toting instrument cases small and large, from piccolos to tubas.

At least they weren't wearing their plumed hats in the building.

He checked the flight's status again. It blinked to ARRIVING. He had a little time. With one eye on the parade of travelers starting to trickle in from the gate area, he tapped his most frequently used contact.

"Hello?"

Leah's voice sounded way less enthusiastic than usual.

"Hey. Bad time to call?"

"No, no, of course not. Never." She sounded more engaged when she asked, "Are you back from the wilderness?"

"I am. Got in late last night. Are you—"

"Lose anybody along the way?" she interrupted.

"Nope, all present and accounted for."

"Well, that's good."

She definitely didn't sound right.

"Leah, what's going on over there?"

"It's nothing."

Eli thought he heard an indignant "Hey!" in the background. Before he could ask, Leah amended her answer.

"Patrick's here."

Ah shit, not again. "Need backup?"

"Everything's fine," she said in what was clearly a forced congenial tone. "But you can come over now, if you want."

Eli cursed the miles between them. "I'll be there as soon as I can, but I'm not in Willow Cove right now. I'm in Syracuse. Victoria's decided to come back early. I'm delivering Blanche."

"Oh."

Silence.

"Leah? You still there?"

"Yeah," she said quickly. "Sorry. It's fine. Whenever you can get here. Tell Blanche I'll miss her. I've gotta go."

Leah disconnected the call just as Eli looked up and spotted a familiar figure coming toward him. Victoria looked weary—understandable after a transatlantic flight and a hop from JFK—but something else was different about her. Her normally statuesque frame was hunched a little, her hair dull, her complexion a bit drawn. Eli tried to catch Victoria's eye, but she kept her gaze, hidden by her trademark huge sunglasses, trained on the floor. She nearly passed him by until he reached out a hand to touch her arm.

"Victoria."

She stopped short with a gasp, her long, slender fingers at her throat. "Eli! My God, you startled me. I almost didn't recognize you."

So Jenna had been right all along—a fancy haircut and some nice clothes really did make a difference.

"I'm sorry," she said, shaking her head as if to clear it. "I'm just tired."

Huh. Not the fancy haircut and nice clothes, then. All right.

"It's really good to see you," she added.

Victoria set her massive shoulder bag down and draped her

arms around his neck, falling so heavily on him he nearly stumbled back.

"Everything all right?"

"Yes, of course." Detaching from him, seemingly with effort, she straightened up, self-consciously brushed her hair down, and took off her sunglasses, revealing weary eyes.

"How was your trip?"

"Fine. Long."

There was a silence. An awkward one. Eli hoisted the crate, bringing Blanche to eye level. "Somebody's excited to see you."

"Oh."

Okay, Victoria definitely didn't look happy to see her cat. Or maybe not unhappy, just distracted. It took her a few seconds before she worked up the energy to say, "I hope she wasn't any trouble."

"Nah. We're buds. She does tend to hog most of the bed, though."

More silence. No "Thank you for taking care of my cat" either, Eli noted.

"So can we go?" Victoria prompted. "My suitcases should be at baggage claim by now. It took so long for everyone to get off the plane."

Eli hesitated. It was as if Victoria had never said anything about wanting to talk. "Sure, yeah."

Eli peeked in at Blanche and whispered to her to make sure she was calm, then hoisted Victoria's bag onto his shoulder. He moved to take her elbow, but Victoria scooted ahead of him onto the escalator. He double-timed to catch up to her.

"Hey. Hey, hold on." This time Eli did catch her arm, and he held it gently. "I don't think you're okay. I mean, obviously something's wrong."

"Oh, I didn't mean to scare you with that text. I'm fine, really."

"Mm, not sure I'm buying it." After he dragged her two large suitcases off the luggage carousel, he said gently, "I don't want to talk in the car, I want to focus on you. Let's get some coffee, all right?"

He handed Blanche's crate to Victoria, who accepted it absently, almost as though she'd forgotten her pet was in it, while he managed the rest of her luggage.

They'd only gone a few steps, however, before Victoria said, "Eli, I'd rather just go home, if you don't mind."

"Not without telling me what's going on first."

Chapter 31

Leah's hands and feet tingled and her head was fuzzy. She couldn't seem to clear it. She wasn't sure why. So Eli was meeting Victoria. Was that what was bothering her? She took a moment to examine her feelings. No, she trusted Eli. He was simply returning Blanche. But he was an hour and a half away. That made her gut twinge. She decided to ignore it, insisting to herself that it was okay. What in the world would he do if he were there, anyway?

She looked up from her phone and took in Patrick's expectant, slightly belligerent expression as he stood by the door. Well. Eli's presence would just make her feel safer, was all. But she'd handled plenty on her own before, and she could do it again. Even though, for the first time in a very, very long time, she realized she'd rather not do it all on her own.

"You done? You aren't waiting for your boyfriend, are you?" His eyes were tiny again. Leah could tell he was assessing the situation to the best of his ability. "Because you can't sit around here waiting for him to come rescue you."

"Nobody rescues me, Patrick."

"You want me to elect you?"

"Wh . . ." It took Leah a few seconds. "You mean evict?"

"Jeez, fine, evict, whatever. Just go."

Still muttering to himself, Patrick yanked open the front door. The exit was blocked.

"Let's do up this bitch," Jenna boomed from the front step.

Jenna, Ben, Delia, Gray, and Gillian were bunched up on the small stoop, the throng bristling with wood and metal. They had brought the tools to her. They bustled into the house, crowding Patrick back from the doorway and halfway into the living room, and Leah felt a giggle bubbling up in her chest.

"Guys . . ." Leah began, but she didn't know how to finish the sentence.

"We heard you needed help," Gillian said. "So here we are."

"Speaking of which," Jenna growled, crossing to Leah and poking her gently in her collarbone, "why didn't you call us? We had to hear from Eli and Ben what you were up against? Are you kidding right now?"

"I didn't want to bother you."

"Well, you'd better get over that," Delia said, just as definitively as Jenna. "This group might be a collective hot mess, but we take care of one another. You're family, lady."

Family.

Delia didn't think twice about tossing off that word, not noticing it struck Leah's heart hard enough to bring tears to her eyes. Leah turned her head away and took a shaky breath. She adored this giving, kind, and loyal crew. She'd started with Eli, but somewhere along the way her affection had expanded to encompass all of them.

"Oh hey, what is this, a party?" Patrick asked. Nobody bothered to answer him, so he persisted, "So, like, is there cake at least?"

"We're helping Leah with the house, Patrick," Jenna answered in a measured tone. "Because you aren't."

Patrick paused, processing again. All he could eventually come up with was, "I didn't say that was okay."

"Hey, man," Ben cut in mildly, "we're just here to make some repairs. Trying to make it all good."

"I don't want some weird army in—"

"Your house," Leah finished for him. "Yeah, I've heard."

"So okay, all of you, you know . . ." Patrick made a large sweeping gesture toward the door. "Get out?"

"Don't be stupid," Leah blurted out before she could second-guess herself. "These are my friends, they're here to help, and you're throwing them out?"

"No," Patrick snorted. "I'm throwing them *and* you out."

She drew herself up to her full five-two height. "You're the world's biggest asshole."

"Oh, real nice. That's the thanks I get for letting you live here for, like, years, rent-free?"

Leah used to be hurt when he said things like that; now she was just pissed off. Her friends, who were hearing this nonsense for the first time and so were a few levels of Patrick-hating behind her, were shocked. Leah's heart lifted a little as they instinctively drifted closer to her, protective. Family.

"Don't you dare talk to me about living here for free," she snapped. "I've been paying the bills for months. Electricity and water and heat, all winter. That's a small fortune. Not to mention I didn't ask for a dime when I was taking care of Mom for a *year*. So you can just shut up and back off."

"You sure talk big when you've got backup."

"Damn right she's got backup," Gray said in a low voice, stepping in front of Leah, coming nose to nose with Patrick, and seeming to inflate to twice his already impressive size. He crossed his arms to show off his muscles to their greatest effect. "Now, do you really want to continue this . . . *discussion*? Because if you do, you're going to have to take it up with me."

"And the rest of us," Ben chimed in, forming a phalanx with Gray. "But you're going to leave Leah alone from now on."

"You know what? Fix your own damn house," Jenna said, dropping a large wrench perilously close to Patrick's foot.

Leah glared at Patrick and said quietly, evenly, "Go to hell," and then marched down the hallway to her bedroom.

In true foster-kid fashion, she was packed up in less than five minutes. She didn't even pause to zip up her backpack, just flung it over her shoulder and yanked her duffel bag off the caved-in twin bed.

"I'm sorry, Cathy," she whispered. "I did my best. I hope it was enough."

Leah held her head high as she walked down the hallway to the front door. Patrick stepped in front of her. Gray stiffened, on high alert.

"You better not have taken anything that isn't yours," Patrick said.

She defiantly looked him in the eye as she calmly scooped up the dusty old VCR from the side table.

"I sold this to Gillian a while back. It's hers." She held the appliance out to her friend, who took it with a wicked look at Patrick.

"I think that's called stealing," he said. "I could call the cops."

"Just try it and I'll destroy you in court," Delia growled. With a wink at Leah, she added, "I'm her lawyer."

"You're out of retirement?" Leah murmured.

"For you I am. So do you feel lucky, Patrick?"

Patrick's peaked brows over his small eyes revealed even he wasn't sure how he'd backed himself into this corner.

Ben bumped him out of the way, and Delia and Gillian stayed tight beside Leah as she walked to the door.

"And she wasn't your mom!" Patrick shouted after her.

Leah didn't even bother to answer, because she knew in her heart that Cathy was indeed just that. She had been blessed to have two women to call mom in her life. Despite their flaws and imperfections. Even if they'd both left her earlier than she'd wished.

Once they were outside, Delia said, "Come on, you're staying with me."

Leah let her hastily packed backpack slide off her shoulder. She knelt to zip it up as she said absently, "Oh, no, I—"

"You can stay as long as you like. Do you have something to wear to the anniversary party tonight? If not, you can borrow something of mine."

Leah paused in her busyness and blinked at the mention of the anniversary party. "I can't believe you all came to work on this house on the same day as the party."

"Oh, please," Jenna scoffed. "Everything's been set to go for ages. We've got hours to get ready—just need to change and collect Mom and the girls. We'll meet you at the restaurant."

"Right," Delia went on, all action. "And after the party we'll have a sleepover. Pizza, s'mores. Girl talk. You can wear my bunny slippers."

Leah didn't answer. Her head swam as she stared at several items in her hand that she'd discovered in her backpack.

"Leah? You okay?" Ben asked.

She didn't answer Ben either. Because she couldn't quite form words as her entire existence telescoped to the nondescript, cheap, creased notebook that she had taken out of the nightstand drawer in Cathy's bedroom and squirreled away with her things. She'd almost forgotten she'd put it in her backpack the previous week, hiding it from Patrick in case he accused her of theft. That was laughable, as the notebook was basically junk, but she wouldn't have put it past him.

The contents were an impersonal account of Cathy's last couple of months: a set of lists, marked off by days, of her medications, the time she took them, whether or not she took them, and whatever food she'd been able to eat. Nothing of consequence, just a record she and the hospice nurses had been able to refer to from shift to shift, visit to visit, but Leah found it difficult to look through it all the same. She didn't need this to remind her of what her foster mother's last days had been like. Cathy had slept a lot, was restless when she wasn't asleep, barely ate. Occasionally she would have lucid moments, which were stranger, because the introspective and kind and grateful Cathy had been so different from the Cathy Leah had grown up with.

But two things had just fallen out of the back pages. One was a photo of her, fifteen years old, with long hair and a tan, dressed in shorts and a striped T-shirt. She was standing in what appeared to be Cathy's front yard, flanked by her little foster sisters. Leah didn't even have any memory of anyone taking that photo. Cathy had kept it all these years. And here Leah had thought she didn't keep photos of anyone.

The second item was even more remarkable, and Leah couldn't quite wrap her mind around the implications.

As she studied it, she was suddenly aware of being surrounded by five people who cared about her and were probably extremely concerned that she was kneeling on the damp driveway, staring at a piece of paper. What had Jenna just said? And Delia? Something about a party. And a sleepover. And bunny slippers.

"I . . ." Leah's vocal cords seemed to fuse together. "I can't," she fought out.

Her words came out more forcefully than she expected or intended, and she felt a little ashamed when the group exchanged confused glances.

"I'm sorry," she murmured. "That's not what I . . . I just . . . need a minute. I can't . . . I'm sorry."

And she yanked open the creaky door of her old Honda, threw her bags in, and drove away.

Chapter 32

"I feel so stupid," Victoria said, still rooted in one place while the bustling travelers swirled around her, including the marching band, who seemed to be enjoying themselves wandering around the forecourt instead of going through the security checkpoint to catch a flight.

"Okay," Eli said, on high alert now, because this wasn't like Victoria. She was always confident, calm, and assertive, not restless and distracted like this. "Okay. Let's break it down. I'm pretty sure this isn't the case, but I'm going to ask anyway. Is it about your work, your research?"

Victoria shook her head slightly.

"Didn't think so. I might be going out on a limb here, but does this have anything to do with the guy you mentioned? Fabrizio?"

Victoria's eyes filled with tears.

"Right," he muttered. "The last time we talked, you were so happy. What happened?"

"He . . . he wants to marry me."

"Wow." Eli wasn't sure what he'd been expecting, but he was positive it wasn't that. He took a beat, then asked, "Get a lot of that, don't you?"

Cracking a joke at this point was a risk, but Victoria finally smiled. "I'm so sorry. I shouldn't be talking to you, of all people, about this."

"Why not? We're . . . you know . . . old news. I don't mean that in a bad way, though. You've moved on and so have I. It's okay." And he meant it.

Victoria didn't ask about Leah, likely because she was still wrapped up in her own drama, but she did look at him closely, as if seeing him for the first time since she'd gotten off the plane. "You seem different."

"I think we've both changed. But we're talking about you now. He asked you to marry him and . . . ?"

"I don't know." It came out as a whisper, almost lost in the noise of the terminal.

"You're comparing you and him to what happened with you and me, aren't you? You shouldn't."

"I can't help it. I mean, your proposal was so sudden."

"And I regretted it for a long time. I apologize if I put you in an uncomfortable situation by doing that."

"You were speaking from a good place, though. Even if I wasn't there with you."

"And his was sudden too, is that it?"

"Yes." She sighed and cast her teary gaze upward. "I don't know what's going on in my head right now. I mean, what you and I had, it was good, right? It wasn't perfect by a long shot, but it was, you know, nice. I have to admit, I thought about us . . . you know, after. I wondered if I'd made the wrong decision, because who can really expect more than that from a relationship, you know? I thought sweeping, passionate true love, that just didn't happen."

"And then you met this guy."

"With Fabrizio, it's so much more than 'nice' or 'okay.' It's everything."

"So you want to marry him."

"I want to marry him."

"But?"

"It's so scary, it's so fast, it can't be right. Nothing could be that easy."

Eli's head—and heart—were filled with Leah when he said, "I think it can be. With the right person."

"But his life is there, and mine is here."

"There's art in Rome, I hear. Maybe not as good as the stuff in the North Country of New York, but . . ."

Victoria actually laughed, although her brighter mood was short-lived. Sober again in a blink, she went on, "I didn't trust anything that seemed to be that easy. I freaked out so bad I got on a plane, and here I am."

"Miserable."

"I thought I did the right thing, but now I'm not so sure."

"Honey, true love is huge. And yeah, it's scary, but it doesn't mean you're supposed to run away from it. It's so rare, you should be running toward it."

She stared at him with a touch of panic. "What if it's too late?"

"If it's true love, it's never too late. You should call him right now, and then you should turn around and get back to Rome as soon as—"

"Vittoria!"

The shout didn't register with Eli, not right away, but it did with her. Victoria went rigid, her head cocked like a spaniel.

"Vittoria!"

Someone ran up to them, panting, inadvertently nudging Eli back. He obliged—not that he had much choice—and took in the sight of what slowly dawned on him was the guy in Victoria's photos. The man was tall and lithe, with olive skin and wild dark curls that reached his collar. He was impeccably dressed, from his leather dress shoes to his mirrored sunglasses, which he whipped off dramatically.

"Fabrizio," Victoria breathed. "What are you doing here?"

What followed was a barrage of Italian, peppered with numerous instances of "bella" and "cara," that Eli wouldn't have been able to make out in a hundred years. Eli wished he knew what Fabrizio was saying, but then again, he didn't really need a direct translation. He'd obviously chased Victoria all the way from Rome. This guy meant business.

It apparently was worth the effort: whatever he was saying seemed to unravel Victoria bit by bit; her stance became less stilted, her shoulders relaxed, her expression softened, and her eyes welled with unshed tears.

Seemingly completely unaware of the travelers slowing down to stare at the scene unfolding in the middle of the terminal, Fabrizio grasped her hand. She let him. He dropped to not one knee, but both, and continued his petition. A crowd gathered to watch the show.

"Hey." A large man in a Dinosaur Bar-B-Que T-shirt and khaki shorts nudged Eli. "What's going on?"

Eli's eyebrows shot toward his hairline. "True love, I think. Passionate, sweeping true love."

Fabrizio's torrent of words slowed, finally, leaving a few spaces here and there for Victoria to respond. She hadn't yet. She was shaking her head in amazement, one hand lightly covering her lips as if to safeguard what might come out. Or she was speechless. Well, if this guy had come all the way from Italy for her, of course she'd be speechless.

"Vittoria," Fabrizio said again, shaking her hand a little and switching to heavily accented English, "please. I love you. If you come back to Roma with me, I give you . . . everything."

Eli felt a laugh bubble up in his chest. His hopes were rising for Victoria, but he couldn't help being just a little amused. He wondered what "everything" entailed. He decided to hazard a guess. "Your Vespa?"

"Si. Yes! Yes!" The other man didn't even glance over his shoulder to see where the suggestion was coming from. "All of them. Even my, come si dice, vintage Vespa. All for you."

"And your villa in Tuscany, don't forget."

"Yes!"

"I knew it," Eli said, openly laughing now.

Finally Fabrizio looked over his shoulder to see who was talking. He rose to his feet and turned to Eli. "You are Elias, no?"

"Si. That's me."

"I have heard so much about you."

"I'll bet."

"You will know, then . . . this woman, she is . . . perfetta."

Eli could figure that word out. "Of course."

"Bellissima."

And that one. "Very."

"How do I make her love me?"

Eli looked past him to his ex, who still had her hand clapped over her mouth. "Oh, I think you already have. You followed her all the way from Rome?"

"Si. We fight. Argue. Some. Un po'. I did not think she would leave me. What should I do?"

Eli blinked, took a breath. "I don't know. Looks like you might need a dramatic gesture to close the deal."

"Che? Scusa?"

"A dramatic gesture. You know, a big . . ." Eli stretched his arms wide, then realized demonstrating physical size about an abstract act wouldn't make any sense.

"Animale?"

"Ani—oh, you mean like a big stuffed animal? Maybe. But you might have to go more, uh, drammatico than that."

"Oh, si, si."

"Wait, that was a word?"

"Now?"

"No time like the present, my friend. It is an airport, after all, and you've already run through it. Time for the final act."

Fabrizio gave him a confused look.

"Ask her again," Eli prompted him in a whisper.

"Yes?" the other man asked, unsure.

"Trust me."

Fabrizio took a breath and turned back to Victoria, dropped to his knees again, and pulled something out of his breast pocket.

The ring flashed under the fluorescent lights. "Ti prego, per favore. Ti prego."

Eli was surprised when Victoria's eyes flicked to him, questioning. He smiled at her reassuringly, and it seemed to tip the scales. The crowd of people that had gathered started cheering when Victoria nodded so vigorously it looked like her head was going to fall off her neck. If the passionate kiss between Victoria and Fabrizio wasn't Eli's cue to leave, the moment the marching band struck up an impromptu rendition of "All You Need Is Love" was.

"Just like the movies," Eli murmured under the flutes twittering away.

Eli set his ex-girlfriend's bag down quietly but kept hold of the cat carrier. If she still wanted Blanche—and he doubted she did—she knew where to find him.

Eli backed away from the scene smiling, but thinking that grand gestures in real life looked pretty cheesy.

～

"What's going on?"

Eli charged into the restaurant, still surging with an adrenaline rush that had gotten him back to Willow Cove in record time. How he'd avoided a speeding ticket was something he'd marvel about later.

Now was not that time.

The only person there besides the serving staff was Gillian, dressed impeccably but fidgeting with worry. The minimalist restaurant was transformed by the whimsical luck theme Jenna had opted for and Leah had made a reality. All the guests entering the riverside restaurant and bar would have to walk under a ladder. Open umbrellas bloomed in the corners. Three black cats from the animal shelter lounged in a huge, fancy cage—only because they'd violate health codes if they were allowed to wander around. The cats were available for adoption, and the hope was they'd find new homes with some of the partygoers.

It was all unique and beautiful and everything they'd planned, yet Eli could only focus on Gillian and the text she'd sent, which had disjointedly rattled off something about Leah getting into it with Patrick and that she had disappeared.

"Have you heard from Leah?" she asked, wringing her hands.

"I texted her to tell her I was on my way back, but she didn't answer."

Gillian filled him in on the day's events. "Something happened with her, honey. I don't know what. I guess because Patrick threw her out of the house?"

"And nobody knows where she is now?"

"Delia and Gray have been driving around looking for her. They'll find her."

"I can't wait around till they do."

~

Everywhere Eli checked in the small town—which suddenly seemed to encompass far too many square miles—revealed no sign of Leah. He checked Thousand Island Dressing, but it was closed; Dickie's, which was open but bare, with even Dickie planning to attend his sister and brother-in-law's anniversary party; Poppin' Locks; the Magic Maids headquarters off Main Street . . . nothing. He drove to his cabin, hoping she considered his place a refuge.

But his driveway was empty and his cabin was dark.

"Dammit," he muttered.

The worst thought imaginable broke through the fog of worry: how she used to talk about leaving town. How she said there was nothing for her here. What if she still thought she didn't have a place in Willow Cove, especially now that Patrick had evicted her? What if all this was his fault? He should have told her how strongly he felt about her weeks ago, should have discussed their future with her. Playing it safe, hiding the depth of his feelings, just because it had blown up in his face with Victoria . . . what a waste of time. Now he was prepared to drop to his knees and . . . well, not employ a marching band, but . . . honestly, Fabrizio had the right idea. It wasn't about the grand gesture; it was about opening your heart and not apologizing for it.

His phone rang, and he hurriedly yanked it out of his pocket. "Yeah?" He cleared his throat. "Yeah, hello?"

"Eli? Did you find Leah? Gray and Delia didn't."

He sighed heavily. "No, Jenna. She's not anywhere."

"Well, she's *supposed* to be with us."

Leah was supposed to be a lot of things, namely wrapped in his arms right now. But she wasn't. What the hell. The town was only so big; where could she . . .

Then he realized.

"Jenna, I've gotta go. Just go to your party, and I'll keep you posted."

Chapter 33

"So. What's going on?"

Leah couldn't help it; the sound of Eli's smooth voice, deep as the river she was watching go by, made her heart squeeze. She wanted to spin around and run to him, but she forced herself to stay where she was, leaning on the railing of the bridge where she first saw him last summer. It was far cooler than that day, no recreational boats on the water now, but she still felt that August day in her bones, saw it overlaid on today like a double-exposure photograph. Only this time she wasn't hiding in the boathouse.

"Just watching the gorgeous sunset."

Eli's footsteps grew closer, and then he was beside her, elbows on the railing, the heat of his body warming her side. She'd been standing there so long, she was practically frozen in place. As if he knew how cold she was, Eli took off his suit coat and draped it over her shoulders.

"Everyone's looking for you. What with the party and all."

Leah fidgeted, searching for words to explain.

"Don't worry about it," he said. "They can wait a few more minutes for us. That is, unless you're skipping town tonight."

She didn't want to admit that she'd considered it. After all, that was what she'd done all her life: a phase of it ended, she moved on, just as she'd trained herself to do. When she'd driven away from her friends earlier that day, gut aching, she wondered what would happen if she pointed her car south and drove away from Willow Cove, out of the North Country, away from these people she loved so much they could break her heart in an instant. She'd left places, left people behind in the past, sometimes for exactly that reason. It only hurt for the first hundred miles or so, she'd learned. With this crew, it might take two hundred miles. But it would still fade.

That thought had only stuck around for a moment, and that was progress, wasn't it? She was able to let a negative thought come into her head and then let it go, replaced it with the memory that her friends had called her "family." She didn't have to leave if she didn't want to. These choices were hers to make—or not make—and she intended to make the choices that would make her happiest. The idea of leaving Eli, leaving her new friends, leaving Willow Cove . . . none of that made her happy.

So she'd only gotten as far as this bridge, standing where Eli and Victoria had stood last summer, staring at the boathouse where she'd hidden while they broke up. She realized it was one of her favorite spots in Willow Cove, because even if Eli had had a bad day in this spot last summer, it was the first place she'd seen him, and that had changed her life forever. For the better.

"Leah?" Eli whispered, a tremor in his voice. "I don't know exactly what Patrick did to upset you earlier, and you don't have to tell me if you don't want to. I just want you to know that I begged you to stay before, and I'll do it again. I'll do it as many times as I need to, to convince you that you belong here. With me."

Leah turned to him, looked up. She loved his eyes, loved his face, and hated to see him so worried. Especially over her.

She leaned into him and closed her eyes. "I know," she whispered back. "Don't worry. I'm here."

He put an arm around her shoulders, gently, tentatively, and she let him.

"It's my fault, isn't it? Because I went to meet Victoria?"

"No," she said. "Of course not."

"She needed some help. She needed a friend."

Eli was just the type to go running to help anyone who needed it, even an ex-girlfriend. She knew that and loved that about him.

"I figured if all else failed, Blanche could give her some fuzzy comfort, but apparently the last thing she wanted was to get covered in cat hair."

"She didn't take Blanche back?"

"Nope. Blanche now owns me permanently and is sleeping peacefully in the middle of my bed now."

"Oh. Good. Did you help Victoria?"

"I don't know. I'd like to take credit for talking her through her problem, but it was more Fabrizio's doing."

"Who?"

"Fabrizio." Eli rolled the R dramatically. "Not bad, huh? I learned that from good ol' Fab. Her fiancé."

Unable to play it cool in the wake of that bombshell, Leah gasped, "*Fiancé?*"

"Quite a guy. They're on their way back to Rome as we speak. I'm sure they'll be very happy together. Hey, do you think my crash course in art means I can teach the subject? The college is going to have an opening in about, oh, five minutes."

Leah desperately wanted to joke along with him, but she couldn't quite manage it.

"Look . . ." Serious again, Eli sighed. His voice was soft but earnest. "I'm so sorry I wasn't there for you with the whole Patrick thing."

"It couldn't be helped. It's okay."

"But you're not okay."

Leah wasn't sure how to explain the roller coaster of emotions she'd gone through in just one day. "I had a lot of thinking to do," was all she could manage.

"You've scared a whole lot of people, you know. Delia and Gray spent hours together not even fighting while they searched the town for you."

Leah winced. "I'm so sorry. I wasn't thinking."

"Well," Eli said with a shrug, "who knows? Something good might come of that."

She laughed softly. "Maybe."

"So. I heard stories from everyone else, but your point of view is the most important. Do you feel like telling me what got you all freaked out earlier?"

"Nothing . . . it's stupid."

"I'll bet it's not."

Leah nervously tucked a curl of hair behind her ear and glanced down at the little notebook she still clutched tightly in her hand. She hadn't let go of it since finding it in her backpack earlier.

"This belonged to Cathy. I used to keep notes in it when I was taking care of her. I found it in her nightstand drawer. It's not important, it just happens to be the last thing I have that's connected to her. Don't tell Patrick. He'd kill me if he found out I took it."

"He'd be angry you took a notebook?"

"Hey, earlier today he threatened to have me arrested for taking the VCR, so . . ."

Eli snorted. "He did not."

"He absolutely did. Anyway, I realized I didn't really want to keep it. I thought maybe I'd burn it. Not in a mean way. As a kind of farewell ritual, like the funeral Cathy never had."

"That's a nice idea. You can do it at my house. You can use the woodstove. Or the fire ring in the yard." When Leah didn't answer him, Eli asked, "Not what you had in mind?"

"I found this inside it."

She showed Eli the photo of herself and her foster sisters, and his eyes widened.

"Oh my God, is this you?" Eli took it from her gently and studied it. "You said Cathy never kept photos."

"She didn't."

"But here this is, after all these years. She must have really loved you and your foster sisters."

"I . . ." Leah couldn't complete her thought, and her constricted throat wouldn't let her anyway.

"And that?" He pointed to the other item she held in her hand.

The piece of paper was even more surprising than the photo. She handed it to him and waited while he read it.

"A will," he murmured in awe. "It leaves the house to you."

"The house belongs to Patrick," she insisted immediately, as though Patrick repeating it all those times had hypnotized her into parroting it.

"This says otherwise. Cathy signed it. And whose signatures are these? The witnesses."

"Her hospice nurse and a social worker. They came to see her a lot."

"Is it real? I mean, legitimate? Legal?"

She shook her head. "I have no idea."

"If it is, though—"

"That's why he kept insisting it was his house, even though nobody was arguing the point. It might even be why he was going through all the boxes I'd packed—maybe she told him she'd written a will and he was looking for it. Or maybe he was looking just in case."

"So . . . this is great, right?"

Leah shrugged. "Eli . . . all my life I've been taught that nobody loved me. Nobody cared about me. My mom did, sure, but she was fighting her illness. So nobody was looking out for me." She held up her hand to stop him from insisting that she was worthy of love. That wasn't the point she was trying to make. "It was just my reality, and I learned to live with it. But today I found out that Cathy really did love me."

"Enough to leave her house to you."

"I don't even care about the house. The fact that she had this picture of me and my foster sisters for fifteen years, and it was by her bedside last year . . ."

"She loved you. She was happy you were with her. And it *is* important that she left her house to you, because it shows she appreciated you and was looking out for you. She wanted to make sure you were okay after she was gone."

"Eli, I don't know how to handle all that."

"I'm sorry. Help me understand?"

Leah took a wavering breath. "I always wanted Willow Cove to be my home, but I never felt like I belonged here, not really. That was why I left when I aged out of the foster system. When I found out Cathy was sick, I knew I was only going to stay as long as she needed me, whether it was till she was back on her feet or she . . ." She swallowed heavily. "Anyway, after Cathy died, I knew I only had a little time before Patrick threw me out, and I had to take care of myself again. That day you were standing here with Victoria, and I was in the boathouse?" Eli nodded attentively. "I was making seventy-five dollars to paint the inside of that boathouse. All those jobs I worked, so many that you called me Kirk? I told everybody it was to get me through till the tourist season, but actually I was scrounging every penny just to save up enough money to leave as soon as I could."

"I'm glad you didn't."

Staring up at him, she whispered, "I didn't dare hope that something would happen that would allow me to stay, so I stuck to my plan. And then . . . then . . ."

"We happened."

"No, I got attached to your family and friends."

"Hey, now. Them first?"

"Sorry." She shrugged, fighting a smile despite everything. "You were off in Victorialand for a long time. They were more welcoming."

"Well, don't ever tell them this, but I guess they were right and I was wrong."

"That's true."

"Anyway . . . ?" he prompted.

"Anyway, I started hoping maybe I could stay. Then there was you, and your friends called me family, and—"

"And now you have Cathy's house."

"I don't want the house. I would never live in it."

"You don't even want to try to claim it?"

"Even if that paper is legal, Patrick would contest it. He'd raise hell in court until he won. It's not worth it."

"That's too bad. Because it looks like Cathy wanted you to have some reward for what you did to help her."

"I don't need that either."

"The money from selling the house could pay for school in Florida."

She stepped closer and pushed down his hand that was holding Cathy's hastily written will. "I hear they have good schools in New York too."

Eli's eager, hungry gaze drank her in. "So you're definitely staying?"

"That's what I'm trying to ask you. Because it's not just about a house. It's about belonging. Do I belong here?"

Eli kissed her. In a voice tight with emotion, he whispered, "If you're asking me if I want you to stay, the answer is yes. I said it before, and I meant it. I mean it even more now. I don't know what I'd do without you. Besides," he choked out a laugh, "I think everybody else would kill me if I let you go. But I can't let you go. I don't want to let you go. You don't have to fight for that house, but please stay here. Be with me."

Leah reached up to wrap her arms around his neck and drew his head down to hers. Eli's suit coat flumped off her shoulders, landing on the boards of the bridge, but it didn't matter. Eli warmed her to her soul. "I love you, Eli," she whispered against his lips. "I want to be with you."

His strong arms held her close against him. Then he let go a whoop.

"She loves me. Wow."

Leah laughed softly, her forehead touching his.

"I love you too," he murmured. "I've loved you for . . . I don't know how long."

Leah let him pull her close again, until she had no idea where she ended and he began. It didn't matter anyway. The touch of his lips, his hands warm on her back, and most of all the emotion Eli was pouring into their kiss was everything. She loved him. She couldn't live without him, and now she didn't have to.

Eli broke their kiss only to trail a series of lighter kisses down her neck to the hollow of her throat, making her knees weak. But that was just fine; Eli was holding her up, as she knew he would whenever she needed him to. No, more than that. He held her together, made her whole. She kissed him again. And again. And again. She never wanted to do anything else for the rest of her life.

It was Eli who reluctantly pulled back. "You're cold. We should get out of here."

With the sun nearly down and a stiff breeze starting to blow in off the water, Leah wasn't about to protest. She let Eli put his jacket over her shoulders again, wrap his arm around her, and lead her away.

"We're not going to watch a movie, are we?" she asked.

"Nope," Eli said immediately, grinning from ear to ear. "Never. Again."

"What? You'll never watch another movie for the rest of your life? I find that hard to believe."

"Not if it's going to turn into a lesson or anything, no."

"Don't worry; you've graduated."

"Thank God. Besides, we have a party to go to."

Chapter 34

When Eli and Leah walked into the restaurant—after a bit of convincing from Eli that Leah looked beautiful whether or not she was dressed for the occasion—he was immediately surrounded by friends and family, but he didn't find himself in the middle of a love fest.

"Where the *hell* have you been?" Jenna demanded of her brother, but she didn't wait for him to answer, instead turning to Leah and smothering her in a tight hug. "Can't believe you just up and left. Honestly. Anyway, Eli, I need you to kick some ass. The kitchen screwed up."

A drunk Dickie wandered past, declaring, "Thass what you get when you don' hire me."

"Oh, shut up, Dickie," Jenna sniped. "We didn't want chicken wings for once, all right?"

"Wass wrong with chicken wings? Hey. You think you're too good for me, doncha? You always did," he grumbled.

"Give it a rest, why don't you? I was your fifth-grade girlfriend. It was, like, literally a century ago. Stop taking it out on me already."

"But I still love you, Jenna," the barman whined.

"Hey, Dickie, how about some water, huh?" Eli suggested, clapping him on the back, gently turning him toward the bar as he did so, and then giving him a slight shove to set him on his new course. He subtly gestured to the bartender on duty, who nodded.

"Idiot," Jenna muttered, all but drowned out by Delia and Gray.

"You found her!" Delia exclaimed, rushing up to the group. "Thank goodness!"

"We've been looking everywhere," Gray said at the same time. "Of course you'd find her faster, though." He put his hand on the top of Leah's head affectionately. "You scared us half to death."

Delia didn't exercise the same restraint. She hugged Leah and scolded, "Don't ever do that again, you hear me? I mean it."

Leah gave Eli a good-natured strangled look over Delia's shoulder, which he found downright irresistible. He wanted to prise Delia off his girlfriend—he loved that word, "girlfriend"—and pull her to his side again.

"About what I said earlier," Delia went on, now pushing Leah away slightly so she could grip her shoulders and give her an *I mean business* glare. "You're staying with me. As long as you like. S'mores and bunny slippers definitely included."

Eli blinked. He'd been so relieved Leah was staying in town, he hadn't given a thought about *where*, exactly, she'd be staying. Before his brain engaged to stop him, he found himself saying, "Well, you could always . . . I mean . . . I just thought . . . I mean we . . ."

"I know," Leah whispered, moving away from Delia and wrapping her arms around his waist. "But I don't want to move too fast and blow up what we just started."

"Stop making so much sense," he murmured back, kissing her temple.

"Well, somebody's got to. But ask again later, okay?"

"You're damn right I will. Blanche would yack a hairball into my shoe if I didn't."

"So this," Jenna said, flicking her index finger from one of them to the other, "this means good things are still happening?"

Eli smiled down at Leah, and his heart swelled at her happy glow.

"They are," she said, blushing the pink he loved so much.

"I'm really happy for you."

"Well, thanks, but this is your day. You look beautiful, and your husband looks very dashing. And your sweet girls . . ." Leah hesitated, because the sweet girls were slaloming through the crowd despite being trussed up in crinoline-laden party dresses, coming close to knocking over elderly guests as Alyce fruitlessly chased after them.

"Our sweet girls are being spawns of Satan today."

"But you love them."

"As one does, in those rare moments when one doesn't want to send them to boarding school in Lithuania. You'll understand soon enough."

Leah was speechless, but Eli cut in. "Okay, slow your roll, there, sister. One thing at a time. Why don't we deal with the food issue right now and talk life events some other time, okay?"

"You know what? Screw the food. If it's not good, people can drink until they don't notice."

"Or you could trust your beloved husband to take care of it," Ben said, coming up behind Jenna. "I talked to the manager—he's on it, and he's apologetic, so he gave us this." He produced a bottle of champagne.

"Thank you, beloved husband." Jenna accepted the bottle and signaled to a passing server for glasses. "Okay, enough stress. We're celebrating. Not just this marriage, which has lasted way longer than anyone expected . . ." She raised an accusatory eyebrow at her friends, who nodded, not even a little ashamed, since she and Ben had ended up proving them wrong for thirteen years. "But also . . . everything. Family. Friends. Friends who are now family." She gave Leah a significant look. "Who are sticking around, right?"

"I am, I promise," Leah said, and Eli's heart swelled even more.

"And we'll put up a force field at the town line to keep Patrick out," Gray said.

"That might be a good idea."

"Why? He didn't do anything else, did he?" Ben demanded.

"No, but . . ." Leah looked at Eli, who gave her an encouraging nod. "Delia, I might need your help after all."

Delia's eyebrows flew up as she quickly scanned the paper Leah handed her. "Cathy's house is yours?"

"Patrick is going to contest this."

"Let him try, girlie. What did I say before? I promised to destroy him in court over a VCR; imagine what I'd do for a whole-ass house. And I'd love it. I'd love it so much, I'd do it for free. I mean, I'd do it for free for you anyway, but . . . you know what I mean."

"Thanks. I just hope . . ."

"What, honey?" Gillian prompted.

"I . . . okay, this might sound weird, but I don't know how to stay in one place for very long. What if I don't figure out how to do it? How to fit in?"

Delia gasped "What!" as Gillian squared her shoulders and fixed Leah with a steely glare.

"Now look, kid," Gillian said, "first of all, you've got us. When we said we're family, we meant it. Besides, you think any of us have it easy? I'm a transplant from Philly, don't forget."

Ben snorted. "Oh, honey. If I could fit in, especially after marrying Jenna . . . I mean, you might not have noticed, but our melanin levels are different, and for some reason that bothers some people."

"And me—you think it's been easy for me?" Gray demanded. "This town still don't know what to do with all this fabulousness."

Eli laughed. "Well, maybe if you calmed your wild ways and settled down?"

"You would deny the population of Willow Cove of . . . of . . . *this*?"

"Maybe they're ready to let you retire," Leah said with a sidelong glance at Delia, who was still scrutinizing the will.

Gray rolled his eyes. "Oh, what do they know?" But he cast his own surreptitious glance Delia's way, and Eli and Leah exchanged a knowing look.

Leah seemed to be mollified. "You're right. I'm worrying too much. I'm grateful for everything. I love all of you."

"But you love me best, right?"

Eli slid an arm around her waist, pulling her close, and Leah went willingly, beaming up at him, drinking him in.

"I do," she said softly. "Just as you are."

Acknowledgments

Authors always have so many people to thank for getting their latest book baby in tip-top shape. I have so much gratitude for everyone who contributed to this book. Giant pink and purple fuzzy hearts to . . .

Glynis Astie for the Big Idea when we just happened to be in close proximity to a Very Famous Actor: "He's *really* tall. You should write a book with a tall hero that he can play in the movie version." Done and done, my friend. *The Rom-Com Agenda* wouldn't exist without you!

My cousins Mary Benvenuto and Nina Burgess for helping me understand what it's like to survive a Thousand Islands winter. Any errors in describing just how dang cold it is there are my fault alone.

The very kind, welcoming (and unsuspecting) residents of Clayton, New York, for patiently answering all my weird questions about life in the Islands.

Alyse, owner of the McKinley House Bed and Breakfast in Clayton, for giving this writer the gorgeous turret room. It was perfect!

Store manager Rebecca, who recognized a heartbreak of a scene when it unfolded in front of her—good eye, my friend—and shared the story with me. I hope Sad Valentine's Day Teen has finally found someone who appreciates him.

Editorial consultant Angela James, for helping me figure out this story's purpose. Because sometimes you need help with the big picture.

Editor Alex Sehulster and everyone at St. Martin's Griffin for getting *The Rom-Com Agenda* on its feet and out the door!

As always, Jordy Albert, agent extraordinaire, for finding my books a wonderful new home . . . and for listening to me whine, like, *all* the time.

JAYNE DENKER is the author of romantic comedies. When she's not hard at work on another novel (or, rather, when she should be hard at work on another novel), she can usually be found frittering away stupid amounts of time on social media.